PRAISE FOR BARRY SIEGEL

Lines of Defense

"ENGAGING . . . Expertly judged writing, thoughtful observations, warm and likable characters."
—*Kirkus Reviews*

"THE WRITING IS EXCELLENT, AS ALWAYS."
—*Booklist*

Actual Innocence

"[A] TOUR DE FORCE . . . A powerful contemporary tale, enriched by surprising examples of how the law works and how it fails."
—*Los Angeles Times*

"GRIPPING AND COMPLEX . . . Highly atmospheric . . . A lush, hypnotic setting."
—*Detroit Free Press/News*

The Perfect Witness

"OUTSTANDING . . . . A cliff-hanger of a story . . . A haunting thriller . . . with artfully drawn characters caught up in a tangle that pulls even tighter as the story progresses."
—*The Seattle Times*

"BOLD AND CLEVER . . . Often the best courtroom thrillers take us beyond the usual murder case to grapple with larger and more complex matters."
—*San Francisco Chronicle*

Books published by The Random House Ballantine Publishing Group are available at quantity discounts on bulk purchases for premium, educational, fund-raising, and special sales use. For details, please call 1-800-733-3000.

LINES OF DEFENSE

BARRY SIEGEL

BALLANTINE BOOKS • NEW YORK

A Ballantine Book
Published by The Random House Ballantine Publishing Group

Copyright © 2002 by Barry Siegel

www.ballantinebooks.com

ISBN 0-345-43822-1

Manufactured in the United States of America

First Hardcover Edition: August 2002
First Mass Market Edition: May 2003

OPM 10 9 8 7 6 5 4 3 2 1

To Marti and Ally—still and always, my special girls.

LINES OF DEFENSE

ONE

In La Graciosa, ten miles from the sea, the most luminous summer evening can still suggest winter's chill. The central plaza's park benches, its bear statue, the winding creek, even the *asistencia* itself can abruptly vanish behind a low, thick wall of fog. Cars crawl then, blinking futile headlights. Pedestrians step with care, searching for familiar landmarks. Muffled voices blend with the smell of kelp. Invisible feet crunch on gravel.

"Goddamn, Jimmy, you know where we're going?" Douglas Bard, Chumash County sheriff's detective, peered into the mist.

"Of course I do," promised Jimmy O'Brien, editor of La Graciosa's *News-Times*. "I can find my way to JB's blindfolded."

"Just what I'd expect of a journalist. No doubt you've memorized each step from the newspaper to the tavern?"

"That would require far too much concentration. I'm just following the smell of whiskey."

"All I smell is seawater."

"Jesus, Doug, how can you be a detective if you can't find your way to JB's?"

In truth, Doug Bard could find his way anywhere, for he held in his mind an intricate image of Chumash County. When all else failed, this mental map guided him through the densest fog. He savored La Graciosa's misty insulation. To him, it felt like the protective embrace of home.

"That's why I need you, Jimmy. You're better than a guide dog. Without you I couldn't—"

A burst of static from Bard's two-way radio interrupted him. At first he heard only a crackly electronic hiss. Then a distant voice. Jake Baum, the sheriff's dispatcher.

Trouble at Ollie Merta's house . . . not sure what's up . . . urgent open call . . . Whoever's listening, get on out there . . . need all the help we can get tonight . . . Repeat, this is urgent . . .

"Ollie Merta?" Jimmy frowned. He knew Merta as a kindly if peculiar old man. Not someone to have trouble at his house. "What's that about?"

"I don't want to know," Doug said. "I'm off duty."

"As are all your colleagues."

Jimmy had a point. It was early Sunday evening, so there were only two deputies working. Likely, one would be trying to resolve another of the Clackhorns' sorry domestic disputes, while the other would be in bed with the Foghorn's barmaid, his radio turned off. Bard gazed in the direction of JB's, then turned and started for his car. "Okay, Jimmy, you win. Hold a stool for me at JB's, I'll be there just as soon as I can."

"What do you mean, hold a stool? I'm coming with you."

"Why bother?" Bard asked. "Haven't you already closed tomorrow's paper?"

"I can reopen it if I want. That's the awesome power of a small-town newspaper editor."

Ollie Merta's home, ten miles from La Graciosa's central plaza, sat by itself in a tranquil, oak-thick dell framed by the eastern foothills of Chumash County. Bard kept his foot heavy on the accelerator despite the fog. Heading down a twisting country lane, he and Jimmy could see a pink glow in the distance. Black smoke began to fill the sky as they closed on the house. Rolling around a final bend, they found three county fire trucks and four sheriff's patrol cars, their blinking red lights piercing the mist. A dozen men milled about while radios screeched.

The fire was out. Merta's house, drenched now and smashed apart, had burned half to the ground.

"Christ," Bard said, sitting motionless behind his steering wheel.

Next to him, peering through the windshield, Jimmy counted the officers. "Nearly everyone with a badge or siren seems to have shown up."

"Even the honorable sheriff himself."

Doug climbed out of his car and walked over to Sheriff Howie Dixon. He studied his boss, holding back, waiting. Dixon had a bristly crew cut, a barrel chest, and hands like catcher's mitts. He didn't get out in the field much anymore. He preferred the comfort of his office, where he could swivel about in his high-backed leather chair and work the battery of phones that kept him linked to everyone who mattered in Chumash County. At the moment he looked indisposed, as if suffering from indigestion or an aversion to the smoky night air.

"Goddamn it, Doug," Dixon said. "What's that reporter doing in your car?"

"As you know, Howie, Jimmy isn't a reporter anymore. He's the editor of the *News-Times*."

"Reporter, editor, what the hell. He's the press."

It's obvious you can and will print anything you see fit. That was Dixon's standard response whenever Jimmy O'Brien sought his comments about a controversial investigation. When out-of-town reporters left phone messages, he offered even less. "You do whatever you wish," he'd write to them, "but I have no intention of spending county money on a long-distance phone call to you."

Bard watched Dixon seethe as Jimmy climbed out of the car. "O'Brien was with me when the call came in," Doug explained. "So I let him hitchhike. He'd have made it out here by himself anyway."

"Maybe so," Dixon snapped, "but he'll have to stay back. This is a restricted zone right now."

Bard looked toward O'Brien. "Hear that, Jimmy?"

"Hear what?" the newspaper editor called out. "You know my ears aren't so good."

Dixon turned away and gazed at the smoldering house.

"There's a body inside," he said, talking softly now. "I assume it's Ollie. Been so hot, we haven't pulled him out yet."

Bard stared at the sheriff. "He's still in there?"

Dixon nodded and shifted on his feet.

"Still too hot?" Bard asked.

"The fire crew just went in for him."

Bard stepped toward the ruined home. He steeled himself for whatever he'd find. Fire victims, burned a blackish brown, grimy and blistered, were among the worst corpses to look at. Sometimes there was no face left at all, no ears, no hands or feet. You were supposed to deal with death in a clinical manner, not project a personality on the body. But looking at such victims, Bard always thought, That's someone's husband or mother or child.

Squinting, handkerchief to his mouth, he entered what was once Ollie's living room. Smoke filled his throat and made his eyes water. He moved slowly, feeling his way with his hands. He sank to his knees when he reached Merta's body. Ollie lay curled on the floor in the shell of a bathroom, watched over by two silent, ash-covered firemen. Recognizing Gergin and Turloff through their grime, Bard murmured a greeting. With relief, he saw that they'd quenched the fire before it had entirely consumed Merta. He still had a face. You could tell it was him. His shaggy brows and thick gray mustache were burned off, but those were Ollie's big funny ears, that was Ollie's round gnomish body. A lifelong bachelor, he'd lived alone, in his own way. Watching him ride his small mule along the Graciosa Creek horse trail, it was easy to consider him eccentric. Merta wasn't the least bit disagreeable, though. Not to Bard, at least.

He rose and continued stepping through the wreckage. Charred shelves, blistered cans, mounds of ashes—slowly he worked through the residue of Ollie Merta's life. A pile of toasted books, a stack of old melted record albums, a scorched computer . . . Bard stopped. In a corner of the kitchen, a crumpled form half-hidden under charred beams caught his eye. He walked over, sank again to his knees. For an instant, he felt dizzy. Another body. This one much smaller, under five feet. The burned ribbon in her hair looked pale blue. A little girl. No more than ten or eleven. Just about the age of Bard's daughter.

"Two bodies," he called out. "Not one."

Sheriff Dixon was suddenly at his side, bending over. Shock spread across his broad wrinkled face.

"A little girl," Bard said. "Any idea who she is?"

"Who says it's a little girl?"

Bard looked up at Dixon. "I do."

Another figure suddenly appeared beside Dixon. In the gloom, Bard squinted, trying to see who had joined them. Keen dark eyes set in a pale oval face stared back. Usually, Chumash County District Attorney Angela Stark wore her long raven-black hair pulled across her scalp, but now it fell loosely to her shoulders. Instead of her customary business suit, she was wearing a black-matte jersey dress and three-inch heels. The dress clung to her body. Fresh from another high-powered dinner party, Bard figured. His eyes moved slowly down her legs.

Stark said, "What are you looking at, Bard?"

Bard nodded at the small form. "A second body. Ollie Merta wasn't alone. As I was telling the sheriff, it's a little girl."

A tremor played across Stark's face, or so it seemed to Bard. In the gloom, he couldn't be sure. Studying her now, he saw only her customary steel, a steel that usually came tempered with a good deal of impatience. The DA rarely responded to a dispatcher's call. She wasn't one for fieldwork, preferring to contemplate the big picture, which—she made plain—she felt Chumash County sorely lacked. She spent considerable time at legal conferences, plotting possible runs for statewide office. She liked her action fast paced. Being under pressure galvanized her, as did the promise of any intense experience.

"It's a privilege to have the DA herself on the scene," Bard said. "On a Sunday night, no less."

Stark ignored him. Her eyes rested on the little girl's

charred body. "Merta volunteers at the elementary school," she
said. "Teaches music or something. Maybe she's a student."

With that, Stark turned slowly, surveying the ruined house.
"What a horrible accident," she muttered, as much to herself
as the others. "What could have happened? Maybe Merta left
the stove top on. Maybe Merta was smoking a cigarette.
Maybe Merta fell asleep."

You've just got to think it through, she liked to say. The
Ricco drug case was a prime example. Two people in a Ford
Bronco, the driver in front, a passenger in back. The cops saw
a bag of cocaine sail out a window. The driver's defense attorney insisted it was the rear-seat passenger who did the throwing. On a hunch, just before trial, Stark decided to call up
Ford. It turned out that with this model Bronco, the back windows didn't roll down. The DA didn't even have to fly out an
expert. As soon as she informed the defense, the driver pled
guilty.

Stark moved step-by-step through the smoldering room.
"Look here," she said, pointing. "I'm willing to bet the fire
began there on that couch. Here's a cigarette butt. You can see
where it started, where it spread."

Bard tried to hold his tongue. Even though Angela was a
crackerjack prosecutor, she had a taste for closing cases
quickly. For a mix of reasons—impatience, civic boosterism,
and political calculation chief among them—she either went
for a swift conviction or didn't wade in at all. In this, she fit well
with the spirit of Chumash County, which liked to cast itself
as a crime-free oasis on the Central Coast. Bad things weren't
supposed to happen around La Graciosa. When they did, they
were often painted as something else. When that didn't suffice,
they were addressed and moved along with dispatch.

Bard understood and usually tried to cooperate. Everyone benefited, after all, if their county prospered. He'd lived
around La Graciosa all his life. So had his father and grandfather, both honored veterans of the sheriff's department. His
dad, Oscar, had made it all the way to deputy chief. Bard, his
fellow cops—they all owned property here. They all had kids

in the county schools. They all had pensions and medical plans. They all had a stake in this place.

Sometimes, though, Angela Stark got on Bard's nerves.

"Why are you assuming it's an accident?" he asked.

Stark pointed a warning finger. "Watch yourself, Bard. Don't be a cowboy. I believe you've heard that advice before."

She could look striking sometimes. Raven hair against that pale skin, eyes bright as candles. Men often offered her their business cards when she spoke at conferences, telling her they admired her wit. She invariably tossed them out, muttering that she hadn't been all that funny.

"Yes," Bard allowed. "That's true."

She walked toward him, her manner softening. "Look, Doug, I'm the prosecutor here. Howie's the sheriff. We're the ones paid to make the decisions."

"That's also true."

Stark offered a faint smile. "I'm no angel of mercy, God knows. I like putting people in jail. But I don't like wasting our time and energy. We have limited resources. We have to deploy ourselves wisely. We have to make choices."

"That we do," Bard agreed.

"This cigarette burn in the couch. I'm surprised you didn't notice it."

"You're too quick for me."

Stark's eyes ran once more around Ollie Merta's ruined house. "Can you think of anyone who'd want to harm this old man? Or anything of his you'd want to steal?"

"Not a thing."

"Well then." She strode off, finished with him. Bard looked toward Sheriff Dixon. "Who called this in?" he asked.

"Neighbor farther up the canyon saw the flames. Notified the dispatcher."

"They put out an open call to all available hands?"

"Yes."

Bard glanced around at the others now stepping through the wreckage. He spotted two of his colleagues on the force, Bruce Spraker and Josh Ericson. He waved them over. "What do you think?" he asked.

Spraker resembled a Chumash State grad student, with his steel-rimmed glasses and watchful brown eyes. Ericson had a white mustache and a face webbed by age. They both stole looks at the sheriff, vainly trying to get a reading before responding. Eric had a career in front of him, Josh a pension to protect.

"Not sure," Spraker said. "Arson team is still on its way."

"They're rather late to the party," Bard pointed out.

"We couldn't track them down on a Sunday night," the sheriff explained.

They heard the coroner's van roll up on the gravel driveway. A moment later, a two-man team entered the house, pushing a pair of gurneys. As Bard and Dixon walked outside, Jimmy O'Brien rushed up. "What you got?" he asked.

"I've got a journalist who's violated a restricted zone," Dixon said. "That's what I've got."

"Just tell me if—"

Dixon put a meaty hand on Jimmy's arm. "O'Brien, I'll handcuff you to Doug's car unless you go back there on your own."

"Come on—"

Bard stepped between the sheriff and Jimmy. He'd bailed his buddy out of jail twice in his life, and didn't want to go for three. "Jimmy," he said, giving him a look. "Back to the car."

Sensing in Doug the promise of a later briefing, Jimmy retreated. Bard turned to Dixon.

"Who called the DA?" he asked.

Dixon ran a hand through his crew cut. "Lord knows, not me. I suppose she heard the dispatcher, just like all of us."

"Looks like she was at another big-time dinner party."

"So maybe that sort prefers to listen to police chatter over their chardonnay instead of Frank Sinatra. Hell, does it matter?"

"It doesn't. I'm just wondering." Bard studied the facade of Merta's home. He walked to the charred front door, knelt, and pulled a flashlight from his back pocket. "It looks like this was kicked in," he said. "Doorjamb's splintered. And this looks like a boot mark."

Dixon leaned over Bard's shoulder. Doug's flashlight guided his eyes. "Yeah, we saw that. It's obvious a fireman did that. We just haven't figured out which one yet."

"No doubt you will, soon enough."

Bard rose and began circling the house. Ollie Merta lived a modest life. His home was no more than a bungalow, really—wood frame, rolled composition roof, small porch, two cramped bedrooms. Merta had used one as an office, Bard surmised. He'd seen a blackened computer in there. A fax and a printer, too. What was it that Merta did, exactly? How did he live? What mattered to him? Bard didn't know. Mainly as a hobby, Ollie kept a few sheep out back of his house, on the steep pasture that climbed into the foothills. He wasn't a farmer, though, or even a gardener. That much was clear. There was little cultivation here: no flowers, no fruit trees, no vegetables.

Bard stopped amid the brush at the south side of the house. Something had glinted as he'd waved his flashlight. He leaned over, yanked at the chaparral. He went to his knees and yanked some more. His hand brushed against something metallic. An empty beer can. The local Graciosa Brew.

"Funny," Bard called out, showing Dixon what he'd found. "Merta didn't drink."

Dixon shrugged. "So he had visitors."

Bard blinked in the gloom. It was hard to believe this was a summer night. Hard also to describe its appeal. You had to have a feel for the Central Coast. "For that matter," he said, "Merta didn't smoke."

Once more, Angela Stark was at their side. Bard wasn't sure when she'd joined them. "How do you know?" she asked.

Bard brushed back the lank black hair hanging over his forehead. He had a rugged face, crooked nose, and engaged, clear blue eyes, which taken together some women at JB's found attractive. He was clad, as usual, in faded jeans, scuffed boots, and a leather jacket. He carried no gun. Guns, he liked to say, didn't look good on a plainclothes cop; the bulge of an unholstered revolver in a pants pocket just wasn't his style.

Bard examined Stark now. He offered the lopsided grin that so confounded his bosses when they tried to rein him in. "To be a detective," he said, "you've got to know your people."

A gray sedan rolled up to the house. Out of it spilled a man and woman, coats askew, hands clutching the air. "What's happened here?" the woman called out. "Oh my God . . . Oh my God . . . Where's our daughter . . . ?"

Harvey and Cynthia Cooper. She was a yoga instructor, he the proud proprietor of a small winery located some dozen miles beyond Ollie Merta's cabin. Angela Stark knew them well. She stepped forward. "Harvey, Cynthia. Don't tell me. Was Marilee with Ollie? Was Marilee in Ollie's house?"

Cynthia Cooper stared wild-eyed at the burned hulk. "A piano lesson, she was taking a piano lesson . . . We couldn't get her right after, so Ollie was baby-sitting . . . Where . . . Where's Marilee?" She started toward the house, but Sheriff Dixon stopped her.

"Don't go in there, Mrs. Cooper. You don't want to see. There's been a terrible accident."

At that moment the coroner's team emerged from the ruined home, pushing the two gurneys, each bearing a blanket-wrapped body. The Coopers wailed and lunged but again Dixon held them back. Doug Bard, unnoticed, approached the bodies, his back to the others. He held up a hand to stop the coroner's men.

The fog had lifted now, leaving a dark hazy sky. Bard raised the blanket on one gurney, then the other, studying the blackened yet still recognizable faces of Ollie Merta and Marilee Cooper. Both of them were curled into the fire victim's usual pugilistic position, arms bent and fists clenched as if ready to fight. This, he knew, didn't mean they'd been alive at the time of the blaze; all bodies react similarly in a fire, the muscles contracting in response to furious heat. Bard couldn't keep his eyes off Marilee. Yes, she must have been eleven, same as Molly.

Didn't Molly have a school chum named Marilee? He ought to know, Bard thought. He didn't, though. Not for sure.

He shouldn't touch the bodies, he understood that, but he couldn't stop himself. He cupped the little girl's face in his hands. He moved his fingers along her cheeks, down her neck. Then he sensed something.

Marilee's throat felt odd around the larynx, as if the cartilage and muscle there had been compressed. He bent closer over her. Now he spotted what looked to be three slivers etched on the side of her throat, each the size of a fingernail mark. He lifted her eyelids and examined the mucous membrane lining the inner surface. He saw there a cluster of small red dots. He pulled back and looked at Marilee's entire face. There were no smoke stains around the nostrils or in the nose, no blistering or marginal reddening of her skin.

"Our firefighters extinguished the fire too soon," Bard called out. "They left some evidence."

TWO

They were still asleep when Doug Bard knocked. Sasha, hearing him, rose and eased the front door open. There she stood, blinking through clouded eyes. For pajamas, she was wearing a man's powder-blue dress shirt, half-buttoned. Over her shoulder, on the side table in the living room, Bard could see an empty wine bottle and two glasses.

"It's so early," Sasha murmured.

He liked her drowsy like this. He tried to see her now as he once had. For a moment at least, he was not an ex-husband, but an admirer. The haunting gray eyes, the air of dramatic languor, the arch expression that at once beckoned and spurned. By the time she'd come along, he'd grown weary of jabbering girls who spilled their needy emotions all over the dinner table. Sasha never did that. She never lost command of herself. The first time they met, at a party they both thought tedious, she looked at him with shared, amused intimacy. He'd been helpless, and in truth, unwilling to protect himself. He'd learned how. It was Sasha who first grew weary and restless. It was Bard who walked, though, when he realized he'd lost her.

"I need to ask something," Doug said.

Sasha glanced over her shoulder into the house. He wondered whether the second wineglass stayed the night.

"Molly's still sleeping," she said.

"I'll talk quietly."

She looked at her watch, ran a hand through her tangle of dark brown hair, then moved aside.

He went first to Molly's room, stepping lightly, holding his breath. From the doorway, he gazed at her. She lay curled in a half circle, one arm hugging a pillow, the other flung out across the mattress. Straight dark blonde hair half covered her face. He wanted to pull the hair back; he wanted to see her eyes and nose and ears. He could feel Sasha's hand on his elbow, pulling him from the room. Reluctantly, he turned and walked out.

They settled in the living room. The wine bottle and glasses were gone now. Bard stared at the fireplace.

Sasha had her fans, there was no arguing. In business as with friends, she defended her turf, yet always with a preternatural calm. People read whatever they wanted into her strong blank mystery. One mesmerized guest, sitting with her on the floor at a friend's New Year's Eve party, likened her to a Zen master. Bard thought of her more as a wistful, landlocked soul. Once in a while, though, at least in their early years, she managed to kick up her heels.

I can't believe what we've become. That's what she told him the night he left. *We've been playing against each other for too long now. I don't know how we ended up on opposing teams.*

"Marilee Cooper," he said. "Do you know that name?"

Sasha tossed her head, trying to shake herself awake. "Marilee . . . Marilee. Yes, of course. Molly's friend from school. They're in the same class. They have play dates together, and a girl-power club. Molly adores her."

Bard nodded, saying nothing.

Sasha waited him out. The Sphinx, he used to call her. She reached for a pack of Marlboros and cracked it against her forearm. Still a smoker, a pack a day. The nicotine didn't help. If you touched her shoulders, you felt the rigid muscles.

"What about her?" Sasha inquired, restless now with the silence. "Why do you ask?"

"She's dead. A fire out at Ollie Merta's house. She was there for a piano lesson."

Sasha drew on her cigarette. A hand rose to the collar of her shirt. "And Ollie Merta? What happened to him?"

Bard studied her. What an odd first response. "He's dead, too."

Sasha's eyes half closed. "My God. How?"

"They think it's an accident. Merta smoking on the sofa, falling asleep."

"Ollie Merta smoking?"

"You knew him?"

Sasha waited a beat. "A little. He taught music at Molly's school. He taught Molly the piano. Molly knows him far better than—"

"Knows who?" Dressed in pale blue flannel pajamas, Molly stood at the entrance to the living room, rubbing her eyes. "Who do I know?"

She's grown another half inch at least, Bard thought. She doesn't stop. It had been only ten days since he'd seen her. He wanted to wrap his arms around her, but he held back, waiting to see which mood she was in this morning. Daddy's little girl or precocious prepubescent with lots of attitude—he never knew.

"Hey, Molly girl," he said.

She came to him and curled into his lap. At eleven, she had to bend her legs to fit, but she made it. "Love you, Daddy," she said, sounding distracted.

He pulled her hair back now, as he'd wanted to in her bedroom. Her face was round, her nose and ears delicate, her eyes an uncommon blue-green. He cupped her cheeks in his hand, and kissed her forehead. She endured that for a moment, then said, "So tell me, who do I know?"

Bard glanced at Sasha. "Molly," he said. "Something bad has happened. It's about one of your friends."

She sat up and looked toward her mother. "Who?"

Sasha gripped the arms of her chair, unable to speak. Bard sympathized. For so long, he'd wanted to insulate Molly from the world. If he had his way, he'd have kept her in a bubble. He didn't have his way, though.

"Marilee Cooper," Bard said.

Molly climbed to her feet. "What about her?"

Bard took Molly's hand. "There's been a terrible accident, sweetheart. A house fire. She got caught in it. She's dead."

Molly pulled her hand away. Children are more resilient than you think, he reminded himself. Also, not so protected as they seem. Especially Molly. Her shy and winsome style could easily fool.

"Who else?" she asked. " 'Molly knows him far better' . . . That's what Mommy was saying when I came in."

"Ollie Merta, the piano teacher."

Molly's face drained of color. "Ollie taught us music. He was my friend."

"Molly—" Bard began.

"Marilee and Ollie," she continued, as if memorizing the answer to a test. She was trying to act grown-up, he knew that. Yet her chin trembled now. She collapsed back into his lap, her arms around his neck. He could feel her tears on the side of his face. "Marilee and Ollie," she whispered again. "Marilee and Ollie."

Bard held her, trying not to move. The moment recalled another one for him. They were up in the foothills, at a friend's ranch. Molly was four, a sickly four. She came back from a hike drawn and hot with fever. He scooped her up, and instantly she fell asleep in his arms. He didn't want to disturb her, so he just sat there all through the afternoon. Four hours later, she awoke, the fever gone.

"How did it happen, Daddy?" Molly still clung to him.

"Well, they say—"

"It was an accident, honey," Sasha interrupted. "They think Ollie Merta fell asleep smoking a cigarette on the sofa."

Molly kept talking to her father. "Were you there? Did you see?"

"Yes."

"Tell me what they looked like."

That was so like Molly. She had to stop at every car accident or flashing ambulance light. She needed details, a chronology, a history. Normally, he obliged. Not now, though.

"It wasn't pretty," he said.

"Tell me," Molly urged.

Sasha held up two hands, like a crossing guard at Molly's school. "Actually, don't. Spare us the details."

A notion seized Molly. "Why were you there, Daddy? You only investigate murders and stuff like that, don't you?"

"Yes, that's right. But this was a big deal for a Sunday night. They weren't staffed. They put out a general call—"

"Are you going to investigate it?" Molly asked. "Are you going to make sure they know what really happened?"

Bard wondered how to answer. Before leaving Ollie Merta's house, he'd tried his best to get on the case, but Sheriff Dixon had refused. There's no damn crime here, Dixon fumed. I can't waste you on a house fire. Doug had already pushed his boss hard twice this month, so he didn't this time. He'd forced himself to back off.

"I want to investigate it," he told Molly. "But the sheriff needs me on other cases. More important cases."

Molly pulled away from him and stood up. Her eyes clouded; her mouth gathered into a pout. He'd been getting this type of angry disappointment increasingly from his daughter. "You have more important cases?" she asked.

"Molly—"

Bard couldn't finish. Molly was flouncing off. "I'm going to be late for school, Daddy. Gotta go."

"No, wait a sec, I'm just—"

Over her shoulder, Molly called out, "Daddy, you're so down the drain."

He looked at Sasha, who offered only blank eyes. He asked, "Is that her newest line?"

The high beep of Bard's pager stopped them all. He pulled it from his belt and stared at the flashing number. He couldn't place it. "Excuse me," he said. "I need to borrow your phone."

A soft, tentative voice answered on the first ring. Bard recognized Agnes Dellon, one of the sheriff's department booking clerks. More than once, Agnes had favored him with sympathetic looks when he was getting chewed out by Dixon. "I'm calling from home, and you don't know where you heard this," she said. "But I figured you'd want to know that they're about to do the autopsies on Ollie and Marilee. Bit of a rush job. They woke Virgil up."

"Virgil Wilcox is going to do the autopsies?" Bard asked.

"Well, he is our county coroner."

"When is he starting?"

"An hour from now."

Bard hugged Molly as he rushed for the front door, ignoring the distant look in her eyes. "Love you," he called out. "Gotta go."

With little notice, change had come to La Graciosa, storefront by storefront, day by day. It was still little more than a ranching, farming, and fishing outpost, cupped in an insulated canyon, bypassed by both the railroad and the interstate highway. The Santa Lucia Range, as always, rose to the northeast, a lesser row of volcanic peaks seaward. The small brick central plaza remained, as did a handful of cafés and bars with patios backing onto the meandering Graciosa Creek. The familiar adobe and tile was mixed with split timber, reflecting the town's roots in both the Spanish mission era and frontier ranching days. Yet to Doug Bard, La Graciosa had started to feel different, almost like a stranger.

There was more energy around, for one thing. Chumash County was hopping. Long-fallow ranches had stirred to life, filling with newly bought cattle herds and the cowhands who came with them. Two or three of the creekside cafés had acquired themes, and salad bars, and suburban branches. On the road out to Pirate's Beach, a fifty-acre plot full of dusty chaparral had turned into a tony retail center stocked with Banana Republics, Crate and Barrels, Williams-Sonomas. A hundred-acre bluff just north of Pirate's Beach had lost its trio of rusting water tanks, then sprouted luxurious condominiums whose earth tones blended naturally with the terrain. Another bluff, directly above Pirate's Beach, now featured a thicket of red-flagged surveyors' sticks.

The impetus for most of this had been an aggressive real-estate venture capitalist firm from San Francisco, working in tandem with obliging Chumash County commissioners. The usual tree-huggers and slow-growth advocates had howled, but they'd been easily outmaneuvered by a far quieter band of business and political leaders. An unstoppable band, Bard figured. Wave of the future.

The sun, low in the sky now, fought through the haze as he made his way across La Graciosa's plaza. At least the visionaries hadn't touched the two-hundred-year-old *asistencia* yet. There it rose at the far side of the plaza, a fortlike quadrangle with adobe walls and clay tile roof. Once the assistant chapel and backup headquarters for Mission San Luis Obispo de Tolosa to the north, it now housed not just the county jail but also the sheriff's station, the district attorney's office, and La Graciosa's solitary courtroom. The jail and sheriff shared the west wing, a low, long run of rooms fronted by a colonnade of eleven pillars.

That's where Bard headed. He punched open the thick timber entry door, then strode through a warren of small rooms with whitewashed plaster walls and pink-hued, hand-laid cement floors. At Sheriff Dixon's office, he turned the doorknob without knocking, and walked in.

Dixon, as usual, was swiveling about in his high-backed leather chair, talking on one of his telephones. He frowned at the sight of his uninvited guest and slowly hung up the phone. Bard looked around. The sheriff's office, once the padre's study, was larger than the others, with a big window overlooking the quadrangle's inner courtyard and an ancient Spanish oak.

"Do we have an appointment?" Dixon asked.

"Let's make one."

"I already have an appointment. Elsewhere. Got to go."

"Let me join you."

"You've got cases assigned to you, Doug. Go deal with them."

"I will. Right after we're finished at the morgue."

Recognition showed in Dixon's eyes now. "So that's what this is about."

"Let me watch the autopsies with you, Howie. It's not my case. I'll just be an observer."

Dixon massaged his temples, as if trying to rub Bard from his mind. He rolled backward on his padded chair's wheels, and swiveled toward the window. He wasn't from Chumash County. A Los Angeles police captain who took early retirement, he came north more than a decade ago, lured by the Central Coast and a job as director of security for Peabody Enterprises. That had kept him busy for a good five years—the Peabodys, four generations strong, had fingers in everything from cattle-ranching to banking and real-estate development. Then Sheriff Dan Wizen had up and died suddenly. For a while there was talk of Douglas Bard being appointed to replace him until the next election. Eventually, Howie Dixon's name also started floating around, and the Peabody clan let it be known he was their choice. For show, the county commissioners held a public hearing before picking Dixon. With the title of sheriff in front of his name, he won easily at the next election.

"Why are you so interested in this?" Dixon asked. "It's obviously a terrible accident."

"No doubt."

"So why push your way in here?"

Bard groped for an answer. "I guess it's because a little girl died. A little girl who was one of my daughter's best friends."

"I didn't know, Doug." Dixon's expression softened as he weighed options. "If I say you can't come, are you going to threaten to quit again?"

Bard had done that twice: once right after Dixon got appointed sheriff, then again when Angela Stark wouldn't prosecute a dirtbag swindler he'd nailed. Both times, Dixon had persuaded him to stay. We need your type even though you're a pain, the sheriff had said. We need folks who like to put felons in jail.

"Whatever it takes," Bard replied now.

A grudging smile spread across Dixon's face. In a department of twenty-eight, Doug had been the leader in felony arrests for five years straight. He didn't mind cutting corners or overlooking niceties. He did not, thank God, think of himself as a shining white knight.

"Yes," the sheriff said, "that's what it's always about with you."

"Always."

Dixon studied him. "If I let you attend the autopsy, you'll let go of this right after, you'll get back to the cases that need chasing?"

"Absolutely."

Dixon rose slowly, his palms held up in unwilling surrender. "Okay, then, come along."

The coroner's morgue was another thing that had not yet changed in La Graciosa. It occupied odd-shaped quarters just beyond the sheriff's office, quarters that Bard thought might once have been the *asistencia*'s stables. Dirty white tiles covered the floor, stainless steel crypts lined the walls. A double bank of fluorescent lights hung from a low ceiling. Marilee Cooper's body lay on a steel autopsy table, wrapped in a sheet.

"Ready to roll?"

Bard turned to see Virgil Wilcox, the Chumash County coroner, shuffling into the room. At seventy, he looked slower and bulkier than ever. His hair, what was left of it, formed gray patches at the sides of his skull. His nose, broad and red, featured a maze of broken blood vessels. His ample belly, held in by a wide leather belt, curved like a beach ball. The coroner's part-time job paid little in Chumash County, so they were fortunate to have Wilcox. At least he was a physician, which was more than you could say about many small county coroners. That he wasn't a forensic pathologist usually didn't matter. Only rarely did Chumash County's coroner have occasion to examine violent, unnatural, or suspicious deaths. When he did, Wilcox could always spend the money to call in an outside specialist.

Sheriff Dixon clapped the coroner on the back. "Guess we're ready to roll, Virgil."

"What do we got here?" Wilcox asked. "What do you need?"

"The arson team has already ruled this an accidental fire,"

Dixon explained. "They say Merta fell asleep smoking a cigarette while the little girl was watching TV in the other room. So from you, Virgil, we just need the usual general evaluation and cause of death."

"D or C?"

Dixon hesitated. Autopsies were classified into four types: A full autopsy, A, used in obvious homicides, went the whole nine yards with witnesses, extensive photography, and X rays. A standard full, B, used often when families requested autopsies, usually did without the witnesses, photography, or X rays. A localized autopsy, C, focused on specific areas, such as a gunshot wound to the head. A simple physical exam, D, involved a visual survey and sometimes blood and urine specimens, but no incisions.

"Your call, Virgil," Dixon said. "But I'd imagine a C."

"You got it."

Bard stepped forward. "Excuse me, but I hadn't heard about that arson report."

"Since you're not on this case," Dixon said, "you wouldn't have."

Wilcox squinted. "Almost didn't recognize you there, Bard. Standing back in the corner and all."

Bard stepped yet closer. "I was trying not to intrude."

The coroner was snapping on a pair of rubber gloves. "DA's office called, filled me in, so I'm ready. Let's get going, okay? I've got a golf date in two hours. If I miss tee-off—"

"Who called—" Bard started to ask.

Sheriff Dixon put a hand on his shoulder. "Doug's just observing here, Virgil. Let's not get distracted."

Wilcox turned to the body. "Shouldn't take long. Deaths caused by fire generally result from inhalation of noxious gases and fumes. We can easily establish that without a full autopsy. I just need to draw some blood really. We'll find carbon monoxide in the blood. That'll tell the story."

"Excuse me," Bard said. "Isn't that so only if the body was alive at the time of the fire? Otherwise, you won't find carbon monoxide, will you?"

Dixon and Wilcox both stared at him. "Are you thinking

this little girl didn't die in the fire?" the sheriff asked. "You thinking she was already dead?"

Bard shrugged. "Just a hypothetical."

"Arson squad has called this an accident," Dixon reminded him.

"As I say, just a question. I was only wondering."

Dixon's hands curled with regret. "I shouldn't have let you come, Doug. You're slowing us down here."

"What's more," Virgil added, "you're on your way to making this a lot more expensive than it need be. If you manage to complicate things, Howie here will have to hire a grand-a-day pathologist."

"Which is money I don't have to spend," Dixon snapped.

The coroner had his hand on the corpse now. He pulled back the sheet. Bard flinched at the sight of Marilee's thin charred body. The black-brown skin looked as if it might crackle when touched. The hair was seared to the roots. The eyelids, forced shut, were a fierce red. For an instant, he imagined Molly on this table, but beat back the notion. Then came an impulse to rewrap Marilee in her sheets. He couldn't stop himself. Slowly, he approached the table.

He'd seen his share of autopsies. He understood why Virgil Wilcox might want only to draw blood and be done with it. The work of forensic pathologists is not glamorous, at least not the part Bard had witnessed. With knives and saws, they slice open torsos, roll back flaps of skin, crack skulls, plunge hands into viscous innards. They pull out spleens and livers and kidneys, they weigh them, they dice them up. Black bile oozes, blood drips, odors assault. The first time he'd seen a doctor carve open a body shoulder to shoulder, then sternum to pubis—the huge Y incision that starts an autopsy—Bard had rocked on his feet. Worse still was the moment the doctor had popped the skull. He started from behind the head, slicing from one ear to the other, then folding back the scalp. Next he picked up an oscillating saw and cut through bone, across the forehead to the ears, and around to the back of the head. Finally, he pulled off the skullcap and held it high in the air, triumphant with his bounty. All this on the body of a three-month-old. The dead baby, a mere carcass by then, his brain and insides exposed to pale yellow light, weighed fifteen pounds.

Bard was standing across from Virgil Wilcox. The coroner was drawing blood. "This is obvious," Wilcox said. "Classic example of carbon monoxide intoxication."

"How so?" Bard asked.

Wilcox pointed. "Look at the postmortem lividity. Nice and pink, just like you'd expect if the girl was alive and breathing during the fire. Textbook example. This is how it usually happens. Death by inhalation. Bodies don't burn that easily. It's amazing, really, how durable they are. They resist the flames. It's the gases that get you, way before the fire. You gotta inhale, after all. Can't stop yourself."

Bard leaned over the body. The color Wilcox called nice and pink, he'd call faintly pink. Grayish pink. "Her color could be a little brighter. Don't you think, Virgil?"

Wilcox frowned. "Looks pink enough to me."

Dixon came to Bard's side. With a hand on his elbow, he moved him back. "If you want to stay in here, Doug, you'd better let Virgil do his job."

Bard stepped around to the coroner's side of the table. He pointed at Marilee's throat. "Feel her larynx," he suggested. "Don't you think the cartilage and muscle there have been compressed? Look also at those little slivers on the side of her throat. Don't those look like fingernail marks?"

Wilcox bent over. He poked and prodded. "No, can't say the larynx feels unusual . . . and can't say those are fingernail marks."

"Doug, what are you driving at?" Dixon demanded.

"Compressed larynx and fingernail marks suggest just maybe you've got a strangulation here."

"But she died in the fire—"

"Did she?" Bard interrupted. His hands touched Marilee. He lifted her eyelids and pointed to the mucous membrane lining the inner surface. "Look, there, at those small red dots. Virgil, aren't those what you boys call petechial hemorrhages?"

"That's just artifact. You see that all the time—"

"Oh," Bard said. "I thought they were presumptive evidence of strangulation."

The odor and close air in the autopsy room had turned Sheriff Dixon's broad face a shade of gray. It happened to even the toughest cops. "Damn it, Doug, you're not a pathologist."

Why did Dixon need to have it this way? Maybe he was right, Bard reasoned, but how could he be so sure? Bard cupped Marilee's face with his hands. "Look at her, Howie. There're no smoke stains around the nostrils or in the nose. There's no blistering. There's no reddening of the skin."

"So what?"

"I believe you would see all that if she were alive at the time of the fire."

Virgil Wilcox's face started to puff up. "Howie is right, Bard, you aren't a pathologist. You're not even a doctor. I am, though. So if you'll step back, I'll do my job. Think I'll ventilate her a little. I'm sure that'll make you happy."

Virgil's payback time. The coroner was going to cut Marilee open just to see if he could turn the detective green.

Bard steeled himself. Virgil picked up a wickedly long, thin knife. He moved with surprising speed for a man of his age and girth. With two sweeping motions he had Marilee exposed from breastbone to groin. A yellowish-brown fluid began trickling out of her. The liquid pooled and ran through drainage holes at each end of the autopsy table. Wilcox paid no attention to the ooze around his hands. With a scalpel now, he was slicing sections from the inner linings of Marilee's throat and lungs. He weighed the samples on a scale, then placed them on a small dissection stand that also had drainage holes.

Sheriff Dixon asked, "What's that you're doing, Virgil?"

"I'm going to test to see if these segments were live flesh at the time this girl died."

"And if they were? Will that settle things, Virgil? Enough to write her up?"

"I'd suspect so, but we'll want to wait for the blood results."

Within twenty minutes, Wilcox had all of Marilee's organs

scooped into a clear plastic bag. "Ready for the next one?" Dixon asked.

Wilcox glanced at his watch. "Yes, let's bring him on."

The two of them slid Marilee's body onto a gurney, which they began rolling to one side of the room. Bard stepped in their way. "Hold on," he said.

He came to the top end of the gurney. He forced himself to look at Marilee. It was harder now to imagine her as someone's daughter. To see a body split open, with the insides dug out, was a humbling experience. Autopsy rooms were not conducive to thoughts of a human soul. Marilee resembled a dressed deer. Bard reached for the sheet crumpled at the foot of the gurney. He pulled it over her body.

"Okay, Doug." The sheriff was wobbling on his feet. "It's time you get back to all those case files sitting on your desk."

"If I could only—"

"This isn't your job, Doug. You're not a pathologist. You're a detective."

Bard turned to leave. "I can't argue with that, Howie."

THREE

From the central plaza, looking two blocks down a cobblestone side street, Douglas Bard watched the stream of chattering children bounce up the steps of La Graciosa Elementary School. Some turned to wave at parents before disappearing behind the school's tall red wooden doors. Others bolted back down the incline for one more hug and kiss. Through the damp early-morning mist, Bard strained for a sight of Molly, but couldn't find her in the crowd.

Only rarely did he get a chance to take his daughter to school. Under the custody agreement, he had her every other weekend, and most Wednesday evenings. He took her boating whenever he could, and on Saturday nights they camped out in Pecho Rancho State Park or roasted marshmallows in the big stone fireplace of Doug's secluded Apple Canyon home. During the school week, when Sasha wanted Molly back in her own bed, they usually did what Molly liked most—shop in the regional mall north of town, then eat pizza and Caesar salads at Spark's Italian Café. Bard especially looked forward to school plays and open houses. That's when he and Sasha and Molly went out as if they were still a family.

Two days had passed since the county coroner's ruling. Accidental fire, Virgil Wilcox had ruled, concurring with the arson squad. Death caused by carbon monoxide inhalation. Marilee's family had accepted that finding, and Ollie Merta had no family. There'd been a pair of funerals, the little girl's drawing almost every student at La Graciosa Elementary. The cases were closed now. More accurately, the cases were never opened.

Bard told himself that was fine. He had a full plate; there were plenty of jerks and mutts to wipe off the streets of La Graciosa. He didn't need another run-in with Dixon and Stark. You can't pout and fire off rockets every time folks disagree with you. It's the DA's and sheriff's bat and ball, after all. Bump up against them once too often, you lose your job. Without a salary, Bard couldn't eat, and worse, couldn't pay his paltry share of child support. What he'd abhor most about that was enduring Sasha's pity.

"Well, praise the Lord—there most certainly will be no crime committed around here this morning." Jimmy O'Brien clapped Bard on the back as he settled beside him. "What priority we folks get here in the central plaza. Top detective in the department, on patrol duty. Or is this a stakeout? Am I blowing your cover?"

Involuntarily, Bard's eyes turned to the school. Jimmy followed his gaze. "I see," he said, with less clamor now. "It is a stakeout. How's Molly these days?"

"As usual."

"Am I supposed to know what that means?"

"No, you're not."

They sat in silence, watching the town fill up. They knew almost everyone they saw, or at least recognized their faces. At the shops, owners were opening their doors and pulling brooms along the sidewalks. At the cafés, waiters were raising umbrellas above patio tables overlooking the creek. At the bear fountain, a half dozen joggers gathered over croissants and steaming cups of fresh-brewed coffee. Everywhere, earnest-looking professionals in slacks and skirts and blazers rushed off to work or appointments.

They didn't used to rush, Bard thought. That was also something new in La Graciosa.

"Okay, Doug," Jimmy blurted. "What's bothering you?"

"Hell, Jimmy. This town is changing too damn much. All of Chumash County, for that matter. Week in, week out. Creeps up on you. When did all this get decided? I don't recall ever being asked for my okay."

Jimmy shot him a look of mock alarm. "You mean they

didn't consult you? My God, what an oversight. We'd better see to that."

"Yes, please do, Jimmy. I'm the oppressed class. Aren't you newspaper types supposed to do stuff for us?"

"Indeed we are. Comfort the afflicted and afflict the comfortable, that's our mission. Why, I'll—" Jimmy stopped, diverted by the sight of someone crossing the plaza. He pointed. "Great timing. Here's who should hear your complaints."

Bard looked up. Bruce Hightower, chairman of the Chumash County Board of Commissioners, appeared as usual to be a man in a hurry. He was a lean six-footer whose broad shoulders and narrow waist gave him the look of an athlete. One hand held a cellular phone close to his ear. As he talked into it, he managed still to recognize and wave at passersby. The cast of his eyes offered reassurance wherever he gazed.

"What a politician," Bard said.

"Not only," Jimmy pointed out. "More than that."

True enough. Hightower didn't just talk, he made things happen. He'd waded in almost as soon as he arrived in Chumash County seven years ago. First he did volunteer work for various community action groups. That led to an appointment on the county planning commission, then election to La Graciosa's city council. He served one term there before running for the county commission. The venture capitalists up north loved him, for he enthusiastically supported development in Chumash County. It was growth on his own terms, though—growth that recognized a certain scale and relation to the environment. Hightower supported only those projects sensitive to the Central Coast's natural world. In this way, he managed to draw lovers of the outdoors and a strong local economy into one tent.

"Many of our fellow citizens consider Hightower to be a visionary," Bard allowed. "A boon to all the Central Coast."

Hightower was rushing by them now. Spotting the detective and newspaper editor, he raised a hand and slowed down. "Hey there, Jimmy, gotta run, late for an appointment, but let's talk soon. Lots of exciting news about the Pirate's Beach project."

"Anytime you want," Jimmy called out.

Bard watched Hightower turn a corner and disappear. He knew the man only by sight and passing nods; Hightower wasn't yet a commissioner when the county board made Dixon sheriff. "Jesus, Jimmy," Bard said. " 'Anytime you want'?"

"He is head of the county commission, Doug."

Bard just shook his head. Jimmy studied him. "What's really up, Doug?"

Bard tried a lopsided grin, but couldn't quite get it into position. "I didn't win the lottery again this week. My game plan is wobbling way off course."

Jimmy didn't even smile. "I saw you at Marilee Cooper's funeral. Then again at Ollie Merta's. That's a lot of time in church."

"They were good people. I was paying my respects."

"Doug, you can't stand church. You can't stand crowds."

"Yeah, well—"

"Come on. I was with you at Ollie Merta's, remember? You were acting like there was something up."

"Accidental fire, that's what was up. Horrible tragedy."

"Well, Doug. I just don't think so."

"You ran the story, Jimmy. Above the fold on page one, with photos. Virgil Wilcox called it, you printed it."

"What do you call it?"

Bard looked out across the plaza. A sacred sense of duty, that's what his father always talked about. *You stand by those you work with. You stand by your community.* How often had he heard that instruction?

Unwelcome images of the late Oscar Bard filled Doug's mind. His feet up on the kitchen table, in his boxers and undershirt. His hands reaching for cleaning cloths, lubricating oil, and a selection from his gun collection. The MAK-90 maybe, or the SKS with the thirty-mag clip—the one he kept "in case things get really bad." Oscar always thought things were likely to get really bad, even in bucolic La Graciosa. To his dying day, he kept a .25 caliber six-shooter stuffed in his boot, and a 9mm on his pickup's floorboard. It's either that, he explained, or succumb to all those punks who want to whack you on the head and you're supposed to like it.

Oscar wasn't entirely paranoid—he was a good enough cop to have made real enemies, and those enemies, once released from prison, had occasionally come looking for him. Guns and the police department—only they stood between the Bard family and unspeakable mayhem. *You stand by those you work with. You stand by your people.*

What the hell, though. Bard spoke softly. "I think they were already dead when the fire started, Jimmy. I think they were strangled."

Jimmy stared at him. He'd trimmed up since his early days as a reporter, acquiring along the way a few serviceable wool suits and a handful of gray hairs. Still he suggested a walrus, with his big gut and broad face and bushy mustache. "Jesus," he said. "What a story to keep from me."

Bard turned on him. "There's no story. This is off the record. Just you and me talking."

"You're supposed to make that clear at the start of a conversation with a reporter."

"Don't horseshit me, Jimmy." Bard's voice was rising. "You know our deal."

"Take it easy. I'm just giving you trouble."

Passersby in the plaza were studying them now. Bard hadn't realized how loud he'd gotten. "Let's get out of here," he said. "Hell, let's go out to Pirate's Beach."

They drove northwest along the country road that followed Graciosa Creek to the sea. Coming around a curve, in a pass between two hills, Bard tensed. Here was where you once would catch your first glimpse of the ramshackle village that sat on Graciosa Bay. Now, instead, the view was of those earth-toned condominiums, set deftly into the contour of a sheer cliff, as if they'd been carved by the winds and sea. You had to swing past them before you could see Pirate's Beach.

At least it was still a hamlet. A scattering of simple wood-frame homes dotted the weed-clogged hillside and descended to the single main street. A row of ragged seventy-year-old storefronts faced the sea. The familiar seedy bars and cafés—Gordo's and Rick's and Tasha's—kept their front doors propped open with stools and gaudy signs.

Yet among them there had sprouted in recent times a handful of boutiques that went by names such as Country Goose and Sheepy Shop and Timberdoodle. Two buildings had been torn down, a third had been boarded up. A bulldozer sat ominously on a rise to the east.

"More of this stuff to come," Jimmy said. "Lots of venture capital still pouring in. Someone means to tear down this whole place and build themselves a La Jolla of the Central Coast."

They were on the boardwalk, heading south. Bard looked around. The grocery store that first opened its doors in 1922 still survived. So, too, did the ancient fishing pier and the solitary Seaside Motel and the grimy Foghorn Beach Pub.

"I like Pirate's Beach as it is," Doug said.

"Yep, me, too. But you got to give it to Hightower's staff. They've maintained some standards. Those condos look like they've been here for centuries, and these new shops, well hell, they're a lot healthier to walk into than Gordo's, for chrissake. Besides, all this development has kickstarted the county. Chumash was dying on the vine. We needed something."

Bard kept walking. For eons, Pirate's Beach had needed nothing but the rolling hills to the east, the vast immaculate sand dunes to the south, the spit of land that reached seaward to the north. Now all that wasn't enough. "I get it, Jimmy. Booming economy, tony merchants, shops full of upscale customers—what comes with that? Lots of advertising in the local newspaper, that's what. Jimmy, my man, you're thinking like a goddamn capitalist. Maybe you should have stayed a reporter. Editor in chief has made you entirely too responsible."

Jimmy searched for a response. In his leaner days as a

bachelor, he'd lived for a while in a hut on Clam Beach, not far from here. He'd hiked the adjacent Chumash Dunes with his lawyer buddy, Greg Monarch. Greg was gone now, retired from the law, living on an island in the Puget Sound. Jimmy was married; Jimmy was a father. There was no returning to the past.

"Well, maybe I have changed," he said. "But so have you. You're no outlaw. You own a house, you have a daughter—"

"I pay child support. And my ex-wife occupies the house."

"All the more to my point. You have responsibilities, so do I."

"Come on, Jimmy. We're still good for something when there's cause—"

"Are we? Good God, my man, not more than thirty minutes ago you told me you thought an accidental fire was really a double murder. Then you pledged me to silence."

Bard looked out at the sea. "What other choice is there, Jimmy? As I'm regularly reminded, I'm a cop. It's my job to collect the evidence. Other people decide what to make of it."

He'd enrolled one summer at the Chumash State law school. He'd had it in mind to bust out of his box. Textbooks, though, made his eyes blur. He'd lasted just eighteen months of night classes.

"I'm not always right," Bard said. "There are people who know more than me. I'm frequently reminded of that, too. I'm also reminded that we all live here together, that we're all part of a community, that we all need to row together."

"Ah yes." Jimmy was grinning. "You have any idea how often a small-town newspaper editor hears about rowing together?"

"How do you handle it?"

"I take rowing lessons."

They'd reached the end of the boardwalk. After studying the tide, they scrambled down to the sand, and settled on boulders beside the sea. Waves sprayed salty water on their faces. In the distance, brown pelicans and great blue herons skimmed the ocean's surface, watched blankly by a pair of harbor seals sunning themselves on a sandspit. Bard asked, "Did you know Ollie Merta?"

"A bit. Funny old guy. Stuck to his own path. He used to come by the newspaper office to propose stories. Ended up fixing three of my computers one day. He knew all sorts of odd stuff."

"Like piano playing," Bard said. "He taught Molly. She knows everything from Bo Diddley to Buddy Holly. Molly thought he was cool." Bard paused. "Molly knew Marilee, too. They were buddies."

"What's happened, Doug? What's going on?"

"Come on, Jimmy, you know."

"Okay, okay. We pretend bad things don't happen here. But this isn't your usual small-time airbrush deal."

"That's true." Bard's feet dug into the sand. "Still, we're just doing what's best for Chumash. We all prosper then. You sell ads, my property values rise, Bruce Hightower gets re-elected. The future looks bright."

"Are you sure they're wrong about these deaths?"

Sometimes Bard resented Jimmy's ceaseless questions. "No, not really, not entirely. I bluffed them a bit. I'm not a forensic expert."

"Well, then."

"Well then what?"

"What say we find out for sure?"

Bard looked sharply at Jimmy. What say, indeed. *Molly thought he was cool.* It must have been so satisfying to be the object of Molly's warm regard. Ollie must have relished his state of grace with these children.

"I'm not even on the case, Jimmy. Hell, there isn't any case."

"You're right. There's no case. There's just two people dead. A funny old man and a sweet little girl."

A sweet little girl. Bard thought of what he saw lying on a steel table in the county morgue. Bard thought of Molly, scrambling up the steps of her elementary school.

What say indeed. Bard had to admit, he felt eager. Everywhere he looked, familiar stories were getting altered. Why not one more?

"It won't be easy," he warned.

Jimmy grinned. "Who wants easy?"

Lost, he threaded his way among the stately brick buildings, each six stories high and covered with ivy. Since his undergraduate days and passing stab at law school, Doug Bard rarely visited the Chumash State University campus. He never had felt comfortable here. Overearnest philosophizing and professors with smug knowing looks did not stir his soul.

Bard was looking for the health science building. He crossed a grassy quadrangle, passing clutches of coeds dressed in thin halter tops and cutoff blue jeans. Their expressions didn't encourage questions. He turned east on a brick path that wound among a grove of stately oaks. At its end, he finally saw the modernistic glass and metal structure that had been described to him.

He chose the stairway over the elevator. On the sixth floor, he located Room 617. A small index card in a slot on the door confirmed he had the right office. *Dr. Peter Garrity, Associate Professor, Forensic Pathology.*

Garrity opened the door at the first knock. Bard found fierce brown eyes boring into him from just inches away. Garrity was tall and thin, with close-cropped graying hair. He held a Bible open in his hand. "Just reading my Psalms for the day," he declared. "Bard, I assume? Come on in."

Bard stepped into a small room, no more than nine by twelve feet. Towering piles of books and magazines rose against two walls. Open files lay scattered on the carpeted floor, pages spilling from them. Garrity's desk occupied one corner, dominated by what looked to Bard to be an authentic human skull.

"Here, here," Garrity said, sweeping loose files off a chair. "Sit here."

Bard stared at the Bible as he sat down. "Not only the wonders of science interest you?"

"The wonders of science?" Garrity's eyebrows arched. He tapped the volume in his hands. "Nothing compared to the wonders in here."

Bard offered an expression that he hoped indicated interest. "As you know, I came—"

Garrity interrupted: "Bard, have you thought much about the Book of Genesis?"

"Not recently."

" 'Where is your brother?' "

"I don't have—" Bard, an only child, started to answer.

"That's what God asked Cain in Genesis," Garrity continued. "And Cain said, 'I am not my brother's keeper.' And God said—"

This time Bard interrupted: " 'Abel's blood cries out from the ground.' "

Garrity stared at him with such ferocity, Bard thought he'd angered the professor. Then a faint smile slowly spread over the pathologist's face. "That's right. That's very good, Bard."

"We've worked together before, Dr. Garrity. On some of those cases where the county calls you in to consult or do an autopsy. I had the Swerdlow case with you. Also those two convenience store clerks that Jason Pine killed."

"Yes, yes, of course. Knew I'd seen your face before. Pleasure to work with you again. What does the county want me to take on this time?"

"Well, actually, it's not exactly the county who's interested in your services."

"I don't understand."

"I'd just like your advice."

"You?"

"It's a case I think they maybe got wrong."

Unease and confusion showed in Garrity's narrow face. "I'm not being retained by the county? You're end-running your bosses?"

"That's about it."

Garrity rose. "I don't work for free, and I don't snipe at my colleagues."

Bard stayed in his chair. "Tell me this, Doctor. Do you often find that victims' blood cries out from the ground?"

The question stopped Garrity. His hand crept toward the Bible that now rested on his desk. "Often enough," he said. "Especially with the little ones. I've opened up lots of little babies. When I see multiple bruises and a bowel full of pus, I think bad thoughts."

"What about when you see a compressed larynx and fingernail marks on the throat?"

Despite himself, Garrity's eyes traveled to the file Bard held under one arm. "That what you got in there?"

Bard slid the file across the desk. Garrity stared at it. "You supposed to have possession of this?" he asked.

"No. But nothing's missing down at the sheriff's. I made a copy."

"Virgil Wilcox handle the case?"

"Yes."

Garrity snorted. "Virgil Wilcox doesn't know his ass from his elbow."

"What about a murder from an accidental death?"

Garrity's fingers touched the cover of the file. "You say you've got a compressed larynx and fingernail marks in here?"

"Also lots of small red dots underside of the eyelids."

"Petechial hemorrhages?"

"I'm no expert, but that's the way it looks to me."

Garrity sank back into his chair. He opened the file, and began turning through the pages. He stopped at a color photo of Marilee Cooper's body. He picked up a magnifying glass and squinted. "Did you see this body in the flesh, Bard?"

"Yes, sir."

"Did you see any smoke stains around the nostrils or in the nose?"

"No, sir."

"Did you see any blistering or marginal reddening of the skin?"

"No, sir."

"Did you see what Virgil here calls 'nice deep pink' lividity?"

"No, sir."

"Neither do I, Bard."

"So what does all this mean?"

Garrity's eyes blazed. "It means Marilee Cooper's blood cries out from the ground."

Sheriff Howie Dixon stood at his big picture window, staring out at the ancient Spanish oak that dominated the *asistencia* courtyard. Behind him, Chumash County DA Angela Stark paced across his office, talking steadily. At the conference table, Virgil Wilcox sat beside Stark's chief deputy DA, Cassie Teal.

Let's consider how this unfortunate story got in our county's newspaper. Where might it have come from? What led Jimmy O'Brien to Peter Garrity? What led Peter Garrity to this case? Any of you want to lay a bet?

Dixon turned from the window and sat down. He glanced at the bank of buttons blinking furiously on his phone, which made him thankful that he'd put all his calls on hold. He wasn't ready to deal with anyone just yet. Once more he studied the newspaper that lay open across his desk. "Questions Raised About Merta House Fire Death" read the banner headline in the La Graciosa *News-Times*. Under it, Jimmy O'Brien's story, rich with quotes from Peter Garrity, identified pointedly as "the county's own outside expert in forensic pathology." *Fingernail marks . . . crushed larynx . . . signs of strangulation . . . suggests Ollie Merta and Marilee Cooper were already dead when the fire began . . .*

Dixon hadn't always cut corners as they did here in Chumash County. There'd been rough spots during his tenure as Los Angeles police captain, but they usually had to do with coming down too hard on the gangbangers who mugged and stole and pushed crack to schoolkids. Sure, there'd been some setups, some guns placed in victims' hands, some teeth kicked in, some wild stories told poker-faced up on the witness stand. Yet always toward understandable goals; always the ends justified the means. They played it differently up here. Sometimes, they didn't fight crime in Chumash County with any kind of means.

He hadn't realized that when he first arrived. He'd proved a quick study, though, while at Peabody Enterprises. They liked that about him, and they liked even more how he kept order when trouble did arise. They liked him so well that they rewarded him with the sheriff's office. What the hell, he'd figured. He had bought himself a nice piece of land on an ocean bluff ten miles up the road, and he needed a steady income to make the payments. Why not coast a little—at least compared to LA—while keeping a salary and badge? If that's what they wanted, that's what he'd give them.

If only Angela Stark hadn't gotten herself elected DA. What a piece of work. You couldn't slack off or slip anything past her. Nor could you ever satisfy her many demands. Yet he was obliged to try if he wanted his job, a fact she never stopped reminding him. *I'm your keeper, Howie.* She always said that with an ironic roll of the eyes, but she meant it. He didn't doubt the ruthless edge in her. Once, she told him to float a rumor that one of her political enemies, a grimly puritanical local judge, was humping his bailiff in chambers. When Dixon pointed out that it wasn't true, Stark said, I know. I just want to watch the bitter old prune deny it.

Only in one instance had Dixon seen Stark's talents fail to win her what she wanted. During the primaries two years ago, she tried to get the Democratic Party's nomination for state attorney general, but lacked the needed bankroll and good-ol'-boy connections. Coming from a backwoods county didn't help. Nor did being a single woman with a law degree from the local state college. Stark emerged from the experience with some biting tales about "fat-cat corporate lawyers" in San Francisco who liked to lament their profession's mounting greed while consuming hundred-dollar lunches at the Clift Hotel. As restless as Chumash County made her, she seemed to prefer it to big-city boardrooms. Dixon couldn't help but laugh when she told her stories. He would have voted for her if she'd made the ballot.

"Sheriff, how about joining our discussion over here?"

Dixon looked up to see Stark waving him toward the conference table. He rose slowly and walked over. "I was just rereading Jimmy O'Brien's article."

"Any notion where it came from?" Stark asked.

Dixon hesitated. "I'm not sure."

"Not sure? Howie, you must be having a senior moment. Don't you recall that Doug Bard brought O'Brien out to Merta's house that first night?"

Dixon tugged at his ear. "Bard didn't actually bring Jimmy out there to the fire. O'Brien tagged along after he heard our radio call. If Bard hadn't given him a ride, he could have followed Doug out anyway."

"And since then?" Stark asked. "What's Bard's involvement been with Jimmy O'Brien on this case?"

"Doug says O'Brien tried to pump him, as always. Doug says he gave him nothing. O'Brien found Dr. Garrity on his own."

"You don't say."

"Doug's a cowboy, but he's always argued from within. Code of honor matters to him. His buddies matter."

"There's always a first time."

"Come on, Angela. I say back off of Doug. He's a pain, but the best goddamn detective I have."

Stark raised an eyebrow. "My goodness, Howie, you are feeling frisky today." She moved closer to him. "I will repeat. I don't believe Bard. I'd like to know—"

"What does it matter?" Cassie Teal interrupted. "The story's out. The question now is, what do we do?"

All eyes turned to her. The deputy DA possessed little of her boss's verve. She had reserved, pale blue eyes, a head full of dark blonde curls, and an oblique way of looking sideways at people. She also had Angela Stark's ear, for reasons unclear to others in the DA's office.

Cassie Teal rose and walked over to Dixon's desk. With one hand, she grabbed the newspaper, with the other, a pile of phone messages. "Look at these quotes from Marilee's parents and the school. Look at all these calls. 'If there's been murder here, we want justice . . . Our Marilee's killer needs to be caught . . . Ollie Merta deserves better than this.' "

Silence fell. A hard memory filled the room. They all knew Cassie Teal had once been a defense attorney, had once represented a child killer, had once endured a scorching wave of similar comments.

"I'll tell you one thing we don't do," Angela said. "We don't let this become a repeat of the Joseph Wallace case."

Dixon scowled at the memory. Cassie's hand went to her forehead.

Joseph Wallace's murder, committed a good year before Stark and Dixon took office, had been a particularly cold-blooded affair. Late one night, high in the Santa Lucia foothills, marauders set fire to Wallace's barn. When Wallace rushed out to save the horses tied inside, six bullets slammed into his face and chest. Chumash County law enforcement responded with even less vigor than usual, no doubt because Wallace was a universally disliked member of Santa Barbara's landed gentry who'd bought his way into central California, then started diverting water from the upper Graciosa. By the time someone thought to summon a forensic team, a rainstorm had washed away all evidence. The murder was never solved, never avenged.

Cries of outrage from Wallace's powerful friends had welled from across the state. Their protests had brought severe criticism upon Chumash County, particularly in the LA and San Francisco newspapers. Who's running things up there? the Los Angeles *Times* demanded. What's happening on the Central Coast?

During her tenure in the DA's office, Stark had managed to quell such questions. Statewide, she'd built a solid reputation, particularly for her ability to pit drug suspects against each other until one flipped. Stark had no intention now of inviting renewed condemnation from big-city voices.

She said, "Believe me, we won't be having another Wallace case around here."

Cassie turned to the coroner. Wilcox's eyes were half-closed, more in retreat than weariness. "Virgil, any way to refute Peter Garrity, or at least counter? You did call these accidental deaths, after all. What is Garrity talking about?"

Wilcox pulled a handkerchief from his pocket and began patting his moist forehead. "Same stuff Bard brought up at the autopsy. It's always a subjective call. He sees gray-pink, I see cherry red, that makes all the difference. What I think we should do is—"

Angela Stark interrupted. "I'm not interested in what you think we should do, Virgil. The question is, can you refute him? Can you counter him?"

Wilcox studied the backs of his hands. "An expert opinion can always be countered. Happens all the time."

"That's right," Angela said. "In law school, we studied some classic examples of conflicting expert opinions. What was that one in England? The Fox case?"

Virgil offered it eagerly, as if he'd already been researching his defense. "Yes, the Sidney Fox case of 1929. It's in all the texts. The great pathologist of England, Sir Bernard Spilsbury, contended that Fox had strangled his mother before she was burned in a fire, even though he'd never seen a strangulation with fewer signs. Spilsbury based his opinion in part on a bruise he claimed he saw, which he didn't preserve and wasn't visible at a later time. Spilsbury won the battle of persuasion against Sir Sydney Smith, the great pathologist of Scotland. Fox was charged with and hanged for strangling his mother—"

"The point," Angela said, "is that pathologists' opinions can differ greatly, and be based on nearly illusory evidence."

Wilcox hesitated. "Well now, there are certain fundamental concepts—"

"Christ sakes, Virgil!" Sheriff Dixon was stirring finally. "Virgil, did you or did you not find carbon monoxide in these people's blood?"

Wilcox wiped his forehead again. "No . . . Not exactly . . ."

Dixon slapped the table with his palm. "Why didn't you mention that in your report?"

Wilcox grabbed a copy of what he'd written. "I guess I forgot. But if you take a look here, you'll see I based my finding on something else. Remember those sections I took from the girl's throat and lungs? I did a microscopic examination of them. I determined that those sections were live flesh at the time the fire consumed her."

Dixon studied the report, then handed it to Stark. She said, "Virgil, do you think this will hold up under much scrutiny?"

"Well, that's hard to say."

"Virgil," Cassie Teal asked, "how many cases in the literature are there of people meeting death by incineration who do not have carbon monoxide in their blood?"

"Let's see . . . well . . . I'd say two or three."

Dixon slammed the table again. "How did you think you were going to defend this finding, Virgil?"

Wilcox turned melancholy eyes on his interrogators. "I didn't know I'd ever have to. I didn't know Garrity was ever going to review this case."

"Then we are in one hell of a jam," Dixon said. "How do we backtrack without looking like fools or worse?"

Cassie Teal said, "This is what comes from not paying for a full-time qualified pathologist."

Stark shook her head. "No. This is what comes from working in a Central Coast backwater." She sat still, working that notion as if she were communing with some higher order. Then came a faint smile. "I have it."

"What?" Dixon asked.

Angela turned to the coroner. "You have really fouled this case up, Virgil."

Wilcox gasped for breath. "I fouled this up? But when I got the call . . . I assumed—"

"That's your problem, Virgil. You assumed."

"I . . . but . . . you . . ."

"I'm afraid you screwed up big-time, Virgil. Sheriff Dixon and I based everything on your ruling. You're the medical expert, you're the one we had to rely on." Stark lifted the phone messages from Dixon's hand. "What are you going to tell Marilee Cooper's parents, Virgil? What are you going to tell Ollie Merta's students? What are you going to tell the citizens of Chumash County?"

The coroner's face had turned a chalky white. He vainly looked to Dixon for an answer. "This hardly seems fair—"

Stark asked, "You like your job, Virgil? You want to keep being the county coroner? You want to keep being a doctor in La Graciosa? You want to keep your medical license?"

Wilcox stared wildly at the DA. "Yes, of course."

"Then what are you going to tell Chumash County's citizens?"

"I . . . I'm going to tell them . . . I . . . What am I . . . ?"

Stark placed a comforting hand on his, which was now shaking. "You're going to tell them that new evidence came to light after your initial ruling. Belated lab test results, additional blood samples, extra bodily gases, whatever makes sense. You will say you rushed your judgment so as not to prolong everyone's grief. You will say you now see that you've inadvertently made a terrible mistake. You will say you're horrified to have erred, but you're gratified to finally reach the truth."

Wilcox frowned. "Everyone will think me incompetent."

"No, Virgil, they'll think you're human. They'll understand."

"What about the arson team?"

"They, too, will be seen as human."

Color began to return to the coroner's face. "You think they will?"

"Most certainly."

Wilcox worked matters around in his mind. "Okay. That's what I'll say."

"One other thing," Stark added. "You're going to announce that you have changed the death certificates for Marilee Cooper and Ollie Merta."

Cassie Teal asked, "What are we going with now, Angela?"

"Homicide by strangulation."

"That'll stir folks up plenty," Dixon said.

"Exactly." Angela Stark rose, full of energy. "And we're stirred up right along with them, Howie. The DA is dismayed and outraged that a killer is loose. The DA vows to see that justice is done. The DA will not stop until she has avenged the deaths of Ollie Merta and Marilee Cooper."

FOUR

"I win the bet," Douglas Bard hollered into Jimmy O'Brien's ear.

"Hell you do," Jimmy yelled back.

They were in Bard's twenty-three-foot Sea Ray, two miles offshore, heading south down the coast from Pirate's Beach. With a northwesterly twenty-knot breeze at his back, Doug fought to keep his bow at an angle to the waves. Two dolphins were hitching a free ride on their wake while pretending to escort them. One soared out of the roiled seas while the other dove under their boat. Doug glanced back at their fishing poles, lashed down in the aft cockpit. He studied the dark clouds rolling in from the west. The sea, five feet now, was building.

"Don't know if we're going to catch those albacore after all," he said. "Not a day to get too far from port."

"You spineless landlubber."

"If I had something bigger than this bathtub toy, I wouldn't hesitate."

"What do you want, an eighty-foot Carver?"

Bard had his dreams, but they didn't reach that far. A boat he could live on, that's what he had in mind. And someone by his side as they cruised up the coast. Neither seemed likely at present. The rustic log cabin where he lived, deep in a wooded reach of Apple Canyon, provided the insulation he desired but not the community. Apart from his dates with Molly, Bard's social life consisted mainly of Thursday night poker games with fellow cops and the occasional visit to JB's Tavern with Jimmy.

"A Grand Banks 32 would do just fine," Bard told Jimmy.

He throttled back and turned into a slow wide curl. Soon his bow was pointed for home. "I repeat," he said, "I won the bet."

"How so?"

"Dixon called me in. If I had any free time, he let me know, it would be okay by him if I worked the Merta case a little."

"Oh, yes," Jimmy bellowed. "Dixon must be sucking air just about now. Angela Stark must be busting his balls to find a killer."

"He did mention something about our DA."

"I bet."

Three chaotic weeks had passed since the district attorney declared Ollie Merta and Marilee Cooper's deaths to be homicides. La Graciosa, unaccustomed to random savage violence, had grown ever more gripped by a fever of fear and sorrow. At the elementary school and the Cooper family's church, anguished crowds gathered for special ceremonies. At one, a priest lamented "this horrible plague that has descended upon us." At another, La Graciosa's mayor, Billie Tompkins, demanded that "the perpetrator of such a violent and senseless crime be quickly apprehended."

Angela Stark tried her best to face into the wind. The first week, she stood by Marilee's parents as they held a press conference, begging through tears for information leading to their daughter's killer. The second week, she spoke at a La Graciosa Elementary School assembly. On Monday of the third week, at a Rotary Club luncheon held in the back room of Stella's Café, she promised "quick results and certain justice."

There'd been nothing else she could offer, though. They had no real leads, let alone breakthroughs. Dixon had put two veteran detectives in charge of a task force, but Victor Baynes and Andy Akers hadn't even pulled anyone in for questioning. By midway through that third week, signs of agitation—in letters to the editor, on radio call-in shows, at lunchtime talk around the plaza—were everywhere.

"I trust we'll soon see the guilty arrested," declared Mayor

Billie Tompkins. "I trust punishment will be swift and appropriate."

Stark chose then to retreat from public view, leaving Sheriff Dixon to catch the inevitable flak. He sent half his force to chase down all the unsourced clues and anonymous tips that had started pouring in, but managed only to break his payroll budget with costly overtime charges. He persuaded the county commissioners to offer a $10,000 reward for information leading to an arrest, but managed only to flush out every two-bit hustler angling for easy bucks. "Now look, goddamn it," Dixon finally snarled at one of the perfunctory press conferences he was obliged to hold every other morning. "We'll catch them when we catch them."

Later that day, Dixon was seen being led into Angela Stark's office. Those passing by in the next hour could not avoid hearing raised voices from behind the DA's closed door. By dusk, Dixon had summoned Doug Bard.

Once you finish chasing down all those felony files on your desk, maybe you could help Baynes and Akers work the Merta case a little. That's how the sheriff had put it to his star detective.

Jimmy started counting with his fingers. "Hold on, Doug. Figure it out. You don't win the bet. It happened right smack between our picks."

"You bet it would take four weeks before they'd invite me in."

"And you bet two weeks. It's been three weeks."

"Actually, twenty days, to be exact. Fact is, twenty-one days would make it a draw, flat even. But twenty days makes me the winner. Closer to two weeks than four."

They were nearing the dock at Pirate's Beach. Jimmy stared at the western sky. Bard had been right to come in; a nasty storm was approaching. "Okay, okay, you win. But, Dougie boy, now you've got the bat and ball. Your turn to play."

He sat beside the fireplace in the house where he had once lived, high in the chaparral-thick foothills east of town. In his mind, Molly—still a laughing toddler—yanked at his pant legs as she staggered across the floor. In his mind Sasha stood beside him, a hand on his shoulder, smiling in that way she had, amused and knowing. Neither daughter nor ex-wife was present, though. He'd let himself in with the key he still possessed. They'd be home in half an hour, he calculated. He could wait.

Time passing meant little to him now. How long had it been since he quit the family? He couldn't say. The memories were a blur. So many good moments. The three of them off Pirate's Beach, exploring the bay in their small runabout, then almost getting lost in the vast Chumash Dunes. Molly riding in a backpack on his shoulders. Sasha walking by his side . . .

Yet there were bad moments, too. It all depended on what you wanted to remember. His fault as much as hers. She grew, she changed, she launched her own career. You could say she turned away from him then, or you could say he just couldn't handle her mounting devotion to a job. Financial management, investments, that's what she did. Ginnie Maes, REITs, Q-tip trusts, limited partnerships—anything that built wealth for her clients. If only he'd felt more comfortable in her world. If only he could have gone where she wanted to go. Yet he lacked her enthusiasm for business schemes and county politics. He had nothing to say to owly investment managers and boisterous developers. Instead, he sat at JB's with Jimmy O'Brien, or did whatever was needed to throw no-good mutts into jail.

What else did he know, coming from a family of cops? He served in the Marines, as did his father and grandfather. He left the service with only two career notions, fireman or policeman. In time, he did aspire to being more than a cop, but by then he was trapped: the world had changed. Sheriffs, police chiefs, most of the managers above him—now they all seemed to have fancy graduate degrees in administration or communications or something. Those that didn't, like Sheriff Dixon, had intricate ties to the county's power structure. Smug young squirts or tough old-school schemers, that's who graded his papers now.

The feel of the fabric under his hand caught Bard's attention. Silk, he judged; a sofa covered in gun-metal blue silk. Sasha had recently redecorated, without sparing the expense. He looked around. The chairs with ivory inlay and velvet cushions were new. So was the silver chandelier. Sasha was clearly doing well.

That's what she always wanted. Or rather—that's what she'd eventually come to want.

Bard had no trouble summoning an image of Sasha in their early days together. For their first date, she showed up at his door in dusty jeans and hiking boots, and marched past him with a skinny beagle named Sam by her side. Sam went everywhere with her back then, as he soon learned. Sasha struck him as such an outdoor girl, his lady of the canyon. He was only half-right. While attending Chumash State, she lived up in the mountains and often rode her horse to school, Sam following and sitting patiently outside her classrooms. Yet she grew up in a gritty blue-collar Oakland suburb. Her father, an auto mechanic and bookie, taught her to repair cars and take bets. "Family is everything," he told her. But also, "you're on your own in this life."

Sasha brought chicken soup for Bard that first day, because he had a cold. In his kitchen, she baked brownies. Only a faint glint in her eyes gave away that she'd spiked the brownies with a dash of supergrade Central Coast grass. She thought it would be cool to get a cop stoned. Bard did, too. She felt like home to him.

"I've been told by some guys I'm cold," she warned. That didn't deter him. She wasn't cold with him. She simply took care of herself; she didn't rattle. He liked that. There were, he sensed, subterranean forces beneath her cool.

Only later, after they married, did he come to see how hard it was to tap those forces. The closer he tried to get, the more she resisted. Bard's watchful eyes bothered her. So did his comments and questions. "When I'm dealing with other people," she told him, "I can put on any act that's needed for the particular situation. I can always outwit them. Not you, though. You present a challenge. You're too goddamned perceptive about me."

"So what?" he asked. "What's the matter with me seeing you whole?"

"I'm not into losing myself. I don't want to forget how to function on my own. I don't want to depend on you every day of my life."

Then Molly was born. Sasha took a leave from work, and for a time they were as content as a family could be. Their hut in the Chumash Dunes, their boat, their baby. But Sasha was counting the days until Molly was ready for preschool. When that moment came, she shed her blue jeans and beagle, and enrolled in a Chumash State graduate program.

Stocks, bonds, real estate, commodities—soon she could go on about such matters for hours. Mortgage securitization particularly fascinated her. "You make mortgages into securities," she explained at the dinner table one night while reaching for the paillards of veal. "A bank purchases mortgage portfolios, then places them in trusts, or in newly created corporations. The trust or corporation issues securities—they call them mortgage pass-through certificates. The debt payments to the mortgage holders are paid with the cash flow from the mortgage portfolios. The clients basically get the difference between the payments they receive from the individual mortgages and the coupon they pay on the pass-through securities."

"Could you pass the gravy?" Bard asked. Then, "What if the economy tanks? What if the mortgages don't get paid?"

Sasha shrugged. "We call in the lawyers."

He listened with wonder at the start, impressed and, he had to admit, even aroused by her mastery of matters so foreign to him. Talk of her work never stopped, though. It mounted, in fact, after she graduated and landed a job at a brokerage firm up in San Luis. Then she often came home late, exhausted but flushed with her day. He vainly tried to adjust, to fit in with who she'd become. The truth was, he'd rather have her attention, he'd rather spend their evenings together barricaded from the world.

She wanted those evenings, too—but only on occasion. She just wasn't inclined to hold hands all the time, not even with the man she loved. That wasn't how she'd climbed out of her dad's oil-splattered garage. That wasn't how she meant to get where she was going.

From mortgage securities she expanded to private financing packages for apartment buildings. Then she moved on to a real bonanza, radio-station licensing deals. "It's a great way to make money," she explained to Bard, "at least until someone hollers and they change the law. If you own a radio station and you sell it to buyers with a twenty-percent minority interest, you get to defer capital gains. Which means that buyers—my clients—can grab a terrific deal. In negotiating a purchase price, we get the sellers to knock off part of what they're saving in capital gains. Everyone wins. And these radio licenses are a gold mine."

A gold mine, and also a power base in isolated regions of California. The dominance of Sasha's investors in the Central Coast radio market eventually drew the attention of people with political connections in Sacramento. Soon the big San Francisco investment firms came calling, dangling lucrative job offers before Sasha. There was just one hitch—the jobs required a move to the city, or constant travel. Bard objected to both prospects.

"What about me?" Sasha asked. "My job enriches my life. It's something I want. It's something I expect to share with my husband."

He tried to talk about other kinds of sharing, but his efforts usually sparked another argument. The bottle of Black Bush in the kitchen became Bard's refuge. Sasha spent her evenings on the phone. Molly stayed in her room.

Which parent first turned to more comforting arms was hard to say. Bard found passing solace with a winsome booking clerk down at the station, and for a good while didn't notice that Sasha now was staying even later at work. Only when he called her there one evening near midnight, and learned from a security guard that she'd left hours ago, did he realize what was going on.

Enough, he decided. He'd rather walk away than play it this way. He had his bag packed by the time she got home. I guess guns and crooks turned you on for only so long, he told her at the front door.

She'd managed well enough without him. In time, she opened her own shop, what she called an "investment boutique," just off the plaza in La Graciosa. Lillo, Inc., she named it; Lillo was her maiden name. She put her clients in everything from sedate index funds to Silicon Valley startups. "Diversification never appears that smart," she advised them, "but over the long haul, it's a much surer way to build wealth."

Bard could see she was thriving. A year or two ago, she rented the adjacent storefront, knocked down a wall, and doubled her space. She had five employees now. She rarely talked to him about her career anymore. Their usual topic was Molly.

The sound of a key, metal against metal, interrupted Bard's reverie. He looked up to see Sasha and Molly standing in the doorway.

"Oh, Doug," Sasha said. "You let yourself in."

"Little too cold and windy to sit outside. I needed some shelter from the storm."

Sasha gave him a look. "Glad you found it."

Doug vainly tried to catch his daughter's eye, but she was busy with a purple plastic Game Boy. "Hey, Molly girl."

Molly didn't even turn her head. She was wearing tight blue jeans, a light pink T-shirt with dark pink roses, and light pink Adidas tennis shoes. Her long dark blonde hair was pulled into a ponytail. In her ears were light pink flower earrings, on her wrist a purple Baby-G watch. Her long nails were painted light pink. Bard squinted. Was Molly wearing light pink eye shadow? He decided not to ask. On this day, Molly seemed disinclined toward that type of inquiry. One of her giving-off-attitude episodes.

"So let me guess," he said. "Pink is maybe your favorite color now?"

That won a brief glance. "Daddy, you're funny."

"What happened to blue? I thought blue was your favorite."

Molly rolled her eyes. "That was so five weeks ago."

"What about Adam?"

Adam was in sixth grade with her. She'd gone bowling once with him and two other kids, Bard chaperoning. Only the ugliest boy would fall for you, Adam had told her, an eleven-year-old boy's ardent overture. She didn't miss a beat with her comeback: And that would be you?

"Adam?" she said now. "Come on, Daddy. This is today."

"Yes, it is."

Bard turned to include Sasha. "I'm on Ollie and Marilee's murder case. The sheriff has asked for my help."

Molly's eyes opened wide. He had Sasha's attention, too.

"You're going to catch Marilee's killer?" Molly asked.

"I'm going to try."

No more attitude. She came to him and threw her arms around his waist. "I told them at school you would. Our class, we named a star for Marilee. Afterwards, I told them my daddy would fix everything. Just ask my daddy, I said. That's what I told them."

His hand settled gently on the back of her head. He feared that the wrong move would drive her off. "I can't fix everything, Molly girl. I can't bring Marilee back to life. But I will try to catch whoever killed her."

Sasha was at their side now. "What makes you think the killer is within a thousand miles of La Graciosa? No one around here would have strangled Ollie and Marilee. I bet your killer is long gone. It's quite a task you've taken on, Doug."

"Yeah, well. I'm task oriented."

"What a wonderful job you have. What a career."

"Job, yes. Wouldn't call it a career. Not like yours, at least."

"Let's not start."

"All I meant—"

The phone began to ring. Sasha picked it up and turned toward the kitchen as she began talking. *Yes, yes, Burt. But keep in mind, if there are no earnings or dividends, then a security can be worth almost anything. You have to be able to measure a security's future income stream and then discount it back to the present. If you can't, you're flying blind. What I suggest . . .*

Molly, at Bard's elbow, tugged at him. "Daddy, what do you think happened? Why did Marilee and Ollie have to die?"

"If only we knew, sweetheart. There are bad people in this world. There aren't a lot of them, and they're not everywhere, but one of them came to Ollie Merta's home."

"Why did he pick that home?"

Why indeed. Why Ollie's little cottage, lost down a narrow country road? There never had been any signs of a burglary. For that matter, there wasn't much to steal at Ollie's except for a fifteen-year-old stereo and a five-year-old computer, and both had been left to burn in the fire. This wasn't random violence, either. Hard as it was to imagine, someone wanted Ollie Merta dead. Marilee Cooper, Doug surmised, had simply been at the wrong place at the wrong time.

"Molly girl," he said, "I don't know why he picked Ollie's home."

Her eyes were filling. "Promise me, Daddy. Promise me you're going to catch the killers."

When she was little, it was so much easier to promise. What she wanted was in reach; he could deliver then, he didn't have to let her down. Later—to avoid disappointment, he imagined—she'd stopped asking for his promise. Now here she was, once again.

"It's hard to promise something like that," he said. "I don't know who he is or where he is. Besides that, I think there's some people in this county who don't want this case to get solved. I think some people—"

"Doug, hello, excuse me." Sasha was standing at the entrance to the kitchen, the phone in one hand, a lit cigarette in the other. "Could we maybe not go on like this with Molly?"

"Why not?"

"It's a lousy civics lesson."

"Maybe that's for the good."

"I grew up with lousy civics lessons. I'd rather she not."

"But you turned out just terrific."

She gave him a look. "Doug."

"Okay, okay." He heard aggravation in his voice, which he hadn't intended.

Sasha heard it, too. She set the phone down, snubbed out the cigarette. "There I go again, Doug. Every time I assert myself, I alienate you."

On the fifth day after the DA announced a $10,000 reward for information leading to an arrest in the Merta-Cooper murders, the phone rang in Doug Bard's cubicle at the Chumash County Sheriff's Department. Reaching for it, he knocked over a paper cup half-full of hot coffee.

"Goddamn it," he snapped.

"Oh, sorry, sir." The voice on the phone sounded timid, and alarmed. "I . . . I must have the wrong number . . . or maybe this isn't a good time . . . I'll call back—"

"No, no," Bard gasped, mopping up the steaming coffee, which was now dripping off the desk and onto his trousers. "I wasn't talking to you. I wasn't talking to anyone, actually. Who is this?"

Silence for a moment. Then, "My name isn't important."

Bard reached for a pen and a pad of paper. "Okay, Mr. Unimportant. What's this about?"

"Those two murders. The house fire out at that funny old fella's house."

Fair enough. Ollie was a funny old fella. "Do you have information for us?"

"Well now, what about you? I heard you guys had ten grand for someone with information."

Someone with information. That would be nice, Bard thought.

If asked, the state sometimes lent counties a forensic psychologist in murder cases. Shrink goes to the scene, to the autopsy, pores through the police reports, makes out a general profile of the type of person the police should be looking for. Bard had passed on all that. He had no interest in such profiles. No interest, no confidence. They were so broad. Once you learn the language, you can apply it to any case. It's like going to the hostage school the FBI runs. What do you learn after two weeks? Wait the asshole out, that's what you learn.

Instead of studying psychologists' profiles, Bard had been prowling grimy East Chumash neighborhoods full of shacks, trailers, used car lots, and pawnshops. The pawnshops he especially liked. Lots of stuff came up there. He'd looked around those shops. He'd looked for anything, but mainly, he'd looked for a particular pair of boots.

Someone had kicked in Ollie Merta's door, and someone had left a bootprint. Chippewas, size eleven, with diagonal tread—a terrific clue, a lovely clue. It wasn't from a fire-fighter, as Dixon had assumed that first night; their standard-issue boots didn't come close to resembling the print. Who, then? It was like a warped Cinderella story. Match a pair of boots to Ollie's door, you're on your way.

But Bard hadn't made a match. He wasn't on his way.

"Yes, we do have ten grand to give away," he said to the timid voice. "But it depends on what information."

"It's not what I know myself. I think someone else knows."

"I don't believe the ten grand would be for you, then."

"Yes, sure, that's okay. I just thought you should know."

"Know what?"

"This fellow I sometimes work with, he . . ."

"He what?"

"He mentioned that he knew something about the murders at Ollie Merta's house."

"Who is this fellow?"

"You won't tell him how you got his name?"

"What would I tell him? That Mr. Unimportant called me? I don't know who you are. I'm already starting to forget this phone call."

"Okay, then. His name is Eddie . . . Eddie Hines."

"Where would I find him? He have a job somewhere?"

"No, he just does day labor once in a while. The rest of the time, most of the time, he hangs out at the Foghorn, down at Pirate's Beach. You know the place?"

The good old Foghorn. Home of whiskey-voiced women

and stringy-haired bikers. One of the county landmarks that
Bruce Hightower's crowd hadn't torn down yet. "Yes, I know
the place," Bard said. "What does Eddie Hines look like?"

"Skinny kid, early twenties. Crew cut, bad skin, funny little
wisp of a mustache, like he can't really grow one."

"Thank you very much, Mr. Unimportant."

The Foghorn Beach Pub, framed by a pair of modern stucco
boxes, resembled a woozy stranger who'd wandered into the
wrong party. The single-story wood-frame building had once
been painted bright purple, but only fragments of faded color
now decorated the splintered gray wood. Inside, as it had for
three decades, a faded green carpet half covered a sticky parquet floor. The plain wooden bar faced a long, grimy picture
window that offered customers a perennially blurred view of
the beach.

Bard scanned the row of stools at the bar. High-mileage
gals, guys with monster shoulders and grimy undershirts, old
gray gents with crusty eyes and red noses . . . but no skinny,
bad-skinned crew cut kids. Bard turned to the three billiards
tables that occupied a rear quarter of the Foghorn. There he
was, alone, lazily poking at a ball.

Eddie Hines was wearing jeans, an oversized Lakers
T-shirt, a Giants baseball cap turned backward. Pink pimples
clustered on his chin, providing bright contrast to his sallow
skin.

"Eddie Hines?"

The kid jumped at Bard's question. "Who are you?"

Bard didn't want to scare him with a show of authority, so
he left his badge in his hip pocket. "I'm Douglas Bard. Chumash County Sheriff's Department."

Hines's eyes widened. Bard couldn't tell whether he was
scared or amazed. "I . . . uh . . . I've always wanted to be a
cop," Hines stuttered.

Bard had run his name through the computer before coming out to the Foghorn. Hines was twenty-two, an eighth-grade
dropout from Chumash Middle School. He had a minor

record of misdemeanor thefts, nothing more. "Yeah, well," Doug said, "maybe if you help me, I can help you."

Hines was nearly vibrating with excitement now. The billiards stick slid from his hands. "Help you with a case? That's what you want?"

"That's what I want, Eddie."

They sat at a small table near a window with a view of the beach. Bard ordered them each a mug of Graciosa Brew. He waited until Hines had swallowed half his glass. Then he said, "I understand you may have information about the two murders over at Ollie Merta's house. If what you have leads to arrests, there's a ten grand reward in it for you."

Hines started choking on his beer. A rivulet of pale gold liquid trickled down his chin. "You say what? You understand what?"

"That you know something about those two murders."

Hines looked wildly around the Foghorn. "I didn't do anything."

It occurred to Bard that he was talking to a young man with a microscopic IQ. This one was even dumber than the usual mutts and jerks. "I didn't say you did anything, Eddie. Just that maybe you had information. If you want to collect ten grand, if you want to be a cop, you've gotta show us you're good at cracking cases."

"If I want to be a cop." Eddie chewed on that. "Ten grand for real?"

"For real."

Eddie sat up straight, ran a hand through his crew cut. "Yes, okay, I can tell you something, I can help you."

"What do you know, Eddie?"

"I was drinking beer with two buddies one night. Out in the Chumash Dunes over there. Me and two buddies. They were saying all kinds of stuff about the burning house. How they were there or something. Or how they knew who killed old man Merta and the little girl."

"Who were your buddies, Eddie?"

"I just know the names they go by, that's all. One, they call him Squeaky. The other is Hotwire."

"Squeaky and Hotwire?"

"Yeah, that's who I was with."

"Last names?"

"I don't know any last names."

"You have an idea where I can find them?"

"Not really. They just hang out on the street. Maybe if we drove around we could find them."

Bard drained his beer glass and started to rise. If the kid's IQ topped seventy-five, he'd be surprised. "That's not enough help, Eddie. That's not enough to get you ten grand."

"Wait." Hines's bony hand clutched Bard's wrist. "I think these guys saw him."

"Saw who?"

"The guy who did it. By the moonlight, they told me. By the moonlight they saw a guy running from the burning house."

Bard slowly sank back into his seat. Informants didn't have to be geniuses, they just needed to have the goods. Half the time they could barely write their name. If he let that disqualify them, he'd never crack a case.

Bard pulled out a pad and pen. "Did they describe this man, Eddie? What else did they say?"

Eddie turned wary. "We were drinking, man. I can't remember what all they said."

Bard stared at him, waiting. It never ceased to surprise him how well silence worked during an interrogation. People naturally rushed to fill the void.

"I . . . I think they said he was a big guy," Eddie offered. "Yeah, a real big guy with lots of hair."

What more was there to tap here? Bard had no idea what Eddie really knew. Maybe he had nothing else to give. Or maybe he had plenty, but was scared about dragging in his drinking buddies.

"That doesn't narrow it down much, Eddie."

"I don't get even part of that ten grand?"

"Not a dime, Eddie. We need enough information to make an arrest."

Eddie drummed the table with his bony fingers. "Tell you what. I'll get you that information."

"How you going to do that?"

"I'll do some detective work for you." Eddie grinned. "I'll track down Squeaky and Hotwire."

Relief, however grudging, spread across Sheriff Dixon's face. His meaty hand settled on Doug Bard's shoulder. "Good work," he offered. "Finally we have a lead."

Standing before the two men, Angela Stark didn't look nearly as pleased. "Don't celebrate yet," she warned. "Your buddy in there still needs to talk to us."

They were in the bowels of the *asistencia,* in a viewing chamber adjacent to an interrogation room, hard by the county jail. Through a one-way window, mirrored on the other side, they were watching Eddie Hines stare at a box that sat on a table inches beyond his reach. "Here's the ten grand reward," Doug had told Hines moments before, when he carried in the carton. "Just so you know it really exists."

For three days now, Hines had been hanging around Bard, promising information without ever coming up with anything. He'd left word for Squeaky, he might be seeing Hotwire tonight, he thought he remembered what his drinking buddies had said . . . In the end, Eddie Hines just kept hanging. Doug didn't mind, mainly because he sensed that Eddie wasn't bluffing. Eddie had something inside him, something he kept almost saying. He was too scared, though, of either the cops or his buddies or someone else. Bard had finally decided to share Hines with Dixon. "Don't know what we've got here," he said, "but I think we ought to find out."

Now they were trying. The defense attorneys could wail as loud as they wanted, the judges could lecture about laws and ethics, but what the hell. Bard never had qualms about using whatever scam would get jerks to talk. So they cut some corners, so they riled the ACLU. A box of cash would just be the start with Eddie.

Bard rose from his chair and headed for the door. Before he got there, it swung open. The deputy DA, Cassie Teal, walked in. Bard stopped. They'd been adversaries more than once when she was a defense attorney. Especially the time she represented her child killer.

"Why, Cassie," he said. "I get to work with you again?"

She barely looked at him. "It appears so, Doug."

"Well, I guess this is better than working against you."

Teal nodded toward Eddie Hines, behind the window. "Better go to work, Doug."

Bard reached for the door. "You're right. Time for Act Two."

Through the window, the others watched as Bard entered the interrogation room, accompanied by a female deputy sheriff dressed in street clothes. "Eddie," he said, "you know that little girl, Marilee Cooper, who was killed in Ollie Merta's house fire? Well, this is Marilee Cooper's mom." Turning to the deputy, he added, "Eddie is going to help you, Mrs. Cooper."

Eddie's eyes swung back and forth between the box and the plainly distraught lady. "Yes, ma'am . . . I'm going to help you."

The lady came to Eddie's side. Her hand touched Eddie's arm. "Thank you so much, Mr. Hines. I am so grateful to you."

Bard escorted her out and returned to Eddie. "Now then," he continued. "I have someone else for you to welcome today, Eddie. Remember your old middle-school buddy Petey? Petey Montrose?"

Eddie's face lit up. "Petey? Sure I remember Petey."

"Good. We've got Petey here to see you. He's going to tell you how good it can be to help us out on a case."

Scanning Eddie's rap sheet, they'd seen that Petey Montrose had been his partner on a couple of break-ins. Then they'd found Petey sitting in the county jail on a two-bit burglary charge. Bard had wandered over to Petey's cell. You can walk right now, he told him, if you help us with Eddie Hines.

Petey had smiled at that. He was short and chunky, with a pointed goatee and a silver earring. Tell me my lines, he'd said.

Now Bard led Petey into Eddie's interrogation room. The

former school pals exchanged high fives. Bard backed out and rejoined his colleagues.

"Hey, Eddie boy, they tell me you can help yourself like I helped myself," Petey began.

In the viewing room, Angela Stark joined the others before the window. "Come on, Eddie," she whispered. "Listen to your pal."

"What do you mean?" Eddie asked Petey. "You helped yourself?"

Petey grinned. "I'm doing time now, but not for long. They're letting me out, giving me money."

Eddie's eyes widened. "How come?"

"My second cousin killed a kid down in South Chumash. Told me all about it. So when I landed in jail, I offered the cops a deal. I give you a killer, you let me go. They liked that. Soon as they arrest my cousin, I walk. Jesus, Eddie. They're going to give me a ten grand reward, and a whole new identity, and a ticket to Costa Rica."

"They are?"

"Eddie, don't you see? If you help solve those murders you know about, you can get the same kind of deal. We kick out together. We could go live like rich men in Costa Rica."

"Oh, man."

"We could be the kings of Costa Rica. You got to help, too, though, just like I did. You got to tell them what you know."

Eddie nearly bounced out of his chair. "I'll tell them everything . . . I'll tell them everything I know . . . I'll—"

"Well, Eddie," Petey interrupted, "what is it you know?"

Eddie looked around the room. He lowered his voice. "I didn't tell that Detective Bard everything. It's true, I was drinking beer with two buddies that night. But we weren't in the dunes, we were in the foothills, out back of that old man Merta's house. Drinking beer, shooting squirrels, shit like that. By the moonlight, we all saw him. We saw this guy running from the burning house."

"Not just your buddies saw this guy, Eddie? You saw him, too?"

Eddie picked at the pimples on his chin. "I didn't want to

tell that to the cops. I didn't want to tell them I was there. I thought I'd get in trouble."

"They need a real eyewitness, though. They won't be mad at you, they won't get you into trouble. They'll thank you, man. They'll pay you big bucks."

"Is that what you were, an eyewitness?"

"Yep, that's what I was. My cousin didn't just tell me about the kid he killed. He came to me right afterwards in his bloody clothes."

Eddie's voice rose. "My guy had blood on him, too."

"You saw him that close up?"

"In the moonlight, it looked like blood."

"You were there, Eddie? You didn't just hear this from the other guys?"

"I was there. Swear to God, I was there."

"I was able to tell the cops my cousin's name. Where he lived, how to find him."

"Me, too," Eddie cried out. "I can do that." He was out of his chair now, over at the table, his hand rubbing the top of the box full of money.

"You know who it was, Eddie?"

"Sure I do. I've just been afraid to tell. Afraid of being a stool pigeon, afraid of what this guy would do to me."

"I wasn't afraid, Eddie. They keep killers locked up forever. It's either him or you behind bars, that's how I figured it."

"Yeah . . . That's how I figure it, too."

"Who was it, Eddie? Who'd you see?"

In the viewing room, Angela Stark, standing behind Bard, gripped the back of his chair. "A name, Eddie," she coaxed. "Give us a name."

Bard could feel her hand brush his shoulder. He could feel her breath on his neck. At the same time, he sensed someone's eyes. Turning, he saw that Cassie Teal was watching them, not the window.

"I've seen him around town," Eddie was saying. "But not often. He lives way up in the foothills. Some weird kind of mountain man. Big old guy with a thick red beard. Nasty when he's drunk. In a tavern once, I saw him swing on a fellow."

"A name, Eddie. I gave them a name."

Eddie had the look now of a poker player laying down a full house. "Jed Jeremiah," he said. "That's who I saw running out of Ollie Merta's house."

Jed Jeremiah. Stark raised a fist. *Yes.*

Bard had to admit, despite Eddie's goofiness, it made sense. They all knew Jeremiah. He had a temper, he had a violent history around town. He also lived high in the foothills directly above Ollie Merta's home. What's more, he was a large man with a full thick beard.

I think they said he was a big guy . . . a real big guy with lots of hair. That's what Eddie had told him days before at the Foghorn.

Sheriff Dixon's arm curled around Bard's shoulder. "Way to go, Doug."

Angela Stark placed a palm over the back of Bard's hand. "Not bad, Detective."

Only Cassie Teal remained silent. Her head stayed down; her pencil flew across a yellow pad. She was taking notes.

FIVE

Douglas Bard let up on the accelerator pedal as he drove the winding single-lane road that threaded through the wooded hills east of La Graciosa. At first all was dark and dense, the sky obscured by thick stands of live oak. Then, as he climbed higher, the foliage thinned and he could see glimpses of blue water through the forest. After a few more turns, he was out from under the lush green canopy, climbing above the tree line in a landscape of chaparral and boulders.

Jed Jeremiah lived up here. Bard knew that much just from checking property records. He'd plumbed his memory and the pages of Jimmy O'Brien's newspaper for other details. References to Jeremiah popped up in the *News-Times* every four months or so, mainly because Jeremiah had a habit of drawing attention whenever he came to town for supplies. He invariably ended up at JB's Tavern, where he spun tales, drank heavily, pounded on JB's piano, and brawled with whoever got in his way. Sometimes, Jimmy O'Brien managed to share a drink with him without getting into a fight. "Solitary" and "bristly" were the words *News-Times* accounts most often used in front of Jed's name.

They were apt choices. Little was known about the man. As Jimmy understood it, he'd wandered aimlessly in his youth, finally ending up mining on the Merced River. There he'd married and settled down for a time, until his wife died suddenly of an influenza that deepened into pneumonia. Her death turned him, for good. For a decade now, he'd lived alone on the small rocky ranch he'd bought in the high hills

above La Graciosa. He mainly ran cattle there, but also
hunted—for food to eat, and coats to sell. Even when sober,
he was not unwilling to fight. When challenged, they said he
could get mighty ired. They also said he measured elbow
room in square leagues.

Jeremiah was no stranger to La Graciosa's jail. Jimmy had
reported the details of one particularly memorable visit in his
"About Chumash" column.

> *Jed Jeremiah, cantankerous shepherd and moun-*
> *taineer, came to town Friday to get a quantity of to-*
> *bacco, ammunition, and staples, and to imbibe a few*
> *gallons of "sheepherder's delight." By Saturday night he*
> *managed to get a sufficient quantity of whiskey aboard*
> *to get him in a quarrelsome mood, and after wandering*
> *around he ended up at JB's Tavern. There he felt exceed-*
> *ingly frisky, and manifested his feelings by whacking the*
> *head of another man. He was taken into custody and*
> *lodged in the town jail for disturbing the peace. He had*
> *on his person one of the largest and most disagreeable*
> *looking knives we have ever seen.*

Bard hadn't told Jimmy that Jed Jeremiah was now their
prime suspect. He wondered how Jimmy would play that item
in his "About Chumash" column.

The detective's tires crunched on pebbles and kicked up
dust. The paved road had turned to dirt, and narrowed into
hardly more than a path. To the right, the headwaters of the
Graciosa trickled down the mountainside, gathering energy
for its long march to the sea. At a curve, looking down, Bard
saw only a dark green blanket, the abundant crowns of the
oak forest. Looking straight ahead, he saw only dust. Then,
around a bend, rose Jed Jeremiah's cabin. And, standing before it, Jed Jeremiah himself.

Mountain man, indeed. Jeremiah was somewhere over six
feet, straight of build and thickly muscled. He stared at his uninvited visitor with fierce, sunken eyes that framed a promi-
nent nose, long and slightly turned up. He had a tangle of

gray hair and a wild reddish-gray beard. In his arms, cradled as if a baby, he held a Browning Stainless Stalker rifle. Bard knew that the 7mm Magnum contained four cartridges, each longer than Jeremiah's index finger.

Bard set the brake and climbed out of his car. "Hey there," he said.

Jeremiah just stared. His hand slid up and down the length of his rifle.

Doug watched with fascination. That was exactly the way Oscar Bard had handled his weapons. As if he were fondling them. Doug vainly tried to fight off the memory of himself at age eleven, being ushered into the thick oak forest for afternoons of enforced target shooting. There Oscar lined up his arsenal, including two assault rifles bought before the feds banned such weapons. They used the pistols mainly, the Colt .45 and the .40 caliber Glock. Oscar's prize was a .45 Springfield semiautomatic, trued and chamfered with a smooth two-pound trigger and a stainless satin finish. A work of art, Oscar called it. Perhaps the most beautiful handgun he'd ever seen.

Here with Jeremiah, Doug as usual was unarmed. He didn't like the way gun-and-badge cops relied on intimidation and the power of their office to extract information. The more you wave your gun and badge, he reasoned, the less people are going to tell you anything. Bard preferred to rely on persuasion. He believed he had at least a chance of getting most folks to talk. He tried not just to convince them to talk; he tried to convince them to confess. Selling jail, he called it.

"Jed Jeremiah?"

The mountain man nodded slowly.

Bard left his badge in his pocket. "Douglas Bard, Chumash County Sheriff's Department."

Jeremiah let his rifle slide toward the ground. "I've seen you around town. In the general store, at JB's." His eyes ran up and down his visitor.

Bard watched Jeremiah watch him. "I'm not packing, Jed."

Jeremiah chewed on that. After a moment, he set his rifle on a log. "Well then, this isn't an official police visit?"

"Actually, it is, Jed. We need to talk."

Jeremiah stiffened. "Talk? What about? That damn ticket?"

From his records scan, Bard knew about the "ticket." Jeremiah had been caught guzzling beer while barreling down the interstate at eighty-five miles an hour. The cop who pulled him over found a .38 caliber pistol in the glove compartment.

"I'd hardly call that just a ticket, Jed. But that's not what I'm here about."

"What, then?"

"That house fire down at Ollie Merta's place."

Jeremiah's gaze swung around to his rifle. "I don't know anything about that fire."

"What about the two people who died in that fire? You know anything about them?"

"You mean Ollie Merta and that little girl, Marilee Cooper?"

"Well now, I see you at least know their names."

"They're in the newspapers."

"You get newspapers up here, Jed?"

Jeremiah reached for his rifle. He turned toward Bard. "I was just about to go grizzly hunting when you drove up. If you want to join me, we can talk on the way."

On the far side of Jed Jeremiah's hardscrabble ranch, the land descended along a long gradual slope and turned greenly fecund once again. They walked through foothills thick with oak and sycamore, sage and manzanita. Purple lupine dotted the sides of the trail; groves of willow and poplar crowded the creek they were following. All was silent, save for the chatter of birds overhead.

"You really have grizzlies up here?" Bard asked.

Jeremiah spat. "Wish I didn't. They can be a bother. I'd have to hunt them even if I didn't want to. One winter, they started coming right into my corral. Darn if my best calves didn't start disappearing. I'd come out in the morning and find bear tracks instead of cattle."

"What did you do?"

Jeremiah peered at him with suspicion. "This isn't why you've come up here."

"Tell me anyway," Bard said. "Tell me about the bears."

"Why you want to know?"

"I just like a good bear story."

Jeremiah appreciated that explanation. Yellow crooked teeth showed through his beard. "Okay then."

First, he explained, he killed his oldest horse for bait, and dragged the carcass to where he figured the grizzlies would like to find it. Then he rigged a setup gun, running a string from the trigger to the dead horse. That night he went to bed thinking he'd for sure solved the matter. He hadn't, though. At dawn he came out, saw from the prints that the grizzly and three cubs had circled and recircled the bait without ever touching it. Instead, they'd headed off to the corral where they killed themselves another calf.

"Damned if those grizzlies didn't figure it out," Jeremiah said. "They breakfasted right royally."

While he talked and marched, Jed swung his rifle around as if it were a machete. "That was too much. I'm afraid I got a mite wrathy. Went after those bears with the largest caliber gun I have. Killed the old varmint plus one of the cubs."

Yes, Bard could see how Jed might draw an audience at JB's. He could also see how Jimmy might find him colorful copy. But Bard had often watched this kind of charm curdle in an instant.

He said, "Word is, you get a mite wrathy all sorts of times."

Jeremiah stopped. "Only when someone crowds up on me, Bard. Only when my rights are being overridden."

"Like that winter eight years ago, Jed?"

The mountain man's grip tightened on his rifle. "Yes, that's right. Like that winter eight years ago."

Bard had refreshed his memory in the courthouse files after seeing certain *News-Times* articles. These pieces weren't colorful items in Jimmy's column; these had made page one, above the fold.

They'd had no more than three inches of rainfall that season. Feed was scarce; livestock on ranges died from starvation by the thousands. Men who owned sheep grew desperate to find food for them. A Basque shepherd named Andre, prospecting the hills, came upon Jeremiah's pastures. They must have suggested an oasis, for Jed had taken claim on a mountain creek, cleared a field, and planted oats to feed his own stock. Andre didn't hesitate to run his sheep right out onto Jeremiah's land.

Late that day, Jeremiah, patrolling on horseback, caught Andre and his flock red-handed. This hadn't been the first trespassing trouble for Jed. The Basque shepherds, particularly, were notorious for appropriating other folks' feed. He rode up to Andre. "I want them sheep taken off my grass," he declared.

In the taverns of La Graciosa, there was dispute still over what followed. The courts ending up fixing on Jeremiah's version. As Jed told it, Andre, rather than comply with his request, produced a revolver and aimed it at him. Jeremiah, in response, raised his rifle and shot the shepherd dead. Dan Wizen, the sheriff back in those days, came for him the next morning. Jed was jailed, but two weeks later, at a preliminary hearing, Judge Martin Hedgespeth ruled that Jeremiah had shot in self-defense. Charges were dropped; Jeremiah was let go.

Bard said, "You know, Jed, not everyone bought your self-defense story back then. Some folks think you planted that revolver on the shepherd."

Jeremiah's eyes narrowed. He started toward Bard, wielding his rifle like a club. Bard imagined this to be the way he came at the Basque shepherd. No wonder Andre pulled a gun. Bard, having only his hands, instead stepped aside. Jed spun toward him but was now off balance. Bard reached up and grabbed the Browning's barrel. "You're in enough trouble," he said, "without assaulting a police officer."

They stood together for a moment, each holding part of the

rifle. Then Jed let go, and slowly settled on a tree stump. "We're making too much noise to get any hunting done anyway," he said. "Might as well get this settled."

"Good idea."

"What exactly are you aiming at here, Bard? First you say something about the Merta house fire, now you're back eight years with the shepherd."

Bard sat down next to him. "If you got wrathy enough once to kill a man, it seems likely you could do it all over again."

Jeremiah, in fact, looked as if he could do it right on the spot. He glared at Bard. "I had nothing to do with what happened down at Ollie Merta's."

"You are known to get wrathy, Jed."

"Why would I get wrathy with Ollie Merta?"

"He ran a few sheep out back of his property. His house sits straight down the mountain here from you. Way I figure, maybe you had yourself another trespassing problem."

"But I barely knew Ollie Merta."

"So you did know him."

"So fucking what." Jeremiah's brow was flushed now.

"Jed, we have an eyewitness who saw you running out of Ollie's burning house."

"You have what?"

Bard let the question hang for a moment. Jeremiah's throat had sounded parched. "Jed, why don't you just tell me what happened?"

"What happened? This is crazy. I'm not going to talk about this."

Jeremiah was kicking at the dirt. Bard watched his scuffed muddy boot swing back and forth, digging into the hard dry earth. In an instant, Bard reached out, put a hand on the boot. A Chippewa. Looked to be size eleven. He said, "Good strong pair of boots you got there."

Jeremiah yanked his foot back. "Just a pair of boots."

"Whoever killed Ollie and Marilee kicked in Merta's front door. Left a bootprint. Tech boys say it was a Chippewa, size eleven."

"Not these boots. I didn't kick in any door."

"Same type, same size, Jed."

"No . . . not mine."

"Think of that little girl, Jed. You didn't know there was a little girl in there with Ollie, did you? That must be an awful ache for you."

"I've got no ache, Bard. Not about this, not about anything."

"You ever had a sister, Jed? How would you like to see your little sister burned to the bone? Strangled and broiled? You've got to make this right, Jed."

For a passing moment, Bard imagined that Jeremiah meant to do just that. Felons with decent hearts were the most likely to break. Jeremiah wasn't evil, but not only evil people kill.

"Talk to me, Jed."

The moment, if it ever existed, passed. Jeremiah was sputtering. "Talk to you? . . . All I've ever wanted was to be goddamn left alone. I want no part of your world down there. That's why I'm up here, where I can control my life. Now here you are, busting onto my land—"

"We have an eyewitness, Jed."

"He's lying to you."

"Is he?"

Jeremiah jumped up. He grabbed his rifle from where it lay next to Bard. He pointed the muzzle at Bard's belt buckle. "I tell you, man, I don't want any part of your world. I want you out of here. I want you to leave me alone. I want everyone to leave me alone."

Bard rose slowly, ignoring the rifle. "Is that why you attacked Ollie Merta, Jed? Because he wouldn't leave you alone?"

"No!"

"Then why, Jed?"

"Goddamn you to hell, Bard."

It usually would have worked by now. Not this time. Bard saw he wasn't going to move Jed. Jeremiah would always claim his innocence.

Maybe he was innocent. Maybe Eddie Hines made up

his entire story. But Bard didn't think so. Eddie Hines was too stupid to conjure an entire eyewitness account, too stupid to name such a suitable suspect as Jed Jeremiah. Eddie couldn't think that quickly on his feet. Hell, Eddie couldn't think at all.

Bard had seen Jeremiah's kind of stonewalling before. If you believed everyone who refused to confess, you'd have a lot of empty jail cells.

Bard said, "Give me your boots, Jed. Let me take them to the lab. Let me see if they match. That will settle things."

"My boots? Jesus."

"The sheriff's department, they're building a case against you. They have an eyewitness, they have two first-degree murders. They can't just let this drop. I can get a subpoena, seize those boots. But you can make it easier on all of us. Give me the boots, let me test them."

They were on the trail now, heading back to the cabin. Jeremiah kept his eyes fixed on where he was stepping. "You going to execute whoever you catch?"

"The death penalty would be likely . . . unless we get some cooperation."

Jeremiah stopped and sank onto a fallen log. He yanked off his boots, threw them at Bard, then rose and began walking home in his stocking feet. Over his shoulder he said, "When you kill me I'll be dead, and I still won't have done it."

At dusk, Jimmy O'Brien and Douglas Bard walked the brick path that paralleled Graciosa Creek as it wound through the center of town. The familiar scent of jacaranda mixed with kelp still filled the air. Through the rear windows of cafés and taverns that backed onto the creek, they could see other signs of what hadn't yet changed in La Graciosa. There in McMarty's Saloon were the red tablecloths and the antler heads and the ancient ceiling fans. There at the Graciosa Brewing Company were the red and black tiles, and the Rockola jukebox, and the boxy light fixtures that descended on long poles from a high ceiling. There at Nora's Café, hanging from walls, were clothes for sale, "wearable art" made by local quilters. There at Bobo's Tavern, pasted to the wall behind the bar, were hundreds of confiscated phony driver's licenses.

Don't ask me, Bobo's bartender had once told Doug, when asked how he spotted the phony licenses. *I can't tell it's phony unless a black guy shows me a card with a photo of a white guy . . . or a guy shows me a picture of a girl . . . Sometimes you can't tell then, either.*

"Nothing had better stop us from JB's tonight," Jimmy said.

"Nothing will."

"Good. You have reason to celebrate, I hear."

Bard stopped. "What do you mean?"

"Come on. Word is, you cracked the Merta case. I hear an arrest is imminent."

"Where the hell do you get your sources, Jimmy?"

"Aha. So I'm right. Howie and Angela must be so thankful."

"Let's say they have expressed their appreciation."

"Who's the suspect?"

Bard started walking again. "When there's something to announce, you'll hear."

Jimmy raced to catch up. The effort left him puffing. "Cut that out, Doug. We're not talking for a story, crissake. Do I have to say stuff like 'off the record' to you?"

Doug watched the creek roll by. What the hell, Jimmy would hear somewhere else soon enough. "Jed Jeremiah . . . that old mountain man up in the foothills."

Jimmy did a double take. "Jed Jeremiah? Good God."

"We've got a case against him, Jimmy."

"I imagine so. He's no Quaker. He's been in more than one scrap. He plumb scares me, tell you the truth. But Jesus, Doug. Good God."

"You just like him because he gives you great copy."

"Maybe so. That's true. I've got a soft spot for mountain men who hunt grizzly and play honky-tonk piano. Still, it's hard to imagine."

"Murder is always hard to imagine."

"What I mean is, Jed's just a throwback, that's all, not a wild animal. Your early Western type. He's got principles. He's got his own code of honor."

"But it's his own code, not Chumash County's. My point exactly."

"What do you have on him?"

"A history of shooting poachers on his land."

"Ah yes, the Basque shepherd. Well, okay. Plenty around here still doubt that self-defense claim."

"There's more."

"What?"

Bard stopped at the foot of Carmel Street, where the creek sank into an underground tunnel and began its ten-mile journey to the sea. Across from them, on the far side of the creek, rose the Apple Canyon Inn, a freewheeling mix of adobe and split timber. Cars were pulling up at its entrance. Those climbing out were dressed in tuxedos and long black dresses. The sound of a string quartet floated across the water.

"We have an eyewitness," Bard said. "Someone who saw Jeremiah running from Ollie Merta's burning home."

Jimmy let out a long whistle.

"Ollie Merta kept some sheep," Bard continued. "His house sits in the valley directly below Jeremiah's ranch. This likely was an old-fashioned California grazing ruckus turned deadly."

"Well, I'll be damned."

"There may also be a boot—"

Jimmy stopped Bard with a hand on his arm. He pointed across the creek at the Apple Creek Inn. "Look what we have here."

Bard turned. Out of a pale green Pontiac, part of the county's fleet, climbed Bruce Hightower. The commission chairman stood alone and motionless for a moment, looking with approving eyes at the scene before him, at the Inn and all the guests streaming toward its entrance. Following him out of the Pontiac, one long black-stockinged leg at a time, came Chumash County DA Angela Stark. Her hair fell loosely over her shoulders. She leaned into Hightower, grasped his hand. Her mouth was open, her smile directed up at him. Hightower lightly draped an arm over Angela's shoulder.

"Those two are an item?" Bard asked.

"Where you been, Doug? She's been his main squeeze for months."

"I didn't think Angela Stark was inclined to be anybody's main squeeze."

"She's head over heels, apparently. She's by his side at all the big hoo-ha parties these days. They travel together in the highest circles. That's where they met, at one of those political dinners. Turned a few heads that night, from what I heard. The two of them, out on the dance floor."

"Angela Stark?"

"Angela Stark."

"What's going on tonight?"

"Political back-scratcher, disguised as a high-end charity fund-raiser."

Just then someone else at the Apple Canyon Inn's entrance caught Bard's eye. She was climbing out of a new silver Lexus GS 300. When had Sasha bought that? It suited her, Bard thought. Her gray eyes matched the car. She ran a hand through her tangle of dark brown hair. She'd come alone.

"Good God," Jimmy said. "Isn't that your ex-wife?"

Sasha noticed them from across the narrow creek and waved, looking oddly pensive. She called out something, but Bard couldn't hear. Then she turned toward Bruce Hightower and Angela Stark, catching up to them as they passed through the hotel's front door.

"Yes, it is," Bard said. "Sasha is getting around now. Just like she always wanted."

They started walking again, thirsty for JB's. In strained silence they followed the brick path, both disinclined to talk more about Jeremiah. As they reached the tavern, Bard could see through the front window a potbellied stove, a kerosene lamp, billiards tables, branding irons, steer horns. He could hear JB's, too—the sound of Dave Murphy on honky-tonk piano, Shirley singing her dirty blues, cowboys clanking their mugs of brew.

"Not the highest social circles of Chumash County," Jimmy said, "but it will do for the likes of you and me."

SIX

The buzzing of her intercom drew Cassie Teal's attention. Angela Stark herself was beckoning. Cassie punched a button. "Just finishing something up. I'll be right in."

She sat back in her chair, not yet ready for the DA.

Not bad, Detective. That's what Angela had said to Doug Bard. In her mind, Cassie Teal reviewed the moment. Angela, touching the back of the detective's hand. Angela, bestowing her uncommon approval. To receive something so rare was a heady experience. Cassie wondered how it felt to Doug Bard.

She knew how it was for herself—curious, to say the least. It had been ever since she'd landed here in the DA's office.

Cassie pushed away from her desk and a mountain of paperwork. Angela could wait. It all could wait.

Cassie had started in Chumash County as a criminal defense attorney, and to her mind, she'd been a damn good one. Even the celebrated Greg Monarch referred occasional cases and talked of a possible partnership. She sat on key committees of the county defense bar, she pioneered use of DNA evidence, she provided pithy quotes and analysis to inquiring reporters.

Then came the Hernandez case.

It began on a Saturday night three years ago, around Christmas. A fifteen-year-old girl, Shari Malone, decided to have a sleepover at her friend's house after a day of shopping. The friend's parents went out and various boys dropped by, turning the sleepover into a drinking party. Near midnight, Shari left with twenty-one-year-old Cal Hernandez to get more beer. They never returned. Shari's parents filed a missing persons report late the next day.

By then, Hernandez was already in custody, arrested on another matter—brandishing a handgun at a convenience store. Shari, police soon learned from a witness, had been with him during that late-night altercation.

Hernandez no longer looked to the cops like a guy caught waving a gun. Hernandez looked like a guy who'd made Shari Malone disappear.

He needed a lawyer, and right away. The court clerk called the public defender they had on retainer—Cassie Teal. Within hours, late on Monday night, she was sitting in a holding cell down at the *asistencia,* talking to her new client.

Cal Hernandez had a round boyish face, a chubby build, and arms covered by incongruous tattoos, mainly snakes. He lacked guile, and seemed to have no appreciation for the seriousness of his situation. He talked openly about Shari Malone from the start. He told Cassie everything. How he'd tried to have sex with Shari, how Shari had resisted, how he'd strangled her, how he'd dumped her nude body in a drainage culvert way up in the mountains. When he finished talking, Hernandez leaned forward and placed his hand on Cassie's. There was something he needed to make clear, something important: He hadn't raped her. He would never rape a girl.

Cassie drove home in a daze. She knew Hernandez had killed Shari, and she knew exactly where he'd dumped the body. Yet the law required her to be a fierce advocate for her client; the law also barred her from violating lawyer-client confidentiality. Instinctively, she'd advised Hernandez against volunteering anything without a deal. That was standard operating procedure. All the same, she lay awake most of the night, staring at her ceiling. The next morning, she watched as Chumash County began organizing a massive search for Shari.

How to honor both her legal and moral obligations? Cassie wrestled with that question for much of Tuesday. Late in the afternoon, she went to District Attorney Angela Stark.

She offered what the lawyers called a "hypothetical." If my

client did indeed kill Shari Malone, and if my client were willing right now to lead authorities to her body, would the prosecutor agree not to seek the death penalty?

It was the only strategy available. The best Cassie could get Hernandez was life without parole. And the only bargaining chip she had was the location of Shari Malone's body. The ploy didn't work, though. Angela Stark sized up Cassie instantly, Cassie and the cards she was holding. Stark wouldn't respond, wouldn't say yes or no. She let Cassie twist in the wind.

The search began early the next morning, a Wednesday. Some 300 sworn officers and citizen volunteers gathered at a command post before fanning out. They scoured the immediate areas around La Graciosa; they dragged Graciosa Creek; they marched through brush in the surrounding hills and backcountry. One day passed, then two. "We're looking in all the obvious places," Detective Douglas Bard, chief of the command post, told reporters.

It was Thursday, near dusk. Christmas Eve. Angela Stark chose that moment to reject Cassie Teal's deal, forty-eight hours after it had been offered. The lawyers were at an impasse now. As the search continued all Christmas day, Cassie spent hours consulting with the best legal minds she could find across California. Many insisted it would be unethical to disclose any information without a deal, and illegal to breach confidentiality. Others told her it was nonetheless the moral thing to do.

Christmas night, she walked the streets of La Graciosa, oblivious to the gentle revelry all around her. At noon the next day, she watched as stymied authorities announced they were calling off the fruitless search. "Shari's still out there somewhere," Detective Bard told reporters. "If only we knew where."

That was it for Cassie. An hour later, she showed up in Angela's office. "Okay," she told the DA. "We'll take you to the body."

They drove out in Stark's county car, Cassie beside her in the front, Bard in the back with a handcuffed Cal Hernandez.

Some thirty-five miles north of town, high up a winding mountain road, Hernandez pointed to a large drainage pipe. "In there," he said. Bard went first. He studied the naked, strangled body. Then he turned and stared at Cassie.

She never tried to duck. To Jimmy O'Brien and the other journalists, she explained everything as clearly as she could. "It was a very difficult situation," she said. "Generally, an attorney is subject to discipline for violating the confidentiality privilege. On the other hand, I had extreme concern for Shari Malone's family, and for the feelings of our entire community."

It didn't help. Nothing did. The drumbeat of outrage mounted by the hour throughout Chumash County. Some wanted criminal charges filed against Cassie. Some wondered whether Shari was still alive when dumped in the culvert. Threatening phone calls began pouring in. Soon came the hate mail. When three roughnecks showed up one afternoon at the office suite Cassie shared with another attorney, Louis Brody, she felt compelled to call the police.

By the time of Hernandez's arraignment, Cassie was reeling. She decided to withdraw as his lawyer. "Too time-consuming," was what she told the court. In truth, the dilemma she'd faced, and the onslaught of negative opinion, had pulled down the pillars that held up her professional world. She no longer felt able to justify, in her own mind, what she did as a criminal defense attorney. On the TV news one night, she watched Doug Bard saying, "I think, as a person, morally, you would have some ethical obligation. Cassie Teal literally does nothing and allows us to be days behind in finding this girl's body." Rather than throw a shoe at the screen, she thought: He's right.

Cassie believed she no longer could function effectively as a criminal defense attorney. Nor did she want to. She needed now to make amends. She wanted to be embraced by her community, not banished. She wanted to convict child killers, not hide their victims' bodies.

To Cassie's grateful surprise, Angela Stark responded quickly when she asked for a job in the DA's office. It turned out Angela appreciated the skill with which Cassie had tried to navigate her perilous course. She respected Cassie for the standoff she'd forced. She saw in Cassie someone else who didn't let moral qualms stop her from doing what was necessary.

The intercom buzzed again. Angela's impatience crackled through the speaker. "Cassie, I'm still waiting."

Cassie's high heels clacked on the concrete hallway as she walked to the DA's office. At Stark's door, she knocked.

"Come on in," Angela called out.

Cassie pushed open the door. Before her, the DA sat in a chair, head down, hands folded on her lap. On either side of her, also with their heads down, were Marilee Cooper's parents, Harvey and Cynthia.

"We've been praying," Angela said. "Praying for Marilee's soul, and praying for justice."

Cassie didn't know what to say. As far as she knew, both Stark and the Coopers were nominal Catholics at best, not overly devoted. She had never imagined Angela ever praying. She looked at Harvey and Cynthia. Both had pale skin and red eyes.

"Would you care to join us?" Cynthia asked.

"I . . . I . . ." Cassie couldn't find any words.

Angela rose. "Never mind, Cassie. I called you in because I want you to meet the Coopers."

Cassie extended a hand to Harvey, grateful for something to do.

"The reason I want you to meet them," Angela continued, "is because I've decided to make you my second chair for the prosecution of Marilee's killer."

Cassie asked, "Have we caught the killer?"

"You were there. You saw what Doug Bard accomplished in that interrogation room."

"Yes, I was, but—"

"Cassie, when you have an eyewitness actually naming a killer, you can't just sit on your hands."

"Of course, I understand that, but—"

"Cassie, I want you to get ready to convene a grand jury.

We're going to indict Jed Jeremiah for the murders of Ollie Merta and Marilee Cooper."

Down dark narrow canyon roads they drove, Douglas Bard at the wheel, Eddie Hines beside him in the passenger seat. They'd been at this for two hours. Eddie wasn't doing any better now than at the start. He still couldn't show Bard precisely where, in the hills above Ollie Merta's house, he and his two buddies drank beer and shot squirrels. He still couldn't find his buddies, Squeaky and Hotwire. He still couldn't fix on a time for all they saw.

Bard said, "A few holes in your story, Eddie. Not enough details."

Eddie looked close to tears. He'd been trying so hard to please. He'd promised to be Bard's eyes and ears on the street; he'd wept over that little girl's death; he'd talked on and on about becoming a cop.

"I want to help," he whined. "It's just that everything gets confused in my head."

Bard didn't doubt that. He made allowances for Eddie's slowness. He'd spent lots of time around dumb mutts, after all. He knew about their confused heads; he knew most of them could barely string three sentences together. He also made allowances for Eddie's dreamy boasting. Eddie claimed to have been in the Marines, for instance, but didn't have a clue who Chesty Puller was. Hell, Bard reasoned, there weren't enough jail cells to hold everyone who lied about their military experience.

Still—something about Eddie had started to trouble him. The punk was having too good a time. Sheriff Dixon, protective of his eyewitness, had authorized a motel room for Eddie, just to keep him on a short leash. Which meant a free telephone, cable television, unlimited room service, and a constantly replenished bar. Eddie had been having a goddamn ball. One night, Bard dropped by his room to find a party going on. Another time, he found Eddie in the motel parking lot, test-driving a used Cadillac that he planned to buy with his reward money.

Bard was accustomed to gaming mutts like Eddie Hines. Back in the *asistencia* interrogation room, that's what he'd thought he was doing. In recent days, he'd grown less certain. He couldn't shake the haunting notion that Eddie was possibly gaming *them*. That would mean Eddie was something more complicated than a sloppy stupid mutt. It didn't seem likely; Eddie barely knew how to tie his shoes. Yet Bard had to admit it was possible. Anything was possible.

Bard looked over at Eddie. There he sat, staring vacantly out the window. The mutt's mouth hung open. Not just his jaw but his whole body had gone slack. No, it wasn't possible. This idiot couldn't possibly be gaming them. He was just doing what came naturally in a county-paid motel room.

"At least show me Ollie Merta's house," Bard said. "Take me there, Eddie. Show me that you know where it is."

Eddie started pointing and directing. They descended through two canyons, then wound their way southeast of town into a broad expanse of farmland. At a T-intersection in the middle of a cabbage field, Eddie pointed to the left. They weren't following a straight path to Merta's, but Eddie did have them in the right reach of the county. As they approached the unmarked country lane that led to Merta's, he hesitated, frowned, and pointed the wrong way.

"You almost did it," Bard said, "but you blew it on that last turn."

Eddie trembled. "I was drunk . . . It was dark."

What the hell, Bard reasoned. That's the way it is with these stupid jerks. They're always drunk; they're always trying to figure out where they were on such and such a night. That didn't make them liars, that made them utterly lame. You polish this one up, help him practice his lines, show him where Ollie Merta's house is, you could still have a believable witness. Cops and prosecutors did that all the time. A dress rehearsal, that's all they—

Suddenly Bard stopped the car. A notion so simple had only now occurred to him. How had Eddie gotten out to the foothills behind Ollie Merta's house that night? They were driving around now, but Eddie didn't own a car. Surely

Hotwire and Squeaky, whoever they were, didn't own one, either.

"You had wheels that night, Eddie?"

Hines blinked in confusion. "What do you mean?"

"How did you and your buddies get out to Merta's house? Don't tell me Hotwire has a car."

"No way."

"Then what, Eddie?"

Hines worked that question around a bit, looking worried. "We stole one. We stole a car that night."

"And afterward?"

"I dunno. I think they ditched it."

"What kind?"

"Chevy . . . a Chevy Blazer."

Bard drove straight to the sheriff's station. Together he and Eddie marched into the records room. Within minutes, the clerk there—Angie Bourbon, a busty sharp-tongued computer whiz—had the relevant record on her screen. Bard leaned over her shoulder, careful to keep his nose out of her cavernous cleavage. He squinted.

"Guess what, Eddie," he said. "There's not a single stolen car report for the whole month Merta died. Not one car went missing in all of Chumash County."

At dusk, Jimmy O'Brien threaded his way through the crowd gathering on the central plaza. It was Thursday, almost time for the start of the weekly La Graciosa farmer's market. Even more than in years past, he relished these evenings when the town closed Carmel Street to cars. Here was something, by God, that would never change: Farmers opening pickup trucks and card tables laden with the region's fresh produce; local restaurants firing up enormous oakwood barbecues full of ribs and tri-tips; street musicians competing with jugglers, magicians, belly dancers, and anyone else who thought they could perform. On one corner, fathers lifted toddlers to their shoulders to watch a puppet show. On another, Chumash State students gathered around a trio playing the blues. The energy and diversity delighted Jimmy.

"What are you grinning about?"

Turning, Jimmy found Doug Bard by his side.

"The farmer's market always does that to me."

"Me, too."

"Hey," Jimmy said, as they neared the east end of the blockaded road. "You smell what I smell?"

Doug lifted his nose. It was hard to ignore. He inhaled the odor of the region's speciality, barbecued tri-tips. "I want some of that."

"Let's go," Jimmy said, pointing the way.

There it was, at the very end of the blockaded street, half-hidden under an arcade. Mamma Depo's red-oak chuck-wagon. Bard threw down a ten-dollar bill. "Hey, Sanchez," he called out to the man with the spatula. "Good to see you're back in action. Let's have two of those gorgeous tri-tip sandwiches."

Sanchez grinned as he turned his meat over the coals. Sweat damped his T-shirt and rolled down the sides of his face, but a red bandana around his forehead kept his eyes dry. "Cost me a bundle to get to code," he said, handing over two hot foil-wrapped packages. "Then another bundle to convince the inspectors to appreciate all I'd done. But at least I'm back."

"Stay put," Bard said. "Jimmy here will write you up a big feature."

"Marketing!" Sanchez cried.

"Marketing," Jimmy promised.

At the end of Carmel, Jimmy and Doug settled on a plaza bench to eat. Steam rose as they unwrapped their sandwiches. Doug moaned as he took his first bite.

Jimmy left his sandwich on his lap. He said, "Inside word I hear, Stark is preparing to take the Merta case to the grand jury. She means to indict Jed Jeremiah."

Bard chewed slowly, swallowed carefully. "You've got better sources than me."

"You still certain you have the right man, Doug?"

Bard kept chewing. "Certain as I can be."

When they finished eating, they rose and walked back up

Carmel. They stopped at a corner where a pair of matronly belly dancers were competing for attention against a man swallowing a flaming sword. Bard looked about restlessly. In the distance, approaching down Carmel Street, two familiar figures caught his eye. "Excuse me," he told Jimmy. "I see some people I know."

Sasha and Molly spotted him approaching from fifty feet. Molly waved but didn't run toward him as she used to. "Hey, Molly girl," he said when he reached them. "I was—"

He stopped, realizing suddenly that Sasha and Molly weren't alone. In the crowd, he hadn't realized there were others walking with his daughter and ex-wife. Two others: Angela Stark and Bruce Hightower. They all stood frozen now in awkward silence. Sasha stared unhappily at the ground; Angela Stark studied the crowd.

"Let's see now," Bard finally said. "Do we all know each other?"

Hightower thrust out a hand. "Sure we do. You and I have crossed paths before, Doug. Remember? I'm Bruce Hightower."

Bard slowly raised his hand to Hightower's. Yes, of course they'd crossed paths. There'd been several occasions—everything from commission hearings to county fairs. He hadn't thought Hightower noticed him, though. He also hadn't thought that Hightower knew Sasha well enough to be walking her down Carmel. Her and Molly.

"Now I recall," Bard said.

With a roll of her eyes, Stark said, "Doug is one of the best detectives we have, Bruce."

Hightower, ignoring her tone, regarded Bard with appreciation. "So I've heard. We're all grateful for the work you do. You must have such stories."

"One or two."

A cellular phone started ringing. Hightower reached into his pocket. "Excuse me," he said, stepping away. "I think that's San Francisco calling."

Bard felt the transfer of Hightower's attention. Whoever

was on the other end of this call now had it. He watched the commissioner as he murmured into the phone. Despite his apparent ease, this man never quite stood still. Always the head turned, or a hand waved. Bard tried to recall all he knew of Hightower.

Not much, he realized. There'd been only vague references to what he'd done before arriving on the central California coast. To some he mentioned some kind of retail business, to others he talked of fund-raising for various charitable organizations. No one paid too much attention, in truth. His eagerness to tackle grassroots community issues had quickly earned him friends and supporters. Soon enough, his ability to attract venture capitalists had carried him into the inner echelon of Chumash County. The political, business, and social circles had all embraced him, and he hadn't resisted.

He had even assumed their ways. He attended the local Episcopalian church; he played golf with old-money land barons; he helped with a youth camp; he sat on the boards of various civic associations. Hostesses throwing dinner parties came to consider Hightower a primary catch. It was at one of those parties, according to Jimmy, that Hightower had met Angela Stark.

"Yes, Bruce," Angela was saying, with no trace of irony now. "You really should hear Doug's stories sometime." Hightower had put his phone away. Angela's hand curled around his elbow. "He has a particularly interesting one to tell."

Bard studied the DA. He'd never seen such a public display from her, mild as it was.

"Is that so?" Hightower asked.

"The Merta-Cooper case," Angela said, a gloat in her eye. "Expect some big news any day."

"Daddy!" Molly's arms wrapped about Doug. She squeezed, and stood on tiptoes to touch his cheek with her lips. "I was right when I told everyone my daddy would fix things."

Over Molly's head, Bard watched Hightower exchange

amused glances with both Angela and Sasha. "Congratulations, Doug," he said. "Nothing better than a daughter's hug."

Hightower was suddenly getting hard to bear. Bard thought he heard condescension in his voice. Also in Angela Stark's, with her supercilious dance over her star detective. They made his teeth hurt.

Bard turned to Hightower. "I can't be as enthusiastic about your work. Don't much like what you're doing to Chumash County."

Then, to Sasha, he said, "What is he to you, another client?"

She shot him a familiar look. "Yes, Doug, a client. That shouldn't be so hard to understand. Bruce's committee oversees Chumash County's investment portfolio. And if you will recall, my field is investment management."

Sheriff Howie Dixon closed the file he'd been reviewing. Doug Bard's reports on Eddie Hines and Jed Jeremiah made for interesting reading. Bard sounded now as if he were starting to doubt his own case. But you could have doubts about virtually every case. Dixon knew he would never have made it to captain in the LAPD by waffling. Nor would Peabody Enterprises ever have tapped him for a prime security job up here on the Central Coast.

If only he'd kept that job; if only the Peabodys hadn't wanted their man in the sheriff's slot. That's how they'd explained it. You do this for now, they urged. We'll take care of you later.

Do this. Every week, it seemed, he learned more what that entailed. They had to resolve Ollie and Marilee's murders, that much he knew. They had to convict someone.

Dixon clutched at a spot just below his rib cage. Damn indigestion was kicking up again. Doctors gave it a more fancy name, gastro reflux something or other. All Dixon knew was, it burned like hell. Made him want a transplant for his entire insides. He reached in a drawer for his pills.

"If you gave up beer and barbecue, Howie, you wouldn't need those."

Dixon looked up to find Cassie Teal standing in his doorway. He'd been puzzled and more than a little appalled when Angela hired her. Teal's role in the Hernandez case had enraged him. But she'd won him over in time.

"Doesn't anyone knock anymore?" he asked.

"Not in La Graciosa, Howie. You know that. We don't much like appointments or closed doors."

"It is different up here. Years ago, I recall there being actual criminal acts being committed in LA. We don't have crime in Chumash County, do we?"

Cassie gave him a sideways look. "Now, now, Howie. Stay on the bus."

"Of course. I just let go of my strap for a second there."

"We do have the Merta-Cooper murders, you know. We have admitted they exist."

"Yes."

"And we are about to prosecute."

Dixon nodded at the files in her hands. "You've been reading Bard's reports?"

"Yes. Angela feels they're enough to take to a grand jury."

"What does that mean? You guys always tell me a good prosecutor can get a grand jury to indict a ham sandwich."

"True. The real question is, can we get a trial jury to convict?"

The answer came from across the room. At the doorway, Angela Stark said, "Of course we can."

She took three long steps into Dixon's office, and settled into a chair before his desk. Cassie sat beside her. The DA held a file in her hand. She tapped it on her knee. "Do you two have any doubts?" she asked.

"We were just evaluating the case," Cassie said.

Angela looked back and forth at them. "We have an eyewitness who saw Jed Jeremiah fleeing the house. We have Jeremiah's past history. We have a probable motive."

Cassie asked, "That motive being?"

Angela nodded at Dixon. "You tell us, Howie."

The sheriff opened the file on his desk and leafed through the pages. "Ollie Merta's shepherding, just below Jeremiah's property. Possibly on Jeremiah's property. Jed, as we know, has a hair up his ass about trespassers."

"All we have to do is connect the many dots," Cassie observed.

Angela said, "Come on now. That's what it's always about."

"Forgive me." Cassie tried to keep her tone light. "I thought being a prosecutor was about justice. That's why I switched sides."

Angela looked amused. "Don't worry, Cassie. You're on the right side now. We don't defend murderers in this room."

Dixon liked that. "Angela for attorney general. You're our law and our order."

"What I am," Angela said, "is someone who doesn't like crime. Who doesn't like people getting hurt. Who doesn't like people getting killed."

"Bravo," Cassie murmured. "Really."

She'd watched Angela once in the courtroom. It was the Conklin murder case, the one where they'd never found the body. The defense attorney, during his closing, argued that the supposed victim might even still be alive. "See that lady over there," he cried out, pointing randomly to a woman among the courtroom spectators. "Maybe that's her." All heads turned but one—the defendant's. Stark noticed immediately, and rose to her feet. "An intriguing notion," she said. "But why do you think the defendant, alone among us, didn't turn to look? Because she knows the victim is dead." The jury took only twenty minutes to convict.

"I'll agree that we're on the right side," Cassie said. "Just one question, Angela. Do we have any—"

A knock on the door interrupted them. Doug Bard entered the room.

"At least you knocked first," Dixon muttered.

Stark said, "Doug is here at my invitation. I'd like to get all the issues resolved as soon as possible."

Bard was halfway across the room before he noticed Cassie Teal. He stopped. "You're still on this case?"

She held his gaze this time. "Yes, Doug. I'll be second chair, if that's okay with you."

Bard sat down by her side.

"I see why you lead our county in felony arrests," Cassie told him. She held up his file of reports. "That was a clever game you played with our eyewitness. Even if it wouldn't pass a smell test."

Bard shrugged. "I found you a suspect. Isn't that what you wanted?"

"Yes, Doug," Angela said. "It is what I wanted. We're terribly grateful."

Bard turned his attention to the DA. He thought of her as she was the day before, at the farmer's market. He thought also of Molly standing on tiptoes, hugging him for finding Marilee's killer.

"Thanks for your gratitude," he told Angela. "But I think there are some problems with the case."

She appeared only mildly interested. "Doug, this is your case."

"Nevertheless, I now have doubts."

"Doubts? Please, Doug . . . We all have doubts. If we gave in to them, we'd end up curled in a ball most of the day. You have to land somewhere finally, or you'll never put anyone in jail."

Bard said, "But I've turned up some contradictions."

"Contradictions?" The notion amused Angela. "I know lawyers who can keep fifty of them in their head, yet talk as if there were none at all."

"That's a good thing?" Bard asked.

"For a lawyer."

"Which I'm not."

"Exactly." Angela spoke to him now as a teacher would to a student. "We've gone over this before, Doug. Your job is to investigate and present us with the evidence. My job is to decide whether that evidence merits filing charges. In this case, I've decided it does."

"Think you have the right person?" Bard asked.

"Yes, I do. Jed's our man. In fact, he's your man—you arrested him."

Bard felt a headache coming on. "That's true. He's my

lead, I brought him in. But I'm starting to think Eddie Hines is nothing but a nonstop liar. He wants the reward money. He wants to be a cop. I've done three drive-arounds with him. He can't even take me to Ollie Merta's house. Why not? Maybe because he's never been there."

Angela turned to her sheriff, inviting his response. Dixon obliged. "He's just a dim light, Doug. Doesn't know where he goes, how he got there. But he knew enough in the box with his buddy Petey. That was obvious—"

"How could he even have gotten out to Merta's?" Bard asked. "He doesn't have a car. Nor do his buddies. He says they stole one, but no cars went missing that month in all of Chumash County."

"Come on, Doug." Dixon's hand drifted to his midsection. "You know police reports on that kind of stuff don't always get written up."

"Don't you see?" Bard's voice was rising. "We wrote the script in there. Not just for Petey but for Eddie, too. You take away the script, he doesn't know anything. When all is said and done, this is absolute bullshit."

"Doug." Stark's patience was wearing thin. "I don't understand. This is your case. You pushed it, you cracked it. I've been singing your praises all over town. Precisely what are you pulling this time?"

"I wouldn't call it pulling. I just never stopped investigating. What I came up with most recently doesn't smell good."

"Christ, Doug," Dixon said. "You aren't ever going to get a case that smells like a rose."

"True enough, but you don't have to take one that smells like shit. Eddie Hines is just a manipulative little liar. He's been playing us for what he can get. He's—"

"We've already decided," Stark interrupted. "We can't just wring our hands forever. Douglas Bard, I promise you, we will indict and try Jed Jeremiah for the deaths of Ollie Merta and Marilee Cooper."

"Even if he's innocent? Even if—"

"But he's not." Angela was glaring now. "Doug, we need a united front here."

"Do we have a united front?" Bard looked over at the sheriff. "Am I the only one with doubts?"

Howie Dixon shifted silently in his chair, preoccupied with a memo on his desk. Bard stared at the side of his face until the sheriff acknowledged him. "The battle is about to begin," Dixon said. "It's time to put away our doubts."

At Bard's side, Cassie Teal stirred. Without thinking, he turned to her. She looked at him for a long moment, then said, "No, you're not alone, Doug. I have doubts, too."

Angela's hand floated to her temple. "Pray tell, Cassie."

Teal slowly thumbed through her file. "I'm sorry, Angela. I understand how useful this Petey Montrose setup is, and how well it will play to a jury, but it just feels kind of unconvincing to me. Maybe Doug is right. Maybe this Hines fellow began to talk because he wants to be a cop, he wants a job, he wants to be somebody."

"Exactly the case," Bard said, trying to hide his surprise at Cassie's support. "Eddie was just making up stories to impress Petey and get his reward and go be the king of Costa Rica. If he can't match Petey's stories, he loses ten thousand dollars and misses the plane ride to San Juan. If he can't—"

Angela interrupted, still focused on her assistant DA. "What else, Cassie?"

Teal thought before she spoke. "Angela, we all liked hearing this story because it was what we needed. And I know how committed you are to Marilee's parents. We all want so much to solve these murders. But I'm just not sure we have enough. It would be so helpful if we had some sort of physical evidence."

"Physical evidence?" Angela looked around the room. "That's what we want?"

Bard ignored her. He understood now what bothered him most. "Worst thing about this," he said, "the guilty guy's still out there. We put Jeremiah in jail, we're not out there looking for the real child killer. And if we're not looking, we're not going to find him. We're not—"

Cassie stopped him with a steadying hand on his arm.

Bard, following her gaze, turned to the DA. Angela was holding up a single sheet of paper.

"Douglas," she said, "there's just one flaw in your theory. I have here the lab report on Jed Jeremiah's boots. The boots you were clever enough to spot and obtain for us."

Bard stared at the document. In his mind he saw Jed Jeremiah yanking off those boots.

Cassie asked: "What does the report say, Angela?"

The DA scanned the pages in her hands. "A perfect fit . . . The boot on Jeremiah's foot exactly matches the print on Ollie Merta's front door."

SEVEN

The sea surged against rugged cliffs dense with Monterey shale. Ancient sand dunes rose out of bluffs thick with ice plant and verbena. Rough trails wound through wooded stream canyons, ending in fields lush with fiddlenecks and California poppies. Bruce Hightower looked about, arms lifted to the sky. "This is why I'm here," he said. "This is why I came to Chumash County." By his side, Angela Stark smiled uncertainly.

At Hightower's insistence, they'd been hiking in Pecho Rancho State Park all Sunday morning. Now they stood above a perilous slope that descended to a hidden surf-splashed cove. The sun, directly overhead, had turned their necks pink and damp with sweat.

"Let's slide down," he urged.

She peered over the edge. "How will we climb back up?"

"We'll answer that question when we have to."

She looked at him with a touch of wonder. "You're always living in the moment. How can you just plunge ahead without calculating where you're going? Don't you ever worry over how things will turn out?"

"Why should I? Everything always works out just fine." He winked at her. "If not always as expected."

"For you, maybe. Not for everyone."

"We're going to rock this county, Angela. You and me."

"Only this county, Bruce?"

"No, not just this county."

It was a mantra they shared. His words, as always, stirred her. "What's our boundary, Bruce?"

"No boundary."

"No boundary," she repeated. Her eyes half closed. "Oh my."

It had taken a while for them to meet, although she'd noticed him almost from the start. He stood out in Chumash County. He wasn't like the men born and raised on the Central Coast, the men she'd grown up with. He spoke out, made things happen. He'd been around, that was clear.

Their paths finally crossed the day she stopped by to watch final preparations for a county fair on the Memorial Day weekend. It was a warm, still Friday afternoon without a breeze, even in the meadow halfway to Pirate's Beach where they held the fair. She wore a cotton sundress, sandals, a floppy straw hat—almost a disguise for the county prosecutor, but one she enjoyed. For a while, she walked among the stalls, talking to volunteers as they set up booths and fences. When she had her fill of that, she settled on a shaded bale of hay to watch.

He was unloading cartons from a truck. The boxes were big and heavy, yet he seemed hardly to strain. In the heat, he'd pulled off his T-shirt. He was wearing only khaki shorts and hiking boots. She looked at his chest, at his arms and shoulders. He was taut and muscled, but not overly so. He had a flat, hard stomach. His hair, light brown, hung over pale blue eyes.

It was those eyes that most drew her attention. They were full of humor and energy, as if he were having fun lugging those boxes. Yet there was something more there, something she recognized—a restlessness. This was not a man who planned to stay in Chumash County forever.

She rose from her bale of hay, intending only to walk by, but he caught her looking at him. "Bruce Hightower," he said, dropping a box and sticking out a hand.

She studied his hand, then shook it. His skin felt warm and rough.

"Those boxes must be heavy," she said. "You should get some help."

He grinned, friendly and challenging at once. "How about you?"

On impulse, she took off her straw hat and shook out her

hair. With two steps, she was at the pile of boxes. "Come on then. Let's get working."

They spoke little more that first day. She lifted boxes with him for half an hour, until they'd emptied the truck, then picked up her hat and walked away. That night, alone in the house she rented a few blocks off the plaza, she kept trying to push the thought of this man out of her mind. He wouldn't leave, though. The sense of a coming adventure consumed her. She felt roiled and intoxicated. She'd not been close with a man since she walked out of her brief marriage to a fellow law student who, she discovered too late, lacked even a semblance of imagination. She hadn't felt deprived one day since. Until now.

The county fair lasted three days. Each morning, Angela found a reason to stop by just before lunchtime. On the second day, she brought him a sandwich. On the third, she asked him why he no longer took his shirt off while he worked.

He laughed out loud at that. Plainly, he liked her brass. The quality that intimidated most of the men in Chumash County seemed to interest him. Angela thought him a solid, confident man, sure of himself, sure of where he was headed.

On that third day, something happened that only bolstered her opinion. Little Gloria Bulger, the ten-year-old daughter of a clerk in Angela's office, fell off a ladder while hanging red, white, and blue bunting. For minutes that seemed endless, she lay on the ground unconscious, turning blue, blood trickling from the corner of her mouth. Her mother clutched her, paralyzed by hysteria, while other frantic adults milled about and searched for cell phones. Then Hightower, with Angela at his heels, reached the scene. He rolled the girl onto her back, holding her head with the body as one unit. He loosened her collar. He opened her airway. With a palm on her forehead, he pressed to tilt her head back. With two fingers, he lifted Gloria's lower jaw to bring her chin forward. He placed his ear close to her mouth, watching her chest and stomach. "She's breathing," he said. "Just got the wind knocked out. Bit her tongue. That's the blood."

By the time the paramedics arrived, Gloria was sitting up,

blinking at the crowd around her. "Everyone here knew what to do," Hightower explained to Angela as they sat in the shade. "They lost their heads for a while."

Later that afternoon, Angela's pager began beeping. Without looking at it, she reached into her purse and punched it off. Hightower was talking just then about his past and his plans. There'd been a divorce, and a child he couldn't see because his ex-wife had gone abroad. There'd been a couple of business ventures gone wrong, mainly because of partners whose low ethics and high greed he couldn't abide. He preferred public service now. He knew what he wanted to do. The city council, the planning board, the county commission— all stepping-stones toward his vision, toward a rejuvenated but preserved Chumash County.

"I'm going to rock this county," he told her.

Even then, she had her question: "Only this county, Bruce?"

She told him about her abortive attempt to get the nomination for state attorney general, and why she'd been denied, and why she wanted to try again. He not only understood, he had his own stories to tell about getting throttled by the good-ol'-boy circuit. Soon they were sharing wicked riffs about big-city lawyers they knew who made a million a year by giving good meetings. "The key to it all," Hightower pointed out, "is pretending that you really know something. Also, being able to sit around the conference table for six hours without keeling over."

Time crawled for her after the fair, a number of weeks with no further contact. Then one night they found themselves at the same political fund-raiser, a dinner at the country club. He held back at first, cautious around the county bigwigs. She, managing to pass him in a hallway outside the bathrooms, gave a long steady look. He asked her to dance. They clung to each other before all the guests, unwilling to let go.

He brought her home that night. His house sat perched on a bluff ten miles north of town, where a point of land met the sea. It wasn't large or ostentatious, in fact it was a simple rough wood dwelling, but it amazed Angela, for it had been designed to follow the land's natural contours, to fit in with

the cliff and the surrounding forest. The grounds were un-
tamed, with carved pathways snaking among towering old
coast cypress trees. There was a driftwood-colored fence, a
stone arch, and flagstone laid in wooly thyme. The house's
original foundation, Hightower explained with obvious pride,
was sea-worn granite, drawn by horses from a little cove below the cliff. A poet-carpenter had built this house with his
own hands. When he died, his estranged daughter had sold it
to Hightower without a second thought. He'd thought it a
steal—as well as a perfect example of what he advocated.

Inside, Hightower had added a layer of insulation and plaster, but Angela still considered it fairly rustic. Off the entry,
there was a single bedroom on one side, a library on the other.
She walked on pine-planked floors to a narrow stairway,
which led down, following the form of the cliff, to a barnlike
kitchen and dining area. Wood-framed French doors opened
to a broad flagstone terrace shaded by bougainvillea and wis-
teria. A brick fireplace rose on one side of the terrace, set into
a wall covered by a jumble of vibrant orange thunbergia
vines.

Angela stepped out onto the terrace. There, at the edge,
facing the sea, she saw a telescope trained to the dark skies.
She went to look through it. A bright hot sphere loomed before her eyes. "That's Venus," Hightower explained. "You
need something like this Meade DE to see her with any clarity. It's my one indulgence. This electric controller lets me
track whatever's moving across the sky. Four speeds, four di-
rections, all night long. The optical system is a dream. We can
count the rings of Saturn."

"Do you do that often?"

"Whenever I can't sleep."

Inside again, Angela found herself drawn to the library,
where two wing-backed chairs in khaki twill flanked a
rock fireplace. There was also a worn leather couch, an old
kilim area rug, and a Chinese armoire full of stereo equipment, but it was the books on the oak shelves lining the walls
that caught her attention. Hightower's interests were so eclec-
tic: history, poetry, urban design, fiction, anthropology. There

were novels in their original French, among them Balzac's *Le Père Goriot* and Camus's *L'Etranger*. There was a complete collection of T. S. Eliot. There was Alice Munro's *Friend of My Youth*. There was a book about the Cree Indians of northern Canada, and another about the Melanesians of the South Pacific. There were Conant and Dewey on educational theory, Erik Erikson's *Young Man Luther*, Paul Goodman's *Growing Up Absurd*. There was even Angela's favorite, the reason she'd become a lawyer: Harper Lee's *To Kill a Mockingbird*.

"Who would have guessed," she told Hightower. "You're a woodsman, astronomer, and professor when you're not a politician."

"I just like to read," he said. "And study the sky."

His bedroom was comfortable but simple, little more than a Shaker-style poster bed set on a seagrass rug. He led her there, then waited. Understanding that was his way, she took his hand and pulled him to her. He pressed against her, she pressed back. It was difficult to say who was more excited. He tugged at her skirt as she reached for his belt. They fell backward toward the bed, not caring where they landed. Afterward, they lay side by side, listening to the sound of the ocean far below.

"Come on," he was saying now. "Let's slide down."

She turned toward the sea and the perilous slope. The blue-green waters beckoned. "Okay. Let's slide down."

They started on their feet, but took most of the slope on their backsides. He reached the cove first, then helped her over the rocks. He brushed the dirt off her and tucked her shirttail back into her hiking shorts. When he finished, his hand stayed inside her shorts. She could feel his fingers, moving slowly.

"Let's swim," he said.

She looked around. "I can see the headlines. Chumash County DA arrested for indecent exposure."

"Maybe there'll even be a photo with the story." He undressed her as he spoke. When he finished she said, "Now my turn."

She was expert with his buttons and belt buckle. In an instant she had his clothes off. She couldn't stop looking. His body reminded her of a Greek statue.

They dove under the waves and stroked toward the horizon. The chilly water startled her, but she said nothing. One hundred yards out, they turned parallel to the shore. Overhead, birds of all kinds—pelicans, cormorants, sandpipers, sooty shearwaters—soared and plunged. Angela rolled onto her back to watch them. A movement off to the side caught her attention. She swam toward it and laughed. Sea otters with inquisitive noses, studying them from the shelter of a tiny grotto. Bruce and Angela swam toward shore.

On the beach, she stretched out under the hot sun, savoring the feel of wet sand on her skin. She ran her hand along her thighs, then slowly up her stomach to her breasts.

"Admiring yourself?" Bruce asked.

She knew he'd been watching. "That okay with you?"

"Perfectly fine."

She waited a moment, then said, "Everything else fine?"

"What do you mean?"

She tried to choose her words with care. He'd been so upset recently. He'd taken to screening calls, to keeping his cell phone turned off. He avoided the plaza now whenever he could, sometimes walking blocks out of his way. This was so unlike the Bruce Hightower she knew, the man who handled tree-hugging environmentalists and grasping venture capitalists without breaking a sweat.

She said, "All your work, Bruce. Your vision for Chumash County. That's what I mean."

He showed her his reassuring grin, even as his hands dug into the sand. "Everything's fine," he said. "Like I told you, things work out, if not always as expected."

The East Chumash County hamlet called Pozo suggested to Douglas Bard the ruined remnant of someone's long ago dream. There must have been a vision, some notion perhaps of an inland retreat from La Graciosa's coastal fog. It was dry and fog-free here in the highlands, but consequently dusty and parched. Farther to the north was land full of rolling hills and towering oaks, vineyards and orchards, farms and fishing lakes. Here there were only lizards, snakes, rusty trailer homes, and faded splintery shacks. The main street, three blocks long, featured a motley mix of curio shops, taverns, and fast-food stands.

Bard walked past them all, staring into windows. He'd started in East Chumash in the days after the murders, searching pawnshops for a pair of boots. Now he was back, searching not for shoes but for men. Two men: Hotwire and Squeaky. He didn't know if they even existed, but if they did, he imagined they'd be here.

Pozo was a backwoods refuge for those who had reasons to hide, those who preferred not to have an address. Sheriff's deputies made it a regular stop whenever they had a pile of warrants to serve on folks they couldn't find. It could get a little wild in Pozo. Once Sheriff Wizen drove out to look into reports that somebody was firing off a fully automatic AR-15 rifle in the woods. Not true, he was advised by Pauline Hussey of Pauline's Pozo Pawnshop; it was only a semiautomatic. Pauline was the hamlet's unofficial mayor. Often, deputies would just phone her when they had a warrant, and the suspect of the day would be produced without further comment.

Bard had decided against calling Pauline. He preferred a face-to-face visit today.

There's nothing more to do ... We've got our case ... Stark's taking it to a grand jury. That's what Sheriff Dixon had told them. Bard wasn't as sure. When the sun was high, he worked the files they gave him, and kept his mouth shut. But in the first and last hours of the day, he still pursued other possibilities.

Despite the matching bootprints, he couldn't convince himself beyond a doubt that they had Ollie and Marilee's killer. Labs could get things wrong, and labs could differ among themselves. Angela was going too fast for him; Angela was too certain, too determined. Thoughts of Jed Jeremiah filled his mind. In his wallet now, right beside Molly's, he carried a photo of Marilee Cooper.

Bard stopped in front of the Pozo Pawnshop. Through the door, he saw Pauline sitting on a stool behind her front counter. He stepped inside. She looked up. "Detective Bard," she bellowed. "Come on in."

From Pauline's ears hung diamond earrings the size of Ping-Pong balls. Her dress, a white sheath, glittered with metallic strips. Her bouffant reflected a pale blue hue. She appeared perilously vulnerable in a Pozo Pawnshop. Yet Bard knew a rifle rested on brackets just out of sight below the counter, inches from her fingers. She'd used it four times in six years, by Bard's count.

"How the hell you doing, Pauline?"

"Probably a whole hell of a lot better than you, sweetie pie." She grinned wickedly. "Which isn't saying much."

"Shoot any of your customers recently?"

"Just a couple who didn't pull their wallets out fast enough."

Bard looked around. Pauline's shop was plain and not overly organized. Unfinished shelves lined the bare white walls; boxes and counters filled the chipped parquet wood floor. The shop's stock reflected what townsfolk had to pawn: guns, rings, stereos, televisions, carpentry tools, kitchen appliances. It was the tools in pawnshops that always left Bard muttering. To pawn your way of making a living always struck him as the last act of someone both foolish and doomed.

He hesitated. He knew Pauline liked to swap small talk before providing leads, but he hadn't the time. "I'm after a couple small-time mutts," he said. "Drifters from the coast."

She slowly slid off her seat, looking disappointed at being denied her day's gossip. "We got a lot like that up here."

"They'd have come up within the past month, I'd say."

"Okay, that narrows it a little. You got names?"

"Only what they go by, and that may have changed. Hotwire and Squeaky."

Pauline hooted. "A tony pair, I take it."

"Real classy."

"What they look like?"

He had only what Eddie told him. "One skinny, short. The other big belly, lots of hair."

As she chewed on that, recognition showed in her eyes. "Holy tamoly. They maybe came in couple weeks ago. If it's them, they pawned an old Colt .45, collected fifty bucks. Never came back for it."

"There'd be some paperwork, wouldn't there?"

She hesitated. "This doesn't get traced to me now, does it, sweetie pie?"

"I don't even know you."

She reached under the counter—her fingers brushing the rifle, Bard imagined—and came up with a file. She opened it and leafed through papers. At one, she stopped. "Here it is," she said.

Bard studied the scrawl. They hadn't used Hotwire or Squeaky, if it were them. They'd used a single name, Harold Jones. Imagination wasn't their strong suit, apparently. He looked at Pauline. "You happen to hear what these guys called each other?"

She'd been waiting for that question. "Didn't call each other anything. This Harold Jones, he's the big belly. When he gets the fifty bucks from me, he turns to the other one. 'Let's hit the saloon,' he says. They all do that. Pawn something, then turn around and hand the proceeds straight over to Buster. He sits there in his tavern waiting for them like a spider after flies. It's quite a show. You learn a lot, Detective. I'll tell you."

He strained to make out the last lines on Harold Jones's pawn slip. There it was, beside his name. Where it asked for a phone number, he'd instead listed an address: *Louise's Boarding House, Room 406.*

"Hey, Pauline," Bard said, "which way to Louise's?"

He found them sitting on the front porch, clutching open cans of Graciosa Brew. Behind them an unlatched screen door banged faintly in the breeze. Louise's Boarding House, a rambling wood-frame collection of wings and levels, looked to be built in at least four sections, each added to the original unit as expansion became necessary. By counting windows, Bard estimated twelve bedrooms, none more than eight by ten feet. Someone had recently slapped on a nice coat of dark green paint. The boarding business must be booming in Pozo.

"You Hotwire?" Bard asked the one with a big belly.

Big Belly frowned at that. He had a full round face, a wild tangle of brown hair, and a single gold earring. "That's not my name," he said, "but I'm called that sometimes."

Bard turned to the skinny one. "You Squeaky?"

He appeared a little sharper than his companion. "Who's asking?" he said.

Doug pulled out his badge this time. "Detective Bard, Chumash County Sheriff's Department."

Hotwire and Squeaky were unhappy, but not surprised. "What we do?" Hotwire asked.

"Nothing I know of," Doug said, "except hide from me."

Squeaky took a pull from his beer bottle. "Why you say that? We don't even know you."

"Oh, but you've heard of me. You know I've been looking for you."

"No law against traveling around," Squeaky pointed out.

Bard smiled. This wasn't going to be hard. "None at all. I'm just happy to catch up to you guys finally."

Hotwire said, "Still don't understand why you've been searching for us."

Bard glanced back and forth at them. He dropped the smile. "I understand you might know something about the murders and fire at Ollie Merta's house."

"What murders?" Squeaky asked. "What's an Ollie Merta?"

Bard spoke with care, not wanting to put words in their mouths. "I understand you were up in the foothills of Boxer Canyon one night about a month ago, somewhere behind Merta's house, drinking beer and shooting squirrels. I understand you saw something."

Hotwire sputtered. "You understand . . . ? You understand . . . ?"

Squeaky was rocking back and forth. "What the hell you talking about? I've never hunted squirrel in my life. I can't stand squirrels. I can't stand sitting in the woods. I've got allergies, man. One night there, I puff up like a balloon. You'd have to rush me to the emergency room."

Bard nodded at Hotwire. "What about you? You got allergies, too?"

"Allergies?" Hotwire had lost the entire thread. "What are you talking about?"

Squeaky slammed down his beer can. "Yes, just what are you talking about? You've been asking after us for weeks now. How come? How come you think we were up in those hills watching people get murdered?"

Bard had no choice but to show his hand. "The buddy you were drinking with up there told us."

"What buddy?" Squeaky asked.

"Eddie Hines."

Hotwire looked at Squeaky. Together they said, "Eddie Hines?" Then they started laughing.

"What's so funny?" Bard asked.

Squeaky said, "Man, Eddie Hines just wishes we'd let him come drinking with us sometime. Eddie Hines is the town clown. Eddie Hines is the neighborhood moron."

From the far side of the *asistencia* courtyard, Doug Bard spotted Marilee Cooper's parents leaving the prosecutors' wing and turning into La Graciosa's central plaza. For an instant, he felt an impulse to chase after them, to warn them about all his budding doubts. The moment passed as he imagined their alarmed expressions. Instead, he turned and headed for the door from which they'd just exited. He stepped through a winding hallway that led him to an empty reception desk. He glanced at his watch—lunchtime in La Graciosa. He looked about, saw no one. He leaned over to study the bank of blinking lights on the reception desk's phone console. Beside one, he saw Cassie Teal's name. He punched the button.

"Yes?" Cassie asked.

"Doug Bard out here," he said. "I think we ought to talk."

She was standing at the open door of her office when he got there. Seeing her made him stop short. Until she'd sided with him against Stark, she'd just been that goddamn lawyer in the

Hernandez case. Now he had to rethink his view of her. Her pale blue eyes inspected him from under a mass of blonde curls, unblinking but lit with humor.

"How can I help you, Douglas? You interested in applying for the job of receptionist?"

They'd never been alone before, he realized. They'd always been in meetings with colleagues.

"Maybe we can help each other."

She weighed that notion for a moment, then stepped aside, and waved him into her office. Bard looked around. Novels, not law books, filled one wall of shelves. *Madame Bovary* . . . *Tender Is the Night* . . . *The Red and the Black*. Behind her desk hung a sketch of Charles Dickens, an artist's proof by Jack Coughlin. On the far wall there was a framed map of the Channel Islands National Park, a wilderness preserve that rose some twenty miles off the coast, well south of Chumash County.

So different from Sasha's office, Bard thought. He nodded at the map as he sat down. "Santa Cruz is my favorite of those islands."

From across her desk, Cassie looked at him with interest. "You've been out there?"

"More than once. Autumn's the best season. No fog, no summer crowds, lighter westerlies. Great hiking, great fishing."

"How do you get there?"

"I've got a Sea Ray. Just a twenty-three-footer, but it does the job."

"Where do you anchor?"

"Depends. Cueva Valdez . . . Lady's Harbor . . . Baby's Harbor . . . Potato Bay . . . Coches Prietos."

Cassie nodded her approval. "You do know the islands."

"Were you testing me?"

"Sort of."

"Since I passed, may we go on to the next level?"

"Which is?"

"The Merta-Cooper murders. Jed Jeremiah."

She played with a pencil on her desk. "Everyone's favorite topic right now, at least with me."

"I saw the Coopers coming out."

"Yes, the Coopers. They want justice, they want resolution. As does Angela Stark, of course. Not next month, not next year. Right now."

"When do you go to the grand jury?"

"Any day."

Bard looked up and beyond Cassie, at Charles Dickens's grand head. There was, he thought, such sadness in the writer's eyes. "You're a fan of Dickens?"

She followed his glance, and studied the profile on the wall. "That was a present from someone who thought I was."

"He was mistaken?"

"Sort of. It's the man as much as his writing that moves me. He used to walk the streets of London for hours, late into the night. Always searching."

"Searching for what?"

Cassie shrugged. "Who can say? I know only that at the moment of his death, a single tear welled from his right eye and trickled down his cheek."

Bard said, "I guess we should talk a bit about the Hernandez case."

"What's there to talk about?"

"I tore into you pretty badly back then."

Cassie gave him a sideways look. "Just back then? Seems to me you're still at it."

"We searched for four days, some three hundred of us. I headed the command station. All the while, you knew. It's hard to forget something like that."

"I understand. But you need to understand, too. I was just doing my job. I couldn't violate client confidentiality. I had to be a fierce advocate for my client. I had to protect his interests."

"Jesus, what a job."

"That's why I quit it, Doug. That's why I joined the DA's office. Defending killers is necessary and honorable, but I found I no longer had the stomach for it. Truth is, defending Cal Hernandez changed my opposition to the death penalty. After weighing the moral issues against the brutal facts, I decided that Cal Hernandez quite simply had forfeited his right to life."

"Now that's not hard to understand."

Cassie smiled faintly. "You should be delighted, Doug. I've come full circle. I'm like you now. I want to throw all the lousy jerks in jail. Or strap them to a chair."

It surprised Bard to realize that he didn't feel delighted. He shifted in his seat. They sat in silence for a moment. He said, "If you indict Jed Jeremiah, I think you may be indicting an innocent man."

Cassie appeared to be enjoying a private joke. "I'm told that all the time. Usually it's coming from a defense attorney, though. Not my own detective. Not the detective who cracked the case."

"I cracked the case because your boss wanted it cracked."

"Do you always obey Angela Stark?"

"Do you?"

Cassie hesitated, then spoke softly. "You know I don't. You saw me side with you the other day."

Bard found he couldn't keep his eyes off her. She created mystery through her reserve. He wondered what chaos he might find beneath that demure exterior.

"You had it nailed, Cassie. Eddie Hines is a moron, just as you said. How did you put it? 'We all liked hearing this story because it was what we wanted.' "

Cassie held up a hand. "But please recall what I also said. That we only have Eddie Hines's word, plus circumstantial. That it would be so helpful if we had physical evidence. Well, now we have physical evidence. We have the bootprints. That changes the equation."

Bard was at the edge of his chair. "I found Eddie Hines's pals, Squeaky and Hotwire. They insist they weren't with Eddie. They called Eddie the neighborhood moron."

"That doesn't convince me. Those pals aren't the kind who'd want to be linked in any way to a murder investigation. Bottom line, to repeat—we have the physical evidence now."

"I think you're making a mistake."

"You're not the judge or jury, Doug. You're also not the defense attorney, which is how you're sounding."

"You're right." Bard came around to her side of the desk. He stood inches from her. "I'm just a cop. A street detective. That's what everyone keeps reminding me."

She looked up at him. "You made this a murder, Doug. You brought us an eyewitness. You brought us a suspect. You can't stop things now."

"I'm still investigating."

She rose. They stood face to face. She was taller than he'd thought. With impatience she said, "The train has left the station, Doug."

A tangle of power cords and audio cable snaked across the Pirate's Beach boardwalk. Rows of folding chairs filled the hamlet's main street, closed off to cars this morning by bright yellow sawhorses. A wooden platform rose at one end of the street, furnished with a microphone and a high three-legged stool. As Jimmy O'Brien watched, Bruce Hightower climbed its steps.

A public "town hall" meeting. That's how they'd billed this. A chance for citizens to talk directly to the county commission chairman about the latest proposed development at Pirate's Beach. Apparently, it was a chance much valued: Some two hundred Chumash County residents had turned out.

Jimmy, watching them settle into folding chairs, saw a wide mix. There were the usual no-growth activists, some of them foothill longhairs down from their hemp farms, others pragmatic political organizers bearing clipboards and precinct lists. Yet there were also fourth-generation homeowners, and more than a few sophisticated young patrons of La Graciosa's sushi and cappuccino shops. Jimmy spotted several proprietors of the ten-acre "gentleman rancher" parcels that developers had carved out of a twenty-thousand-acre cattle spread. One he knew grew kiwi and grapes; another raised purebred Arabians. They'd come not to protest, Jimmy figured, but to make sure they had a hand in deciding what would get built.

That the developers hadn't fixed on a particular project yet, but were already waging a campaign for approval, amused Jimmy to no end. Here was a clear sign of the slow-growth forces' mounting influence. Jimmy had explained it all for readers in his "About Chumash" column.

> *In the last few weeks, roughly five hundred acres above Pirate's Beach owned by a consortium of investors have become the center of a battle between those who would develop it and those who want their "sacred spot" forever preserved. The developers, who two decades ago might have pushed a project through with little public input, realize that nowadays it's in their best interests to get residents involved. Because most of the hillside properties are zoned residential, they're not protected by Chumash County's SOAR law, which requires a countywide vote on the development of farmland. So the developers could simply move ahead with the standard process if they chose. Instead, they're holding a series of public meetings to discuss potential projects and find one that residents will embrace. If they come to some conclusion—and many involved concede that's a big "if"—the landowners say they plan to put their development plan to a countywide vote. "To a certain degree, they're acting as if this is under SOAR laws," points out county commission chairman Bruce Hightower. "In Chumash County, they've learned that's the approach the public wants."*

What they'd actually learned, Jimmy knew, was that this was the approach Bruce Hightower wanted. Jimmy marveled at the commissioner's savvy: He was manipulating both the developers and the citizens, while appearing to promote only an admirable exercise in responsible democracy.

Jimmy's eyes fell on a dozen easels that lined the Main Street sidewalk. Each bore an architect's sketch of a possible housing development. Jimmy walked over to them and worked his way down the row. He had to admit, these weren't the most awful plans. No big stucco boxes, no garish monuments to bad taste. Instead, here were various subdued combinations of adobe and tile, many in the style of haciendas, all scattered among wide reaches of open space. Their design certainly showed Hightower's influence: He was forever championing residential complexes buffered by parkland and centered around internal courtyards. Not quite the proper backdrop to Gordo's or Rick's or Tasha's, but what the hell, those honky-tonks were doomed anyway. Maybe it was time for something new. Something that actually drew folks with money. Something that led to more advertisements in the local newspaper.

"I guess we're ready to get started."

Jimmy turned to see Bruce Hightower up at the microphone. Hightower had come to Pirate's Beach today in old khakis and a flannel shirt. He stood with his hands in his pockets, his feet planted in a way that suggested he owned the stage that held him aloft. He surveyed the crowd with approving eyes.

"I hope you've all had a chance to see those drawings over there," Hightower called out. "They ought to give you some idea of what the developers have in mind for Pirate's Beach. We're going to be passing out information kits. They'll give you more details. You'll have plenty of time to study and think on all this. I want to remind you, there is no set plan yet. The developers want our public input. That's why we're having these meetings. What I want to do today is introduce a representative from the developers and show you their various ideas. First, though, I'll answer any questions you might have."

A scattering of hands shot up instantly from amid the crowded rows of folding chairs. Hightower pointed at one of the fourth-generation ranchers, a sturdy middle-aged man with a bald head and rough reddened skin.

"Mr. Hightower, I'm intimately familiar with the beauty of this land. I love it, and it means a great deal to me. I worry so much about what might happen here. How can we be sure no harm will come?"

As he responded, Hightower pointed to the hills above Pirate's Beach. "Why would anyone want to destroy the natural beauty of this sacred spot? I have talked personally to these landowners. They won't want to wreck that extraordinary ridgeline. No, I can't really see where these hills would ever be leveled off or overbuilt. Just look up there. Whatever housing they build would be limited by the landscape itself. Those rugged slopes, those nearly inpenetrable thickets—they are our surest, finest protection."

More hands thrust into the air. The questions rained down on Hightower.

Why do the developers need so many consultants if there are no plans yet?

I worry about the public relations polish of these meetings. Don't these developers mean to sugarcoat it and make it go their way?

Aren't these people just leading us to a predetermined but yet undisclosed conclusion?

Hightower listened with abundant patience. Over and over, he reminded his constituents that these developers could do this their own way if they wanted, but have agreed—"at the request of your county commission"—to hold these meetings and even submit to a countywide vote. This is far more than public relations, he told them. This is a real commitment. We may all go home unsatisfied in the end, but we owe it to ourselves and our county to give this a try.

What's in it for us?

Why not just leave this land alone?

Aren't we better off opposing anything they propose?

Now Hightower methodically offered a lesson in environmental history. "This land has never been well preserved," he explained. "Long ago, these hills were the site of controlled burns by the Chumash Indians. Since the arrival of the Spanish, they've been a place to graze cattle and pump oil. The oilmen and cattle's legacy is everywhere now. Look up there at the eroded streambanks. Look at the ruined wildlife habitats, the trampled meadows, the barren rangeland."

Heads turned as Hightower again pointed to the hills. "We can make these big-city developers pay," he declared. "We can make them pay for an expensive, much-needed environmental cleanup. That's what's in it for us. That's why building wisely is better than doing nothing."

In the silence that followed, a middle-aged woman with a blue scarf rose from the front row. Jimmy recognized her as the owner of a small foothill farm full of sheep and apple trees. "Mr. Hightower," she said, "here's what I'd like to know. Who actually is developing Pirate's Beach? Who owns all this land here?"

Hightower nodded his approval. "Good question, very important question. The fact is, a whole bunch of investors own this land now. On their behalf, a venture capitalist firm has been acquiring parcels for several years from our local families. RC Cummings, Inc., up in San Francisco. They've formed a corporation just for this project. Pirate's Beach Investments. A representative from RC Cummings, Albert Donner, is with us today. I'll be bringing him on shortly. Their role is explained in the information packet we'll be distributing. As you'll see—"

"And your role?" the middle-aged lady called out. "Your role, Mr. Hightower?"

He nodded again. "Another good question. The fact is, I'm here today because I care about how Chumash County grows. And I'm here because I'm your elected representative. In the end, my job is to represent the will of the people. One of the reasons why we're here today is to measure that will—"

"But haven't you already decided that you support this project, Mr. Hightower?"

Hightower's smile seemed effortless. "What project? Remember, there is no project to support yet. Please understand, I'm just trying to get us to recognize and weigh all the issues. What I'm trying to be is a facilitator, a central switchboard. Investors in Chumash County's future need someone to talk to. So do our citizens. That's why—"

"What if we refuse to play along? What if we refuse to come to these town meetings?"

An ever so faint flicker of impatience began to show in Hightower's eyes. He glanced over to the side of the stage, then turned back to his questioner. "That would be a mistake," he said. "The time to strike is now. We've gotten all the landowners to work through RC Cummings, and to agree to this process. That's never happened before. If this falls apart, if this current approach fails, we may end up with piecemeal, unsupervised development. That would be a tragedy in my opinion."

Others in the crowd were waving eager hands now. Hightower lifted his eyes beyond the front row and began pointing. On came quite different questions.

When will this happen?

If we could offer executive housing up here, couldn't we entice all sorts of businesses to relocate?

I'm not sure about Abercrombie and Fitch, but how about an Old Navy down on the main drag?

Jimmy, looking closely at the front rows, attempted to locate the middle-aged lady with the blue scarf, but no longer could. She'd disappeared, swallowed up in a surge of bodies near the platform. Jimmy now realized that half the county's power structure was present. All the other commissioners—Bud Conklin, Ward Delwood, Horace Wright, Delbert Hardy—had showed up, as had all the important ranchers, merchants, pastors, and arts patrons. Even Henry Aston, the elusive Peabody in-law, had made an appearance. As Jimmy watched, the whole gang climbed to the platform. Hightower passed the microphone to Aston, who never spoke publicly. Yet here he was. "We are so pleased with this chance to help shape a vision of our future . . ."

Jimmy turned away. He couldn't stop the clock, didn't really want to, but he'd heard enough. Better get a brew at the Foghorn while it's still standing, he reasoned. Past Gordo's and Tasha's, heading toward the pub, he stopped in front of the newly opened Country Goose. For years it had been a Fosters Freeze. Jimmy peered through the windows, straining to see just what it was this shop sold.

"I didn't think you were a Country Goose type of guy, Jimmy O'Brien."

The voice came from over his shoulder. Sasha Bard was standing behind him. They weren't friends, but they went way back together, to Doug's early months with her. That provided a bond closer than friendship. "I don't have a clue what this place sells," he said. "I was just investigating."

"How come, Jimmy?" There was a playful challenge in her voice. "Who are you shopping for?"

"I'm here for the town meeting, actually."

"Of course."

"And you?"

"The same."

"But I'm covering this for the paper."

"And I'm just an interested citizen."

Jimmy hesitated. He never knew exactly what to say to Sasha. He'd seen her rise and speak firmly before the city council, the planning commission, the coastal board. He'd heard her dissect those opposing what she wanted, which was usually a cable franchise or a new apartment building on the fringe of Chumash County. Progress or die, she liked to say—which will it be? In those public moments, when it was needed, she held nothing back. Yet she wasn't always like that. More often she just studied the scene, dragging on a cigarette. Whenever Jimmy found himself in close quarters with her, she clammed up entirely.

"I suppose you're in favor of this project here," he said. "Lots of investment potential."

Before answering, Sasha scanned the crowd and all of Pirate's Beach. "You'd be far wiser to invest in Chumash County land than the stock market," she said. "Even the blue chips lose twenty percent overnight when someone sneezes in the executive suite. But this"—Sasha waved her arm all about—"this is only going to grow. You've got finite land, an expanding population, rising demand. It's a no-brainer."

Jimmy said, "If only I had money to invest."

"The plight of the journalist. You should have been a lawyer."

There didn't seem to be anything more to say. Jimmy started to back away. She stopped him with a hand on his arm. "What do you hear about Doug?"

Jimmy didn't understand. "About Doug?"

"The Merta case, Jimmy. Ollie Merta and Marilee Cooper's deaths."

"Ah, the murders . . . He's finished investigating, far as I can tell. They have their man. They're going to the grand jury."

"I see."

"Why do you ask?"

Sasha was peering into the window of Country Goose. "No big reason. It's just that Marilee was friends with our daughter Molly. And Ollie Merta taught music to Molly."

Jimmy recalled something now. A dustup a while back at the elementary school, some parents disturbed that this odd Merta fellow was mingling with their kids. A "confirmed bachelor" was how one mother described him; another, in the parking lot, was heard to mutter about "that dirty old man." Hadn't Sasha gone to bat for Ollie? Hadn't she torn into those nervous, ignorant parents at a PTA meeting one night? Jimmy recalled a speech of hers dotted with multiple references to stuffed shirts and narrow minds.

He asked, "Weren't you friends with Ollie, too?"

"Molly was friends with him," she said. "I just knew him."

With trepidation, Doug Bard drove the winding, climbing single-lane road that snaked through wooded hills to Jed Jeremiah's ranch. He'd known for days now that he'd have to come for Jeremiah. The DA wanted Jed in jail while the grand jury probed, just to make sure he didn't run. Howie Dixon had found the means—that citation for driving with an open beer can and a loaded pistol. Doug had balked at first, asking that they send someone else to get him. No, Dixon had replied; he's your man to pick up.

True enough. Bard couldn't argue. He couldn't ask another deputy to slap the cuffs on Jed. He didn't want to, in truth. He had to talk to Jeremiah. Even though he had little notion what to say.

Bard's tires once more crunched on pebbles and kicked up dust as he pulled into Jeremiah's front yard. Jed's cabin seemed even more ramshackle than usual. A pane of window glass had cracked and gone unrepaired. Chickens ran amuck looking hungry. Tools lay strewn about in the high grass. Bard climbed from his car just as Jeremiah emerged from the cabin.

They stood in silence for a spell, the yard between them. Then Bard stepped toward the cabin. Jeremiah held his ground.

"I'm not talking to you anymore," the mountain man said. "Talked too much as it is."

"That's okay. I didn't come to ask you questions."

"What then?"

"Your boots matched the print on Ollie Merta's door. They've got a case against you. They mean to take it to a grand jury real soon."

Jeremiah tugged at his beard as he slowly sank onto his porch step. "I'm not going back out into the world. They will just have to leave me alone."

"They won't." Bard paused. His hand slipped to his side, the pocket of his leather jacket. This one day he was packing, but his Glock 9mm was only a prop; he'd left the bullets in the car. "Jed, I've come for you. You're under arrest. I have to take you down to the county jail."

Jeremiah stared blankly at him. "I'm not going."

Bard kept his hand at his side. "Not for the murders right now," he continued, as if Jed hadn't spoken. "I'm picking you up on that old charge. The beer and the pistol. Just a way to hold you until the grand jury acts."

"You think I'd run?"

"I would if I were you."

"Is that an invitation? Should I get up right now and just start moving?"

"No. I'd have to shoot you."

Jeremiah's eyes traveled to Doug's hand, still resting on his jacket pocket. "You'd do that?"

"Yes."

"You son of a bitch."

"I've been called worse."

"I don't think you have it in you. How many men have you shot?"

How to answer that? He'd never pulled a trigger in Chumash County since becoming a cop. With the Marines in Vietnam, he couldn't say. They'd worked in the dark most of the time.

"I don't rightly know."

Jeremiah didn't appear to hear. He'd moved on. "What happens now?"

"I need to search you, Jed. Then I need to cuff you. After that, we'll drive down to the county jail."

"If I don't cooperate?"

"That would just make things worse for you."

"How could things be any worse?" Jeremiah kicked at the ground. "I don't understand why a man can't defend his own turf. I don't understand what's happening."

"I'm sorry, Jed. That's part of what I came up here to say. Fact is, I'm not sure what's happening, either."

Jeremiah looked at him. "We were so happy for a while."

"We . . . ?"

"Me and my Suzanne. My wife."

"Oh."

"First we thought it was just a bad cold. Then the flu. Then, coming around three one morning, she just shot up in bed, crying out, grabbing at her chest. Hurts mighty bad, she kept saying. It was so black outside that night, no moon, not a star. So I waited. Pneumonia they said, when I finally got her to the clinic. You came too late, they said." Jeremiah spat. "She died that afternoon."

"Jed—"

Jeremiah waved him off. "What the hell. Let them come take me. Let them put me in jail."

"Only if you're guilty."

Jeremiah's thick gnarled hand clutched Doug's arm. "That I am."

Doug examined the fingers wrapped around his elbow. After a moment, he reached over, grasped Jed's wrist, and snapped on the handcuffs.

EIGHT

At the sound of the 10:20 recess bell, Molly Bard raced from her classroom. She made it to the foursquare court just ahead of two boys. "Girl power today," she squealed. Her buddies Kate and Rebecca and Torie arrived a moment later, carrying the ball. The boys sauntered off, saying they didn't want to play a girl's game anyway. Molly and her pals hooted, then began to sock the ball back and forth.

From a corner of the La Graciosa Elementary School playground, Doug Bard watched. An oasis, that's how he thought of this place. He wished that Molly could live here forever. If he had his way, she'd never leave the shelter of the ancient oaks that formed a canopy over the school's campus.

If he had his way. Angela Stark was taking her case against Jeremiah to the grand jury in three days. That's all the time he had left to change her mind. He had two notions: figure out why someone wanted Ollie Merta dead, and figure out why Jeremiah's boots matched the print on Ollie's door.

First, Ollie. He'd heard that a guidance counselor here at Molly's school, Sally Dyle, had befriended Merta during his days teaching music. Dyle might have particular insights.

Bard started across the playground toward the central office. His course took him within Molly's line of vision. Twice, three times she socked the ball. Finally she saw him. She raised a tentative hand in greeting. But when he started in her direction, she gave him a look. He called out anyway. "Hey, Molly girl."

She took four steps toward him, close enough for him to hear her lowered voice. "Daddy, don't embarrass me."

"Saying hello does that?"

She looked appalled. "Daddy, you don't get life sometimes."

He had to agree. He stepped back, saying no more but still watching her. A boy strolled over, his shirttail out, hair hanging in his eyes. His head reached to her shoulders, though they were in the same grade. "What an ugly painting you did for art class," he taunted. Over her shoulder, walking away, Molly said, "It's a portrait of your face."

These poor boys, Bard thought. What they're in for.

"May I help you?"

Bard looked around at the fourth-grade teacher, serving this hour as playground monitor. "I'm Molly Bard's dad," he said. "I'm here to see the guidance counselor."

He and Sally Dyle could barely fit together in her cramped cubicle. He sat with his knees up against the edge of her desk. A half cup of cold coffee rested at her elbow beside an ashtray full of cigarette stubs. Dyle was a plump, brisk, forthright woman in her late fifties who had no marriage rings on her finger or family photos on her desk.

"What can I do for you, Detective Bard?"

Tell me about Molly, he thought. Tell me how she is, who she is. Out loud he said, "I understand you knew Ollie Merta fairly well."

Sally snapped a pack of cigarettes on the back of her hand, then withdrew one and lit up. "These aren't allowed in here, but I think all of us should regularly break one rule or another. Hope you don't mind. I'll hold this over here."

"That's fine."

"Ollie Merta . . . You're investigating his death?"

"Yes."

She appeared to appreciate being sought out as someone with inside information. "Poor Ollie. I didn't know him well at all, but I guess I did know him better than most. He liked to talk to me. Nothing profound, he was just a lonely man."

Bard tried to imagine the connection. Both brooked no cant, he figured. Both broke certain rules. And both lived in empty houses. "Were you aware of any threats, anything that disturbed him?"

"Nothing."

"What can you tell me about Ollie Merta? His past, what he did here, people he knew."

Sally held her cigarette gingerly, and inhaled deeply. "You mean people who might want to kill him?"

"Yes."

"I can't imagine anyone would. Ollie was a bit eccentric, but not in a cranky way. He had no close relations or friends that I know of."

"What were his interests? What drew him in?"

"He loved to be with the kids. Maybe because he had none of his own. He was also full of curiosity. He'd have sat in on some classes if we'd let him."

"What else?"

"Let's see, he was a whiz with computers. He built them himself, wiring together components he bought from catalogs. Then he donated them to local schools. We got three from him. He'd come by to hook them up and teach us how to use them. That's how he got to be the music teacher. One day he just sat down and started playing at the school piano. When we saw how he got the kids to sing along to stuff like 'The Naughty Little Flea,' we knew we had our man."

Sally beamed with the memory. "He tried to act reluctant, but oh was he pleased when we asked. 'Okay, okay,' he said. 'I guess I'll be the pied piper of La Graciosa Elementary.' "

"You say he was a whiz with computers?"

"Sure was."

"Any idea where that came from?"

"None. He never said."

"Or where he came from, what he did before he moved to La Graciosa?"

Dyle stubbed out her cigarette. "He told me he was a U.S.

Customs border guard up in Canada. You know, the guy who asks tourists whether they're bringing any fruit or alcohol back into the country. Did that for thirty years. Most of the time, he worked the British Columbia border near Vancouver. Off days, he loved riding the Washington State ferries through Puget Sound. That was his life."

"He said nothing more about his work?"

"What more was there to say? Up there near Vancouver, way he told it, you don't see many serious smugglers. You see lots of families. You see bags of illegal peaches."

"How about what he did here in La Graciosa?"

"I never got a clear answer. 'This and that,' he'd say. Fair enough, but he seemed to have a comfortable means of support. Those computers he gave away were only part of it. You could just tell, he wasn't overly worried about money."

"Did he have a job?"

"It seemed so to me. But whatever it was, he didn't go to an office. He worked at home, in solitude. Something to do with all his high-powered computers, that's what I always figured. Whenever I came by his home, he'd have at least two of them running in his study."

Bard looked up from the notes he'd been taking. He recalled only one charred hulk in Merta's study. "At least two computers?"

"That's right."

"You're sure?"

"Sometimes there were three."

Bard studied his notes. *Whenever I came by.*

"Ms. Dyle, how often did you visit Merta at home?"

Sally reached for another cigarette. She began fussing with her lighter. Twice, three times she spun the wheel. She couldn't get it to work. "Just on occasion," she said. "Usually to drop something off, pick something up. I live out that way."

Bard moved to the edge of his chair. "Ms. Dyle, when were you last there?"

A pile of papers drew Sally's attention. She reordered the

pages. Reaching for a paper clip, she knocked a pen off her desk. "This isn't important. I—"

"Ms. Dyle, at this stage, we don't know what's important or not. We just need to explore."

She clutched at the collar of her sweater. "I can't recall exactly."

"Please, Ms. Dyle. Tell me what you know."

"I know nothing."

"Whoever killed Ollie may still be out there."

Sally blanched at that. With unsteady hands, she finally got another cigarette lit and inhaled deeply. The nicotine didn't seem to improve her nerves.

"All these questions about Ollie Merta," she said. "But a little girl died, too. I knew Marilee Cooper better than Ollie. Quite well, in fact. No sweeter girl existed. She wanted to be a veterinarian."

"Okay, Ms. Dyle, for Marilee's sake then. When were you last out there?"

"For Marilee's sake . . . ?" She sat still for a while, lost in that notion. When she turned to him, there were tears in her eyes. "Okay . . . for Marilee."

"When, Ms. Dyle? When were you there?"

"That day . . . that last day."

"The day Ollie's house burned down?"

"Yes."

"What time?"

"About seven P.M., I'd say. I didn't visit, I was just driving by, on the way back to my house. The road cuts away from Ollie's place. I'd say I was a good fifty yards off, with a thick stand of oaks obscuring my view. So it wasn't very clear. Hardly clear at all. It was dusk. I could barely see."

"What were you able to see?"

She'd inhaled halfway down the cigarette now. She crushed it into an ashtray. "I saw a figure running toward his house."

"Toward, not from?"

"Yes, I'm certain."

"Could it have been Ollie?"

"No, no. Ollie had a bad hip. Ollie wouldn't have been running like that."

"A big man, then? A big husky man with lots of hair and a tangled red beard?"

"No, I don't think so. He was small, with a brown kind of cape wrapped all around him. He moved like a dancer, really. Or a deer. Just slid along, so fast, yet so effortless. That's what struck me, that's what I noticed most."

Or a deer. Bard wished he hadn't heard that, wished she hadn't said that.

"Ms. Dyle, could it in fact have been a deer?"

"Yes, I believe it could have. That's why I never came forward to tell anyone. The more I dwelt on it, the more I thought it was a deer."

Bard rose, and stuffed his notebook in his back pocket. She wouldn't sway Dixon or Stark and she wouldn't be any good on the witness stand. Still. At the door, he turned back to her. "Ms. Dyle, whoever is charged with these murders will have a defense attorney. Do you mind if I give this lawyer your name?"

In her confusion, she tried to light the wrong end of a cigarette. She dropped it into the ashtray. "Tell me, Detective Bard . . . Just whose side are you on?"

From La Graciosa Elementary School, Bard jogged the three blocks to the central plaza. There he slowed to a fast walk. At the entrance to the *asistencia,* he drew a breath and pushed open the door. He wound through the narrow corridors, past the prosecutors' offices, past the sheriff's, past the coroner's. At a plain unmarked door, he stopped. He tried the doorknob; it turned in his hand. He walked in.

Rick Gordo looked up from where he sat at a table in the middle of a room that served as Chumash County's spartan crime lab. Boxes, bottles, and test tubes filled shelves that lined all four walls. A large black refrigerator stood next to a pair of sinks. An industrial-strength blender rested on a counter. Glass piping snaked from an oval cistern that hung from the ceiling.

"Careful," Gordo muttered. "Don't knock anything over."

Bard stepped gingerly. Gordo was okay, he just liked to act grumpy all the time. With the limited resources they gave him, he had a right to complain. Being chief of the crime lab in Chumash County was not a particularly satisfying job. More than half the time they had to outsource matters to larger, more sophisticated labs. Gordo wore a perpetual frown along with his customary suspenders and green eye-shade. Over a beer at JB's, though, he had no trouble enjoying himself.

"This place always reminds me of my high school chemistry class," Bard said.

"A class which you no doubt failed."

"Pulled a C minus, if I recall."

"A mercy grade, I imagine. Probably a middle-aged female teacher. You batted your sixteen-year-old eyes."

"Something like that."

Gordo waved Bard to a chair. "Let's see. Let me guess why you're here."

"Tell me about the bootprints on Ollie Merta's door, Rick."

"What's there to tell? The big-city experts say they matched the boots you pulled off Jed Jeremiah."

"The big-city experts?"

"Hell, yes. You don't think we'd leave a matter like this to our own little county crime lab?"

"Not a surprise, but I didn't know."

"No, not a surprise at all."

"Walk me down the trail."

Gordo turned to the window that gave onto the *asistencia* courtyard. "There's no story here, Bard. They sent the prints to the experts, the experts said bingo. Done and done."

Doug understood. Gordo was a grump, but not a rene-gade. He hadn't survived twenty-five years in his department by bucking the brass. And he needed to survive now. His wife was sick; she'd been hospitalized three times this year. The diagnosis was uncertain, but not the need for medical insurance.

"Okay," Bard said, "no trail to walk. But what happened here inside this crime lab?"

Gordo kept his eyes on the window. "Nothing. It went straight to outsourcing."

"I don't think so, Gordo."

"Who the fuck cares what you think?"

"Come on, Gordo. Off the record."

"Man, that's a good one. Off the record. What the hell does that mean?"

"It means I protect you. I learn this again from a second source. I hear this again from someone else."

Gordo chewed on that, then turned away from the window. "I don't for a skinny second believe you can do that, but give it a try, okay?"

"A deal."

Gordo pulled his chair close to Bard's. "You're right, it started here. Donny Garber, our ID guy, looked at the prints and boots first. Donny Garber says the boots don't appear to match the marks on the door. That's his judgment."

"Where's his report?"

"Don't be naive, Bard. I told him to write up his conclusions. Didn't happen, though."

"What did happen?"

"When Sheriff Dixon hears about our findings, he calls Garber to his office. They have a chat. Garber decides not to write a report. Garber decides he no longer is so sure of his judgment."

"Then they outsource it?"

"Yes."

"Where?"

Gordo's amusement grew. Thumbs hooked his suspenders. He leaned back in his chair. "The question is, where first."

"We went to more than one lab?"

"It's no big deal. We've done this plenty of times before."

"Tell me about this time."

"First we send the boots and prints to the state crime lab, where some forensic scientist hotshot says Jeremiah's boots, quote, 'could have at best' made the impression on

the door, but that another shoe, quote, 'very well could
have made the questioned print.' Not good enough. So next
we send it to a lab up in Washington that's supposed to
have this even hotter hotshot. He's willing to say Jed's boot
'probably' made the print. Still not good enough. So finally
we find this gal who calls herself a forensic foot and shoe
specialist."

"A what?"

"Yeah, that's what I asked. Name is Roberta Kabal. A professor somewhere, some kind of anthropologist. She's achieved
the dream of every entrepreneur—no competition. She's the
only person in the world who can say for sure who made a
footprint. Claims every human foot in the world is different,
each makes unique impressions inside a shoe, which transfers into wear patterns on the outside of shoes that are just
like fingerprints."

Bard whistled. "Prosecutors must love her."

"And pay her. She charges five hundred dollars an hour,
five thousand a day to testify. Since 1980 she's testified
twenty-five times, and has never reached a conclusion that
didn't support the case of whoever hired her."

"The queen of quackery."

"Not bad, Bard. I'll have to use that line."

"Her report on Jeremiah?"

"She advised that Jed's boots unquestionably made the
print on Merta's door."

"That's our basis for saying the boots match the prints?"

The humor drained from Gordo's face. He rose, and paced
across the room. "No, it's not. Both the other two outside experts eventually revised their opinions. Both now say the
print and boot 'most probably' match."

"And our very own Donny Garber?"

"Donny sees a match now, too. Donny doesn't remember
ever thinking otherwise."

Bard marched past the prosecutors' secretary before she
could speak. He flung open Cassie Teal's door. She looked up
from her desk without surprise. "Come on in, Doug."

"I'm already in."

"Farther in."

"Okay, I'm farther in."

"So sit down, Doug."

Bard dropped into the chair in front of her desk. "Let's talk about Jeremiah's bootprint experts."

"What's there to talk about?"

Bard hesitated. He didn't like the idea of lying to Cassie, but he needed to protect Gordo. He chose his words carefully. "I have a source at the state crime lab. A pal who likes to tell me what's what."

She pushed papers around on her desk. "Do you, now?"

"Yeah, I do. What I hear is, our own lab guy says it's not the boot. We don't like that answer, so there's no paper written. We go to a second guy, up there at the state lab. He says maybe. We go to a third. He says probably. We find a fourth, a real fruitcake. She says, Yes, sir. She also says, That'll be ten grand. We write a report only on Ms. Yes—"

"And your point?"

Bard studied her. The resolve in her words didn't match what he sensed. "My point is, someone's trying to frame Jed Jeremiah."

"Come on, Doug."

"Cassie, we just shopped around until we found the right expert."

"Don't be naive. You know that's how it usually works. Matching prints is an art, not a hard science. Experts will differ."

"Okay, I'm being naive. But where do you stand on this, Cassie? Are you still comfortable with your physical evidence?"

Again, she appeared amused by a private joke. "As a prosecutor, I am. If I were a defense attorney, I'd be screaming bloody murder."

Her candor startled Bard. So did the thought that now popped into his head. "Maybe you ought to be a defense attorney again."

Cassie barely moved her lips. "I've played that role already, much to your distaste."

Bard said, "I think I may have found another eyewitness."

"Do tell."

"Sally Dyle, guidance counselor at the elementary school. Also Merta's buddy. She told me she was driving by that day, saw someone running to the house who didn't look the least like Jeremiah."

"Have you reported this to Howie or Angela?"

"They wouldn't be interested. Dyle isn't really sure what she saw. It was dusk; she was looking through a forest from fifty yards away. She thinks maybe it was a deer."

Cassie rolled a pencil across her desk. "I see."

"She's not likely to do well on a witness stand."

"No, she's not."

They sat in silence for a moment. Bard asked, "Doesn't Jeremiah need a lawyer now? Is the court going to appoint him one?"

The pencil rolled off Cassie's desk, unnoticed. "The court already has. They gave him Louis Brody."

"Ah yes. Just as I figured."

Cassie's former office-mate had replaced her as chief public defender when she switched to the DA's office. Many in Chumash County had hailed Brody's appointment, knowing him to be a wise and tenacious lawyer. Yet those closest to him had been less certain he was the right man for the job. Time, and a steady stream of painful cases, had rubbed him raw. You could see it in his eyes, standing beside clients he knew were guilty. Clients who sold crack to schoolchildren, clients who'd knifed girlfriends, clients who'd robbed and raped and murdered. Often enough, Brody managed to get their sentences knocked down. Occasionally, he won a sullen miscreant his freedom. Once, a freed client waited only two weeks before jamming a knife into another store clerk's belly.

The Hernandez case had provided a sort of capstone. Brody had supported Cassie during those tortured days, and he'd defended her publicly when it was over. But he'd never been able to spit out the foul taste. He'd never been able to pretend they were engaged in something the least bit righteous.

Cassie's course, switching to the DA's office, hadn't appealed to him any more than protecting a girl's killer. He despised the notion of dedicating himself to accusation and punishment. To rise in court and incite a jury's ugly passions, to beg them to seek vengeance—no, that went against all his reflexes. He lacked the incandescent zeal required of a prosecutor.

That's what he'd told Cassie as she packed up her files and prepared to transfer to Angela Stark's quarters. "I'd go with you if only I could believe," he said. "It's hard to march in the jackboots of authority unless you're sure you're on the side of the angels."

"You know perfectly well I'm not sure," Cassie replied. "But we all have to play roles in this game. The only question is, which one do we choose?"

"Neither . . . none of the above."

Brody took the public defender's job mainly because no one else of any skill or experience wanted it. "These clients need my help," he told the *News-Times* on the occasion of his appointment. "But I'm not going to go around promising them I'll get them off. That just isn't always possible, or even desirable."

Bard recalled those words well. He'd applauded at the time, even while wondering how Brody's clients would feel. "Too bad Jeremiah can't afford one of those expensive big-city defense attorneys," he said now. "Brody is something else."

"Oh, I don't know." Cassie thumbed through a pile of documents on her desk. "Louis has a singular attitude to the law, but he's smart and he cares. I think he cares too much, in fact. That's his biggest problem."

Bard couldn't help but notice her fond tone. He tried to recall what Brody looked like. The scholarly type, wasn't he?

Slow-talking, wire-rim eyeglasses, cardigan sweaters. "You know him well, Cassie?"

She ignored the insinuation. "Well enough to understand his philosophy."

"Which is?"

"Louis likes to say 'I can be passionate about my clients' cases, but I will not carry their anger.' He talks about 'acceptance of responsibility' and 'civility to adversaries.' That sounds reasonable to me."

"But is it effective?"

"It can be. It has been."

Bard rose. "Come with me, Cassie. I'm going to see Dixon and Stark."

"What for?"

"To tell them about Sally Dyle. One last effort to raise some doubts."

"You have doubts. I don't."

"I don't believe you."

"I'm not your ally here, Doug. I'm Angela's deputy."

"So come along in that capacity."

Cassie slowly rose. "Okay, Douglas Bard . . . in that capacity."

Angela Stark studied her watch. Sheriff Dixon shuffled papers. Cassie Teal scribbled notes. A humid, oppressive heat filled the *asistencia*'s conference room. Bard wondered whether they'd ever replace the ancient rattling steam radiators. If they were going to modernize and upscale all of La Graciosa, why not include this building? Why not tear down the two-hundred-year-old *asistencia* and build themselves a plain stucco box with central air and heating? Why not—

"It's no use, Doug." Stark began gathering her files. "We've gone over your objections three times now, and you haven't swayed anybody in here. It's past time that we form a solid front."

Bard's open palm slammed the table where they all sat. He reached for a yellow legal pad. He began writing. *Bootprint.*

He yanked the sheet from the pad, crumpled it, tossed it over his shoulder. "Bullshit," he snapped, "all bullshit." He wrote again. *Eddie Hines.* Yank, crumple, toss. "More bullshit." *Hotwire and Squeaky.* Yank, crumple, toss. "Still more bullshit."

Dixon stopped him with a hand on his wrist. "That's enough, Doug. We get the point."

"The point? The point? How's this for a point: Eddie Hines doesn't have a car. And Sally Dyle saw something at Merta's house."

"You're repeating yourself," Stark pointed out, "and wasting office supplies."

"What Dyle saw sounds to me like a deer," Dixon said.

Bard asked, "You think our fruitcake bootprint expert will play any better on the stand than Sally Dyle?"

"Experts," Angela corrected. "We have four of them."

"After a little shopping around," Bard said.

Angela turned on him. "Look, Doug. You know perfectly well that these lab guys' conclusions can vary. You also know that it's therefore reasonable to get multiple opinions. I've endured enough from you. Now it's got to end. Now it's time for us to move."

"Now?" Bard asked.

"Tomorrow we take this to the grand jury."

Bard looked at Cassie. "We?"

Cassie, ignoring him, spoke to the DA. "It would be nice to give the jurors clear proof of a motive, Angela. Instead of mere speculation."

Angela bit off her words. "Oh, but we will, Cassie."

Bard watched Stark. Just like that other day, she was holding a sheet of paper in the air. "From the county legal archives," she was saying, "found only this morning. It turns out Jed Jeremiah had a dustup with Ollie Merta two years ago. It had to do with Merta grazing sheep on Jeremiah's land. Jeremiah made verbal threats and pointed a gun at Merta. Then he shoved him to the ground. Ollie had the good sense to call the sheriff's department, although he didn't press charges. Doug, you wouldn't know about this because it wasn't a felony. One of the junior deputies went out and took a report. Here it is."

Stark placed the sheet of paper on the table before Cassie Teal. "Does this look like motive to you?"

Cassie locked her eyes on the document. She read to the bottom of the page. "Yes, Angela. This looks like motive."

NINE

Sitting on stools at JB's Red Rooster Tavern, Jimmy O'Brien and Doug Bard watched the television that hung in a corner behind the long mahogany and maple bar. On the local evening news, Angela Stark stood before a microphone, flanked by Marilee Cooper's parents. "I promised you justice would be done in response to these horrible killings," she declared, "and now I'm here to tell you, justice most certainly is being done."

Jimmy reached for his second Black Bush. Doug nursed a Graciosa Brew. Jed Jeremiah's indictment, handed up by a grand jury at midday, was big news throughout the county.

There's no room in this county for brutal killers. There's no room for people like Jed Jeremiah. Justice must be done . . .

"I tell you this," Jimmy said. "Stark has most of my front page tomorrow."

"Why not ignore her? Don't report the indictment. Don't report Angela's press conference."

"That's an idea."

If only it still were, Bard thought. A century ago, before radio and TV and the Internet, a Chumash County editor could make unwelcome events disappear simply by omitting them from the newspaper. Plenty of Jimmy's predecessors had done just that.

"Seriously, Jimmy, how did you handle this?"

"What do you mean, Doug? I told the story, that's how I handled it. I did stick in a sidebar profile of Jed Jeremiah. But along with Jed's grizzlies and honky-tonk piano, I had to mention his limited tolerance for people who get on his land or in his face."

"You coming around to thinking Jed's guilty?"

Jimmy turned on him. "Now look, Doug. Let's get things straight. I have opinions, but I'm not an advocate. What makes my pitiful role the least worthwhile is that I play above the fray. God knows, someone has to, what with everyone else screaming for their side. I still have doubts about this case, but I don't have divine insight. I don't even have a copy of the blasted investigative file. Hell if I know what really happened at Merta's house."

Bard drew a wet line along the bar. "I see."

"It's called integrity, Doug. Not mine, which we know is puny and matters little, but the newspaper's. Which, by God, does matter."

"Okay, Jimmy. I said I see."

"You see? What do you see?" Jimmy was sputtering. "Tell me this, Doug. Do you know what happened at Merta's house?"

Bard weighed that question. He did have the investigative file. Yet he had to admit that he didn't really know, either. Who's the more reliable eyewitness, Eddie Hines or Sally Dyle? Which bootprint expert had it right? What of Jeremiah's temper? How about the way he shot that Basque shepherd? How about the way he threatened Ollie Merta?

The public, skimming headlines and sound bites, assumed that the legal system sliced through such confusion, rendering a verdict with clarity and certainty. It didn't work that way, of course. You could assemble just about any narrative you wanted to explain the available facts. Faced with enigmas, lawyers constructed stories full of certainty.

Detectives did the same. So did journalists. Jimmy thought their jobs were so different, but Bard was struck by how much he had in common with him. With Cassie, too, and even Angela. They all were required to reconstruct experience, usually through many voices, treating witnesses and perpetrators like characters in a tale. They were all, each and every one of them, storytellers.

"I can only surmise," Bard said.

He looked back up at the TV screen. The image had shifted from Stark to Jed Jeremiah's newly appointed attorney, Louis Brody. Bard studied him. He reminded Doug of an English professor he had at Chumash State. He spoke quietly, without a defense attorney's customary flamboyance. *I will be talking to my client. We will progress through the system. We will decide what's appropriate* . . .

The seed of a thought had been tugging at Bard for days now. Time to give it voice. "Louis Brody may be a terrific attorney for all I know," he told Jimmy, "but I still think Jeremiah is going to need additional help."

"Yes, well, sure, let's go hire—" Jimmy stopped. He glanced around the bar as if searching for someone. "God, I wish my old buddy Greg Monarch was still practicing law."

"He's not, though. He left Chumash for some island, didn't he?"

"Yes, he'd had enough."

"So we've got to try something else."

"You've got an idea?"

"Possibly."

"Do tell."

"Whoever wants to help Jeremiah now has to do so outside the judicial system."

"Where outside?"

"From a place where stories can be told that will grab the public's attention. The public's, and the sheriff's, and the DA's."

Jimmy almost bounced off his stool. "Bard, my man, you're going to open your purse? You're going to leak to me? You're going to share the investigative file?"

No. No, he wasn't. Hearing it put so baldly, Doug pulled back. The low mutter of Oscar Bard's words once more filled his ears. *You never break ranks. The department is your family. Cops are your brothers.* They were not words for a son to ignore, for only in those lessons, and during shooting sessions in the woods, had Doug ever fully claimed his father's attention. Night after night in their living room, he'd vainly sought more. Night after night, he'd searched Oscar's face for signals that he was whole, that he pleased Oscar, that he had a place in the world.

"That's not what I meant," Bard told Jimmy. "I'm not handing over police files. You have to get it some other way."

Jimmy stared wide-eyed at him. "What other way? There is no other way. It's you or nothing. It's you or Jed goes down."

"No." Bard glanced around. JB's was about a third full. He sensed attention fixed on them, even though everyone was looking at their beer or their companions.

"Come on, Doug, I can't spin or slant, but I sure can report facts. Especially stuff from an official record. Bring them on, buddy."

"I can't, Jimmy."

"Jesus. Then why'd you raise this?"

Why had he? That was easy. Because something had to be done.

You never break ranks. Bard drained his beer glass, waved for a refill. Oscar's voice wouldn't stop. "Sorry, Jimmy. I was just thinking out loud."

"Damn, Doug, you've got to do more than think."

Bard worked to imagine that. "Seize the day, huh? Shape fate, choose to act?"

Jimmy slapped the bar. "Precisely."

Bard held up his glass, squinted, tried to see through the murky amber fluid to the other side. He couldn't, of course. It wasn't that easy.

"Okay, Jimmy. Why the hell not?"

For a moment, concern dimmed Jimmy's delight. "You understand it won't be too much of a mystery who's feeding me?"

Bard swirled the beer until tiny waves slapped the glass. There would be consequences, of course. Just as there'd been consequences when he, full of hubris, first set out to crack this case.

He said, "I understand."

Jimmy slapped him on the back so hard he almost fell off his stool. "I could get used to this."

*   *   *

From ten miles offshore, the lights of La Graciosa flickered like faint distant stars. Beyond the lights rose the magnificent Santa Lucia Range, a looming black outline against an indigo sky. Winds that day had brushed the natural world to a startling clarity. Standing on the deck of a forty-five-foot yacht, Angela Stark studied the heavens until she spotted Venus. It was faint but visible with the naked eye this night. She'd been mesmerized by Venus ever since seeing it through Bruce's telescope.

Venus was so hot, nine hundred degrees on the surface, and so bright, the brightest object in the sky besides the sun and moon. Its own sky glowed bright orange all day long. Active volcanoes rumbled everywhere. How perfect, Angela thought, for a planet named after the Roman goddess of love. What would it be like to journey there? They said walking on Venus would feel like walking underwater.

"What are you thinking about?"

Angela turned to see Bruce Hightower standing behind her. From within the yacht's salon came the sound of Dinah Washington singing on a CD, and ice clinking in cocktail glasses. Bruce and two other county commissioners were the guests tonight of RC Cummings, the San Francisco venture capitalist firm. The other commissioners had brought their wives; Bruce had brought Angela. She slipped her hand around his arm.

"I was thinking of space travel," she said.

Hightower followed her eye, and saw where she'd been looking in the sky. "You'd better think twice about your destination. Standing on Venus would be nasty. Like standing in an enormous oven filled with choking fumes, but worse. Searing temperatures, crushing pressures, suffocating atmosphere, no water. You'd be fried and crushed to death in an instant. No one's even dreaming of sending astronauts there. You won't ever get to Venus unless you're an automated probe."

"Too bad."

"It is. You know, Venus and Earth formed at about the same

time, from similar materials. We once had similar atmospheres. Now Venus is dry and lifeless and we're teeming. I wonder what happened."

"Is that the kind of thing you wonder about?"

"Sometimes."

"You're so different from the others." She nodded toward the yacht's windows. "The only thing they want to talk about tonight is this boat."

"It's a Carver 450 Voyager. In case they give you a quiz, you ought to know that."

"Got it. A Carver 450 Voyager. But shouldn't I know something about the two staterooms with cedar-lined hanging lockers, the two heads with separate electric-pump showers, the engine-room camera surveillance, the UltraLeather upholstery, the hand-crafted cherry wood trim, the six-speaker Bose surround-sound, the cockpit icemaker, the full service wet bar, the—"

"Okay," he interrupted with an appreciative smile. "You have been paying attention. They'll be so pleased."

They stood together, silent now. They'd gotten good at that, sharing solitude. Sometimes they bought wine and cheese and just walked up the coast, listening to the waves. Neither wanted to say how much their union had rocked their worlds. Life had sharpened, accelerated. Public hearings, country-club parties, even county commission meetings had taken on a new tenor.

Angela relished their pace and their promise for a future. What did Bruce relish, though? She wondered, sometimes.

It gave him pleasure to think he aroused passion in her. That much showed in his eyes often enough. At times, he talked of a persistent loneliness, a self-enforced exile since his marriage foundered. For so long he needed to keep his life simple, he told Angela once. Now he didn't. Which was good, because she sure made things complex.

That she was the county district attorney certainly intrigued him. He liked to talk about the discretionary power she wielded. Whom to prosecute, whom to absolve? Where to draw the lines that divided wrongdoers from proper citizens? You bring order out of chaos, he told her. You give meaning to human conduct.

He wasn't mocking her in those moments, but she suspected he wasn't entirely being serious, either. So she gave as good as she got. Actually, she told him, chaos is what interests me, not order. Complexity so intricate it can't be imagined.

That intrigued him even more. One night he said, "I've never been able to figure out prosecutors or anyone in criminal law. You're always around crime, and you're always around criminals. What's the attraction?"

"Maybe we're all crazy," she suggested. "Or maybe we're just trying to figure out what makes people tick."

Another night he asked, "Is there any crime you might approve of?"

That question stopped her for a moment.

"What about a crime of passion?" he pressed.

"Passion is good," she replied. "But must it be criminal?"

"Not necessarily," he said. "But it's so much more exciting then."

What was also exciting, he made clear, was having the county DA by his side at public gatherings. Especially when the county DA was a striking woman with pale skin and raven hair. He liked the energy about her, the sense of a continuing, high-stakes drama. Also the notion of their "alignment," as he put it. It helped them both. We're turning heads, he often whispered to her as they stood on podiums. We make such a fine pair.

She agreed. As he went about his duties as the county commission chair, she came to regard him as a sort of beguiling outlaw traveling in camouflage. If not an outlaw, at least an outsider. A jazz saxophonist, humming smoky tunes as he presided at hearings over variances for shopping center parking lots.

It turned out that some of the books on Bruce's library shelves reflected where he'd been. The more time they spent together, the more he referred obliquely to his past. It was clear he'd lived in northern Canada among the Cree Indians. He'd worked in the South Pacific, the Samoas, and Fiji. He talked often of unspoiled ways of life, of populations untouched by any form of modern culture. It seemed to Angela that Bruce longed to return somewhere, to a certain place, a certain time. Once or twice, she heard hints that she reminded him of someone from long ago.

He couldn't endure boring dinner parties any better than she. Everyone always ended up talking about immigrants, immigrants and violent crime. At one, a particularly venerable San Francisco business lawyer—who spent his days defending white-collar felons charged with multimillion-dollar frauds—offered up his solution: Blanket deportation for some, mass sterilization for the rest. Enlist volunteers, call out the National Guard, clean out whole neighborhoods. The lawyer delivered himself of this idea while signaling an elderly Guatemalan butler for a refill of the 1961 Château Lafite Rothschild he was pouring. The rest of the dinner guests, listening with forks poised in the air, didn't even notice when Bruce and Angela slipped out of the room.

Now here they were at another dinner party. At least this time they were floating in the black sea on a gleaming white yacht.

"One thing you forgot," Bruce said. "Our friends in there must have mentioned this baby's gorgeous twin Cummins 330B diesel engines. Talk about rocking the place. Those mothers are almost enough to get you to Venus."

"Wish you were rich enough to own something like this?"

He looked out to sea. "No, not really. That's not what I'm after."

"What do you want?"

He took his time answering. "Some kind of success I can be proud of."

"You already have that."

Another long pause. "No. Not really."

She cast about for a comforting response, but didn't understand enough about him to provide one. She knew only that he seemed always to be waiting for something.

"I watched you on TV today," he said. "It must be so satisfying. Indictments, bringing killers to justice."

He even meant it this time, Angela sensed.

She glanced at their guests, silhouettes against the salon window curtains. Their host, RC Cummings's Albert Donner, had brought with him Sasha Bard, of all people. In a lowered voice Angela said, "Sasha's ex-husband wasn't too happy about the indictment."

"That detective? But I thought he cracked the case."

"He changed his mind."

"What does it matter?" Hightower pulled a cell phone out of his pocket. He frowned at the blank screen. "The main thing is, you found your man, you're taking him to trial."

She glanced again at the salon. On the CD, Dinah Washington had given way to Shirley Horn. Someone inside was pulling back the curtains, peering out, looking for them. Hightower started toward the starboard door. Angela grasped his elbow. "No, that's not the main thing," she said. "The main thing is, we're together."

He pulled free, stuffing the phone back into his coat. "Time to visit with our fellow guests, Angela. Let's go inside."

Sasha Bard looked bored as Delbert Hardy leered in her face. The Chumash County commissioner had consumed three Stoli martinis so far, and appeared to have forgotten that his wife was present with him on the RC Cummings yacht. "How's my little businesswoman?" he asked Sasha, his normally pink skin now a darker hue of red.

Sasha sucked on her cigarette and flicked ashes at Hardy's feet. "Your little businesswoman is just fine."

Hardy turned to Albert Donner. "What an excellent choice you've made tonight for companionship, Albert."

Donner offered an easy smile. He looked no more than thirty-five, with a medium build and slicked-back dark hair. "Sasha is more than a companion," he said. "Sasha is one terrific businesswoman. Get her talking about mortgage securities. She'll make your head spin."

Bud Conklin, Hardy's fellow commissioner, called out from the starboard settee where he sat with both of their wives. "Delbert, come on now, you know how much business

RC Cummings does with Sasha's company. They don't do that just because Sasha's a good mate."

The corrections only fueled Hardy. He turned back to Sasha. The Carver's luxurious salon had a spacious, wide-open floor plan, but he acted as if they were squeezed for space. His face loomed in hers. She was wearing a simple black sheath with a V-shaped neckline that particularly seemed to draw his attention. "My little businesswoman . . . You sure have built up your firm, now haven't you?"

Sasha took a step back. His attentions didn't annoy her so much as oblige her to respond. "Yes, I have, Delbert. I provide a local presence for RC Cummings. I tell them where to put their money on the Central Coast. It's been satisfying to play a role in Chumash County's resurgence."

Sasha turned to the salon's window and pulled back the curtain, searching for Bruce Hightower and Angela Stark. A moment later, they stepped through the starboard door. "How are you all doing without us?" Hightower called out.

Hardy lifted his empty glass. Hightower took it from him and placed it in the galley's sink. "How about a tour of the boat?" he proposed.

Albert Donner picked up the cue. He seized Hardy by the elbow. "This way," he said.

A pass-through made the Carver's raised pilothouse accessible from the galley. Donner showed Hardy the six-way Flexsteel power helm seat and the autopilot joystick. "What's this?" Hardy asked, pointing at a monitor.

Donner punched a button. The screen lit up, showing the yacht's engine room. "A surveillance camera. We can keep an eye on the powerplants without leaving the wheel."

Hardy liked that. He was a third-generation rancher from up-country, a cattle baron who'd decided he could better pull strings from public office than from behind the scenes. "Wish I could run Chumash County that way. It would be great to keep an eye on what's driving things while I do the steering."

"You don't need a camera, Mr. Hardy. We at RC Cummings are your eyes and ears."

"True enough. That's what I like about you fellows."

Donner steered him belowdecks to the Carver's lush private staterooms. Each had a queen-sized island berth. Hardy threw himself on one of them and bounced up and down. He resembled the plump sea lions that inhabited the harbor.

They both heard the sound of high heels on teak inlay at the same time. They turned to see Sasha duck her head as she joined them below. The commissioner suddenly jumped up. His reddish-pink cheeks had turned gray. His eyes were glassy.

"Better get topside," Donner urged. "You'll feel better with some fresh air."

Sasha watched Hardy lumber up the stairs. She turned to Donner, and ran a finger along the cherry wood trim. It was awkward with Albert. She knew him originally as a small-time investment counselor in La Graciosa, working for a firm owned by the Peabodys. Then she met him later in San Francisco, after he'd become a major player at RC Cummings. He hit on her up there one night near the end of her marriage. Half-wasted on an expensive burgundy, drawn by his young-jock look, she didn't discourage him. Somehow they ended up on the roof of his office building, near midnight. What she remembered mainly were the lights of San Francisco blinking all around them. In the morning, she made it clear this was a one-time event. Just forget about it, she told him. Nothing happened.

"It seems everything has settled down, Albert."

"Yes, yes, all smooth sailing now." Donner shifted on his feet. His earlier days, mainly spent riding waves on a longboard, showed in the way he held himself. On occasional summer evenings, he still escaped to the sea at news that the surf was up. "What about you?" he asked. "All smooth sailing from your end?"

Sasha hitched up the strap of her dress, which had slipped off her shoulder. "My competition disappeared when Ronny Olson's little shop folded. And your boys have started talking to me again. So yes, Albert, all's fine now."

Again, Donner fidgeted. "Great. I prefer it when things aren't so complicated."

"I wonder how they got complicated."

Donner started for the stairs. "We better get topside, Sasha."

She slid her hand into the crook of his arm. "Yes, Albert. Whatever you say, Albert."

Once more, Cassie Teal read the article splashed across the front page of the La Graciosa *News-Times*. It was the third one this week that Jimmy O'Brien had run on the Jeremiah prosecution. Each had dissected an element of the state's case. First came a withering look at Eddie Hines's veracity. Then an interview with that school guidance counselor, Sally Dyle. Now, today, the story of shopping for bootprint experts.

Queen of quackery. That's what two different law professors were quoted as saying about their forensic foot specialist.

She's a prosecutor's dream . . . She can't be refuted because she has no competition . . . Since no one else in the world can do what she does, who can prove her wrong?

"Enjoyable reading?"

Cassie looked up to find Angela Stark at her door. The DA wasn't happy.

"They're trying this in the papers, Angela. Before we even get to the courtroom."

"As always. The damn defense attorneys have the advantage there. They rush to the microphones, while I can't talk about an ongoing prosecution. You've done that yourself, Cassie. You know what they're up to. They can't control the facts so they try to marshal public opinion and taint the jury pool."

"You can't blame them. Being up against the awesome might of the state and all."

Angela slumped into a chair beside Cassie. In a low voice she said, "I don't feel so mighty. Not all the time. Not now."

Cassie gave her a sideways look. "Join the club."

"Just show me where to sign up."

They weren't anything alike, yet Cassie thought they did share something: a complicity. After all, it wasn't just Cassie who prolonged the four-day search for Shari Malone. For two days, simply to gain leverage, Angela hadn't responded to Cassie's offer. She'd let Teal twist in the wind while three hundred volunteers combed the foothills.

"You ever think of the Hernandez case?" Cassie asked.

"What do you mean?"

"I mean, do you ever feel remorse?"

Angela shrugged. "When a thing is done, it's done."

"If only I could be as wise."

"That's what you call it? Wisdom?"

"It's a way to handle life, at least."

"Yes, it is that."

Angela waited a beat, then continued. "I've been thinking, Cassie. We ought to put up a defense this time. We need to respond to these articles. If Brody is leaking, so must we."

"You think? Won't that just draw loads of flack?"

"We can handle flack easier than these articles. We have no choice. The court of public opinion is almost as important as the one inside the *asistencia*."

Angela was right, Cassie had to admit. As she often was. It surprised Cassie how much she felt inclined to help this prosecutor.

"I guess I agree, Angela. But I don't know what exactly we can leak, or who we'd get to do the leaking."

Angela started gathering up the newspapers on Cassie's desk. "That's easy. We'll leak point by point what we need to counter the defense. As for who will do it—who's better suited for the job than a former defense attorney?"

"Now wait—"

"Cassie, this will be second nature for you."

"Second nature? Believe it or not, Angela, I never leaked when I was a defense attorney."

"Maybe that was your problem."

"Only one of them."

Angela, glancing at her watch, rose. "I'm late, got to go."

"Hey, wait; come on now—"

At the door, Angela stopped. "Buy Jimmy O'Brien a drink," she said over her shoulder. "Buy him several drinks."

Alone, Cassie replayed their conversation. *If Brody is*

leaking—that's what Angela had said. But no, this wasn't Louis Brody's handiwork. Cassie knew that much.

This was Doug Bard. She felt certain. Doug Bard had turned mole. Doug Bard was out in the cold.

To her surprise, the thought electrified Cassie.

Silence fell as Bard walked into the central squad room of the sheriff's department. A half dozen deputies looked away. Two others, Victor Baynes and Andy Akers, studied him without expression. Even Bruce Spraker and Josh Ericson, cops who went fishing with him on summer weekends, had nothing to say.

"Don't let me interrupt," Doug called out.

Victor Baynes spoke first. "That's okay, Bard. We were finished."

Andy Akers spoke next: "We're not real comfortable talking in front of a turncoat."

Since Baynes and Akers had started as lead detectives on the Merta case, Bard understood their moods. For days, they'd all had classrooms each morning to go over where they were, what they'd learned. Bard kept missing them, though. Eventually, he stopped coming entirely.

"You've got it wrong," Bard said.

Baynes rose and approached him. He was a tall, gaunt man with anxious eyes and a perpetual frown. "You're making us all look bad, Bard. You're undercutting everything we do."

Bard, feeling Baynes was standing too close to him, took a step back. "The newspaper went public with this. Not me."

Regret showed in Baynes's expression now. "I was hoping for a more convincing response, Doug."

"We can't always get what we want."

Baynes's regret deepened. "You've put yourself at risk."

"All sorts of things are at risk. Innocent people's freedom. Truth and justice. Capturing a murderer."

Baynes looked away. "If I were you, Doug, I'd worry about myself first."

*   *   *

Bard couldn't stop himself. Driving northwest along the country road that followed Graciosa Creek to the sea, his thoughts kept drifting to a memory of his father.

It was a late autumn afternoon in Doug's rookie year as a cop. They sat across from each other at Oscar's kitchen table. Dirty dishes filled the sink and sprawled across the counters. Oscar lived alone, having lost his wife to cancer six years before. He was wearing khakis, boots, and a buttoned shirt that day, which meant he'd been out somewhere. He'd put on a few extra pounds by then, especially in his belly and his jowls. His face was round and full, his head nearly bald but for a gray fuzz. Before him on the kitchen table lay the MAK-90, a semiautomatic version of the AK-47. Rifle-cleaning time, once again.

"Dad, have you ever actually used that thing on anyone?"

Oscar's thick hands floated to the weapon. "The important thing is to have the option."

"Why, Dad? How come?"

Oscar glared, but Doug saw more unease than anger in his expression. "Power is who has the guns and who doesn't have the guns."

"Our shooting sessions in the forest, Dad. They were to give me power?"

Oscar fairly leapt at the question. "Yes, exactly, that was it. So I knew you were protected. So I knew you could take care of yourself."

They shot at branches and tin cans mainly. The thing was, Doug had been good at it, truly his father's son. He drew more than Oscar's attention out there, he drew his affection. Doug recalled Oscar's thick arm wrapped around his shoulder, his big hand squeezing with pride. If only they'd left it with the branches and cans. But Oscar decided his son ought to know what it was like to shoot at something live.

So they went hunting. First they aimed at squirrels and opossums. Doug didn't do as well with the small moving targets, or maybe didn't want to do as well. He kept missing, session after session. Oscar's impatience grew. So did his disappointment. He made that plain to his son. "You got to be able to pull the trigger," he advised, "if you're ever going to stand on your own two feet in this world."

Finally, weary of such words, Doug did stand on his own two feet. They were hunting squirrels but came upon something else at the edge of a small forest lake. The foliage was thick; Doug could barely see movement, only a vague gray patch near the water. He lifted his rifle, Oscar whispering encouragement in his ear. *Steady now, take your time.* All Doug wanted was for this to be over, for them to leave the forest. He pulled the trigger. Somewhere beyond his vision he heard a splash. They plunged through the woods until they stood at the lake. It was a mule dear, a young doe, shot cleanly through the heart. Her coat was rusty red. Her face and throat were whitish. She had a black patch on her forehead, and a tail tipped with black. Even in this state, Doug thought her so graceful. Her large round eyes stared back at him, unblinking.

"You did it, Son," Oscar said. "You pulled the trigger."

At the kitchen table, Oscar picked up his MAK-90 and began rubbing it with a cloth. "I'm not sure my lessons ever took, Doug. It's hard for me to see how you're ever going to take care of yourself."

"I'm a cop, Dad. I followed in your footsteps, just as you wanted."

Oscar kept rubbing the MAK-90. "A cop who won't carry a gun," he muttered. "Jesus."

"We could call it your greatest legacy."

The road to the sea curved and snaked into a narrow black canyon. Doug's mind drifted from Oscar to Molly. How would he respond if she ran amuck and risked her career, risked her livelihood? Would he cheer her on or would he grasp her by the shoulders and urge her to be smart and play by the rules? He wanted Molly to be brave and autonomous, but like Oscar, he was also a parent. He wanted to know she would always be safe.

Choices. Goddamn choices and their consequences.

A faint blinking yellow light fifty yards down the road claimed Doug's attention. He slowed. For a moment, he thought it was another car. Then he saw it was only a construction sawhorse, placed over an open ditch at the shoulder of the road. He rolled past it. Another hundred feet down the road, halfway to Pirate's Beach, he turned off the main country route. He was driving now on the dark narrow trail that wound its way through Apple Canyon. He climbed and banked along a series of switchbacks. At an unpaved path, he swung onto gravel and coasted the last fifty feet. Here was home, his unpainted redwood cabin set in a dense stand of old-growth.

Inside, the beams were exposed, the walls unfinished. The fireplace rose into a stone chimney that reached to the ceiling. The windows were wide and uncurtained, the furniture a mismatched mix of corduroy and oak. On the way to his bedroom, Bard glanced at his phone answering machine. He saw a blinking red light. He punched the play button.

Daddy, Daddy, where are you? . . . Please, Daddy, please pick up the phone . . . I need to talk to you right away . . .

At first Molly's voice sounded oddly calm. Doug heard her panic only as he kept listening.

Daddy, Daddy, please come quickly . . . Somebody's been calling us . . . Somebody's been following us . . . Somebody's walking around outside . . . Daddy, Daddy, someone's banging on our door.

TEN

For once, Doug Bard railed at La Graciosa's perennial fog. What he usually cherished now presented a maddening impediment. Peering over his car's steering wheel, he couldn't see more than five feet down the country road that led from Apple Canyon into town. Each time he replayed Molly's voice in his mind, he punched the accelerator pedal, only to brake as he found himself hurtling into misty oblivion. "I'm coming, Molly," he muttered. "I'm coming."

There'd been no answer when he called their house. The phone just rang and rang. He'd tried to imagine it pealing through the living room, the hallway, the bedrooms. Where were they? What about the answering machine? Had the line been cut? Had they fled?

The fog thickened as he approached town. Now he was just inching forward. Twice he had to stop entirely and wait for the haze to lift. He thought of Jed Jeremiah, stymied by the ink-black sky as his wife lay dying of pneumonia.

I'm coming, Molly . . . I'm coming.

In the middle of the night, Chumash County felt like a frontier outpost, untouched by modern times. Mountain secrets still hid in these winding murky canyons. Wild boar and wild turkeys, played-out gold mines and rare Sargent cypresses—all could be found here. Climate and geography had always protected La Graciosa. A rugged coastline, a lack of sheltered anchorages, the never-ending fog, the inland mountain range—together, they'd made this region almost inaccessible.

What had happened? Bard wondered. What had made La Graciosa so exposed?

He could see the road now, so he punched his accelerator. Once past the heart of town, he began climbing the eastern foothills, rolling through sprawling chaparral-thick grasslands dotted with enormous Spanish oaks. Sasha had insisted they buy their home here, in the zone above and beyond the fog line where wild lilac and manzanita bloomed in the summer heat. Such starkness and clarity were not his preferences, but he'd agreed. Whatever Sasha wanted in those early days, he'd willingly provided.

Bard screeched to a stop in the darkened driveway of the home where he had once lived. He hesitated for a second, then grabbed his Glock 9mm from the glove compartment. In an instant, he was pounding on the front door. "Sasha," he yelled. "Molly." He kept pounding. "It's Doug . . . It's okay . . . It's Daddy . . . It's okay . . ."

No answer. No lights. No sounds.

He backed away from the door. No, he didn't want to treat this as a crime scene, but instinct told him he had to. He couldn't disturb anything that might provide answers. Just as with Ollie and Marilee, he had to absorb, he had to read the unquantifiable nuances. Anything and everything should be considered evidence. Nothing should be touched or moved.

He couldn't bear it, though.

"Oh, dear God," he cried out.

Just then, the front door swung open. He fell to a crouch and lifted the Glock. It felt heavy in his hand. In the dark, he squinted. A porch light came on. He could see two figures, arms raised. He could see Molly and Sasha, beckoning him toward the house.

They faced each other in three chairs that circled a natural oak coffee table at one end of the living room. Molly slouched low in her seat, her legs flung across the table. Sasha sat straight up, hands clasped together. Doug studied his daughter and ex-wife. Molly looked numb. Sasha looked ready to challenge the world.

"Okay then," he said. "I take it someone came knocking at your door?"

"Duh," Molly said.

"Where were you?" Sasha asked. "What kept you?"

"I got here as soon as I heard Molly's message."

Sasha lit a cigarette. "Well, we don't need you anymore."

Bard watched Molly. She kept her eyes fixed on the oak table. "You okay, Molly girl?"

She nodded without lifting her head.

Bard rose and walked to the fireplace. "Someone here has to start talking. Tell me what happened."

Sasha drew deeply on her cigarette. "What happened is, first we got a phone call. Then we were followed as we took a walk up here in the woods. Then someone came around the house. Footsteps, lots of noises."

"Did you see anyone?"

"Never."

"You didn't look out the window?"

"No, we didn't, Doug. We locked ourselves in the bathroom. That's where we were when you arrived."

"Any idea who it was?"

Sasha flicked ashes into a bowl. "Why don't you tell us, Doug?"

"What do you mean?"

"The phone call, it was about you."

"What was said?"

Sasha nodded at Molly. "You're the one who heard it. You tell him."

Molly pulled herself up and wrapped her arms around her body. Still she wouldn't look at her father. "The person said stuff like 'Tell your daddy to stop pissing everyone off.' "

Bard came to Molly's side. He knelt. He put his fingers on her chin and pulled her face to his. "Anything else?"

Molly turned to him now. "Yes. The person also said, 'Tell your daddy his daughter could get hurt if he doesn't back off.' "

Bard tried to put his arms around Molly. She pushed him away. "Molly girl," he said. "You're my special—"

Sasha was at their side now. "If she's so special, Doug,

maybe you ought to spare her all this. How can you put Molly in jeopardy?"

Bard rose and backed off. "Why say that? Why are you so certain this is about Jeremiah's prosecution?"

"Oh please, Doug. Let's not argue. You know what this is about."

Bard walked to the phone. "Have you had any calls since the threat?"

Sasha shook her head. Bard picked up the receiver and punched in *69 to redial the last incoming call. An instant later, his own cell phone began to ring in his front pocket. "Damn," he said, tossing down the receiver. "I called here before driving over. I'll try to trace this, but I'll bet a buck it came from a pay phone way out in the toolies."

He asked Molly, "What kind of voice? Can you describe it for me?"

"Not really. It was all muffled, like the person was talking through something."

"The person?"

"I don't even know if it was a man or woman."

They sat in silence until Sasha slapped the coffee table and jumped up. "I can't stand playing victim anymore. Let's make this a party." In the kitchen she found a bottle of merlot; at the stereo, an old Van Morrison CD.

With glass in hand, Sasha sang along to "Gloria" in a strong, clear voice. Bard watched with pleasure, as he always did when Sasha wasn't playing the Sphinx. He liked so much the ways she chose to defy fear.

"It won't always be like this," he said. "I promise, Sasha."

She turned the volume up higher. She danced across the room, shouting, "She knock on my door. She knock on my door . . ."

The sight of her kindled memories. Just as she was their first date, after the grass brownies. Just as she was so often that first year.

"Knock on my door," Sasha called out. "Knock, knock on my door."

Molly was smiling now, clapping and swaying to the beat.

Bard said, "We'll get this under control, Sasha."

"Will you?" Sasha stopped dancing, punched off the CD player. She waited, catching her breath. "You're still the only person I can turn to, Doug. Yet you're the cause of this. Quite a conflict."

Bard didn't respond. He didn't know what to say to Sasha. He only wanted to scoop Molly in his arms. "Hey now, Molly girl. I promise I won't let this happen again. I promise I'll be here for you."

The smile washed from her face. "Like you've always been here, Daddy? Is that what you mean?"

"No, I . . ." Bard groped for the right words. "Not like always. Better than that. I promise."

"Who gives," Molly said. "You think I give?"

Bard cupped her face in his hands. "Yeah, I do."

Molly tried to pull away, then stopped. Tears filled her eyes. Tentatively, she leaned toward him. Then she was clinging to him. "I was so scared, Daddy. I'm still scared."

Bard realized that he was, too. On the streets, he never knew fear. In this house, it consumed him. There was something here he could lose. He didn't want to let go of Molly. He never wanted to let go.

They sat in silence for a while, father and daughter. Bard recalled so many other mornings like this. Whenever Molly climbed into his lap, he'd put aside whatever he was doing. He'd make himself keep still, as if his forced repose could freeze time.

A low murmur from the kitchen drew Bard from his reverie. He strained to hear. Sasha was talking to someone on the phone. Another business call. *I know it sounds wild, but there's money to be made. We'll be the Hertz of rental satellites if this works. There are more than two hundred geo satellites up there right now, but one in eight new launches crash, and two in orbit fail each year. We can collect four-million-dollar annual retainers for a time share in a backup, then three mill a month if they actually need one . . .*

Bard closed his eyes. She'd been so uncomplicated when they first met. Then she grew up. That's what happened;

that's what had to happen. Inevitably, they grew apart. Simple as that.

When he opened his eyes, Sasha stood at their side. She spoke firmly. "You need to stop, Doug. You need to leave things be."

"Asserting yourself once again, Sasha?"

A cigarette hung cold from her lips. She tried to strike a match, but couldn't do it. The match tip finally broke and flew off. She tossed the cigarette after it. "Yes, Doug. Sorry if I'm once again alienating you. Can't be helped."

Bard watched the cigarette land and roll along the carpet. He drew Molly even tighter to him. "I think I better stay here for a while," he said. "I think I better move in."

Molly's eyes widened with excitment. Sasha spoke first, though. "I think not," she said. "We've already tried that, remember?"

I believe in God, the Father Almighty, Creator of Heaven and Earth . . . Our Father Who art in Heaven, hallowed be Thy Name . . . Hail Mary, full of grace, the Lord is with Thee . . .

Listening to Sunday services from his pew, Jimmy O'Brien tried to keep still, just as he had as a young boy. Back then, at least, his mother had been by his side, governing him with nudges and glances. Now, he had only his conscience. He rarely attended church, but had felt the urge this morning. After being assailed constantly for the good part of a week, he had a need for solace and absolution.

First, there'd been a televised press conference, called by Marilee Cooper's parents to denounce the *News-Times* for its articles undercutting the Jeremiah prosecution. With Angela Stark at their side, they'd held up copies of his newspaper.

"Trash," declared Cynthia Cooper. "Nothing but trash."

"Jed Jeremiah killed our daughter," proclaimed Harvey Cooper. "Now the *News-Times* wants to let him walk free."

"I prosecute cases only when there's probable cause," Angela Stark vowed. "And that's what we're doing in this case.

To say that I'm prosecuting this case for political reasons is utter nonsense."

Cynthia Cooper spoke next: "Losing your child is one of the most dreadful things that can happen. Angela Stark has helped us through this more than anyone. The very first day after the fire at Ollie Merta's, she came to our home. She prayed with us. She saved us."

Harvey Cooper put his arm around his wife. "As terrible as this crime was, what's gone on since has been even worse. We're dealing now not with murderers but with journalists—educated, intelligent people—and still we are harmed, still we are hurt. Selling papers, not reporting truth, is all the *News-Times* cares about."

At that moment, Cynthia Cooper dissolved into heaving sobs. "We lost our baby . . . We lost our baby and Jimmy O'Brien just wants to exploit our pain."

A day later, the attack continued from within the Chumash County courtroom. The DA, in a written motion seeking a delay in the trial of Jed Jeremiah, harshly criticized the *News-Times* for "poisoning" and "tainting" the pool of jurors. The newspaper's articles, Stark maintained, had served "to sow prejudice among prospective jurors, as well as their friends and families, with whom they will be in contact throughout a trial."

Finally came the after-hours visit to Jimmy O'Brien's office by a small but distinguished group of county leaders. The businessmen in the group threatened to pull their advertising and lead a countywide boycott. Several civic figures warned Jimmy that to get community support, he had to support the community. When Jimmy tried to defend himself, they cut him off in midsentence. They weren't the least interested in a dialogue.

"You're hurting the Coopers," advised Henry Aston, the Peabody in-law who always looked as if he sensed an unpleasant odor in the room. "You're hurting La Graciosa. You're hurting Chumash County. And you're hurting the *News-Times*." Aston clamped a bony hand on Jimmy's shoulder. "Which is to say, Jimmy O'Brien, you're hurting yourself."

•

All around Jimmy now, people were rising from their pews. Services had ended. He jumped up. He no longer remembered why he'd come here. Enough of church, he needed fresh air. He turned into the aisle and strode toward the exit. The vestibule was crowded with departing parishioners. Jimmy had to thread his way. Bumping into someone accidentally, he turned to apologize, then froze.

Harvey Cooper. Next to him, Cynthia. Next to her, Angela Stark. Jimmy couldn't remember ever seeing any of them in church before.

"I . . . I'm sorry," he stammered.

Harvey asked, "What for exactly?"

"I didn't mean to bump you like that."

The trio stared at him. Jimmy tried again. "I don't mean to cause you pain."

"Mr. O'Brien," Cynthia said, "please be aware that what happened to our daughter has affected so many other people. So many children in our town now go through their daily lives full of fear."

"Yes . . ." Jimmy gathered himself. Enough of this apologizing. He'd faced irate readers before. It came with the job. "Yes, I understand. But I think you should understand, also. Despite what Ms. Stark here says, we may not know for sure who did this."

Harvey Cooper took a step closer to Jimmy. Then another step. They were just inches apart. "That's just the point, Mr. O'Brien. You don't know what happened, and can't know. But you act as if you do. The DA here feels she has enough evidence to file charges. What makes you think you're wiser than her? Mr. O'Brien, I believe you're forgetting what job you've got here. You're the reporter in this matter, not the arbiter."

Jimmy felt his throat go dry. Through parched lips he said, "No, I haven't forgotten my job."

"Well then," Harvey Cooper suggested, "maybe it's your integrity you've mislaid."

*   *   *

Douglas Bard aimlessly prowled the streets of La Graciosa. Through the plaza, past the bear fountain, past the *asistencia*. Up the brick pathway that paralleled the creek. Across the wood bridge, down the other side. Into a narrow alleyway. Along a side street paved with cobblestones.

He had nowhere to go. Sasha had rejected his notion of moving in for a while. Jimmy had started backing away. Sheriff Dixon and his fellow deputies had cut him off. Angela Stark was glaring. No one cared that someone had stalked and threatened his little girl.

"Did Sasha file a complaint?" Dixon asked when Bard pressed him. "I don't see anything in the record."

"They called me instead. I am a sheriff's detective, after all."

"Don't know for how much longer, Doug. I'm getting calls."

"From who?"

"People who matter."

"When people who matter get so bent they pick up the phone, I usually figure I'm on the right track."

Dixon ran a chunky hand through his crew cut. "Well," he allowed, "I can't argue with that."

Bard tried to press the advantage. "Hey, Howie. How about arguing with Stark, sometimes? It might even make you feel good."

Dixon shifted in his chair. "We all have our jobs to do."

"Yes . . . but—"

"You're good, Doug. You should do your goddamn job. Just lay off Angela. Don't undercut the DA all the time."

"I have nothing against our DA. My beef is with the case on Jed Jeremiah."

Dixon almost looked amused. "You made that abundantly apparent in the pages of the *News-Times*."

"You don't know that. Jimmy O'Brien has refused to reveal his sources. I bet it came from Louis Brody. It's the defense attorneys who always leak."

"Okay, Doug. I made that same argument to Angela. I'm trying to protect you. But for God's sake, back off."

"Something must be wrong with my hearing," Bard said. "I'm starting to hear an echo all around town."

He was. Sasha, Stark, Dixon, his fellow cops, even an anonymous caller . . . Was there anyone who didn't want him to stop, who he wasn't pissing off? Only Jed Jeremiah, probably. No, that wasn't true. Jed Jeremiah had more reason than any of them to be pissed off.

Bard couldn't stop moving. He crossed back over to the plaza, returning to the creek-side path. He didn't see a soul. Stella's had closed early for lack of customers. It was dusk on a chilly Sunday. Most families were home, gathered around the fireplace or the dinner table. Bard wondered how that would feel.

A judge had granted Angela Stark's request for a temporary delay—"that newspaper has made it terribly hard to pick a jury"—but had allowed only thirty days to let the articles' impact abate. Jed Jeremiah's murder trial would begin within a month. What to do? Maybe he could—

"Hey there."

Lost in thought, and the dim haze of dusk, Bard hadn't noticed the figure approaching from the opposite direction on the brick path. Cassie Teal was wearing scuffed boots, jeans, and a navy-blue parka. Dusk's faint light gave her face a luster.

"Hey there," he said back.

"What are you doing out here alone on a cold Sunday evening?"

"I could ask the same of you."

"I asked first."

"Okay, then. I'm out here because the Jeremiah case is driving me nuts and I'm trying to walk it all off."

She nodded as if she understood. "You've got the heebie-jeebies tonight."

"I guess you could call it that." He hesitated. Something in her expression invited him to continue. "I have nowhere to go. I've managed to make myself a pariah. The creek path is way better than staring at four walls."

"I see." That they were crossing into new territory now

didn't seem to bother her. "I know a little about being a pariah," she pointed out. "Also about heebie-jeebies."

"Yes, I suppose so."

They both allowed themselves tentative smiles.

"You been talking more to the Coopers?" he asked.

"A bit. They're furious over the newspaper articles."

"I noticed." Bard stared at the creek rolling by. The moon, just risen, was casting fingers of white light on the water. "I always thought Marilee's father might kill Jeremiah. Especially if Jed were somehow acquitted."

"Why do you say that?"

"If my daughter were murdered, and I thought the guy who did it got off, I would kill him. I might strangle him right in court. No sheriff's deputy could keep me away from him."

A breeze had picked up. She moved closer to him. "Tell me about your daughter. Tell me about your family."

He didn't want to go there. He didn't want to talk to Cassie about Sasha. "Your turn first. Why are you out here?"

She turned frank eyes on him. "Same as you. Heebie-jeebies. And nowhere to go."

"Is yours all professional angst?"

"Slow down, Detective."

"I just meant, is the Jeremiah case bothering you, too?"

"Yes."

He realized suddenly how hungry he was. Thirsty and hungry. He hadn't eaten all day. "How about a sandwich and a glass of wine at JB's?" he proposed.

She weighed that idea. "No . . . too many people we know there. Let's go farther away. Let's go all the way up the coast."

They sat in silence as Bard drove the winding road that threaded through the coastal hills north of Pirate's Beach. At first they saw the black moonlit sea only when the hairpin turns pointed them to the west. Then the road straightened and began to hug the rim of a crumbling wooded cliff. Now the dark surging water was everywhere, stretching to the horizon, pounding the cliff, claiming the unspoiled sand of the vast Chumash Dunes.

Bard thought of the Lost Pavilion, built in the dunes near here at the turn of the twentieth century. La Grande Pavilion, its original billing, was ballyhooed across America as the elegant centerpiece of a budding seaside community. Instead, it proved to be a lasting monument to the occasional folly of free enterprise.

The notion seemed like such a winning one to speculators: a planned beach town revolving around a stunning pavilion. The developers chose a spot for their colony near Venano Gordo Lake. The pavilion rose in 1905, a dramatic example of the Victorian architecture of the day. Two stories high, dominated by three churchlike towers. The second level was an elegantly appointed dance hall complete with hardwood floor and double-pane glass. The first floor, at first partitioned into offices for the swarming real-estate agents, later became shops, boutiques, and other small businesses. The developers built a large water tank to serve the pavilion and the settlers to come. They ran power lines to each building. They erected a seven-hundred-foot pier. They drew plans for landscaped grounds and cement sidewalks.

Most important to their goal, they subdivided the land around the pavilion into thousands of parcels, with prices starting at fifty dollars. They advertised heavily in the East, trumpeting the good life on the Central Coast. They sold hundreds and hundreds of lots. Hordes of people arrived for the celebration of music and dance that marked the project's official opening. A good number came in horse-drawn buggies, some by way of the beach, some by a gravel road. Many were landowners viewing for the first time the property they had purchased by mail.

Painful reality quickly set in. The colonists discovered they had purchased piles of shifting sand. Marking their property, let alone building on it, was almost impossible. Blowing sand soon obliterated the gravel road. Rough seas washed away the pier. There was no access other than from the beach. At high tide, the site was unreachable. People who bought saw it was hopeless. Nobody could live there.

By 1915, the pavilion was empty, abandoned. Vandals

smashed the windows and tore up the hardwood floor. Nature was even harsher, blowing sand under one corner of the building until it collapsed. Wrecking crews took apart the ruins for salvage. In time, shifting dunes covered all traces of the pavilion. The only sign now of a lost dream came when winter storms occasionally revealed shards of glass or electrical wire.

Bard couldn't help but wonder whether all of Chumash County's new developments might one day meet a similar fate.

"So tell me now about your daughter," Cassie was saying. "Your daughter and her mother."

He couldn't avoid it any longer. Introductions surely were in order. "What can I say? Molly and Sasha . . . I'm afraid they're both upset with me."

"For different reasons, though."

"Yes, for different reasons."

Cassie watched him, saying nothing.

He felt her eyes. "Sasha's upset over what I am, what I'm not. I failed to meet her expectations. Or maybe her expectations were too high. Either way, she got let down."

"I see. And Molly?"

He drove on, following a sliver of moonlight that arced across the sea. "I believe she feels her father abandoned her, abandoned her family."

"You don't think she understands why you left?"

"It's my sense that she thinks maybe it's her fault."

"You can't talk this out with her?"

"That's not so easy with a girl her age."

"My question reveals me then. I know little of families."

"Tell me your story."

"I don't have one, really."

"Everyone does."

"Not me."

"You're alone. That's a story."

She turned from the sea, and studied Doug's profile. "We are getting personal."

"You started this."

"Yes, I suppose I did." She shrugged. "I just never met someone I could stay with for long."

"Why not?"

"I have little patience, I guess."

"For . . . ?"

"Foolish boys, foolish men."

"Why foolish?"

"They're so obvious with their longings. They go on about my eyes or my smile or, God forbid, my soul. They imagine so much."

"They're mistaken?"

"Oh, yeah."

"Why so?"

Her head fell back on the car seat. "Let's just say that hurt can numb all trace of feeling."

He looked at her. He mainly saw yearning. "I don't believe it," he said. "I don't believe you."

Down the road, through a dense stand of sycamore, they could see lights now, and a half circle of parked cars. The clifftop Crocker Bar and Grill overlooked a wild reach of coastline strewn with boulders and tree trunks. The surf pounded wildly here, the thick oak forest crowded almost to the cliff's edge. They were twenty miles north of La Graciosa, in a land even thicker with cowboys and ranchers. "You wanted to go far away," Doug said. "Here we are."

Like dozens of other central California spots, the Crocker's walls were decorated with steer horns and trapper's tools. There was no jukebox, though, nor piano players, nor any familiar faces. Hardly any faces at all: The room was empty save for a scattering of couples, the men with cowboy hats and dark leathery faces, the women with big hair and dangling gold earrings. Doug and Cassie sat in a booth that offered a view to the north. Their eyes followed the coastline. Candlelight played off Cassie's face.

She sipped a martini. She said, "I think I'll tell you about the Bidwell case."

Bard nursed a Black Bush on the rocks. "The Bidwell case?"

"Danny Bidwell. Before I came here. My first year as a defense attorney. Up in San Luis County."

"What happened?"

"I lost. Blew it big-time. They convicted a totally innocent man."

"How did that happen?"

Cassie stared out the window. "He'd been identified by a dozen eyewitnesses, none of whom had a reason to lie. He was also what you, Detective Bard, would call your basic piece of shit punk."

"Very good. You've been listening to me."

"They charged him with kidnapping, robbing, and shooting two men who he supposedly yanked from a restaurant. The victims survived, identified Bidwell. So did eight others in the restaurant."

Cassie traced an outline on her glass. "Jury convicted in an hour. Not totally my fault. It was a fall-down case if ever there was one."

"Any physical evidence?"

"No."

"Did that trouble anyone?"

"Only one person beside me."

"Let me guess. A stubborn irascible old sheriff's detective."

"Yep, you've got it. Detective Jeremy Marlin. Cranky old coot, hard to endure, irritated the hell out of everyone. Had his instincts, though. He just didn't think Danny Bidwell was the type to back out of a restaurant shooting. Not enough balls for that, too much the punk. So after the conviction, Marlin starts flooding the county with photos of Bidwell."

"What happened next?"

"Six months later, a half-drunk gal calls Marlin from some saloon and admits she was there at the restaurant that night with the guy who really did it—and it wasn't Bidwell. Larry Allen did it, she says. Larry Allen."

"A dead ringer for Bidwell."

"Yep, a dead ringer. They boxed Allen, and right there with

the polygraph going, he confesses. Danny Bidwell walks free. End of story."

"You left out the best part."

"The best part?"

"There must have been a hearing for postconviction relief."

"Aha. A cop who knows the law." Cassie drained her glass. "Yes, there was a hearing. All the other cops besides Marlin keep whispering, 'Let sleeping dogs lie.' The judge wants at least a retrial. But the prosecutor won't go for that. He's appalled he convicted an innocent man. That's why Danny Bidwell walks."

"What do you know. A prosecutor and detective are the heroes in this story."

"Yes. Exactly."

"Why bring this up now, Cassie?"

She looked at him steadily. "I want you to understand why I crossed over, why I joined the DA's office. It has something to do with wanting to be on the right side. Unlike defense attorneys, prosecutors are obliged to pursue the truth."

Bard chose his words carefully. "The Hernandez case, that must have been tough."

"I lay awake four straight nights during the search, imagining that girl's body in the culvert."

"Me, too. We've got a bond."

They sat with hands on their empty glasses, searching for the next step. A waiter put plates before them full of T-bone steak and baked potato. Cassie asked for a glass of merlot, Doug for a Graciosa Brew. They picked up forks and knives, and went to work.

"Someone has been stalking and threatening my family," Bard said.

Cassie stopped with a fork halfway to her mouth. "What?"

"Molly and Sasha. Someone followed them, then called, then came around the house."

"The stalker's message?"

" 'Tell your daddy to stop pissing everyone off. Tell your daddy his daughter could get hurt if he doesn't back off.' "

Cassie put her fork down. "Who have you told?"

"Dixon isn't interested. Stark just glares at me. Jimmy O'Brien kind of circles around."

Cassie's hand impulsively covered his. Nothing about her felt numb to him. "You're out there all alone," she said. "Aren't you?"

He didn't want to admit that. He didn't want to say it mattered. It did, though. There were nights now when he lay awake almost to dawn, full of an unexplainable terror. He thought often of Harvey Cooper, trying to imagine this father's grief over a murdered daughter. He thought of Sasha, trying to understand her odd first reactions to news of the deaths. He thought of Molly, trying to know her fear as she crouched in a bathroom, hiding from a stalker.

"There's something I should tell you," Cassie said.

"Another story from long ago?"

"No, this one is more current."

Bard pushed back his plate. The candle on their table had burned half down now. Cassie sat half in shadow. "Tell me," he said.

"It's something that happened during Jeremiah's grand jury hearing. One of our lab technicians pulled Angela aside when he arrived to testify."

"Would that be Donny Garber?"

"Yes, very good. It seems that besides the bootprint on the door, they later found two other prints, in the dirt below a window. Angela was going to present them to the grand jury. But then Garber, an hour before he's due to testify, tells her that he's decided these prints were made by a woman's shoe, size eight. Way too small for Jed. Garber suggests that Angela not have him testify. Angela demurs. She goes ahead and calls Garber to the stand anyway. She just ignores this new information. She avoids asking Garber about those prints."

"And since then," Bard asked, "she's forgotten to tell the defense?"

"She doesn't consider it exculpatory. She considers it irrelevant."

At the same moment, they both became aware of a noise, a

rustling all around them, close and fast. They turned to the window just in time to see a jagged flash of lightning. Then came thunder's enveloping boom. Without warning, a midnight storm had blown in from the sea. Doug slid an arm around Cassie. "Come on now," he said. "We better get home."

ELEVEN

Bruce Hightower slapped the phone back into its base so hard, it bounced. Angela Stark looked up. "You're going to break that," she said. "If you haven't already."

He rose, crossed the room, stared out the French doors at his flagstone terrace.

"You're sure in a mood," she said.

"And what are you in?"

"At least I'm not breaking things." She forced a smile. "Yet."

The remains of their Sunday morning brunch littered the dining table. The mushroom omelet they cooked together, standing side by side in silence at the stove. The toast she'd burned out of distraction. The coffee he'd made too strong by miscounting his spoonfuls.

"Let's not personalize this," Bruce suggested. "We're both obviously bothered by stuff right now."

"That is true."

For him, it was the proposed Pirate's Beach project. Resistance was mounting from both sides. The naysayers had formed a committee—"Opposition Grows to Possible Development" blared a banner page-one headline in this morning's *News-Times*. The developers, in turn, were digging in their heels, resisting Hightower's call for "responsible" proposals. The phone and fax machine had been ringing for hours.

If Angela weren't nursing her own concerns, she believed she'd have more patience for such tumult. She did have her own concerns, though. For one thing, Doug Bard was still challenging the Jeremiah prosecution. For another, Angela's latest bid for the attorney general's nomination was foundering before it even started. The chief fund-raiser for the California Democrats had canceled an appointment; the governor's political deputy wouldn't take her call.

"We'll turn this around," Hightower said. "All of it."

"Will we?" She began to clear the table. "You're the romantic in this room, Bruce. I'm afraid I'm the realist. You're so damn ready for whatever's coming. I steel myself."

At the French doors, he rocked on his heels. His hands were jammed in his pockets. "If we act instead of wallowing, we can shape how things turn out."

Angela looked at him. He seemed as if he meant it, as if he could do it. She wondered how often he had in the past. She was struck by how little she knew of him. "Bruce, what exactly did you do up in northern Canada among the Cree?"

"I lived with them."

"Where?"

"Norway House, little community in Northern Manitoba."

"How'd you end up there?"

"I was just wandering around. It felt like a last frontier, which God knows is what I wanted. So I stayed awhile."

"Why'd you leave?"

"It stopped being a frontier."

"What happened?"

"First the province brought in electricity. You'd think that wouldn't be so bad. What the hell, lightbulbs instead of lanterns or propane. But with the electricity came television."

"No more frontier?"

"You wouldn't believe what happened. Kids started buying those celebrity magazines and coming to school half-asleep. They also stopped playing outside. One old Cree I knew took his son camping, wanting him to reexperience bush living, and damn if the boy didn't ask to go home so he could watch Bugs Bunny. That's when I decided it was time to leave the last frontier."

Angela said, "It sounds like you spent time around those kids."

He looked oddly at her. "Sorry, I thought you knew. I was a teacher. I taught sixth grade."

She tried to imagine him before a class of twelve-year-olds. "No, I didn't know."

He came back to her at the dining table. He sat down, grabbed a pen and a yellow legal pad. "Let's plot some strategy," he proposed.

Within an hour, two sheets were filled with his scrawl, one for him, one for her. He would call a press conference on the bluff above Pirate's Beach; he would organize a weekend camp-out there for local schoolkids; he would dramatize how the area's natural beauty could be both preserved and developed. Meanwhile, she wouldn't take no for an answer; she would fly to Sacramento and knock on doors; she would talk to the Assembly Speaker. Hightower would, too, for Bruce knew the Speaker. Chips would be called in, strings pulled, pressure applied.

Hightower declared, "We're still going to rock this place."

His cell phone rang just then. As he listened, he rose and slowly left the room.

Sheriff Howie Dixon raised a hand, to both protest and soothe. "I know," he said. "I understand."

Angela Stark tapped her desk with the point of a pencil. "Do you, Howie?"

They'd been talking for nearly an hour now.

"I will speak to Doug," he promised.

"Speak to him? My dear Howie, you apparently aren't listening to me. I've been saying that we have to fire this man."

"I *am* listening to you, Angela." Howie shot her a look, all eyebrows and sucked in jowls. "That's the problem."

"Okay, okay." Impatience and appreciation mixed in Angela's voice. "You're right, I know if I fire Bard I'll just get myself another round of headlines. Plus a lawsuit. Plus a lot of explaining to do. I can hear the questions. 'Why did you dismiss your number one detective? Why did you dismiss the star investigator who cracked the Merta-Cooper murders?' "

"Yeah, boss," Dixon said. "Why did you?"

The color rose in Angela's cheeks. "Because he's undercutting us publicly. Because he's trashing our case."

He watched as she stood and went to the window that gave onto the *asistencia* quadrangle. "There are those who might put it another way," he said. "There are those who might say Bard's being fired for raising troubling questions."

Stark turned on him. "Damnit, Howie. Jed Jeremiah killed an old man and a little girl because he's a wild animal who doesn't like anyone prowling on his land. I will not let him get away with that, not in my county. Bard would, though. He's working against me. He's rolling around town acting like he's still looking for a suspect. That's fodder for any halfway awake defense attorney. 'If their own detective isn't certain'—I can hear that speech to the jury even now. Opening argument, closing, they'll sing that song every time they get a chance."

She was right, of course. Dixon knew that. Despite his warnings, Bard hadn't stopped poking around. In recent days, he'd taken the school counselor Sally Dyle on a drive around Merta's house. He'd called the forensic hotshots who identified Jeremiah's bootprint. He'd visited their lab man, Donny Garber. He'd even left messages for Harvey and Cynthia Cooper.

All those folks, in turn, had called Dixon. Some, like Dyle, were simply perplexed. The forensic foot gal was irritated. The Coopers were outraged. Donny Garber was scared.

How had Bard even found out about the bedroom window footprints? Where was he getting his information?

Dixon had to admit, Doug was one hell of a detective. But he was badly undercutting the DA. Dixon understood and even sympathized with Angela. You can't prosecute cases if your own players keep ruining your narrative.

Dixon didn't see how he could protect Bard any longer.

"I'll tell you what," he proposed. "Maybe we can get rid of Doug without firing him."

Stark came to his side. "How?"

"Maybe Detective Bard, all on his own, will decide it's time to quit the force."

*   *   *

Long fluorescent bulbs cast a sickly yellow light. Words, white letters against a blue backdrop, blinked on a row of computer screens. Young men with lots of hair walked about in wrinkled khakis, shirttails billowing. Young women with earnest eyes adjusted their headsets and reached for ringing phones. From inside Jimmy O'Brien's cluttered office, he and Doug Bard studied the *News-Times* city room through a glass wall.

"You ever get sick of this place?" Bard asked. "Looks like it could get kind of depressing."

"It's no worse than your squad room."

"Granted."

"Anyway, I thought it might help to meet here."

"Help who?"

"Me." Jimmy flipped unopened mail into his out-basket. "What can I say, Doug? Here is where I work. This is my life."

Bard studied him. Jimmy's voice was flat. His shoulders sagged as if someone had let the air out of him. "Hell, Jimmy, I didn't think anyone or anything could put you down like this."

"I don't know what you're talking about."

"Tell me what's happened. Tell me who got to you."

"You saw the Coopers' press conference. You saw the DA's motion for a delay in the trial. You heard what the judge said about the *News-Times* in his ruling."

"What the hell, Jimmy. You've taken fire like that before. It usually just makes you dig in your heels."

"You're right."

"What then?"

"Well now . . . Did I mention how I bumped into the Coopers at church? Did I mention how Harvey Cooper looked as if he wanted to drive a knife right through my gut?"

"No, you didn't."

"It's not fun being at odds with some fellow who's just lost his eleven-year-old daughter."

"I know. I'm there, too, Jimmy."

"Well, then."

"You're backing off? No more stories challenging the Jeremiah prosecution?"

"I didn't say that."

"You don't have to."

Jimmy rose from his chair. "Damnit, Doug, I'm going to cover the trial and report the facts with all the resources I've got. But I'm not going on a one-sided crusade. I'm going to be skeptical to all sides. That's my role here. Harvey Cooper didn't convert me, but he did remind me there are other perspectives. I've got to reflect them all."

Jimmy grabbed the day's paper off his desk and thrust it at Bard. "Look at the motto that runs on my front page every day. *This newspaper is first, last, and always what an honest-to-God newspaper should be—a mirror of the life of the public it serves.* That comes from the founding publisher one hundred and ten years ago, Doug. Corny, maybe, but it still holds true. No, I'm not backing off, I'm doing my job. And I'm letting the judge and jurors do theirs."

Bard stared up at Jimmy. "It's the paper's owners, isn't it?"

Jimmy looked as if he were going to bust something. "No, it's not the owners, goddamn it. This is my call all the way."

"But you do have owners, don't you, Jimmy?"

"Well yes, Doug. Okay, fine, the *News-Times* does have owners. Corporate owners, absentee owners, but owners nonetheless. We are a for-profit business, those folks like to remind me. Business has to be earned every day. We must meet our simultaneous responsibilities to readers, customers, advertisers, and communities. We must—"

"Who came to visit you, Jimmy?"

"Who says anyone came to visit?"

"I do."

Jimmy started prowling along the bookshelves that lined one wall of his office. "Let's just call it the hidden power structure of Chumash County. You had your businessmen, your civic figures, your pastors, your—"

"Names, Jimmy."

"Okay, okay. Let's see. There was Shelby Kirkland . . .

Henry Aston . . . Bud Conklin . . . Ward Delwood . . . Hank Curry . . . Daniel Boiles . . . Ken Broderick . . ."

Such a diverse group, not just the usual old-money gang. Some were commissioners, some cattle barons, some merchants, some patrons of the arts. Bard tried to find the thread. "What's their connection, Jimmy?"

"What do you mean?"

"Think, Jimmy, think. They didn't just happen to show up at your door at the same moment. They gathered. They no doubt have gathered on other occasions. Where have you seen this group before? What's their common ground?"

"Common ground? They're all fat and rich, that's their common ground. While I, alas, am fat and poor—" Jimmy stopped and sank back onto his chair. "Wait a sec. I know where I've seen them all together. Up on Bruce Hightower's podium at Pirate's Beach. Hightower's town hall shindig. They were the cheering squad."

"Who spoke the most when they visited you? Who was the leader?"

"That old fart, Henry Aston."

Bard had heard that name more than once at his home. When he had a home. Aston was one of Sasha's best clients.

"What did Aston tell you, Jimmy?"

"That I was hurting everyone. The Coopers, Chumash County, the newspaper . . . and myself. Especially myself."

"Sounds as if you got some good advice there."

Jimmy flared. "I have a family now, Doug. I have responsibilities. It's not like the old days."

"No," Bard said. "I guess it isn't."

From a bench in La Graciosa's central plaza, Cassie Teal watched the noontime crowd begin to gather. By the creek were mothers with strollers and young children. By the bear fountain, young shop clerks and office workers in their twenties. On the steps of the *asistencia*, lawyers and sheriff's deputies. On nearby benches, retirees with sack lunches and college students with bulging backpacks.

Someone, somewhere was playing a guitar. Cassie thought

she recognized a Joni Mitchell tune. *I've looked at clouds from both sides now* . . . How perfect, she thought.

Others complained of how much La Graciosa had changed, but Cassie savored this small town. After searching for home for so long, she felt she'd found it here. She wanted to be a part of something, a part of this place. That's what had made the backlash from the Hernandez case so hard to bear. She could defend herself endlessly on the basis of legal ethics and obligations, but she couldn't wipe away the community's rancor.

"There you are."

She looked up at Louis Brody. He'd suggested they meet on the plaza rather than in "a stuffy office." Now he stood over her with pensive deep-set eyes, clutching a bag of salads and sandwiches from the take-out window at Stella's Café.

She patted the bench beside her. "Come sit down, Louis."

He handed her a tuna sandwich. She handed him a thin file.

"This is full disclosure, Cassie? All you have on Jeremiah?"

She looked at him. There was no accusation in his voice, just a lawyer's routine question.

"All we have that's producible, Louis."

The file sat on his lap, unopened. "Been a while, Cassie. We should stay in touch more."

"Sorry, Louis, the DA's office keeps me pretty busy."

"Yes, I can imagine."

They'd talked little of the Hernandez case since Cassie had left their suite of offices. They still shared memories, though. For two days, as hundreds searched the backcountry, Brody sat beside Cassie, listening and posing questions. Their subject, the contrast between what was moral and legal, consumed them. Brody understood both dimensions but by instinct had his preference.

There's right, there's wrong, he told Cassie. There's good, there's evil.

But it's unethical to disclose any information from my client, Cassie reponded. It's illegal to breach confidentiality.

Rules can't cover all the territory, Brody argued. Rules can be interpreted any way you want. Moral right transcends written rules.

Still, he stood by her throughout all the community outrage that followed. On the afternoon the three thugs burst into their office suite, Brody faced them down without raising his voice. This isn't good for you, he told them. You'll end up sitting in a jail cell next to Cal Hernandez's. Is that what you're after? Do you really want to be soulmates with Cal Hernandez?

It was Brody who called a locksmith to come put in new dead bolts that day, and it was Brody who stepped before the cameras and microphones. *Cassie was just trying to advise her client. That was her sacred duty. She couldn't abandon her client. It's unfortunate the public doesn't understand that.*

"Has it helped, Cassie? Being on the other side?"

"I'm just fine, Louis." She nodded at the file sitting on Brody's lap. "Where are you now? I mean, with this case."

"Ah yes, this case." Brody looked reluctant to turn to the business at hand. "I've been to see Jed Jeremiah twice so far."

"What's your sense of him?"

"Truth?"

"Of course."

"Jed's eyes, they're just about the darkest I've ever seen. He's a rough case. He won't play well before a jury."

"Are you thinking of pleading?"

"I haven't raised it with Jed, and he hasn't said anything. In fact, so far we've talked little about the case itself. Mainly we talk about his life."

"Anything you can share?"

"I think I'll save it for the trial, Cassie. Mainly, it's your usual hard-luck tale. Alone most of his life. His dad died when he was eleven. A stepdad liked to use a belt on him."

"Sounds like you've managed to get close."

"Only on occasion. It's complicated."

"How so?"

Brody mulled that. "Here's the thing, Cassie. There are moments I get drawn to him, when he talks about the life he's lived. Then he explodes again, just spewing violent irrational bile, and I see how capable he is of an angry murder."

They sat in silence. Cassie asked, "Louis, aren't you going to look at this file?"

He regarded the folder on his lap as if it had suddenly appeared. He opened it and started to scan the pages. He shook his head. "It's as I understood. You've got a past history of bad blood between my client and the victim. You've got an eyewitness in Eddie Hines. You've got how many here, let's see, not one but four experts matching Jeremiah's boot to the door. Pretty impressive."

Angela had left the prints at the bedroom window out of the file. Those prints weren't there the day of the fire, she'd argued. They weren't in any of the reports. They must have been made later by those coming around to gawk. They weren't part of the crime scene. They weren't anything.

"Yes, Louis, the state's case is rather impressive. In case you ever do get to considering it, I have to tell you I don't see much room to plea-bargain. I'm sure we'll want first-degree murder. You can't plead into that."

"No, of course not."

"So do you have a plan?"

"I just might."

Cassie looked at him and saw the quiet resolve that others sometimes missed. "Would you maybe want to share that with me?"

The notion amused him. "You mean, as if we still shared an office? You think I'm that confused about what role to play in our marvelous system?"

She gave him a sideways look. "Just thought I'd try, Louis."

Together they negotiated the *asistencia*'s warren of corridors and small rooms. Their heels clattered on pink cement floors; their hands brushed against white plaster walls. Doug Bard, leading Louis Brody to Jed Jeremiah's cell, felt as if he were smuggling contraband into the county jail, even though this man had every right to visit his client.

Brody had called him instead of the jail's central desk.

Cassie Teal suggested I go through you. That's how he'd explained it. They knew each other from several cases over the years, although not well. Bard wasn't that close to any criminal defense attorney. He labored to throw lousy bent mutts into jail, then the lawyers got them out. He did not often find himself standing side by side with someone like Brody.

"I understand you found the eyewitness," Louis was saying. "I understand you got him to talk."

"Yeah, that was me."

"Kind of cracked this case single-handedly, didn't you?"

Bard pushed open a towering double door made of unfinished oak logs. Here was La Graciosa's jail: a small vestibule that gave onto a dozen cells, six on each side, sprouting off a narrow hallway. At a counter in the vestibule sat a pale, thin guard.

Bard, instead of answering Brody, called out to him. "Hey there, Dexter."

The guard nodded and silently reached for his ring of keys. They walked past cells full of street punks all too familiar to Bard. There was Alfredo, there Sully, there the one they called Cougar. All nothing but mutts. Breaking and entering, shoplifting, drunk and disorderly. Not a real felon among them.

Jed Jeremiah, stretched on his cot, lifted his head at the sound of his cell door being unlocked. He sat up. Clearly, jail hadn't set well with him. His eyes were cold with fury; his skin had a sour gray pallor.

"Hello, Jed," Brody began. "I've come again to talk about your case."

Jeremiah didn't acknowledge him. He was staring at Doug. "Look what you've done, Bard . . . Look where you've put me."

Brody tried to get his client's attention. "Detective Bard has been kind enough to escort me down here—"

Jeremiah kept talking over him. "I spend twenty-three hours a day in here, Bard. Alone in this five-by-seven cell. I get out one hour a day to walk around the yard. I can't bear it. I won't bear it."

Bard said, "Maybe you won't have to for much longer."

Jeremiah's calloused hands clenched the edge of his cot. "You wanted to see me get wrathy, Bard. Well, I'm mighty wrathy now."

Brody again tried to intervene. "Anger isn't going to get you out of here, Jed. What we need—"

"Kill me if you want, Bard." Jeremiah looked as if he meant to hurl himself at Doug. "Do whatever you want."

Bard took a step farther into the cell. "The thing is, Jed, you forgot to tell me about your fight with Ollie Merta two years ago. You forgot to tell me you shoved him and threatened him with a rifle."

"Wait a sec—" Brody began.

"And so what if I did?" Jeremiah rose from the cot. "He came onto my property with his goddamn sheep. Then he mouthed off when I told him to leave. The bastard was on my land, Bard. *My* land. I had a right—"

"Is that what happened the day Ollie died, Jed? Is that—"

"Now hold on here," Brody interrupted, moving between them. "That's enough, Bard. You cannot interrogate my client. I didn't know you were going to try that. You'll have to get out now. You'll have to leave us alone."

Bard slowly backed away from Jeremiah without turning his head. "Of course," he said. "You two need to confer. Just holler when you're finished."

At the end of the corridor he stopped and looked around. There was a time, he knew, when these barred rooms held prisoners only until the good citizens of Chumash County got around to lynching them. The first killer brought to justice in this fashion was one Jose Aquilar, a Spanish soldier at the local garrison who in 1800 made the mistake of shooting a trapper in front of two witnesses. Then two Chumash Indians, hauled in for plotting an uprising, were hanged on a beam erected in front of the *asistencia*. Then Lucien Garvey felt the rope for killing a drunken Mexican stranger who one night unwisely waved a $200 roll in the local taverns. They came for Garvey the very night of his arrest, storming the *asistencia,* breaking open the jailhouse door. Garvey begged and shrieked at the end, protesting his innocence, but at the stroke of midnight he was nonetheless sent into the presence of his Maker.

"Hey, Detective, what's happening?"

Bard scanned the cells, searching for the voice.

"Over here, Bard."

He stepped slowly down the corridor. Now he saw. The voice came from the cell adjacent to Jeremiah's. Spiky Samuels was waving at him.

Bard shook his head at the sight of Samuels. He was a scrawny strung-out meth freak with gimlet eyes and long oily hair. Bard couldn't count the number of times they'd arrested Spiky, but it was always for small-time stuff—stolen car radios, shoplifting, sleeping on the plaza. The stuff Chumash County didn't want to recognize. They'd finally taken to parking him in the county hospital's mental ward rather than throwing him in jail. Spiky had fried about 90 percent of his brain cells, and they weren't growing back.

"Hey there, Spiky. What you in for this time?"

"Got in a fight over a six-pack, man."

"They hauled you in for that?"

"Ah . . . well . . . I had to break into a motel room to get it back."

Funny, Bard thought. He hadn't heard about this fight or this arrest. They usually avoided rolling out for such small-time stuff. Bard threw a switch on the wall that opened Spiky's cell door. He stepped inside. He stood in silence, studying this prisoner.

Tell me more about yourself, Jed. Tell me about your dad. Tell me what happened to him . . .

With a start, Bard realized he could hear the conversation in the next cell between Brody and Jeremiah.

What's the point in that?

I just want to understand . . .

This jail was once a dormitory for young Indian girls. Thick oak doors connected each cell to the next. At the bottom center of every door was a small arched hole, cut long ago, probably for drainage. Sound carried well through those holes.

Tell me about your father . . .

Bard could hear Jeremiah pacing about in the cell.

Oh Christ to hell. My pappy?

Yes, your pappy.

Christ.

Now came the squeak of mattress springs as Jeremiah sat down on his cot.

It happened back during the great drought, when I was eleven . . .

Bard knew he should turn away. This wasn't for him to hear; this was private talk between lawyer and client. He couldn't stop listening, though.

Everyone was so desperate, watching their sheep die of starvation. Not Pappy, though. In Jumper Canyon, just the far side of Pozo, he knew feed was plenty. Pappy drove his sheep to that place. Brought me with him, me and Buddy, our shepherd dog. We built a fire, had supper, then laid down in our blankets. We were mighty cold, so high up in the mountains, but we slept. Then Buddy came running up, all in a fuss. Pappy thought it maybe was a stray coyote. He got up, told me to stay put. Next thing I heard was an awful commotion, off in the dark. It wasn't a coyote. It was a goddamn grizzly. The drought had him crazy starved. I jumped up, ran toward the noise, even though I was supposed to stay put. I saw the grizzly walloping Pappy something awful, saw Pappy go down.

Silence for a moment. Bard thought he heard Jeremiah rise from the cot.

Pappy should have kept still then. He knew that anyone who fights a bear gets the worst of it. But you see, he'd heard me come running. He had to distract the grizzly from me. So he fought him. The more he fought, the more the bear mauled him. Run away, he kept calling to me. Run away. I minded, I ran and ran. When I crawled back, the grizzly was gone. Pappy was still alive, but barely. He didn't last the day.

Bard could hear Jeremiah's hand slapping the iron bars of his cell.

Nothing much more to say. You know the rest.

Bard realized now that not only he had been listening.

Spiky Samuels, on the edge of his cot, had his ear turned to the small hole at the bottom of the oak door. The strain of concentrating had wrinkled his brow.

Bard regarded Spiky with a vague unease. When he'd heard a voice calling him, he hadn't thought to look in this cell because he knew it was empty. That is, it had been empty just twenty-four hours ago.

"Who arrested you, Spiky?"

In confusion, Samuels turned from the oak door. "I'm trying to remember. There was two of them. One was a tall bony guy, not very happy looking."

"Victor Baynes? Victor Baynes and Andy Akers?"

"Yeah, that's who, they're the ones."

Bard's unease deepened. Baynes and Akers were on the felony and homicide squad. That's why they'd drawn the Merta murder case. What did they care about a fight over a six-pack?

As he should with a fine Macanudo, Sheriff Dixon took his time. He held the long, thick cigar close to his nose, sniffing. He peeled off the cellophane. From his desk drawer, he pulled a cigar cutter. With precision, he clipped off the end of the Macanudo. Then there was a lighter to swing open. He pushed a button and watched the flame jump up. He held the cigar just over the fire. He inhaled. He closed his eyes with pleasure.

"Sometimes," he said, "things just happen." He glanced over at Doug Bard. "You understand?"

Bard shifted in his chair. Dixon had been toying with him for twenty minutes now. "Not really."

"Ah . . . well . . ." Dixon tapped ashes, inhaled again. "I just mean, we shouldn't read too much into things sometimes."

"Into what things, Howie?"

"Personnel shifts, for instance. Manpower allocation in an understaffed sheriff's department."

Bard steeled himself. He expected something, but didn't know what exactly. "Why don't you just tell me why you've called me here? What are you going to do, fire me? Is that what's up?"

Dixon rolled the Macanudo in his fingers. "No, no, Doug. You're far too valuable, even if you do manage to piss off our DA every week."

"What then?"

"Okay, here it is, Doug. The issue for me right now is proper deployment, given our limited resources. We have very few murders in Chumash County, very few serious felonies. I just can't keep you full-time on the felony and homicide beat."

"I see."

"Doug, do you know how many underage teenagers are drinking and driving in this county? Do you know how many crimes they're involved in?"

Bard didn't, but he knew the numbers were high. There'd been articles, town hall meetings. He himself had spent more than a few moments preparing himself for when Molly would be ricocheting around in some pimply punk's souped-up Chevy. "More than all the county's murderers combined, I imagine."

Dixon put down his cigar. "My point exactly. Which is why we need to refocus our priorities."

"Refocus?"

"We're starting a countywide crackdown on underage kids buying liquor. We're going to put you on a stakeout at several of the convenience stores. See how many of these folks we can catch red-handed."

Bard grinned, trying to treat it as a joke. "You want me to sit in 7-Eleven parking lots all day?"

Dixon remained as impassive as a cow. "That's exactly what I want. That's your assignment now, Doug."

Cassie Teal eased off her accelerator pedal. The road that twisted through this reach of Apple Canyon had suddenly narrowed and turned to dirt. Dense brush crowded up to the sides of her car, which lurched crazily over a welter of rocks and potholes. She'd climbed and turned through this maze just as Doug had instructed. Now she should be there. Her car rolled slowly around a final bend. Yes, there it was, just as he'd described. An unpainted cabin set in a dense stand of

old-growth oak. Cassie exhaled, and loosened her grip on the
steering wheel. What a home. The cabin looked to be no more
than 1,200 square feet. It also looked as if it had been standing here for at least half a century.

He opened his door at the first knock. He was wearing
khakis and a flannel shirt. Over his shoulder, she could see
flames leaping in a giant stone fireplace. "Thanks for coming," he said, standing aside. She stepped inside. The disarray
stopped her. Clothes lay where they'd been dropped. Newspapers, dishes, and a sack of unpacked groceries covered a
dining table.

"This is some kind of bachelor's pad, Doug."

He needed to talk to her, he'd said. He'd proposed meeting
at Stella's Café, on the creek beside the plaza. She'd demurred.
You have too many enemies now, she'd explained frankly. It
wouldn't do for a prosecutor in Angela Stark's office to be
seen hanging around with you. He'd suggested alternatives—
Pirate's Beach, Pecho State Park—but she'd rejected them all.

What then? he'd asked.

How about your place? she'd proposed.

She went straight to his hearth now, and held her hands
over the fire. She'd come from work, and apparently a day in
court. Her hair was pulled into a ponytail. She was wearing a
navy-blue business suit and high-heeled shoes.

Bard said, "You look like a prosecutor."

She kept her eyes on the blaze. "Because I am a prosecutor." Then one hand went to her head, the other to her heels. In
an instant, she was barefoot, with a tangle of curls cascading
down her back. "Still a prosecutor, but at least feeling a little
more comfortable."

He brought out two glasses and a bottle of Saucelito Canyon
zinfandel. They settled in worn corduroy-covered chairs, facing each other before the fire.

"I've been yanked off the felony-homicide beat," Bard
began. "Dixon called me in this afternoon. Put me on the underage drinking beat. I'm supposed to stake out convenience
stores. Bust teenagers who buy six-packs."

Cassie nodded, sipped her wine.

"You knew this was coming?" he asked.

"I sensed something was up. Poking around after the indictment, hammering our lab guys, trying to call the Coopers. That doesn't go over very well."

"I'm just doing my job."

"It's not your job anymore, Doug. The investigation is over."

"Cassie . . . where are you on this?"

"Do you mean am I with you?"

"I guess I do need an ally."

She turned from the fire. "Funny, isn't it, Doug? You publicly denounced me three years ago for defending an accused killer. Now that's just what you wish I'd go back to doing. All because you think you've got a lock on the truth."

Bard didn't know how to respond. They sat in silence. The flames in the fireplace ebbed. Outside, dusk gave way to a black night.

"What are you going to do, Doug? What's your choice now?"

"Every day, I've got to look in the mirror. Every day, I tell Molly to do the right thing. How can I tell her that if I don't do the right thing?"

"What's the right thing?"

"I'm going to resign. I've got to quit."

"You sound determined."

He rose, and paced before the dying fire. "I have no choice."

"Then why call me here? What's to talk about?"

He stopped, came back to his chair. "Quitting is hard."

Cassie looked wistful. "Ah, the human heart in conflict. Instincts versus sense of duty. An eternal story."

He watched her in the firelight, and wanted to lay his head on her shoulder. "Thing is, quitting feels like I'm folding my hand."

"Well, you are, aren't you?"

"They've backed me into a corner. I can't play the game. I've got to quit."

"That's exactly what they want you to do, Doug. This is a setup. You're falling for it. You're playing the sucker."

"Sucker, my ass. I'd be a sucker to sit around 7-Eleven parking lots. I'm not going to do that. I'm not going to bust teenage boys."

"Remember the Bidwell case, Doug. That detective fixed it from within. You can—"

The sound of a beeping pager interrupted them. Cassie checked her purse, shook her head, said, "Not mine." Bard pawed through the debris on his kitchen counter until he found his. Blinking back his panic, he scanned the digital screen. No, thank God, it wasn't Molly calling. It was Jimmy O'Brien. Bard grabbed his phone, punched in the editor's private number.

"What?" he barked into the receiver. "What, Jimmy?"

He listened, then, more softly, asked, "When? . . . Where?"

He scribbled on a notepad. "Okay, Jimmy, I'm on my way."

His eyes were on Cassie as he set the receiver down. "There's been another house fire," he said. "We have another death in Chumash County."

TWELVE

Sheriff Howie Dixon examined the smoldering hulk that once was Benjamin Mire's home. They're not the same, he told himself. This one isn't the least like Ollie Merta's house fire.

No kicked-in front door, for one thing. No bootprints. No little girl. No confusion about cause, either. Mire's ancient furnace had exploded, they could all see that easily enough. The blast itself, even without the resulting fire, would have nearly demolished the cabin. The first lick of flames would have finished it off.

Dixon weaved among the fire trucks and patrol cars. He had Victor Baynes and Andy Akers on this one. He could see Vic now, on his knees by the furnace with their arson tech, Jack McGown. Andy was talking to a pair of firemen.

Mire lived out by the cabbage fields to the south of town, a flat treeless reach where the seaside cliffs descended and the beach widened into the start of the Chumash Dunes. Farmworkers dwelt here, many transients who moved up and down the coast following the seasons. So did those who could afford nothing else, or wanted nothing else.

Dixon stopped the coroner's aides as they were wheeling Mire's body out on a gurney. He pulled back the sheet. Here was something else different. Unlike Ollie, the fire hadn't spared old Ben Mire in the least. Parts of Ben resembled the charred tri-tip you saw on chuckwagons at the Thursday night farmer's markets.

Dixon didn't know much about Mire. Just that he was a retiree and widower from the north who'd settled in La Graciosa about half a dozen years ago. On pleasant days, he sometimes came to the central plaza and sat by the creek, feeding the ducks. Occasionally, he stopped by JB's for a beer, but always kept to himself. He was short and slightly built, with a funny widow's peak and a liking for red plaid suspenders. Dixon once had tried to make small talk with him on the plaza, to little avail. Mire had been polite but painfully shy.

The sheriff reached out and touched Mire's neck, trying to recall how Bard did it. Nothing felt odd, nothing compressed. He bent closer over the body. No fingernail marks on the side of his throat. He lifted the eyelids. No small red dots in the mucous membrane.

Yet more differences from Merta. Dixon allowed himself to relax. No choices to make this time, no compromises. Just a simple, terrible accident.

The screech of tires jangled Dixon's nerves. He turned to see Doug Bard hurtling up Mire's dirt driveway. In an instant, Bard was at his side.

"What do we have here, Howie?"

"We don't have a serial killer, I can say that for sure. Furnace exploded. House like this must have burned like paper."

"Can I take a look?"

"Hell, no. I've got Baynes and Akers on this. You shouldn't even be here."

"Another pair of eyes won't hurt. Just let me—"

A voice from behind Bard interrupted him. "You heard the sheriff, Bard. This isn't your case. Aren't you supposed to be staring at 7-Eleven right now?"

Bard found Victor Baynes's face screwed into a tight, thin-lipped scowl. In return, he offered his lopsided grin. "Just thought you'd want some help, Vic."

"We've got this covered. We don't need an extra pair of eyes."

"Who's to say? Extra eyes came in handy over at Ollie Merta's."

"Actually not," Baynes said. "Extra eyes got in the way."

Dixon stepped between his two detectives. "You've got another assignment now, Doug. Let's get to it."

Bard didn't move. "Howie, you've got someone in Chumash County who likes to set house fires. Jed Jeremiah is in jail, so we know it's not him."

"These aren't linked, Doug. Jeremiah killed Ollie and Marilee. A bum furnace killed Mire."

"Someone's still out there, and we're not looking for him. We won't be, as long as you keep insisting it's Jeremiah."

"Jeremiah is guilty, Doug."

"How can you be so sure?"

Dixon hesitated, glancing at Baynes. "Because Jed Jeremiah has said something that's mighty revealing."

"Said something?"

"Yeah. About Merta being a goddamn poacher. About having to put a stop to Merta's poaching."

"And to whom did Jed say this?"

Baynes answered before Dixon could. "To another prisoner."

Bard pretended to mull that. "Let me guess . . . Spiky Samuels?"

Baynes's scowl deepened. "How'd you know?"

"Lucky guess. Nice detective work, Victor."

He'd suspected that Spiky Samuels's presence in the cell next to Jed's wasn't an accident. *Rent-a-tat,* that's what the defense attorneys called this game. Inmates called it *jumping on the bus.* Often, they testified against people they'd never even met, about crimes they never witnessed. Sometimes the inmates bought case files from outside sources so they'd know what to say, and sometimes the prosecutors themselves provided the needed information. The prosecutors win cases; the informants win early freedom.

Bard knew the game as well as anyone, because he'd played it. Throwing Petey Montrose at Eddie Hines in that interrogation room had been a variation on the theme. It was odd, seeing this scam from a different angle.

"For chrissake, Howie. I've played rent-a-tat with you. You can't get this by me."

Dixon looked weary. "Doug, it's not you we have to get anything by. A judge and a jury will decide this thing. You're not the final arbiter of guilt or innocence. You need to back off. You can't control the whole process."

You can't control the process. Dixon's words stung. The sheriff was right, of course—but what alternative did Bard have now? With inescapable clarity, it occurred to him: When the trial started, he couldn't remain a passive bystander.

Something else occurred to him: What he needed to do was testify for the defense.

Bard reached into his pocket and pulled out his wallet. He flipped past the photo of Molly, past the photo of Marilee. He extracted his badge and handed it to the sheriff. "I quit, Howie. I'm off the bus."

Angela Stark glared at the silent phone. He'd said he'd call, but hadn't. She disliked the emotions this aroused in her, but try as she might, she found now she couldn't entirely control them. He'd done that to her. She'd surrendered something.

In the kitchen, she scooped ice into a tumbler and filled it with vodka. She wasn't much of a drinker, but tonight she thought the alcohol might soothe her. There was a price to pay, she saw now, for this dance with Bruce. There was risk. She told herself she didn't care, that she savored risk. Only by taking risks would she ever pull herself out of Chumash County.

Angela took her drink and settled into an armchair, summoning images of Bruce. There were so many—he bare-chested at the fair, he grinning from behind a podium, he staring into her eyes with wonder that first time they made love. He'd seemed then to be welcoming her into his life. Yet over time, he'd proven chary with that look. It came and went. Lately, it hardly came at all.

Angela raised the glass to her lips. She fixed again on the phone. In the hallway, a clock ticked. It was nearly ten.

When did things start to cool? That one night in particular stood out, that awful night he came home acting so agitated. His mood, the late arrival, everything combined to roil the atmosphere. She tried to calm him, but couldn't find the right words. All evening long, he kept pacing and staring out windows.

Ever since, he'd grown increasingly detached and preoccupied. The tug-of-war over Pirate's Beach seemed to consume him. His cell phone kept ringing at odd hours. There were unexplained meetings with lawyers, sudden trips to San Francisco. At times now, she saw something close to alarm in Bruce's face, as if he felt his life spinning out of control. As if he needed to retreat, to reclaim himself.

The sound of a car on the driveway drew her attention. A moment later, the front door swung open. There he was. She rose to greet him with eyes that smoldered. She didn't mind playing the coquette at times. The lessons you learned at law school about handling jurors weren't all found in law books. A tilt of the head, a tone of voice, a way of looking at someone, they were all fair parts of the arsenal.

"Good thing you're late," she said softly. "I just got here myself."

He exhaled. Tension drained from his face. "We're in synch, at least."

She reached up, ran her fingers along the back of his neck. "Let's see. What should a good mate do here? Ask how your day went?"

He smiled. "You can be more imaginative than that, can't you?"

"I'll try."

Her fingers slid down his back. She kneaded his shoulder muscles as she leaned into him. After a minute, he stepped back. He glanced at the cell phone clutched in his right hand.

"Hey," she whispered, "you're a tough audience."

"Sorry. Let's have a drink."

They sat on the terrace until past midnight, silently sipping white wine. Later, in bed, she watched him, then slid a hand toward him, under the covers. When he stirred, she curled a leg around his.

"Bruce."

"Yes?"

"What happened tonight? I didn't know where you were."

He looked at her oddly. "Where I was? It's you who went missing. You were supposed to meet me at that supper club up in the north end. The local Rotary Club chapter."

Of course. In the rush of her own work, she'd forgotten.

"Angela?"

"Yes?"

"So where were *you*?"

She stared off into the dark. There were no streetlights around Hightower's house, here on the sheer cliffs above the waves. Through the window curtains came only the faint glow of stars and the distant roar of the surf. "Sorry about that. I got distracted. An emergency at work."

"What kind of emergency?"

She rose from his bed and went to the window. He watched her standing there nude, alabaster curves against the sable sky. She felt his eyes.

"Another house fire," she said. "Another death."

He said nothing at first. She could hear his breathing, which sounded labored.

"Who?" he asked.

"An old man in the cabbage fields. Benjamin Mire."

"An accident this time? Or do we have another murder in Chumash County?"

"Accident."

She could hear him exhale. "Well, thank God for that much," he said. "We've had enough damage to our county's image."

"Yes."

Angela turned from the window and walked back to the bed. She slid under the sheets and reached for him. She ran her tongue along his neck; her fingers traced a line up his leg. He shuddered, then rose to her touch.

"I take it back," she said. "You're not such a tough audience."

I have a problem I need to talk about. At the dance contest last week I almost won, but an older girl named Jessica won because she got extra practice with the teacher. I did not get that extra practice. I will never win

*if the teacher gives Jessica the practice she needs, and
doesn't help me one bit. Why does she like Jessica more
than me? Is it because Jessie won three contests and I
only won once? I hate it when Jessie brags. She thinks
she's so cool when she is not cool at all. She does not
even dance well. I think I can dance better. That contest
where we danced to Britney Spears, do you know how
much I wanted to win? It just is not fair!*

Molly sat at the dining-room table, writing in her private
journal. She loved putting her feelings into words. She also
loved being alone inside her head. The whole afternoon, that's
where she'd been.

Now she wasn't. Sasha, emerging from her bedroom,
bolted across the living room, heading toward the kitchen.
"Finished with your homework, darling?"

"Just about. Working on my journal."

Sasha stopped. "Now that must make for an interesting
read."

"It's supposed to be private, Mommy."

"I know. I was just—"

The phone began to ring, interrupting them. Sasha stared
at it without moving.

Three times the phone rang, four, five.

"Mom, aren't you going to answer?"

Sasha stirred. "Yes, of course. It's business. Someone returning my call. I'll take it in the kitchen. You finish with your
journal."

She lifted the receiver on the seventh ring. "Sasha Bard
here."

For a moment there was silence on the other end. Then the
RC Cummings vice president said, "Albert Donner here."

"Oh, Albert. You."

"Yes, me. It's so nice to hear the delight in your voice when
I call."

"It's always a pleasure, Albert. Whether it's evident or not."

"Especially today. I'm bringing you a golden opportunity.
We've got a communications start-up that truly stands out

from the crowd. Maker of optical networking equipment that laps everyone. They've got fiber-optic strands that carry over six million megabits of data a second. That comes down to something like eighty million calls at a time. Interested? You have any investors looking for something right now?"

"I do, Albert. But no way would I recommend this to them. You know perfectly well that the technology is changing too fast. No one knows what will succeed. These technologies compete, and have too many sellers chasing too few buyers. So prices are way low. The Internet doesn't pay the bill. Only four of the forty large network operators show positive cash flow."

"Build it," Albert said, "and they will come."

"Sure. Profits will come. But when? And for who? Sorry, Albert. I'd rather have my clients go watch *Field of Dreams*."

Donner didn't respond. Sasha could hear him breathing. She stole a glance into the living room, where Molly was still working at the table. She lowered her voice.

"I found a note in our mailbox the other day, Albert. Just three words. 'Silence or else.' In big black letters."

Donner took his time. "I don't know a thing about it. If that's what you're asking."

"You don't?"

"No."

"Who's doing this?

"I don't have a clue."

Sasha closed her eyes. When she opened them, Molly was standing in the kitchen, looking puzzled, pointing toward the refrigerator door that her mother was blocking. She wanted something to eat.

"I have to go now," Sasha said.

"Okay then. Give some thought to what I'm offering here. There won't be a second chance."

She heard a click. She put down the phone and turned to her daughter.

"Who was that, Mommy?"

"Just a business client, honey. Here, what do you want?"

She opened the refrigerator. "Will a grilled cheese sandwich hold you until dinner?"

"Sure."

"I'll make it and bring it in to you."

Molly turned away. "You trying to get rid of me?"

"No, no. I just need to make another business call."

"Am I air? Is that what you think?"

"Air?" Sasha smiled faintly. "No, my dear, that never occurred to me."

"Okay." Molly headed toward her bedroom. "I'm going on-line. I've got boys to chat with anyway."

"Only the ones on your Buddy List."

"You think that's safe?" Molly's eyebrows bobbed. "I've got a couple of little hotties on that list."

"Molly!"

"Just kidding, Mommy. Can't you ever tell?"

Sasha picked up the phone as her daughter retreated to the bedroom. She held it in her hand. She stared at it.

She wanted to call Doug. She had to admit that. One night that first year after the split, he left a note while dropping by to pick up his things. *I miss you. I miss us. I miss our life together.* She'd felt the same at the time, but never responded.

Sasha began to punch in Doug's number. Then she stopped.

They'd been so bad for each other. That's what she was forgetting. She was wallowing in nostalgia. Their good days together were long gone.

Acrid smoke from the stove commanded her attention. She'd burned the cheese sandwich to a black crisp. Molly, alerted by the smell, was emerging from her room, heading to the kitchen. Sasha put the phone down. "It's okay, Molly. I'll start another one."

Stella's Café was nearly empty by the time Doug Bard got there. The breakfast crowd, folks with jobs, had scattered to their desks and shops. Bard settled at a table on the creek-side deck. Marie, the ancient waitress who'd worked at Stella's for three decades, came over to pour coffee.

"Think I'll have a spinach and mushroom omelet, Marie."

She gave him a funny look. A toasted English Muffin, devoured on the run, was his usual breakfast. "A slow luxurious morning for you, Detective?"

She didn't know, hadn't heard. He didn't feel like explaining. "Taking some time off, actually. Not a detective today."

"Okay then, Doug."

He leafed through a copy of the *News-Times* while he waited for his food. There was a medium-sized story about the fatal furnace explosion at Benjamin Mire's house. No mention of sinister theories. Also no mention of the Jeremiah prosecution. And nothing, of course, about Detective Douglas Bard's resignation. Did Jimmy even know?

It had been days since he had a job—or a paycheck. His scant savings weren't going to last long. Bard worried more about paying his share of child support than his groceries and mortgage. He wanted Molly to be as much his responsibility as Sasha's, no matter which parent had the bigger bank account.

Bard looked up, searching for Marie and a refill of his coffee cup. For the first time now, he noticed a man sitting at a table on the far side of the patio. He was frowning over a disheveled pile of papers, adjusting his glasses, and sipping a cup of coffee. Bard started to turn away, then stopped. Yes—it was Louis Brody.

Bard rose and approached his table. What the hell, they were on the same side now. "Hello, Brody," he began.

The lawyer lifted his head. "Detective Douglas Bard. What a coincidence. Here i am, reading through the Jeremiah file."

Bard sat down. "It's not Detective anymore. I quit the sheriff's department yesterday."

It took a moment for Brody to digest that. Slowly, he pushed aside the documents before him. "What happened, Doug? Have you become another one who's sick of the whole sorry game?"

"My reason was more particular. It should interest you, Brody. I quit because I think the sheriff and DA are prosecuting the wrong man for the Merta-Cooper murders. I think your client is innocent. I told Dixon and Stark, but they wouldn't listen. So I walked."

Brody slid his chair closer to Bard. "How interesting. Yes, indeed. How very interesting."

"I couldn't testify for the state at Jed's trial. I'm willing to help you with this case. I'm prepared to testify for the defense."

Brody began stirring his coffee. The spoon clanked against the inside of the cup. "Terrific. This is really going to help us. Let's just think here for a minute."

"I'll testify about my investigation. I'll tell them how I came to believe that Jed was innocent. I'll tell them why I reached that conclusion."

Brody kept stirring, lost in thought now. "Sort of like an expert witness."

"Exactly. An expert witness. That's what I am. At least about this case."

Brody stopped stirring. Something appeared to occur to him. He frowned as he reached for a pen and legal pad. He began scribbling notes. "To me you certainly are an expert, Doug. You will be a great help, advising me."

"Wait a second. I don't want just to advise. I'm offering to testify."

Brody kept scribbling. "I appreciate that, Doug. I can't tell you how much. I just hope the judge will let you talk freely."

"Why wouldn't he?"

"The problem, as usual, is with our wonderful legal system. Our rules of law allow witnesses to relate only what they directly saw or experienced. They don't let you spout your opinion. They certainly don't let you say who you think is innocent or guilty."

"Why not?"

"That's the jury's job. Even qualified experts like doctors, who can give opinions about cause of death, can't talk about guilt or innocence. And you, I'm afraid, may not even be what they call a qualified expert."

"But I know more about this case than anyone. I *made* this a case, for crissake."

Brody stopped writing on his pad. "If only that mattered in a courtroom. It doesn't, though, just as so much else doesn't. Doug, look. Don't worry. No matter what, you're going to be a great help to Jed. We'll think of all sorts of ways to make use of your insights."

Bard slapped the table. "They'll listen to me. They'll have to listen."

"Doug, Doug . . . Do you really think if you're allowed to go into the courtroom and say, 'Hey, this guy didn't do it,' that everybody then is going to say, 'Well, that's settled, let's let Jeremiah go'?"

Bard looked around. Marie was heading toward him with his omelet. He no longer felt the least bit hungry. "Maybe," he said. "I'm a detective, after all. I crossed a line. I'm from the other side."

"Maybe so. Maybe you're right. We'll certainly give it a try."

Marie was beside them. "You want this here or at your table, Doug?"

Brody scooped his papers off the table. "Right here."

The smell of eggs turned Bard's stomach. "Jeremiah is innocent," he insisted.

Brody lined up his papers in a neat stack, then slid them into his briefcase. "That may be so. All the same, I have to tell you that Jed has started to talk to me about a deal."

"A deal? What do you mean?"

Brody rose slowly from the table. "What I mean is, Jed wants to plead guilty."

In late afternoon, when he knew they'd be home, Bard knocked on Sasha and Molly's front door. No one responded until he called out. "It's Doug . . . It's Papa."

The door slowly swung open. Sasha stood there, looking confused. "But I didn't call you."

"I just feel like visiting."

"That's funny." Sasha stepped aside and waved him in. "I feel like having you visit."

He found Molly at the dining-room table, doing her homework. She bestowed a smile.

"That's all I get?" he asked.

Her smile broadened. She stood up and came to him, offering a hug. "Love you, Daddy."

"That's better. What you working on?"

"Report about Anne Sullivan."

"Who?"

"You know, the lady who taught Helen Keller."

"Oh, yeah. Can I see?"

She climbed into his lap as he sat at the table with her, reading her work. *Anne Sullivan is a very special person because she was the one who taught Helen Keller to read and write. It was an incredible job for Anne to teach Helen, but she did it . . .*

"Nice work," Bard said when he finished. "Way to go, Molly."

Sasha was at their side now, hands on her hips. Bard wondered if she was going to dance again. Maybe a little Bonnie Raitt this time. He never knew.

She asked, "What are you guys up to?"

Molly climbed off of Doug's lap. "Just showing Daddy my homework." She headed toward her bedroom.

"Where you going?" Bard asked. "Stick around."

"My on-line buddies are waiting."

"Her new recreational activity," Sasha explained. "Instant messaging with the boys in her class. Our daughter is eleven going on nineteen."

Bard smiled but felt uneasy. "How do we know who's really on the other end of the messages?"

"Daddy." Molly looked exasperated. "Get with the program."

"No, really," he said. "There are bad people out there."

"And your point?"

Bard didn't answer her. He could think of nothing to say.

Sasha studied him. "What's up, Doug? Something is, I can tell."

He rose from his chair. "I quit my job."

Sasha and Molly were both staring at him. "When?" Sasha asked. "Why?"

"Yesterday. I had a difference of opinion with Sheriff Dixon."

"Over what? You always have differences."

Bard was looking at Molly. She'd turned her back to them. He put a hand on her shoulder. "I had reasons, Molly."

She could barely speak. "You quit your job? You're not trying to catch Marilee and Ollie's killers?"

"I didn't just give up. I was protesting something. It'll be okay."

Molly said nothing more.

"Molly—"

"It's okay, Daddy. I'm fine."

Sasha asked, "What are you going to do?"

He said, "I'll figure something. Sell boats or fix cars if I have to."

Sasha's expression was unreadable. The dancer retreats, the Sphinx rises. "What were you protesting?"

"That second house fire yesterday, that second death. I think it's suspicious, Dixon doesn't."

Sasha obviously wasn't tracking. "I've been locked in a two-day conference up in San Luis. My rent-a-satellite deal is about to launch. I haven't heard any news for forty-eight hours. What are you talking about?"

"Out in the cabbage fields. Old guy named Benjamin Mire. Supposedly his furnace exploded on him."

"Oh, God." Sasha wrapped her arms around herself.

"You know this fellow?"

"No . . . no, it's not that . . . it's just . . ."

"Sasha, I don't understand."

She retreated toward the kitchen, shaking her head, waving him off. Molly reached out as her mother passed, trying to offer comfort. Sasha pushed her arm away. Bard rose and started toward Molly. Too late, he saw that she didn't want his help. She shoved him, a palm in his belly. She began pounding his chest.

"We can handle this on our own, Daddy."

"But I—"

"Go away, Daddy," Molly cried. "Just go away."

Late that night, Bard walked down the brick pathway that followed the creek. He knew where she lived, a couple blocks this way, then across the wood bridge and up the slope to a rise that overlooked the water. He'd never been to her home, but he'd passed it by several times in recent weeks. Each time, he'd studied it with curiosity. No more than a cottage, really, with a broad porch and a shingled roof. He stood now at its front door. He knocked.

Footsteps. The door swung open. Cassie Teal was wearing a blue silk robe, tied at the waist. She was barefoot. She had a hairbrush in one hand, a hand towel in the other. Fresh from the shower.

"I've sort of been expecting you," she said.

He stepped inside. Her living room, so unlike Sasha's, was full of sisal rugs and canvas twill furniture.

"I assume you heard," he began.

"Oh, yes."

"What do you think?"

"You quit, Doug. Unlike my Bidwell detective."

"I couldn't testify for the state. I had to testify for Jed. But I saw Louis Brody today. He said the judge might never let me on the stand."

"Not as an expert witness. Not to proclaim your opinion about guilt or innocence. I could have told you that. You can offer facts gleaned from your investigation, but not conclusions."

Bard watched her in the dim soft light. Her dark blonde curls, which she'd been brushing, framed an oval face. Her full lips, slightly parted, appeared to be on the brink of a question. Her robe, thin and damp, clung to her body. She looked steadily at him.

"Cassie."

"What?"

"I . . ." He stopped. "A glass of wine would be nice."

She leapt at that idea. "Sorry for my bad manners. Just a minute."

They settled into a swinging redwood bench on her patio. For a good while they sat in silence, sipping their wine, watching the creek roll by. "There has to be a link," he said.

"A link?"

"Between Ollie Merta and Benjamin Mire."

"We've found nothing."

"I'm not sure I'd trust our sheriff's work."

"Come on, Doug, you're getting paranoid."

"No I'm not. Something's up. The stakes are higher than normal."

She didn't believe him, or wouldn't believe him. He saw that, yet he saw something else as well. He plunged ahead.

"I paid a visit to my former family tonight. My daughter was rather disappointed to hear I'd quit. My ex-wife seemed scared of something. Neither wanted me around."

"They told you that?"

"Molly took her fists to me. 'Go away,' she said. 'Go away, Daddy.' "

Cassie winced. Her hand crept onto his. She spoke softly, from out of a memory. "You're alone again. Even more so than before."

"I guess that's right."

She hesitated, trying to decide. Then she came to him, curling into his arms. He could smell her, something musky and redolent of the canyons. He felt her breath on his neck. She wrapped herself around him as if trying to form a shield. He sensed her heartbeat. Her eyes offered such promise.

He whispered, "I'm afraid I'm just another foolish man, looking at you with obvious longing."

"No, not foolish. Not you."

"Even though I imagine so much?"

"Even though."

He leaned over and kissed her, slow and hard. Her robe started to part. His hand moved slowly along her leg. "You don't feel numb to me," he said. Her eyes were half-closed.

She was shivering. She tugged at her belt and her robe fell away. She moved against him, urgent now. The swing bench swayed in the night air.

"Are you with me, Cassie?"

Her voice was thick. "Only for tonight."

THIRTEEN

The pale pink sky of dusk had turned magenta by the time Angela Stark and Cassie Teal emerged from the *asistencia*. It was Sunday night, just hours before the start of Jed Jeremiah's trial. They'd been working since early morning. They had an opening statement crafted, and an order of witnesses, and a schedule of exhibits. Tired but ready, the two prosecutors began to cross the central plaza.

"You have to admit, it's a strong case-in-chief," Angela said. "Eddie Hines's eyewitness account, the bootprint on the door, Jeremiah's fights with Ollie Merta, Jeremiah and the Basque shepherd, what Jeremiah told Spiky Samuels."

"It is impressive," Cassie agreed. "But it can be picked apart."

"That's the defense attorney's job, not ours."

"True enough. But as I've been saying all day, if we want to prevail in court, we need to see this from every perspective."

"Every perspective." The notion appeared to pain Angela. "By all means."

Cassie stopped near the plaza's bear fountain. "Just so we don't get blindsided, Angela. For one last time, let's think like a defense attorney. Eddie Hines doesn't have a car, can't find Merta's house. Someone sharp could have a field day with our bootprint experts' flip-flops. The Basque shepherd shooting is remote in time, and it didn't lead to a conviction. What Jeremiah told Spiky Samuels is vague, and Spiky on cross will make Eddie Hines look like Mother Teresa and Einstein combined. That leaves Jeremiah's dustup with Merta two years ago, nice history but hardly evidence beyond a reasonable doubt."

Angela's eyes were roaming the plaza. "Cassie, we've been over all this. You're simply underestimating our case."

"Am I? Look at what Jed told Spiky. It's so general. *Merta's a poacher, Merta had to be stopped.* He could have been talking about their confrontation two years ago. What would be so much more convincing is a narrative of the murders that provides details no one but the killer knows. That's what persuades juries." Cassie hesitated. "That's what persuades me, too."

Angela pointed at a trio of panhandlers kneeling on the far side of the bear fountain. "Look at them. They're flat out intimidating people into giving them money. I'm told they're waving blades when nothing else works. Damn. I'd like to sweep this county clean of such vermin."

Cassie examined the men as they stared back with red, sullen eyes. They weren't unlike some of her past clients. She thought they radiated as much woe as menace. A question occurred to her. "Angela, have you always been this passionate about fighting crime? How did it start for you?"

Angela shrugged. "Where does anything start? From experience, I suppose. From what we learn about the world."

"Experience?"

"Yes."

Cassie sensed that she should ask no more. They began to step away from the bear fountain.

"How about a quick dinner over at the Brewing House?" Angela suggested.

Cassie couldn't hide her surprise. This was unusual from Angela. "Sure. Brewing House sounds great."

They sat in a corner booth, watching the meat-market antics over at the bar, mainly cowhands wooing shop clerks. Each type was strange fruit to the other, so their talk crackled with foreplay. Angela nudged Cassie when one shop clerk with a wristful of bracelets ran her palm along the neck of a wiry, sunburned cowhand. He was backing her against the bar.

"Oh, God," Angela whispered. "You think that's how we're destined to end up? Standing at a bar, pawing men?"

• "We better get some fellows to marry us, I guess."

"Ha. I tried that already. A handy arrangement, except for the problem of pretending to be alive."

Cassie had heard little of Angela's early marriage. "Yes . . . that is a problem, isn't it?"

Angela slid closer to her in the booth. "It's horrible feeling dead. On the other hand, I'm getting kind of allergic to men asking me why I'm single. I tell them that actually, I'm not. I tell them my husband is out in the garage, sharpening a long knife."

Cassie gave a laugh. "I'll have to remember that."

Angela hesitated. "Cassie, have you ever done something just wild and crazy? You know, something you wouldn't want others to know about? Something you should be ashamed about, but aren't really?"

Cassie wondered how to answer. There'd been a prisoner once, a client on death row. The two of them alone in his cell. She trying to reassure him even as she reported that the appellate court had denied them. He clung to her, dark and brooding and full of need. His skin felt hot to her touch. He pulled her to him with such urgency. She stayed with him as he sank onto his cot.

Cassie said, "I'm not sure what you mean, Angela."

"With a man, for instance. Someone you just met."

Cassie watched the cowboy at the bar. She tried to imagine what Angela ever did that was wild and crazy. "No, not someone I just met."

Angela was watching the bar, too. "Cassie, would you call yourself a passionate woman?"

Would she? Cassie couldn't say. She certainly knew enough about unlived passion. That, she suspected, was Angela's true topic.

"Oh, I don't know. It all depends how you define that."

"Exactly. What I mean is—"

Cassie stopped the DA with a hand on her elbow. She pointed across the room. "We're about to have company."

Sheriff's detectives Victor Baynes and Andy Akers were heading toward them. Akers trailed in Baynes's wake, as if covering his back.

"Detectives," Angela called out. "What a surprise."

Baynes looked everywhere but at her. "We've got something to tell you about the Jeremiah case. Something that should help."

Angela said, "Do you, now?"

"Why don't you sit down," Cassie suggested.

The detectives warily lowered themselves into the booth. Angela signaled for a waitress. "What'll you have?" she asked the detectives.

Both wanted Graciosa Brews. Angela ordered a glass of white wine. Cassie asked for hot tea. In the silence that followed, Baynes fiddled with a fork. The DA let him stew for a moment. "Go ahead," she said finally. "Tell us your story."

Baynes cleared his throat, cracked his knuckles. "This is something I thought you already knew. But just now, not more than thirty minutes ago while we were talking to Sheriff Dixon, it came out that this never got into a report. So I—"

"What do you mean by 'this'?" Angela asked. "Let's get to the point, shall we?"

Baynes kept playing with the silverware. "I mean what happened when we were transporting Jed Jeremiah to the grand jury on that first Saturday."

"Yes?" Angela ignored the wine being placed before her. "What happened?"

"Well now." Baynes drew a breath, drained half his beer glass, and sat back in the booth. The brew gave him the nonchalant glow he needed. "Thing is, Jed kept talking to us that day while we were moving around, and waiting in that holding area. He was all shook up. He'd imagined something the night before, he kept telling us. Like a real bad nightmare, except he wasn't asleep, just kind of drifting."

"A nightmare?" Cassie asked.

Baynes nodded. "In his mind, he'd had an image that an old man was trying to kill him."

Angela and Cassie looked at each other. The DA said, "Do go on, Victor."

Baynes revisited his beer glass, then wiped his mouth with the back of his hand. "Yeah. Let's see, where was I?"

"An old man trying to kill Jed," Cassie reminded.

"Oh, yeah. So Jed put his hands around the old man's neck. Behind him, a little girl started screaming. He turned to grab her, but she only screamed more. He put his hands around her mouth, just to silence her. Finally she stopped screaming, so he let her go. She fell to the ground. That was in a corner of a kitchen, Jeremiah said. He went back to the old man. He was lying in a bathroom, sleeping. Jeremiah started out of the house, but it was all on fire now. Jeremiah thought he was trapped. Told us he snapped out of it then. Jumped right off his cot."

Angela and Cassie again looked at each other. They both knew Marilee had been found in the kitchen, Ollie in the bathroom. There was no way Jeremiah could know, though. Unless he were there.

"Victor," Cassie asked, "how come you never mentioned this before now?"

Baynes eyed his empty beer glass with regret. "We did, we told Howie. But not in all this detail, I'm afraid. We just told him Jeremiah had a dream about killing someone. There was no time for more, everyone was in a hurry, there was such a big rush that day, what with the grand jury starting. Dixon told us not to bother with a written report. He'd mention it to Angela when the prisoner got dropped off. Least that's what we thought he said. So we forgot about it. Didn't know what use it would be anyway. Not much, we figured later, since no one ever said anything."

"Not much?" Cassie asked, signaling for a refill of Baynes's glass.

Akers weighed in. "He means legally. In terms of what could be used in the courtroom."

"I see." Cassie turned to Angela. "Did Howie ever mention this to you?"

"Of course not. You think I'd ignore something like that? Jesus, how could Howie drop the ball?"

"That's just it," Baynes said. "That's why we're here. When we were talking to Howie half an hour ago, we brought up Jed's nightmare, asked what had happened with it. This time we told Howie all the details. He nearly shit a brick, if you'll pardon my French. Turns out, way we told it before, he assumed this dream was about the Basque shepherd shooting. He also thought we'd mentioned it to you. Back then, it turns out, he said *we* should tell you, not *he*."

Angela was fuming. "I cannot believe what I'm hearing."

The waitress came with Baynes's refill. He took another long draw. "Neither can Howie. He's so flaming mad at us, he said we had to come tell you about the screwup ourselves."

"God," Angela said. "How utterly pathetic."

Baynes frowned. "Hey now—"

Cassie interrupted. "Why not at least do a written report, Victor? For that matter, why not give Jed a Miranda warning and flip on the tape recorder?"

Baynes's expression turned blank, a mix of beer and caution. "Jed was just talking like usual. Dixon doesn't always want us to do formal Mirandas in that kind of situation."

Angela ran a finger along the edge of her wineglass. "You know, that makes some sense, Cassie. A Miranda could have just shut Jed up. Or say he waives his rights but is all emotional, we could be getting suppressible evidence. Sometimes we prefer just to get them to talk at the grand jury."

"But you didn't do that," Cassie pointed out.

"Of course not. I didn't know about this, remember?"

"Yes, I remember."

"And besides, Howie didn't realize what he had here." Angela grabbed her wine, raised the glass to her lips. "Incredible. This nearly slipped between the cracks."

"Yes," Cassie said. "It nearly did."

"It's the missing element you wanted, Cassie." Enthusiasm was overwhelming Angela's initial dismay. "A narrative that provides details no one else knows, no one but the killer."

Cassie glanced over at the bar. The wiry cowhand was

pressing himself against the shop clerk's ample backside. She was arching, pressing back, rattling her bracelets. Had that girl ever done something wild and crazy? Something she should be ashamed about, but wasn't?

"Like a recovered memory," Cassie said. "How fortunate we are."

Chumash County's solitary courtroom occupied what had been, a century before, the *asistencia*'s modest church. Set in the corners of its oak-paneled atrium were four private alcoves, once havens for prayer, now handy spots for lawyers to thrash out pretrial issues with their clients or adversaries.

In one such alcove early on Monday morning, Cassie Teal sat with Louis Brody, making full and obligatory disclosure about what they now were calling Jed Jeremiah's "daydream." Brody listened politely as she spoke, taking notes. Then he said, "No way, Cassie."

She tried to appear puzzled. "What do you mean, Louis?"

"What do I mean? Here's what I mean. I'll give Stark and your detectives the benefit of the doubt, okay? I'll say that they genuinely believe Jed Jeremiah is guilty. Maybe he is, for that matter. But they're creating evidence. No doubt about it."

"I might say the same if I were the defense attorney, Louis. Still, that's an outrageous claim."

Brody regarded her with sorrow. "Your suspect gives that kind of statement, you bring in cameras, tapes, lights. You ask him about it before the grand jury. You don't forget about it." He shook his head. "No way. It didn't happen."

"I guess that will be up to the jury to decide."

"Maybe the judge." Brody started scribbling a note to himself. "I think I'll make a motion *in limine*. Try for a hearing on whether this should even be admitted at trial."

"There have been so many delays already. Judge Hedgespeth will not be pleased."

Brody stopped writing. "It will be your fault, unless you give up this daydream thing."

"Not a possibility."

"Well, I'll—"

A voice above them interrupted. "Don't let her out-argue you, Louis. She's good at that."

Cassie raised her eyes to Doug Bard. "Not so very good."

Bard studied the two lawyers, sensing something. "What's happened?"

Brody slid over, motioning Bard to sit down. "You could help us, maybe. Something wonderful just came up for the state. It seems that Jeremiah, back during the grand jury transport, told Baynes and Akers about a daydream he had. A dream where he was strangling an old man and little girl in a house all aflame."

Bard sat down, starting to grin. "Very funny."

"No joke," Brody said.

Bard's grin evaporated. "Why haven't we heard about this before now?"

"That's what I was going to ask you." Brody made a show of thumbing through his notes. "I don't recall you ever mentioning this."

"I never did."

"But you worked right alongside Baynes and Akers, didn't you?"

"For a while, yeah. We worked together until I bailed. A task force, you could call it. Desks together in one room. Each morning we shared what was going on."

"You ever hear anything about Jed's daydream?"

Bard was staring at Cassie. "No. Never."

Cassie looked away, scanning the plaza. "You wouldn't, necessarily. You stopped working with them early on. Besides, I don't think they trusted you. You weren't exactly close colleagues."

Bard kept staring at her. "That's right, we weren't."

Brody rose. "We'll have to thrash this out in court, I guess. It's time."

Standing on the steps of the *asistencia,* Doug Bard watched the lawyers file into the building. All 150 spectator seats, he imagined, would be filled in Chumash County's narrow, compact courtroom. Angela and Cassie would take chairs on one side of a single lawyer's table, Louis and Jed on the other. Judge Martin Hedgespeth would enter from a door behind his bench.

There'd be preliminary motions then, maybe a hearing over Jed's daydream. There'd be jury selection. There'd be opening statements. Finally, the march of witnesses. When the defense's turn came, what would Brody do? Bard wished he could see.

He couldn't, though. Brody had reminded him why: He was going to be a witness at this trial, for better or worse. Witnesses can't be in the courtroom except when they're on the stand. Something else he hadn't calculated when he threw his badge at Howie Dixon.

Bard turned away from the *asistencia* and headed for the plaza, walking with his head down, his hands stuffed into the pockets of his leather jacket. Sensing movement, he looked up. On the far side of the plaza, a familiar burly figure was hurrying toward the courtroom.

"Jimmy," Bard called out. "Jimmy O'Brien, you had better not pass me by."

They met in the middle of the plaza. Jimmy glanced at his watch and the entrance to the courtroom.

"They're just doing preliminary motions this morning," Bard said. "You're not missing anything yet."

"But we're the paper of record here. I have to report everything."

"Everything?"

The question appeared to sting Jimmy more than anger him. He forgot about his watch and the courtroom. He took a step closer. "I thought I explained myself, Doug. I'm not the enemy here."

Bard examined Jimmy's broad ruddy face. It occurred to him that friends more than anyone can disappoint. "You're right," he said. "Whatever our differences, we can't afford to be at odds with each other. Neither of us have that many buddies to spare."

Jimmy offered a wicked grin. "I have one or two more than you right now, Doug."

"If you've got even one ally, you're up on me."

"What the hell you doing quitting your job, Doug?"

"So you've heard."

"Of course."

"You didn't put it in the paper."

"I will, though. When you testify, that's what I figured. We call it a news hook."

"We don't have much time. They're flat out framing Jeremiah now. Baynes and Akers have suddenly recalled that Jeremiah told them long ago about a daydream he had. One that sounds a lot like the murders."

"Suddenly recalled?"

"Just in time for the trial."

Jimmy let out a whistle. "They're sure pushing the envelope."

"You might also find a story in Benjamin Mire's exploding furnace."

"I've already tried, believe me. I checked with everyone about Mire's death. Didn't hear a hint of anything bent."

"You wouldn't."

Jimmy glanced over his shoulder at the courthouse door. A pair of sheriff's deputies, Spraker and Ericson, once Doug's fishing buddies, were watching them.

"Come on," Jimmy said. "Let's go sit by the creek."

They walked to the far end of the plaza, filled now in mid-morning with students from Chumash State and mothers pushing strollers. At one bench, a little girl with a blue ribbon and an old man with a gray mustache were tossing bread-crumbs at ducks in the water. At another, a young couple leaned against each other, watching the current. At a third, a man in a brown cardigan sat by himself. Jimmy and Doug passed them by and settled on a grassy berm at the creek's edge.

Jimmy asked, "How you doing, Doug?"

"I could use a paycheck. I want to pay child support even if Sasha doesn't need it. I also want to eat from time to time.

Maybe even stay dry and warm. Other than money, things are fine. Quitting was no big deal. I just didn't want to be part of that stuff anymore."

"What about Molly and Sasha? How's it going with them?"

"It's not. Molly feels let down. Neither want me around. They made that rather clear."

"Jesus."

"Yeah. What the hell, Jimmy."

"Doug . . ." Jimmy hesitated. "I guess one reason I haven't reported your quitting is I thought you'd reconsider. Are you certain you've made the right choice?"

Bard didn't answer for a while. He studied the ducks, then glanced up the creek. The old man and little girl were packing up, getting ready to leave. The young couple were giggling and whispering. The man in the cardigan was staring at something over Bard's head. Doug sensed that cardigan man had just lifted his eyes from them.

"Maybe I haven't," he said. "But it's my choice. Nobody made me do it."

"No regrets?"

"Right now, all I regret is I can't be in the courtroom, sitting beside Louis Brody."

Jimmy looked as if he wanted to say something more, but didn't. He kicked at the ground, sending a mound of pebbles tumbling into the creek. "Suddenly remembering a daydream," he said. "Good God."

"I laughed out loud when they told me. Thought they were joking."

Another kick. More pebbles slid into the creek. "How come Molly's let down?"

"Once again, her father's a quitter. This time, he's not out catching Ollie and Marilee's killer."

"Holy Mary."

"No big deal."

Jimmy stared out over the creek. "You know, Doug, I've got staffing problems. How they expect me to put out a paper with a handful of pea-green kid reporters, I don't know."

Bard turned to him. "What are you saying?"

"Couldn't pay a deputy sheriff's salary. Couldn't make it formal, on the books. But I need a real investigator. A researcher for my reporters."

Bard gave him the lopsided grin. "I think I know one."

"The state calls Professor Roberta Kabal."

Cassie Teal watched the forensic specialist stride to the stand. She was a short, squat woman with the brisk air of one who understood that time was money. Angela had already questioned the other footprint experts. Despite their equivocation and revised judgments, all had survived Louis Brody's cross. We work in increments, they explained. The picture evolves as we assemble data.

It's going well; it's not going well. Even to herself, Cassie Teal couldn't decide how to describe the early stage of Jed Jeremiah's trial. Judge Hedgespeth had quickly rejected Louis Brody's motion to ban Jed's daydream, saying he'd leave it to the jury to figure its veracity. They'd needed only two days to pick that jury, since Hedgespeth had insisted that they do the *voir dire* questioning in panels, six candidates at a time. The opening statements had taken less than a day.

Ladies and gentlemen of the jury, last April 17 started as a normal day for Ollie Merta and Marilee Cooper . . . but it ended as a nightmare, a nightmare that continues today for Marilee's parents.

Angela Stark was in her element before the jury, articulate and focused. She looked each juror in the eye. She spoke with assurance. She told a story rather than argued.

On that day Marilee went to Ollie Merta's for a piano lesson. Her parents were at work, so she stayed awhile, Ollie Merta being her favorite baby-sitter. They may have shared a snack, or shared stories. Then, suddenly, came a horrible noise . . . someone kicking in the front door . . . someone who left a bootprint on that door . . . a bootprint that we will categorically prove was made by the defendant, Jed Jeremiah.

Louis Brody didn't do badly, either, although he couldn't match the sheer drama of Angela's tale.

You just heard a horrible story. You would be inhuman if you weren't affected. But that horrible story is false and misleading. The evidence will prove this beyond a doubt. Please remember, nothing occurs in a vacuum. Chumash County has been agitated, has been eager to see justice done. But it's not justice that we've found. We've found a scapegoat. We've found Jed Jeremiah.

Cassie thought Louis did particularly well with Jed's daydream.

You will hear about a so-called daydream that Jed Jeremiah supposedly told to two detectives. But you know what, folks? These experienced police officers never wrote a report about this daydream. It wasn't revealed until days ago, months after it was supposed to have happened. I think you will conclude it never happened. You're going to hear from former detective Douglas Bard, a man of integrity who retired from the Chumash County Sheriff's Department because he couldn't abide how the case was being handled. He's going to tell you he would have known if there was a daydream. He's going to tell you that the other detectives never once mentioned this to him. He's going to tell you this daydream flat out never happened . . .

At the end, Louis went and stood as close to the jurors as he could. He spoke softly. *Keep an open mind. I beg you, be fair and impartial.*

Not bad, not bad at all.

It wasn't that simple, though.

Cassie knew what had transpired in the moment after Louis sat down. She was sitting directly across the lawyers' table from Jed Jeremiah. She watched him clutch at Louis's sleeve. She heard him whispering. They'd trimmed his beard and wild tangle of hair, but they couldn't wash the unruly cast from his eyes.

I am a guilty man. That's what he'd whispered. *I want to plead guilty.*

A client right up Louis Brody's alley. There Jeremiah was, taking responsibility for his conduct. Just as Louis always preached. Yet Louis hadn't been pleased. Not this time, not this day.

Quiet, he'd muttered. *Don't say another word.*

Jimmy O'Brien was reaching for his second Black Bush when Doug Bard took the stool next to him at JB's. At the piano, Dave Murphy was pounding the keys; at the microphone, his wife Shirley was bawling about love gone wrong. Jimmy waited until they finished before turning to Bard.

"I'd call it a draw so far in the courtroom," he said. "Shame you can't be in there."

"Maybe I should just forget the idea of being a witness."

"You can't, now. Brody mentioned you in his opening argument. 'A man of integrity.' That's what he said. There's my hook. I'm going to put it in the paper."

"How kind of you."

"Just covering the news."

Bard signaled the bartender for a Graciosa Brew. "What else has gone on in there?"

"Opening arguments, then the bootprint experts. That's it."

"Is Angela handling all the questioning for the prosecution?"

"Yep. Why do you ask?" Jimmy squinted at him. "You wondering about Cassie Teal?"

"Just give me the courtroom highlights."

"Other way around. I'm paying you now. Let's hear what you're up to."

"I've been retracing your steps, I guess. Trying to find Benjamin Mire's trail. There's got to be a connection to Ollie Merta."

"Why got to? That assumes Mire was murdered, and by Merta's killer."

"Exactly. You got it."

"But you don't. Not a hint of a connection."

"Only that they were both older men who lived alone and had some sort of income."

"And were into computers."

Bard slowly put down his beer glass. "Say what?"

"Both were into computers. Both had multiple computers hooked up in their homes."

"I knew Merta did, but I never heard anything about Mire."

"That's because you quit the department, Douglas."

"No, they kept me from Mire's house even when I was on the force. I drove out there the day of the fire. Dixon blocked me from going inside. Dixon and Victor Baynes."

"A shame."

"How do you know about the computers?"

"Let's just say the police reports on that case got mislaid for a while. Terribly sloppy."

Both had multiple computers hooked up. Bard toyed with that, but couldn't connect the dots. He turned to the music. Shirley sang and Dave played on. It was past 11 P.M. Bard signaled for another beer. *Multiple computers . . .*

He'd lost the thread, it suddenly occurred to him. Long ago, at Molly's school, the guidance counselor, Sally Dyle, had mentioned Merta's multiple computers. Back then he'd been more interested in what Sally saw running toward the house. Maybe what Sally saw inside the house held greater import.

"Hey—" he began.

The beeping of his pager interrupted him. He squinted at the readout. This time it was Sasha and Molly.

"Excuse me, Jimmy," he said, jumping from his stool. "Got to go."

FOURTEEN

Sasha opened the door at his first knock. Bard glanced left and right as he stepped inside, hand on his pocket. "Ease up," she said. "There's only me and Molly here."

He prowled through the house anyway, unable to sit down. The remnants of Molly's evening were everywhere—a table full of homework, a crumpled bag of cold French fries, a purple Game Boy. Bard turned to Sasha. "So why'd you page me?"

She'd come from the kitchen. She had a dish towel in her hand. She twirled it in the air. "I thought we might sing and dance a little. Throw a CD on, have another party."

"Come on, Sasha."

"Okay." She was squeezing the towel now, wrapping it around her fingers. "I thought the threats would stop after you resigned. They haven't. I found another in our mailbox tonight."

He started toward her but stopped himself. "This one any different from the others?"

Sasha tossed the towel toward the dining-room table. It fell short, landing on an antique English floral rug. "Whoever it is, this person knows Molly's whole schedule."

She pulled a piece of plain white computer paper from her pocket. On it, Bard saw, was Molly's schedule from morning to night. The order of her classes. Recess, lunch. After school dance. Basketball practice. Play dates. Who drives her. Where, when, how. More detail than Bard himself knew.

"How could someone put this together?" he asked.

Sasha lurched at him, her hands clenched. "Someone's watching her, Doug. Someone knows everything."

He wondered what she wanted to do, hit him or hold him. He grasped her wrists. That would be something, first Molly, now Sasha beating on him. He could think of only one question. "Does Molly know?"

"No. I haven't told her." Her fingers uncurled.

"I wish we could leave it that way. But she has to be told. She has to be on guard."

Sasha pulled away from him. "Dear God, Doug. We're going to make our eleven-year-old fear the whole wide world."

He flexed his empty hands. This latest threat made no sense. "I'm off the case, off the force. The trial has started. Jed Jeremiah's halfway to death row. How could I be causing this?"

"What else could it be?"

Bard looked at her. "You tell me."

She sank onto the sofa by the fireplace. "I don't know."

Once again, the sense came over Bard that he long ago had lost the thread. He'd been blocking off what he didn't want to recognize. He no longer knew this woman—this woman who raised Molly, who guided her, who sent her off to school every day.

Molly's worksheets caught his eye. He bent over them, trying to decipher a labyrinth of numbers assembled under two columns. *Associative parameters . . . Commutational parameters.* At eleven, she'd already passed him by in math. He flipped the pages in her notebook until he reached another subject. Here Molly's handwriting filled three sheets. Her composition had a title. *The Melting Ice of Rivertown.* A short story. Molly was writing fiction now.

"Doug." Sasha sounded so faraway. "Did they ever learn anything more about the fire at Benjamin Mire's house?"

"Why do you ask?"

"Can't I wonder?"

"Square with me, Sasha. Let's not play a game. Let's not—"

"Play a game? *Play a game?* Now look—"

The creak of Molly's bedroom door swinging open interrupted them. She came out frowning and rubbing her eyes. A thin white crust had formed at the corners of her mouth. Bard fought the impulse to grab a washcloth and wipe it off.

"What time is it?" she asked. "You guys did it again. You woke me up with all that fighting."

"We weren't fighting," Bard said. "Just talking like old married folks."

"But you two aren't married anymore."

"Habits die hard." Doug settled into an oak rocking chair and held up his arms. "Come here, sweetheart."

She fell into his lap, too sleepy to think of an alternative. He kissed her on each cheek. He ran his hand through her hair. "Did you change your mind about quitting?" she asked, head buried in his chest.

"That hasn't changed, Molly. It's not going to. I couldn't work at the sheriff's anymore because I didn't agree with what they were doing."

"Couldn't you compromise? Like they tell us to do at school on the playground?"

Bard rocked slowly in his chair. "This was a little different situation, Molly. It's more like when I tell you I expect you always to do the right thing."

She thought about that, then said, "Please don't be mad at Mommy. She's just as sad as I am. Mommy really liked Ollie Merta. They were such buddies. They talked all the time. They talked just about every day."

Bard wasn't sure he'd heard Molly correctly. She had such a deadpan delivery with her jokes, he often got tricked. This happened, that happened, she narrating with fraudulent aplomb. So wide-eyed and cunning at once, so innocent and aware. His daughter was always a silent witness, absorbing them.

"What's that you say, Molly girl?"

"I said, Mommy and Ollie were really close buddies."

She meant it. Bard kept rocking. He glanced at Sasha. She was studying her hands. He turned back to Molly. "How close, sweetheart? What do you mean?"

"Ollie came to dinner almost every Sunday night, Daddy. They stayed up late talking. One time, Mommy visited him in the hospital when he was sick. Ollie mattered so much to her."

Back and forth, back and forth. He swayed in rhythm. It was true, he no longer knew Sasha. Time had worked its magic.

Bard's arms tightened around his daughter. He fought the impulse to rise and rush with her to his car. "Back to bed now, Molly girl. You've got school tomorrow. I promise, no more fighting. We'll keep it quiet."

He stood up with Molly cradled in his arms and stepped toward her bedroom. He could still do that. *I'll carry you until I can't anymore.* That's what he always promised her. Gently, he lowered her onto her bed.

"Daddy," she whispered, "I wish we all could be together during this."

He kissed her cheek. "Me, too. You're my special girl."

Sasha was standing near the phone when he came back into the living room. He didn't think there'd been time for a call. He hadn't heard anything. "Shall we begin?" he asked.

They settled before the fireplace. Bard thought Sasha looked relieved. Either that, or simply fatigued. It must have taken so much energy, he imagined, to keep everything to herself.

"Ollie worked for you, Sasha?"

"Yes." She hesitated. "From home, on his computers. He could follow everything for me, trading and investing. He was a master in the commodities markets, particularly. The Chicago Mercantile. You have no idea how many Chumash County citizens care about the price of hay and livestock."

"Why hay?"

"If you had no rain for months and a few hundred head of cattle to feed, you'd care, too."

"Why not tell me this before?"

Sasha looked blankly at him. She had no answer.

"You're scared about something, Sasha. You've got to tell me. If not for yourself, for Molly."

Sasha's head rolled back on the sofa. "I don't sleep at night anymore, Doug. You should see me. What a sight. Wandering down the hallways, staring out windows."

"We should be together right now. It would help us all. This house is rattling you. Come stay with me, Sasha. You and Molly."

For an instant, he thought she might say yes. She looked as if she wanted to. Instead she said, "Come on, Doug, you know I have never wanted to depend on you."

"That I know."

She was wiping her eyes. "Poor Molly. Poor Marilee. Poor Ollie."

"Talk to me, Sasha."

"Talk to you? That would just make matters worse. We need to leave things be. *You* need to leave things be."

"That's something I've never been good at."

"No, you haven't."

"Sasha, you're in my world now, not yours. You need to trust me for once."

"I used to, Doug."

"Try again."

"That's not so easy. Those days are long gone."

"Forget the nostalgia, then. Just tell your story."

She examined his face. Her hand rose slowly. She touched his cheek, the way she used to. "My dearest Bard. I'm so sorry."

He reached up, lifted her hand off his face. "Your story, Sasha."

She curled her hand around his, refusing to let go.

"God, Doug. I look inside myself sometimes and see ice-cold steel. It scares me. Have I become that bad?"

"I don't know, Sasha. You tell me."

She stared at their entwined fingers, this enforced union. "Okay, I will."

She'd started Lillo, Inc., with just a few dozen accounts, mainly older folks with more land than cash. She put them into REITs and Ginnie Maes at first. Eventually, she edged them into consolidated pools that were buying up options on farmland at the fringes of Central Coast towns such as La Graciosa. In time, the San Francisco venture capitalists saw what Sasha was up to. RC Cummings called, wanting to anoint her their local face along the Central Coast. It was a big break for her. RC Cummings's clients included lots of old-money folks who wanted to invest in tangibles, not high tech. Central Coast farmland qualified as a tangible. Investment capital began flowing from RC Cummings through Lillo to Chumash County—seed money for the revitalized ranches, the luxury condos, the new retail centers. Lillo had just a small finger in the pie, but it was a large pie. Lillo prospered. Sasha prospered.

"It's what I always wanted, Doug. It's where I was headed when I met you, before I got pregnant. I gave it up. Now I was getting a second chance."

"And then something happened?"

"Yes."

"What, Sasha?"

"Ollie was always so diligent. Ollie was always staring at his computer screens."

"Go on."

Sasha spoke now as if reciting a lesson. After a while, RC Cummings started having Lillo handle various security transfers. It all seemed fine, until Ollie came to her one day. He'd noticed something odd—a series of puzzling commodities trades that RC Cummings had instructed Lillo, Inc., to execute on behalf of certain shared clients. Options trades involving grain and cattle that were obviously disadvantageous to those clients. Options trades that bordered on the irrational.

Reserves in grain and livestock are at a seven-year high, Merta told Sasha. But still we're doing options at incredibly inflated prices. It doesn't make sense. There's something fishy here.

Merta had spelled out all the details in a five-page memo. He pulled it from his frayed canvas briefcase.

I wish to emphasize that I do not believe anyone in your office is doing anything deliberately wrong . . . I am afraid I have to say that they simply don't understand what it is they are doing . . .

Merta, as always, had been diplomatic. He never raised his

voice or pointed fingers. He also never told Sasha what she should do.

"What was RC Cummings up to?" Bard asked. "Why the strange trades?"

"I think they were trying to manipulate commodities prices, corner part of the market. That's not uncommon. But this time, it was at clients' expense."

"What did you do?"

Sasha took the question as an accusation. "It's so easy to say, do the right thing, Doug. But life is more complicated than that. RC Cummings was my way in. They put me on an exclusive playing field with its own rules. You violate those rules, you're out of the game."

"I can imagine."

"You can imagine." She sounded doubtful. "I couldn't bear the notion, Doug. Perhaps you can. We're different in that way."

"So you put Merta off. You did nothing."

"Please understand. It's possible that the RC Cummings trades were fancy high-wire acts but totally legit."

"Is that how you figured it?"

"Yes, Doug. That's how I figured it."

"End of the story?"

"No, Doug, you will be happy to know that's not the end of the story."

He waited, saying nothing. Sasha continued.

"Weeks pass, maybe three months or so. One day, my contact at RC Cummings calls with a special request. As a favor to a private client, they want me to backdate certain nonexistent transactions, on my letterhead. My contact says, 'Do me this great favor.' That's what Albert asks."

"Albert?"

"Albert Donner, their executive VP."

"What was he up to?"

"To this day, I'm not sure."

"What did you do this time?"

"What did I do?" Sasha slowly raised a fist in the air. "You'd be so proud of me, Doug. Even though it almost put me out of business, I turned him down."

She told Merta about the request. Over one long weekend, they analyzed their options. Merta followed with another memo. *As you know, I was disturbed even before about RC Cummings's pattern of trading. I then became persuaded, when they sent us this request, that my suspicions were correct.* They agreed she couldn't comply. She called Albert Donner, told him no dice. Donner didn't like that. He tried again. She held firm. After a week, Donner finally backed off.

He did more than back off. He, and all of RC Cummings, fell silent. Lillo, Inc.'s, business with them dried up. Almost overnight, a new investment boutique sprang up in La Graciosa. The new boutique started handling RC Cummings's business. Sasha found herself pushed nearly to bankruptcy. For a good half year, she struggled to keep afloat.

"Then Ollie Merta called me one afternoon. He'd discovered new information. He had another memo to give me. Could he come by the next day?"

"What did he have?" Bard asked.

"I don't know. I never learned."

"Why not?"

Sasha didn't answer right away. Her fingers, sliding along the sofa, brushed his arm. "That evening," she said. "After he called . . . That was the evening of the house fire."

Bard watched her. The Sphinx was trembling. "You must have been so scared. Ever since. All this time."

His words, an invitation, were silently accepted. Sasha leaned toward him, then sank into his arms. Doug held her. He'd not done that for years. They sat without speaking for a long while. He weighed what he knew, what he might not know. Sometime during the night, a question occurred to him. "Sasha, the second fire victim, Benjamin Mire, did he also do some trading for Lillo?"

He could feel her breathing. "No," she said. "But he knew Ollie. They played checkers together once or twice."

A remote connection, but there it was.

They lapsed back into silence. Holding her felt strange and familiar at once. In a drawer somewhere, he had a letter she'd written near the end. *I feel so alone when you're not close to me . . . I want to be back in your arms again feeling loved and secure.* Funny thing was, he couldn't recall her ever before seeking such succor. Near dawn, he asked, "What happened to your business, Sasha? You don't look like someone in bankruptcy."

She roused herself, sat up. "I'm not. Not long after Ollie died, the new competition folded. RC Cummings started doing business with me again. Truth is, I'm flourishing. We may end up owning a piece of a communications satellite."

They looked at each other across a vast ravine. Bard struggled to understand her. Also to divine the truth. "You conceded?" he asked. "Climbed on their bus?"

"Not at all, Doug. I simply pointed out how much I knew of their game. How preferable it would be if we were on the same team. How there'd be no need then to betray confidences."

Bard whistled. "You are something, Sasha. What balls. My lady of the canyon."

"It's a rough and tumble world. You have to identify a company's needs if you want their business."

Pride showed in her cool gray eyes. She saluted herself again with a raised fist.

Such a tough, accomplished woman. Just what she had wanted to become.

"Sasha, who else knows this story? I mean, among those who are still alive?"

"Only me."

Softly Bard said, "I wish you didn't."

FIFTEEN

Jimmy O'Brien vainly tried to smell the money in the room where he sat. All he saw were young men and women gliding silently across a thick carpet, on their way to meetings or their offices. Some were holding documents by their fingertips, as if they were fragile finds from an archaeological dig. Everyone spoke in low monotones. Not a soul displayed anything close to emotion. The notion here, Jimmy imagined, was to project a mastery of yourself at all times. If you raised your voice, you'd be looked at as some kind of deviant.

"I don't see blood on anyone's hands," he said.

At his side, Doug Bard shifted restlessly. "You wouldn't. I've never seen such a bloodless place."

They were sitting in RC Cummings's reception area, waiting for Albert Donner. They'd spent half a day driving up California's winding Highway 1 to San Francisco. They'd chosen the long scenic route so they could satisfy Jimmy's desire to stop at Duarte's Tavern in Pescadero for crab cioppino and ollieberry pie. I can die and go to heaven now, Jimmy kept exclaiming as he wiped his plate.

Hours had passed since then. "It's nearly six," Jimmy pointed out. "Donner is keeping us waiting."

"Why am I not surprised?"

The walls at Royce-Conner were covered with a gray and burgundy fabric. The furniture was glass and stainless steel. In one corner, a bank of clocks showed the time in eight different zones. Bard watched the second hands jerk along their circular routes. There was a risk to Sasha, coming here. But if it was RC Cummings stalking her, she already faced that risk. Better to find out—and to convince them that she didn't have Merta's memo. Bard meant to call off the dogs, or at least find out whose they were.

"Mr. Bard? Mr. O'Brien?"

They looked up into the smooth-skinned face of a man who appeared to be no more than thirty-five. He was wearing a blue blazer without a tie, dark khakis, penny loafers. He was not large, but looked as if he lifted weights in a gym. His neck was a little too thick for his body.

"I'm Albert Donner. Sorry to keep you waiting. Come this way. We'll grab the conference room. Can I get you anything?"

Jimmy wanted coffee. Doug wanted water. Donner fussed over their requests, rushing to track down a secretary. Then he joined them at a large oval table. They were in Embarcadero Four, a high-rise on Sacramento Street. The Bay Bridge and San Francisco skyline loomed out a big picture window. Bard wondered what Donner made in a year, what he was worth. And what, if anything, Sasha saw in him.

"To repeat what we agreed to on the phone," Donner began. "This is an off-the-record background conversation. You want some he!p deciphering certain events in Chumash County. I have agreed to help if I can, but only for your understanding, not a news story."

"That's the deal," Jimmy said.

"And Mr. Bard here, he works for you now? He no longer is a sheriff's detective?"

"Correct," Bard said.

Donner drummed the table with his fingers. "Don't misunderstand my cooperation, guys. This is in our self-interest, you know. We normally wouldn't let you through the front door. But the notions that apparently are floating around, they're so misguided. It benefits us to correct inaccuracies."

"Benefits us, too," Bard said.

Donner glanced at his watch. "Okay, fellows, fire away. What can I tell you?"

Bard dealt only the few cards he wanted to show. He left out the strange commodities trades and the request for Lillo,

Inc., to backdate nonexistent transactions. Instead he vaguely mentioned Ollie Merta's discovery of "certain unknown information" about RC Cummings. From there he went to Ollie Merta's undelivered memo, Ollie Merta's death, and the threats to Sasha and Molly. He arrived finally at Lillo, Inc.'s rise and fall and rise again.

"So much to understand," he said. "So much to wonder about."

Donner had been taking notes as Bard talked. Now he studied them, chuckling at one point, scribbling something in the margin at another. He looked up. "You have such rich imaginations. Incredible, really. You've been watching too many movies. Or whatever you do down there on the Central Coast."

"Maybe we can take this point by point," Bard suggested. "Instead of jumping to the overview."

Donner nodded, seized by a thought. "So you're Sasha's husband?"

"Ex."

"You've drawn this stuff from Sasha?"

Bard leaned across the table. "Let me make something clear, Donner. Sasha has told me nothing about her business with you. She doesn't know about this visit. She doesn't have the memo. She doesn't know what's in the memo. Whoever is threatening her now has targeted the wrong person."

Donner said, "Tell me, Bard. Is that why you've really come up here? To wave us off Sasha?"

"It's one reason, among others."

Donner broke into a grin. "You guys have this all wrong. We're venture capitalists here. We may be rather aggressive in our business. We may push the envelope as far as we can on regulations. We may even break off relations with a company like Lillo if they don't see things our way. But please understand, gentlemen. We have a taste for making money, not killing people or stalking our colleagues. Which, I take it, is what you're suggesting."

"Ollie Merta had learned something," Bard pointed out.

"He'd written a memo. Maybe it would have affected your ability to make money."

Donner shook his head. "I don't think so. There's nothing in our closet that our high-priced attorneys can't solve. That's what lawyers are for."

"They can't solve everything," Bard said, knowing he was fishing. "Maybe Merta was something they couldn't solve."

"Something they couldn't solve?" Donner found that amusing. "How about something they never knew about?"

"What do you mean?" Jimmy asked.

Donner looked back and forth at them. "Don't you see what you've failed to consider?"

Silence. The visitors waited. "Okay," Donner said. "Let me give you a hint. When did you find out Ollie Merta was working for Sasha?"

Bard glanced at Jimmy. "Just the other day."

Donner nodded. "It wasn't common knowledge, was it? No one knew?"

"Right," Bard allowed.

"Which is exactly my point. RC Cummings couldn't have had a beef with Ollie Merta, because we didn't even know the man existed, let alone that he worked for Sasha. We certainly didn't know about any memo. First I heard about all this was when you called the other day."

"But how—" Bard began.

Donner kept going. "That's why I welcomed you fellows up here. You piqued my interest with that talk of a memo. I'd love to see it, to tell you the truth. If ever you find it."

Bard fought a sharp, rising dread. Had he just put Sasha in more danger? He'd assumed Donner knew of Merta, knew that Merta worked for her. That much had seemed evident. What to do now? In his mind, Bard ran through Donner's story, searching for a soft spot.

"Okay, then," he said. "How come you cut things off with Sasha, then reconnected after Merta died?"

"We're a business. We do what's best for us at any one time. Sasha had some problems handling our needs, so we turned to others. They proved even less satisfactory, so we came back to her. We worked out the problems. The timing had nothing to do with Merta. Remember, we didn't know about Merta."

Bard knew Donner was lying, knew they'd rehired Lillo, Inc., because Sasha had them all by the short hairs. Yet he longed for confirmation. "When you say 'worked out the problems,' do you mean Sasha agreed to play it your way?"

Appreciation showed in Albert Donner's eyes. "No, not at all. I think it's more accurate to say we both agreed to play together."

She came to him now under cover of dark, winding her way through Apple Canyon while most of the county slumbered. It was near midnight on Saturday night, one week into Jeremiah's trial. Cassie Teal knew she could no longer be seen with Doug Bard. Yet he'd summoned her. So here she was, bound for his lost cabin in the woods.

The sound of tires on the gravel driveway brought him to the front door. He stood waiting for her, a shadowy outline backlit by his fireplace's faint yellow glow. Neither was sure how to greet the other. They'd not been alone together since the night on her deck.

"Thanks for coming," Bard said, reaching for her.

She held him off. "I don't know why I'm here."

"I'll explain."

They sat in the corduroy-covered chairs near his fireplace. She was wearing baggy dungarees and a sweatshirt. Bard couldn't help but think of her that other night, pulling open her robe.

"I know why Ollie Merta was killed," he said.

"Doug, the trial has started. I'm part of the prosecution team. Talk to the defense."

"I'll get to Brody. But first, I want you to hear this. I want you to see what you're involved in."

Cassie stared at the fire. "I think I know."

"Maybe you don't."

Bard gave her as much of the story as he saw fit. Lillo and RC Cummings. Merta's notice of the funny options trades. The request to obscure certain big land purchases. Sasha's refusal to cooperate. Lillo's plunge into near bankruptcy. Merta's phone call about new information. Merta's death. Lillo's rebound. Bard left out only Sasha's collapse into his arms, and the long night he spent holding her.

"Merta had another memo for Sasha," he concluded. "He wanted to come by the next day and give it to her."

Despite herself, Cassie was drawn in. "She never saw that memo?"

Bard wondered how to answer. In truth, he knew only what Sasha told him. That he didn't fully trust her was not something he wished to share with Cassie.

"No one has it. Unless Vic Baynes and Andy Akers found it." Bard paused. "Or unless it's sitting in the prosecution file."

Cassie looked as if she also wanted to take fists to him. "It's not in our office, Doug. Just what kind of lawyer do you think I am?"

"A prosecutor. At least for the moment."

"For always, Doug. I'm not going to resign. I'm not going to—"

She stopped.

"To quit? Is that what you were going to say, Cassie? To quit, like I did?"

Cassie threw up her hands in exasperation, but rose and came to him. She sat on the arm of his chair, her arm around his shoulder, her hand on his neck. "Okay, yes, Doug, that's what I was going to say."

"Fine . . . fine."

Her fingers caressed his face. "I can do better from the inside, Doug."

He took her hands. "Then go do that. Go tell your boss why Ollie Merta was killed."

"What am I to say? For that matter, what are you saying? That a hotshot San Francisco venture capitalist firm offed Merta to hide some funny bookkeeping?"

"No, I don't think so. Not the company."

"Who then? And for what reason?"

"I don't know exactly. Those options trades and the back-dating weren't what needed silencing. If they were, Sasha could have been the target. It's whatever Merta learned beyond that. It's whatever he put in his memo."

"So who's got the memo, Doug? Where to find it?"

Bard forced himself to answer. "I think Sasha may have a copy. I think Sasha possibly got it from Merta before he was killed."

"That's why she and Molly are being threatened?"

In a way, he'd like to think it was true. Then their peril wouldn't be his fault. "I don't know, Cassie. I can't say."

She took her time. Bard watched her. It was hard to imagine that he once disdained this woman.

"It's so wild," she said. "With what you have, there's no way to see a pattern, no way to make this hold up in court. It looks like a classic example of what defense attorneys do when they don't have the facts or law on their side. They obscure and distract."

"It's something a jury should know."

"You're being naive about the law, Doug. There's lots of things juries are kept from knowing. Verdicts are never based on the whole story."

"Aren't prosecutors officers of the court? Defense attorneys have to do whatever's needed for their client. But I thought prosecutors were obliged to seek truth and justice."

"My dear sweet Doug. Surely you know that truth and justice, like everything else, depends on your perspective."

"Why not see if Angela—"

"Look, Doug. I doubt very much that Angela Stark will want to muddy the waters before her jury. Give them a simple story, told simply. That's always her strategy."

"Okay then, I'll follow your advice. I'll share this with Louis Brody. Jimmy O'Brien, too. We'll see how they play it."

Cassie started to respond but didn't. She rose, went to the

fireplace, stared at the flames. "Hold off on them, Doug. Let me talk to Angela."

"Only if you do it right away."

"By Monday."

"A deal."

They each hesitated now, not sure where else to go. Cassie stayed in front of the fire. Watching her, he recalled again that night on her deck. The feel of her skin under his fingers, the pressure of her legs, the way she breathed.

"Only for tonight," Bard said. "That's what you told me at your house."

"You asked if I was with you."

"Limits on that?"

"Yes."

"So now it would be sleeping with the enemy?"

She smiled faintly. "Or we could abstain."

"What a shame."

"Yes."

Bard started toward her, then stopped. He no longer could put off telling her what he'd just learned that morning. "Cassie . . . Molly and Sasha have been threatened again. Someone knows Molly's schedule minute by minute. So they don't want to be alone. They're going to move in here for a while."

Cassie reached for a poker and fussed with the logs. "It sounds like a wise idea."

"Yes . . . but I—"

"The only solution," Cassie continued. She turned to the door. He followed her out to her car.

"When will we get together again?" Bard asked.

"I don't think that will be possible, Doug. Your cabin here has been the only safe place to meet. Now it's off-limits. Wouldn't you agree?"

In the late-night dark, the television monitor flickered, throwing off light as if it were a fireplace. Angela Stark, seated on the edge of a couch in her living room, reached for her remote control. She pressed reverse. She wanted to watch this again.

I can't stand this anymore. I want it over, I want out.

Jed Jeremiah, on one side of a conference table, was talking to Louis Brody. His voice had an odd cadence, as if he were praying to himself. Louis sat perfectly still.

Out from what, Jed?

From this goddamn trial . . . from this goddamn world.

What are you saying?

I want to plead guilty.

Security reasons—that's how Angela justified the miniature videotape camera that sat hidden in the ceiling of the jailhouse conference room. Each day, dangerous criminals, many violent, were left alone in there with unarmed lawyers. If anyone got hurt, it would be the county's responsibility. The camera was needed for monitoring purposes. The videotapes just provided backup. You could never use them in court, of course. Still, they helped.

Plead guilty of what, Jed? Are you prepared to accept responsibility for what happened in Ollie Merta's home?

I already have, Brody.

Jed, are you truly guilty?

Hell, yes. I'm guilty of every goddamn thing I've ever done. Now come on, Jed—

I'm evil, Brody. Jeremiah leaned across the table, his face inches from his lawyer's. *Don't you see? People have died because of me.*

Brody pulled back. *Jed, try to settle down. What's going on with you?*

Jed showed a double row of crooked teeth. *You never really know what's going on with me.*

Angela hit the pause button and studied Jeremiah's face. His eyes seemed portals into a tortured animal more than the soul of a man. Those who would defend Jeremiah, they should see this face.

"Angela, what are you watching?"

Stark looked up at Bruce Hightower.

"Oh, it's you, Bruce . . . You startled me."

Hightower glanced at the TV screen. Jed Jeremiah's face loomed there, frozen in a twisted grin. "What's that?"

She reached for the remote, hit the stop button, then power off. "Just reviewing something for the trial."

Hightower took the remote from Angela's hand and punched PLAY. Jeremiah's face again filled the screen.

Can you get me out of here, Brody?

I'm going to try. I can't promise any client more than that.

Then let's cut the crap. Let's get this over with.

When you plead, it's to get something less than a death sentence, Jed. That's how it works. But they won't deal.

I want to plead anyway. I'd rather hang than stay in this concrete cave another day.

Don't say that, Jed.

Why not? At least then, I control my destiny.

Hightower hit the pause button. "I don't understand, Angela. Where did this tape come from?"

"Don't worry, Bruce. I'm just doing what's needed. I want that man to pay for what he's done."

"Are you having problems with Jeremiah? I thought you said this case was a lock."

"It is. I just wanted to look at the killer's face." She gave him a playful look. "It focuses my attention."

He didn't respond. He kept watching her.

"Can you understand?" she asked.

Still, he didn't answer. He turned to Jed's image on the TV screen. "What are murderers like, Angela?"

The monitor's glow left her face half-lit, half in shadow. "What do you imagine they're like? They're deranged. Think about it, Bruce. The idea of intentionally killing another human being, it just can't come from someone normal. If it could . . . why, what does that tell us about ourselves?"

Hightower's eyes stayed on the screen. "Makes it hard to idealize human nature, doesn't it?"

She smiled faintly. "A lawyer is never far from evil."

She reached up, unbuttoned his shirt, ran her hand along his chest. "You're the antidote to all that."

He pulled away from her touch. "Angela, we need to talk."

She tried not to show anything—above all, her deep sadness. "Okay, Bruce."

"Sit down," he said.

She sank onto the edge of the couch. She gazed up at him. He was looking at her now, for just this moment, as he had at the start, when he made her the center of the universe.

"What are we going to rock now, Bruce? All of California? The U.S. of A.? The great wide world?"

"Angela."

"Or maybe our boat. I guess it's time to rock our boat."

He clapped his hands, to either quiet her or get himself going. "Angela, I think we've gotten too intense together. I think we need to cool things."

She could hardly hear him over the roar in her ears.

"What do you mean, Bruce? How could we be too intense?"

"There are ways."

"Yes, I suppose there are."

"A hiatus. That's what I have in mind. Time for each of us to get perspective, take a breath."

"I think that's a good idea, Bruce."

He'd expected a different kind of response from her, she could see that. He hesitated, then came to her. He draped an arm around her shoulder, in the way he'd done so many times before. "It's my fault, Angela. Problems I'm having. Baggage I'm carrying. You're one of a kind. What can I say?"

She had an effect on him still, she could see that, too. She had mastery. She spoke quietly, matching his tone. "What can you say, Bruce?"

Louis Brody rose slowly, lost in thought. At the lawyers' table, he thumbed through a pile of documents. A handful of loose papers fell to the floor. Leaning over, he scooped them up. Beside him, Jed Jeremiah watched. Across the table, so did Cassie Teal and Angela Stark. For a moment, Cassie's and Jed's eyes met.

"Defendant is present, counsel are present," Judge Martin Hedgespeth called out from the bench. "Good morning."

Brody looked up from his pages. "Good morning."

Angela Stark said, "Good morning."

Hedgespeth, a fixture for three decades in Chumash County, was neither high-minded nor a rogue. His prime concern was always to keep his courtroom moving, preferably toward a verdict that wouldn't get overturned. He was a politician at heart, more suited for the smoky backrooms of the state legislature than a law library. At seventy-two, he was still wiry, compact, buoyant, and ever on alert for the will of the voters.

Hedgespeth nodded at Brody. "I understand there's a matter you want to place on the record before the jurors are brought out."

"That's right. Yes, Your Honor. Let me explain this in order, if I may. The state's next witness is Mr. Spiky Samuels. Mr. Samuels was interviewed this morning by Ms. Stark, and then Ms. Stark stepped out of the lockup room and announced that Mr. Samuels didn't wish to speak with me. I asked for a chance to hear Mr. Samuels tell me that himself. Ms. Stark refused. So Ms. Stark and I argued. I tried—"

"What's your point, Mr. Brody?" Hedgespeth was glancing at the wall clock.

"My point is that Supreme Court Rule 415 is quite clear on this. The prosecution cannot in any way impede, can't urge a witness not to talk to us. That's impermissible. We want the court to bar the testimony of this witness as a result, because of the conduct of Ms. Stark, which is inexcusable and in violation of Supreme Court Rule 415—"

"Excuse me, Your Honor." Angela Stark was on her feet. "Before he argues his point, could we have him finish his narrative, for the record?"

"Yes," Hedgespeth said. "Fine."

Brody didn't look as if he wanted to. "Well, the next thing that happened, Judge, was that Ms. Stark did invite me in to see Mr. Samuels."

"And what did Mr. Samuels tell you?" Angela asked, taking over the interrogation.

"Mr. Samuels indicated he didn't want to talk to me," Brody allowed.

Angela said, "Surprise."

"But they coached him," Brody argued. "That's obvious."

It was Monday morning. The state had already put the bootprints into evidence. Now they were about to produce the crowning blows: First, Jed's tirade against Merta, courtesy of Spiky Samuels; then, Jed's daydream, courtesy of Baynes and Akers. If Brody had much hope of saving Jeremiah, he had to block these two statements.

"I take exception to the implication that I prevented access," Angela said. "There was nothing improper that happened, and I wish the record to so state."

Hedgespeth again glanced up at the wall clock. "All right now. We need to proceed. Both sides have placed on record their particular points. Mr. Brody, you did get in to see Samuels. I don't see evidence that the state blocked you in any way. The motion by defense to exclude will be denied."

Brody flipped through his documents. Hedgespeth fingered his gavel. Jed Jeremiah made a grunting noise and extended a long leg into the aisle.

"The next matter we have," Brody said, "is also a motion to exclude this witness Spiky Samuels. It's based on his past conduct in another courtroom. He's done this before, Your Honor. When he was in jail three years ago over in El Nido County, he came up with something about another prisoner's case so as to get leniency."

"Hold on now." Angela Stark was back on her feet. "Spiky Samuels's conduct elsewhere, on other matters in other jurisdictions, is not relevant. It's not part of this case, it can't be used or introduced in any fashion—"

"It's in the public record," Brody argued. "At his burglary trial three years ago, Spiky wrote a letter to his brother, telling him what he was going to do." Louis plucked a sheet from his file. Bard had found this and slipped it to him. "Here it is. 'In order to beat the case we have to have stories to give them about someone else . . .' That's what he wrote."

"Now wait," Angela said. "I'm familiar with this matter. Back at that trial, Samuels denied even writing that letter. That's also in the public record."

"But we can prove—"

"What's happening," Angela continued, "is that Mr. Brody is trying to set up a situation totally unrelated to this case. I can see where he's going. If he can't exclude Samuels, he'll wave this letter at him on the stand. He'll try to impeach Samuels with it. But he wouldn't be impeaching anything that Samuels says on the stand today. It would have nothing to do with today's testimony. I maintain he cannot do that. That is impeachment on a collateral issue. That is impeachment based on proof of something he did on a former occasion."

The judge asked, "Would the state like to make a counter motion?"

Angela jumped at the invitation. "Yes. The state moves to exclude this supposed letter they say Samuels wrote years ago. I object to its production at this trial."

Hedgespeth nodded at Brody. "It does seem to be collateral, doesn't it, Counselor?"

Brody stood silent. For an instant, Cassie thought he wasn't going to reply. Then he approached the bench.

"Your Honor," he said, "I'm perfectly aware of the legal arguments about collateral evidence, but I'd like to offer a different sort of argument. Permit me to be simple-minded about this. The state has elected to call a guy who is a liar, and it just seems to me that we ought to be able to show that to the jury. He's created a pattern of lying, where he lies in order to save his own skin. He knows how to manipulate the system by lying, and we ought to be entitled to present that to this jury. I mean, that's a real simple-minded thought, I guess, but that is just the truth, Your Honor."

Brody turned and sat down. The judge rubbed his temples. He wasn't terribly happy to be caught in the crossfire between these two lawyers. The legal issue they were arguing was tangled, full of potholes. Wherever he landed, some appellate panel would likely slap his knuckles. Yet he had to land somewhere.

"Okay now," Hedgespeth began. "After having heard argument of counsel, I'll say this. Mr. Brody, I do like your idea of looking at matters simply. Often I wish it could be done that way. However, the law is far from simple." He stopped, wrote a note to himself. "I find that the material about past events is collateral and does not go to a material issue in the case, so is not admissible. State's motion to exclude the letter is granted. Defense's motion to exclude Spiky Samuels's testimony is denied."

"Thank you, Judge," the DA said.

Hedgespeth regarded her without enthusiasm. "Just to satisfy myself, Ms. Stark, I'd like to ask you something."

"Yes, Your Honor."

"Is there a deal here? Have you ever said a word to Spiky Samuels about putting in a good word for him at his sentencing hearing?"

"No sir, never." Angela was looking right at the judge.

"Did the question or issue of Samuels's sentencing come up in any conversation between Samuels and you?"

"Never."

"What about Samuels and Ms. Teal?"

Cassie, taking notes, froze in midsentence. Angela was turning her way, so was the judge. She rose slowly, and spoke with care. "I think the issue may have come up once."

Angela, her back to the bench, stared at Cassie.

Hedgespeth asked, "And your response, Ms. Teal?"

Cassie could feel Louis Brody's eyes on her. Jed Jeremiah's, too. She gripped the edge of the lawyers' table. "I told Mr. Samuels there could be no deal. I told him that we absolutely couldn't promise him any special treatment."

Angela Stark paced across Cassie Teal's office. Cassie watched from the conference table, where she sat picking at a salad. Court had recessed for lunch after two hours of Spiky Samuels's testimony. It had been a helpful two hours for the state.

"Good thing we managed to get Spiky up there on the stand," Angela said. "Thanks for your support, Cassie. You showed me a lot today. It's greatly appreciated."

Cassie put her fork down. The salad tasted bitter and oily. "What is it we do, Angela? I mean, what do lawyers do?"

Angela stopped pacing. "Oh, God. Let's not go there."

"I need to."

"Come on, Cassie. It's an old story. What we do is shaped by who pays us, what our client wants. Our client happens to be the citizens of Chumash County."

"We're all hired guns, in other words. Willing and ready to take any position."

"You're just realizing that, Cassie?"

"It's hard to stomach sometimes. God, Angela. As spinners, lawyers beat politicians hands down. We change stories, we change sides—"

"And it's not only okay," Angela said, "it's an ethical obligation."

Cassie looked up at her. "There's something I need to tell you. Something that may put a whole new slant on things."

The DA winced, as if kicked in the shins. She sat down next to Cassie. "Here we go again. What do you have?"

Cassie steeled herself. There was no way to bring this up without mentioning how she'd heard of it. Yet there was no way not to bring it up. "I've learned of a possible motive why Ollie Merta was killed. A motive that has nothing to do with Jed Jeremiah."

"What are you talking about?"

Cassie spoke slowly now, reciting. "It turns out Ollie Merta worked out of his house for Sasha Bard's investment boutique. He noticed some funny business going on at RC Cummings, that venture capitalist firm. He did some research, he learned something. He was about to deliver a memo to Sasha Bard when he died in the fire."

She waited for Angela's response. There wasn't one, though. The DA reached for a glass of water. She lifted it to her lips. She sipped. She said, "And your point, Cassie? Are you suggesting that RC Cummings had Merta killed?"

Cassie's question exactly, to Doug.

"No, that doesn't seem likely. I'd vote instead for whoever was the subject of Ollie's memo. Maybe a rogue employee? It's what Ollie put in that memo that got him killed."

"If it even exists."

"What do you mean?"

"How'd you come up with all this, Cassie? What's it based on?"

Here it was, unavoidable. "From Doug Bard. He got it from Sasha."

Angela looked more disappointed than angry. "I see. You're consulting with Bard now?"

"He came to me with the information. He asked that I convey it to you."

"You say he got it from Sasha?"

"Yes."

"Does Sasha have the memo?"

"No."

"How can you be sure?"

"It was pretty clear Doug hadn't seen it. He thought maybe we had it."

"Maybe Sasha hasn't shared it with him."

"No, I doubt she'd keep that from Doug."

Angela rose and resumed her pacing. "I question the veracity of this whole tale, Cassie. You should, too. You're supposed to be providing us the defense perspective, remember? Well, think. This is a classic case of defensive distraction. If not by Brody, then Doug Bard. He cooked something up, and now is trying to plant it wherever it will grow. It's all so wild. Even if it were true, how can you draw a link between this supposed memo and Merta's death? Who but Sasha would even know about this memo?"

Cassie didn't have an answer. She was back replaying Angela's suggestion that Bard had planted this with her. That Bard had used her. *Wherever it will grow.*

"Maybe you're right," Cassie said. "Maybe this is nothing."

Angela was examining her, seized by a notion. "Has Sasha told her story to anyone else?"

"I don't think so. I really believe she's kept this to herself. Doug only recently pried it out of her."

It's not likely she can document anything? Or be willing to come into a courtroom?"

"Not likely."

"It would just be hearsay anyway. Not admissible."

"No doubt."

Angela turned and headed out of the room. At the door, she stopped. "Well then, should we get on with the trial?"

Cassie rose slowly. "It is that time."

SIXTEEN

JB's Tavern was packed. Two drunk cowhands who'd seized the microphone from Shirley were trying to sing their own twisted version of "Cattle Call." At the piano, David was doing his best to help them keep a tune. Behind the bar, JB himself was rushing to fill orders. Jimmy and Doug, unable to get his attention, retreated to a corner table by the potbellied stove. A kerosene lamp hung over their heads, trapper's tools and steer horns loomed on the wall behind them.

"Nothing's working," Bard said. "Every path dead-ends."

Jimmy, watching the cowhands, turned away from them only reluctantly. "How so?"

"Cassie told Angela about Ollie's memo, but our DA wasn't impressed. She made the same point as our friend in San Francisco. Who else but Sasha even knew about the memo?"

"Well, it is a fair question."

"Yeah, I know." Bard finally got JB's attention, and signaled for a couple of Graciosa Brews. He'd stay for only a few minutes, then go check on Molly and Sasha.

"Hey, Doug." Jimmy hesitated. "There's something I've been meaning to talk to you about."

"So talk."

"It's about Cassie Teal."

"That topic isn't off-limits."

Their beers arrived. Jimmy grabbed at his glass. "Yeah, well, okay. I didn't tell you this before, but in court the other day, Hedgespeth went after Stark, asking her whether she'd cut any deals with that jailhouse rent-a-tat. She denied, of course. Through her teeth. Then Hedge asked Cassie the same thing."

"What did Cassie say?"

"She backed Angela. Looked the judge straight in the eye. No deals, she said. No promises."

Bard reached for his beer. His fingers curled around the glass. "That's the way it works. I can't count on the prosecutors to spring Jeremiah. That's obvious."

"Can you count on Louis Brody?"

"Brody's a stand-up guy, actually. But I'd say he could use help."

"You have someone in mind?"

Bard looked at him. "How about you?"

Jimmy's eyes went opaque. He turned to the music. "Goddamn, Doug. After all our talk, I thought we got that settled."

"Take it easy. I was just thinking out loud here. Just trying to come up with something. Didn't really mean that."

"You damn well did mean it, Doug. Now look, I would if I could. But I don't have the goddamn goods."

"Don't worry. We'll come at this some other way."

"Yeah, sure. Don't worry." Jimmy glared at his empty glass and waved for another beer. "There are things you just don't get, Doug. For instance, any story I do would need Sasha's complete cooperation. On the record, for quote, nothing anonymous. You haven't thought of that, have you?"

No, he hadn't. The dread again was rising in his chest. "You won't get that, Jimmy. She's not going public. Not to you, not in the courtroom."

A hint of triumph showed in Jimmy's eye. "Well then. The obstacle is not just me."

"That's right."

Jimmy tapped the bar with his knuckles. "You're some kind of jumpy, Doug. What button did I push?"

Bard wondered. It was easy enough to say he feared for Sasha and Molly's safety, that only Sasha's continued silence kept Merta's killer at bay. Yet that wasn't all of it. He feared also what Sasha knew. He feared Sasha's role.

"Catch you later," Bard said, rising suddenly. "There's someone I have to see."

Sheriff Dixon wasn't alone when Bard pushed open his office door. In two chairs, facing Dixon at his desk, sat Victor Baynes and Andy Akers. Baynes's hand instinctively dropped to his holstered gun at the sight of an intruder.

Bard said, "Do that often on the streets, Vic, you're going to hurt someone."

"You're interrupting us," Baynes replied.

Bard looked at the sheriff. "I need to see you, Howie."

Dixon shook his head. "Not a good time."

"Besides," Baynes said, "you're not even supposed to be in these offices without a guest pass. How'd you get in?"

Bard kept his eyes on Dixon, ignoring the others. Baynes started to rise and come at him. Dixon jumped up and got between them. The sheriff hesitated, then said, "We were just finishing up. Vic, Andy . . . I'll catch you later."

As the two detectives filed out, Bard sat down at Dixon's conference table, grabbed a legal pad, and started diagramming. "Come here, Howie, let me show you this."

He drew the links—Sasha and Lillo, Inc., Ollie Merta, RC Cummings. He listed the sequence of events. He walked Dixon through the story. "Merta had uncovered some funny business, that's obvious. He called Sasha. He had a memo to give her. Then kerbam, good-bye. Old-fashioned grazing war my ass. Others had a better reason to kill Merta."

Dixon puzzled over Bard's sheets. He followed the lines, reread the sequence. "Someone at RC Cummings?" he asked. "You're kidding."

"I know. There's too many missing links right now to draw a conclusion."

"Missing links?"

"That memo, Howie. Where is it? What happened to it?"

Dixon did the same slow burn as Cassie. "We don't have it, if that's what you're asking."

"Okay, you don't. But what about your detectives?"

"Now listen, Doug—"

"I'm asking, not accusing. It's just maybe something to look into."

Dixon sat for a moment. Bard thought he was weighing options. It could be his eternal indigestion, though. Bard never knew with the sheriff.

"My department's not bent," Dixon said. "I won't have you making suggestions—"

"Something else is missing, Howie. Those who know Merta say he always had a bank of computers in his office, at least two or three. But I saw only one the day of the fire. I'm wondering what got carted out before I arrived."

"Just what are you saying about our department, Doug? Christ almighty. Your poor dead father. His picture hangs in the hallway right outside this door."

Ah yes, Bard thought. Oscar's picture. They took that photo in the summer Doug turned twelve, the summer that Oscar drew all those admiring headlines. The first bunch came when Dick Kobar's two-year-old daughter fell down a flight of steps, and Oscar rushed her to the hospital in his squad car with the lights and siren blazing. The second bunch came when Oscar single-handedly captured four bank robbers at gunpoint after a high-speed chase across Chumash County. *Don't give me any bullshit, mister, I want to hear the truth.* That's how Oscar got confessions, towering over his unfortunate subjects, jabbing revolvers in their chests.

His photo, shot at a fancy studio, hung in a sterling silver frame above a plaque that hailed him as a "leader and role model." Doug could never pass by it without recalling another event from that long-ago summer.

It happened late on a fogbound August night. Oscar had been at a tavern with his buddies. He was not normally a drinking man, but he'd had a few beers. He came home past midnight, singing "She'll Be Coming around the Mountain When She Comes." His wife was long asleep, but Doug was up way past his bedtime, watching TV. Scared of getting caught, Doug ran to hide in a downstairs closet just as Oscar threw open the front door.

All the lights were out. In the closet, Doug moved slightly,

making a rustling noise. Oscar heard it. He reached for the
loaded .357 Magnum he kept in a kitchen cabinet. He stood at
the closet, the gun at his side. He yanked open the door. Doug
stepped forward just as Oscar's gun rose. Oscar had his finger
on the trigger. Doug looked down a long barrel, then up at
Oscar. They stared at each other, father and son. *Goddamn,
boy,* Oscar muttered. *I could have killed you.*

"Our department?" Bard told the sheriff now. "It's not my
department anymore, Howie."

"Precisely. That's the problem." Dixon rose. "Get out of
here, Bard."

"Howie, where's the one computer that I saw at Merta's?
The all-burnt-to-hell one? I've checked the evidence room. I
didn't see it there—"

"You what? You were in the evidence room?" Dixon's face
was flushing red. "Goddamn it, Doug, you can't go in there.
You don't work here anymore. You just broke the goddamn
law. I could have your goddamn ass arrested."

"Come on, Howie. Doesn't it occasionally bother you to
carry water for Angela Stark? That Jeremiah daydream business really takes the cake. Jesus, Howie. Don't you—"

Dixon had him by the elbow now. He was pushing him out
of his office, pulling him down the corridor. "I'm going to arrest you if you don't get out of here, Doug. This is an active,
open case and you're a private citizen. I can't even discuss
this with you. Move your skinny ass or I put it behind bars."

They half scuffled and half walked until, at the end of the
corridor, the sight of a door swinging open stopped them. The
door to Angela Stark's office. She was in court; they both
knew that. It couldn't be her. As they watched, a man came
through the portal, bearing an armful of files.

"Well hello there," Bruce Hightower said. "What a surprise. I thought everyone was out to lunch."

"State calls Detective Victor Baynes."

Cassie Teal watched Baynes slowly settle into the witness
stand. Angela stood before him as if they didn't know each
other.

"Sir, would you introduce yourself and spell your last name, please."

"Yes, ma'am. I am Victor Baynes. B-a-y-n-e-s."

"By whom are you employed, sir?"

"I am a detective with the Chumash County Sheriff's Department."

"How long have you been a detective with Chumash County?"

"About twelve years now."

"As a detective, are part of your duties to investigate violent crime in the Chumash County jurisdiction?"

"Yes, ma'am."

"Calling your attention, sir, to the first week of March, did you become involved in the investigation of the murders of Ollie Merta and Marilee Cooper?"

"Yes, ma'am, I did."

"During the course of your investigation, did you have occasion to interview various individuals?"

"Yes."

"Calling your attention, sir, to late May, during the course of your investigation did you interview Jed Jeremiah?"

"Yes."

"I want to call your attention, sir, to June thirteenth. Were you on duty that day?"

"Yes, I was."

"Would you tell the ladies and gentlemen of the jury what, if anything, occurred on that day?"

Cassie's mind drifted. She couldn't help it: she imagined how she'd challenge this cop's testimony if she were on the other side. She looked over at Jed Jeremiah. He was studying the witness with unusual curiosity.

"That was a Saturday, the initial day of the grand jury probe into the Merta-Cooper deaths. I and Detective Akers were in charge of guarding and transporting Jed Jeremiah. We sat much of the time in a holding area with him."

"Did you have a conversation with Jed Jeremiah at that time?"

"Yes, ma'am."

"Would you tell the ladies and gentlemen what Mr. Jeremiah stated to you at that time."

"Basically, Mr. Jeremiah related that he had a kind of daydream. And in this dream, he told us, an old man was trying to kill him. So he put his hands around the old man's neck. Behind him, a little girl started screaming . . ."

Cassie glanced again at Jeremiah. He was whispering into Brody's ear.

"Could you describe how Mr. Jeremiah appeared to you at that time?"

"He appeared very upset and distraught. He kept saying, basically, 'Please tell me this was just a daydream, please tell me this didn't happen.' "

Jed's chair scraped across the floor on the defendant's side of the table. Brody raised a hand to his client's shoulder. Judge Hedgespeth stared them into silence.

"What did you do next?" Angela asked her witness.

"Basically, well, myself and Akers had a little discussion. And at this point I called Sheriff Howie Dixon. We gave him just a brief summary of what had taken place, what we had heard."

"What did Dixon say?"

"Well, what I thought he said was that he'd tell you."

"Did there come a time when you were advised that wasn't what he said?"

"Yes. Just recently, Thursday of last week, I learned that the sheriff had advised me to tell you myself. We each thought the other would. So neither did."

"How did you discover this?"

"During discussions at the office with Sheriff Dixon, in preparation for this trial."

Angela Stark turned toward the lawyers' table. "I have no further questions."

Hedgespeth nodded to Brody: "You may cross-examine."

Jimmy O'Brien, stepping out of the courtroom during a late-afternoon recess, found Doug Bard pacing across the central plaza. "You should have seen it," he said. "Louis Brody sure as hell got riled in there."

"Tell me," Bard commanded. "Give me the story."

"Don't have much time, I'm only out for a recess. State has finished its case-in-chief. Defense is about to start to present its side."

"Okay then, the short version."

They sat down at a bench on the creek. Jimmy began.

"The daydream business drove Brody just about nuts. He really went after Baynes during his cross. Do you have any police reports about this dream? Any office memoranda? A tape recording? Any notes even? No, no, no, no, Baynes says. But Brody keeps asking, again and again. Angela keeps jumping up. Objection, asked and answered. The judge keeps agreeing with her. Asked and answered, move on, Mr. Brody. Louis doesn't stop. Any reports, any tape, any notes? Objection, sustained, move on. I thought old Hedgespeth was going to throw Brody in jail."

"Jesus. How was the jury taking all this?"

"Hard to say. The jurors were paying attention, I'll tell you that."

Jimmy pulled out his reporter's notebook and began reciting.

Tell us, sir, was this daydream tape recorded?

Objection. Asked and answered.

Sustained.

You thought it very important?

Well, possibly important.

You thought it possibly important, but you didn't tape record it?

Objection, Judge.

Sustained.

You didn't write it down?

Objection.

Objection sustained . . . asked and answered.

You didn't write it down?

Jimmy ran his finger along a line of notes. "Here's where

Brody pushed Hedgespeth over the edge. Judge starts banging his gavel. Says, 'Counsel, there is an objection, and it is sustained.' Well, Brody ignores him, keeps going. 'You didn't memorialize it in any way?' he asks. Objection, Stark calls out. Bang-bang goes the judge. Hedge is almost shouting now. 'Apparently you're not hearing me, Counsel, so I will make myself heard. When something is asked and answered and there is an objection, that means you don't ask the question again. Understand?' "

Jimmy slapped his notebook shut. "I swear, Brody had a mind to start up again. Hedgespeth sees it coming, smashes his gavel. 'I'm warning you, Counsel, if you don't understand, I will hold you in contempt. I will have you taken out of here in chains.' That stopped Brody, finally. All of a sudden, he just threw his hands up. 'I have no further questions of this witness, Judge.' That's what he said. Nothing more. Sat down."

"Doesn't sound so good," Bard said. "But what the hell, good for Brody. If I were a juror, I'd applaud."

Jimmy flipped through his pad. "Angela called the sheriff right after Baynes. Howie verified the whole story. How Baynes and Akers called him that Saturday. How he only got a brief summary, how he misunderstood what it was about. How they got confused over who was reporting to Stark. How he forgot all about it. How the deputies reminded him many weeks later."

"Did Louis challenge him at all?"

"Brody tried his best to object, but Hedge kept glaring and banging his gavel."

"What about Jeremiah?"

"He started out all squirmy, then just gave up. Looked like he'd been kicked in the belly."

"Christ."

"Christ, indeed."

A voice calling Bard's name from across the plaza interrupted them. Louis Brody was shouting and waving, charging down the *asistencia* steps toward them.

They rose and met him halfway. Brody grabbed at Bard's

arm. "I've been looking all over for you," he said, trying to catch his breath. "Case for the defense is starting. We're in a jam. I have no other choice."

"What are you talking about?"

Brody was pulling him toward the courthouse. "What I mean is, I'm not saving you. You have to be my first witness. Let's go."

"Could you please tell your name to the ladies and gentlemen of the jury and spell your last name for the court reporter."

"Douglas Bard, B-a-r-d."

Brody stood at his side. "Mr. Bard, what is your occupation?"

Doug couldn't say he was a researcher at the *News-Times,* for that would make too much trouble for Jimmy. He looked around the courtroom. All 150 spectator seats were filled. Many watching were people he knew. Todd Justin, the carpenter. Harvey, over at the hardware store. Madison, Radler, Downing, all from JB's.

"I'm presently unemployed," Bard said.

"Were you previously employed?"

"Yes."

"What was your previous occupation?"

"I was a sheriff's detective, specializing in violent crimes."

"And where were you a sheriff's detective?"

"For the Chumash County Sheriff's Department."

"How long were you with the department?"

"About fourteen years."

"And for how long were you a violent crimes detective?"

"About eight years."

"While you were assigned as a violent crimes detective, did you win any awards within the department?"

"I—"

"Objection," Angela Stark called out. "This witness's resume is irrelevant. He's up here to report facts, not deliver authoritative opinions."

"That's true," Hedgespeth ruled. "Objection sustained."

We're going to try to qualify you as an expert, but it proba-bly won't fly. That's what Brody had advised.

"Are you familiar with the investigation into the deaths of Ollie Merta and Marilee Cooper?"

"Yes, I am."

"How did you become familiar with that?"

"I was on the case almost from the beginning."

"Did you work with others?"

"Yes, Detectives Victor Baynes and Andy Akers."

"You spent hours together?"

"Many. At least for a while. Day after day at the start."

"Now, Detective Bard—"

"Objection," Stark called. "The witness is not a detective."

Doug turned to her. "Now look—"

Brody stepped between his witness and the DA. "Excuse me, Mr. Bard. Let's just continue here, okay?"

"It's just that—"

This time, Hedgespeth interrupted. He did not look happy. "Mr. Bard, in this courtroom, you only respond to the questions asked you. I know you understand that. You've been here before, after all."

Bard drew a breath, angry at himself for letting Stark provoke him. "Yes, Your Honor."

Brody resumed his questioning. "You have heard about something called the Jed Jeremiah daydream. You know what I'm talking about, don't you?"

"Yes, I know what you're talking about."

"Detective Bard, as you were investigating this case, did you ever hear about Jed Jeremiah having a daydream?"

"Objection."

"He may answer if he knows," Hedgespeth ruled.

"No, I did not."

"In the first month after the investigation closed, did you hear anything?"

"No."

"The second month?"

"No."

"The third month?"

"I just heard about it for the first time the other day."

"Do you think it's significant, Detective, that for all these months you never heard about this so-called daydream?"

"Objection," Stark called. "He's not a detective, and not a qualified expert witness. What he thinks doesn't matter."

Bard again was staring at the DA. Hedgespeth had a hand on his gavel. "Objection sustained," he said.

Brody tried again. "Can you tell us what you think of this evidence?"

"Objection."

"Sustained."

"Can you tell us what you think of Eddie Hines's eyewitness account?"

"Objection."

"Sustained."

"Can you tell us what you think of the bootprint evidence?"

"Objection."

"Sustained."

"Can you tell us—"

Angela Stark was on her feet. "I object, Your Honor. I object to all of this. Mr. Brody knows perfectly well these are improper questions."

Brody wheeled on her. "The DA is now objecting to questions before I ask them."

"That is true," the judge said. "Let's do one question and objection at a time."

Brody turned back to Bard. "Can you tell us what you think of Jed Jeremiah being charged for this murder?"

"Object, object, object."

"Sustained."

"Given your analysis of this crime, do you have an opinion as to whether or not this crime was perpetrated by Jed Jeremiah?"

"Objection, Judge, objection."

"Objection sustained."

"You want to tell the ladies and gentlemen of the jury why you left the sheriff's department?"

"Objection."

"Sustained."

"Was your leaving the department related to the DA's decision to prosecute Jed Jeremiah?"

"Objection."

"Sustained."

"Mr. Bard, if you had—"

Hedgespeth finally slapped his gavel. "Enough, Counsel. Enough, Mr. Brody. I've tried to give you lots of leeway, but the DA is right. You do know perfectly well that all these questions are improper. Let's move on now, or give it up."

Brody appeared to be weighing the judge's words. After a moment, he walked to the lawyers' table. There he stood, facing the bench. "Your Honor, thank you very much. For the record, I don't think these questions are improper; in fact, I think they're extraordinarily appropriate. But I guess they're not going to get answered here today. So I have nothing more."

Angela Stark stayed in her seat. She wasn't the least inclined to keep Bard on the stand. "The state has no questions of this witness."

That was it, Bard suddenly realized. For this he had resigned.

He rose slowly and stepped down from the witness stand. As he passed Brody, the defense attorney whispered to him. At first Bard couldn't hear, then he did. "Sorry, Doug," Louis was saying. "But I warned you."

SEVENTEEN

Yellow light poured from the windows of Doug Bard's cabin. A silver Lexus sat on the gravel driveway. The faint sounds of 'N Sync's "Bye, Bye, Bye" rose in the night air.

From his own car, a battered twelve-year-old Jeep, Bard surveyed the scene. He was not accustomed to seeing signs of life in his home when he turned onto his property. He didn't know how to feel. For so long he'd missed and longed for the complicated succor of a family, yet he'd grown accustomed to his solitude.

All walls were closing in on him now. He couldn't fathom what had happened, what was to come. For a moment, he considered driving away.

Instead, he climbed out of his car holding a small bag of groceries—milk, butter, eggs, cheese, bread, the evening paper. He approached his front door. Through the window he could see Molly at her boom box CD player, Sasha coming out of the kitchen. It had been a week since Sasha agreed to move in. Her daughter didn't want to be alone any longer—and neither, she reluctantly admitted, did she. *I'm getting tired of being superwoman,* she'd muttered when she showed up on his doorstep.

They were no safer here, Bard knew. But at least they weren't in that tormented house anymore. And at least the three of them were now facing this together.

He looked at his daughter. She was sticking a headset on, cranking up the volume. She rose, and started dancing to the music in her ears. Left hand on hip, right hand twirling high in the air, turning in a circle. Stop, cross hands across her chest, clutch shoulders. Sway.

Bard's attention turned to Sasha. She stood off in a corner, talking on her cell phone, paying no attention to Molly. A business call, no doubt. Bard tried to imagine the topic.

He opened the front door. Molly waved as she danced past him. Sasha quickly put her phone down.

"Don't you want to say good-bye?" Bard asked.

"I just did."

"Here." He thrust the grocery bag at her. "I stopped for a few things."

"How domestic."

"Stocking up for the weekend."

Bard groped for what more to say or do. If he were alone, he'd pour a beer, light the fireplace, flip through a few magazines. Why not try that? He walked into the kitchen and reached for the refrigerator door.

"What happened at the trial, Daddy?"

Molly was beside him now, her headset off.

"I'd rather not talk about that."

"Hello? I mean, am I air?"

"Christ, can I get a beer at least?"

Molly's eyes widened. Her lip trembled. He hadn't meant to snap at her. This was yet another byproduct of his time in the courtroom. He'd played it so wrong. He'd thought the world would stop when he got on the stand and declared Jeremiah's innocence. Instead, the world was merrily hurtling on without him.

"Sorry, Molly, just give me a minute."

"Sure," she said, edging away. "Take a hundred minutes."

Bard tried to keep his mind on a task. From the woodbox he lifted three logs and a handful of kindling. He threw it all into the fireplace. He lit a match. As the flames leapt, he settled into one of the corduroy chairs. He picked up that evening's edition of the *News-Times*. Skipping over the main headline, yet another report about the fight for Pirate's Beach, he scanned down the page.

There it was, a small story on the bottom left corner.

Jimmy had probably delayed his deadline to fit this in. "Detective Tells of Jeremiah's Daydream, Judge Limits Defense Questions." At least it was only a two-column head. Bard skimmed the account. Victor Baynes's testimony, the cascade of sustained objections to Brody's cross, the defense's dubious decision to open with Doug Bard. *Douglas Bard, formerly a Chumash County sheriff's detective, was not permitted to testify as an expert witness. Currently unemployed . . .*

"Daddy, can we talk now, can I show you something?" Resilient as always to his moods, Molly was climbing onto his lap, knocking his newspaper aside. Bard grabbed for the paper. It ripped as Molly sat down. "Damnit, Molly, can't you be careful?" He pushed her off him, reached for his paper. She stood above him now, trying not to cry.

"I don't know why you're mad at me, Daddy. Please tell me."

"I'm not mad at you, I'm just—" Bard stopped. He drew a breath, trying to gain mastery. He reached for her. "Come here, Molly girl."

She pulled away. Tears were welling in her eyes. "No way."

"Come on, Molly girl."

They were tears of fury, he saw. She hated to cry in front of him. "I'll never do it again," she shouted. "I'll never sit on your lap or try to show you anything."

"Molly girl . . ."

Her voice rose, louder yet. "You don't know what it's like to be a kid. Everyone telling you what to do all the time. My teacher, the school principal. Then when I come home, Mommy is always ordering me around. Now I come to your house, and you're snapping at me. You hate me, you can't stand me—"

"Molly, Molly, I'm not perfect—"

"That's right! That's right! You're not perfect, Daddy!"

The one truth he wanted always to keep from her. Yet the one truth that was impossible to hide. "I'm trying my best, Molly—"

"Try? Is that why you left us? Is that why you quit your job? You always go away, Daddy, that's what you do. Why don't you just go away right now."

Bard looked about for Sasha, but couldn't find her. "Molly girl, let me explain. I was reading something in the paper. You sometimes just need to see that, maybe wait a minute, maybe—"

"Errraaarrhh." Molly, hands to ears, was shrieking to drown out his voice.

"Let me talk to you, Molly. Let me explain."

Now she was pounding the arm of his chair with clenched fists. "Don't keep explaining. I don't want to hear."

He rose. There was no point, he'd have to wait out the storm. "I think I'll go into my bedroom. You can join me when you're ready."

He started to step away. She said something, but her mouth was buried in her arm.

He stopped. "I can't hear you, Molly."

She lifted her face. She spoke softly now. "Going away isn't going to solve anything."

"What then?"

She stretched out her arms. "Hold me . . . Pick me up . . . Carry me."

Hours later, Bard sat with Sasha as Molly slept in the spare bedroom. "You were good with Molly tonight," Sasha said. "You were so patient. More patient than I could be."

He'd thought his patience had failed, actually. But he didn't try to object or correct. "She's not normally like that. I thought it best to let her vent."

"What's the point of us staying here, Doug?"

"Molly wanted to be together, remember? Also, it's easier for me to watch over you two."

"We're all gone during the day. If someone is following Molly—"

"I'm following Molly."

"What?"

"One advantage of being unemployed is I have time on my hands. I've been keeping an eye on her."

"You think that's needed?"

"I don't know what's needed. I don't even know what's truly going on."

He waited, hoping she'd explain more, but she didn't. He decided to ask the question he'd been harboring since he'd come into the house. "Sasha, how'd you get linked up with RC Cummings in the first place? How'd they happen to offer you such terrific backing for your company?"

"I told you. My investments around here, the land options mainly, drew their attention. They wanted in on it."

"The particular way it came about, that's what I'm after. Who made the contact, for instance."

Sasha appeared to be searching her memory. "I think I just bumped into their exec VP one evening. We started talking."

"That would be Albert Donner?"

"Yes."

"Bumped into? Where? When?"

"I can't recall all the details."

What wasn't being said filled the room. She trying to draw a line where she wouldn't go, he holding back regarding his own visit with Donner. Bard thought of the look in Albert's eyes when talking about Sasha.

"Not good enough," he said. "Time is running out. Whatever you're involved in, you have to cross over."

She didn't appear to hear him. "Actually, now that I think of it, we bumped into each other one night at the farmer's market."

"You knew him before, then?"

"Well . . . yes."

"An old flame?"

"No."

"What then?"

"We'd done a few trades up in the San Francisco financial markets."

"I see. A few trades."

"Let's leave it at that, Doug."

"Okay, let's." He tried to let go. "Then you bumped into him down here at the farmer's market?"

"Yeah. No longer is he a small-time trader. Now he's exec

VP of RC Cummings. I tell him what I'm up to, he says he's heard. He offers their help."

"How kind of him."

"What are you driving at, Doug?"

Bard wished he knew. If only he had some training in Sasha's field.

His eyes fell on the *News-Times*'s front page. Staring back at him was Bruce Hightower's face. His story, three columns above the fold, had drawn far bigger play than Jeremiah's trial. In the photo Hightower was smiling and waving. "County Commissioners Approve Pirate's Beach Development."

Bard had skipped over this before. Now he picked up the paper and scanned the article. It didn't mention anything about putting the plans to a citizen's vote. In this account, the county commissioners were the only ones voting.

I'm the gofer now. Just picking up a few things for Angela. That's what Hightower had said when they bumped into him coming out of Angela Stark's office. Another puzzle, another angle to pursue.

"Sasha. You say you'd done a few trades with Donner up in San Francisco. Is that where you first met?"

"Well no, not exactly."

"Where then?"

"I first knew him from down here in La Graciosa. He spent a lot of time surfing at Pirate's Beach in those early days. But he had money to invest even then. He was always looking for local Chumash County projects. That's why he came knocking at my door. Literally, that's what he did. Knock at my door."

"You took him seriously?"

"Only because it was obvious he was fronting for someone."

"Did you know who that was?"

"No, I didn't."

"Not RC Cummings?"

"No, no. They didn't exist back then."

"Do you know who owns RC Cummings?"

"As I understand, it's privately held."

Bard fell silent. Sasha shot him an appreciative look. "These questions aren't bad for a cop."

"Ex-cop," Bard reminded.

He could not sleep. The living room, where he lay curled on the sofa, was black as a tomb. The scent of wood-smoke from the fireplace hung in the air. Beyond the window, a solitary owl hooted. Bard drew deep, slow breaths, hoping for release. Instead, images flooded his mind. Jed Jeremiah, throwing his boots at him. Angela Stark, murmuring, *Not bad, Detective.* Howie Dixon, dragging him by the elbow. Judge Hedgespeth, refusing to recognize who he was.

In Bard's den, a half dozen awards hung on the walls, accolades over the years from the sheriff's department. They meant nothing. How had he ever imagined that they did?

Old Sheriff Wizen, years before, once asked him if he wanted a deputy manager's job. He'd be a desk jockey, pushing papers, giving orders. Bard had declined, preferring the streets. The streets had branded him, though. He could see it in the others' eyes. Sasha's, Dixon's, Stark's.

Not Cassie's, though. Bard's thoughts drifted to her. He stopped himself. No. He couldn't go there.

Sleep tugged at him now. He felt himself sinking into a merciful void. So much he didn't understand. If only they had Ollie Merta's memo. If only Ollie Merta could talk to them from the grave. If only—

Bard sat up. Why couldn't Merta talk from the grave?

His memo might be anywhere. You can burn a memo in the fire. You can fold it five ways and stick it in a cave. You can tear it to bits and swallow it. But you can't so easily dispose of a computer.

Surely Merta wrote his memo on a computer. Surely Merta researched his memo on a computer. Which computer, though? The one destroyed in the fire? Or one of those that's gone missing?

If only Bard knew who took the computers. He'd been focusing on Dixon and his boys. Yet it wasn't likely that they'd managed to cart computers away before Bard arrived at the murder scene. Too many witnesses, not enough time.

The killer then. Of course. If he came to silence Merta, he came, too, for the computers.

But why leave one computer behind to burn in the fire?

Bard threw off his blanket. No. The killer wouldn't have left one computer behind. The killer set the house fire not just to obscure a murder, but to destroy the computer. The one computer he saw.

Merta must have known he was being targeted. Merta must have hidden the other computers.

Talk to us from the grave, Ollie.

Bard jumped up. Through the window he could see the faint light of early dawn. He pushed open the door to Sasha's bedroom—his bedroom. "Sasha, Sasha, wake up."

She rolled over, bleary-eyed. "What the—"

"What do you know about Merta's computers?"

"I . . . what?" Sasha sat up. "What are you talking about?"

"Merta's computers. Where did he keep them? What's in them?"

"Doug, have you lost your mind? It's five A.M."

He tried to slow down. "Okay then. Let me explain."

Over coffee at the kitchen table, they watched not the sun rising but the morning fog descending below the treetops. Bard talked on and on. When he finished, she lit a cigarette. "I don't know, Doug. The only chance for us to be safe is to lay low. You stir things up, they're going to come after us."

"Who's they?" Bard tried not to sound desperate. "Sasha, who are they?"

"I have no idea. Not RC Cummings, not Albert. They don't even know Ollie Merta ever worked for me. But someone obviously does."

Bard again beat back the dread. "Sasha, I have something to tell you. The fact is, Donner does know Ollie worked for you. I went to visit him. I had to find out what he was up to. I made it clear you knew nothing, had nothing—"

"You what?" Sasha's hand went to her mouth. Her eyes flared, a mix of fury and fear. "How could you—"

"I had to, Sasha—"

"You had no right—"

"Now listen, Sasha. Jed Jeremiah is two steps from Death Row because of me. He may blow any time now. If I don't stir things, he's going to hang."

She bit off her words. "And if you do stir things, your daughter may just disappear one day."

Bard sat back in his chair as if gut-shot. He could think of nothing to say. His head swam with terror. In the moment's silence, he heard a faint sound—music coming from Molly's room. The Beatles' "Yellow Submarine." He rose, went to her door, knocked lightly. Molly opened it.

"You like golden oldies this week, Molly girl?"

She gave him her sweet smile. "Ollie taught us this one."

"It's Saturday. You can sleep in. How come you're awake?"

Molly was swaying to the rhythm. "I had the music in my head, so I decided to get up and play it." She peered around him, out at the kitchen table. "Why are *you* guys up so early?"

Bard looked at Sasha and chose to ignore the storm warnings building there. "We were talking about whether I should let Jeremiah get convicted and keep everybody but Jed happy, or whether I should find the real killer and stir up trouble."

"What kind of trouble?" Molly asked.

"Well, like whoever has been bothering you and Mom. Someone wants to keep something quiet."

Molly walked past him into the living room. "Keep what quiet?"

Sasha said, "Doug, please—"

Bard waved her off. "Well, Molly, that's what I don't know quite yet. I think the answer is in Ollie's computers, but we have to find them, the ones that weren't burned in the fire. We also have to figure out how to make them work."

"You mean retrieve stuff and crack passwords?"

Bard regarded his daughter with surprise. "Yes, that's exactly what I mean. How do you know—"

"We study that stuff, Daddy." Molly hesitated. "And Ollie showed me stuff. I know how Ollie's computers work. I probably know better than anyone."

"Better than anyone?"

"I think so."

Bard stood up. He refused to look at Sasha. To Molly he said, "You want to go get some breakfast at Stella's?"

"Doug!" Sasha was pleading. "You can't take Molly—"

"Yes, he can, Mommy." Molly was already heading to her room to change clothes. "I want to help Daddy."

Sasha leapt from her chair. "You're not going without me."

Bard turned wintry eyes on her. "Yes, I am."

EIGHTEEN

From the central plaza, Doug Bard drove southwest along the winding country lanes that led to the rural hills where Ollie Merta's house once stood. The fog hugged the ground now, just as it had the night of the fire. Bard didn't keep his foot as heavy on the accelerator pedal this time. Next to him, Molly peered through the window. She was wearing her customary uniform these days. Pink Adidas, tight blue jeans, a pink peasant blouse, an unbuttoned blue jean jacket. Her hair was pulled up tight into a ponytail and wrapped in a pink scarf.

I don't think you're dressed warmly enough, he'd said as they rushed out of the house.

Well, at least I'm dressed cool enough.

At Stella's, she'd devoured a pile of pancakes and bacon, showing no sign of nerves. Eleven going on nineteen? More like twenty-nine.

"How can you drive in this?" she asked. "What can you see?"

In his mind, he saw a pink glow, then black smoke, then a cluster of fire trucks and patrol cars with blinking red lights. If only he'd let things be back then. Or if only he'd noticed what he should have. Instead, he'd been distracted by the sight of a dead little girl who reminded him of his own daughter.

"I know this region so well," he told Molly, "I could almost drive it blindfolded."

"Mommy was mad that I was going with you."

"I know. She's worried about you."

"Who gives."

"What a way to talk."

Molly fiddled with the radio until she found her station. Britney Spears's voice poured out of the speakers. "Should Mom be worried?"

Bard peered down the foggy road. He could see just fifteen feet ahead. "Maybe. But I don't think so."

"Thanks for clarifying, Daddy."

Rolling around a final bend, they came finally to the ruins of Ollie Merta's home. Nothing had been done to it since the investigators pulled up stakes. It rose now in the mist, a blackened, abandoned hulk. A door, a window frame, the chimney, blocks of bathroom tile, a charred refrigerator.

"This is where Marilee died?" Molly asked.

He looked at her. She was okay; she could handle this. She'd imagined it long enough. Better give it tangible form than let it fester in her mind. "Yes, Molly."

"Where are the computers?"

"I don't know. We have to find them."

They climbed out of the car and began to step through the ruins. If anything, the haze had deepened. Their feet crunched on disintegrating wood chips. Charred stubs of wood jutted into the air, pitched at bizarre angles. Sooty bricks littered the floor. They were in Ollie's computer room now, what was left of it. Bard saw the remains of a long aluminum table, big enough for four computers at least. Under it, a long panel of extended power taps, eighteen outlets in all, broiled a greasy brown. In the corner, a swirl of ruined cable.

"Daddy, where was Marilee?"

He didn't want to show her. He'd brought her here, though, and she was asking. He took her hand and guided her to a corner of the kitchen. He pointed to a bank of blackened beams. "Under there."

Molly squeezed his hand tighter, but said nothing. They walked back past the chimney, then through what was once a wall. They were in Ollie Merta's backyard now. Or rather, Ollie's back meadow. Here's where he must have kept his sheep. His land reached toward a thick stand of sycamores at the rear of his property. The stand climbed into the foothills and canyons, forming the border of a dense mountain forest. Bard looked around, squinting through the haze. He could see only bare outlines of forms. There rose what, a mound of hay? There a toolbin? Off to his far right, Bard sensed something moving. He whirled. A single red squirrel, racing up the trunk of a thick oak.

Bard had both hands on Molly's shoulders now. "Mom was right. I shouldn't have brought you here."

She twisted away from him. "Daddy, I want you to find out who killed Ollie and Marilee."

"They've found him. They're trying Jed Jeremiah."

"But you don't believe he did it."

Instead of responding he scanned the murky horizon. With Molly in hand, he started walking out across the meadow. "If Ollie thought someone might be coming for him, where would he hide his computers?"

"The forest," Molly said.

"How do you know?"

"He used to talk about the mountain forest out back of his house. How some people thought it scary, but he thought it the safest place he knew in the whole world."

"He wouldn't just leave his computers in the forest. They'd get ruined."

"There's a little barn out there somewhere. Like a play-house, but for grown-ups. He told us about that, too. Called it his *Sound of Music* world. Sometimes he'd go to the piano and start playing stuff from that movie."

"*Sound of Music?* Not exactly Britney Spears's material."

"That's what I told Ollie. He didn't care."

She shouldn't be here, Bard thought. She shouldn't be involved. He needed her, though. He put his arm around her back. He felt her arm wrap around his waist. "Let's go into the forest," he said.

The sycamore branches, thick with lobed maplelike leaves, reached out and swallowed them. The sky disappeared, giving way to a green-brown canopy. Tree roots surged out of the earth, forming long low barricades. They heard no sound now but the creak of branches in the breeze. The only signs of life were a scattering of gray fox and mule deer tracks. Bard looked back over his shoulder as they walked, trying to keep his bearings. He wasn't sure he could find his way out.

"This is neat," Molly said.

Stepping slowly among the trees, they followed a narrow winding trail into ever denser foliage. They were moving down a slope now. The pitch grew steeper, forcing them to clutch at branches to keep their balance. Bard thought he heard a faint crunching noise, off to the left; then he didn't. The silence was worse. "We'd better turn around," he said.

"Good luck."

That meant no way, Bard gauged. He didn't want to ask.

"What's over there?" Molly was pointing at a spot ahead of them where the land fell off vertically into a small gorge. Near the edge stood a solitary sycamore with a thick yellow rope tied around its base. The rope dropped over the rim, hanging down the incline.

"Looks like a helping hand from Ollie Merta," Bard said. "A gift from the grave."

They approached slowly. It wasn't a vertical pitch after all, just a steep incline. The rope tied to the tree made it possible to climb or descend. It required some skill and strength, though. "I don't think we can do this," Bard said.

Molly was already tugging at the rope. "I learned how to rappel at summer camp."

Bard looked back along the trail they'd traversed. Retreating didn't appear any more inviting than advancing. He peered over the rim. The forest seemed to open up down there into a small meadow. Just the spot for a cabin.

"Okay, Molly, let's rappel."

Bard tried it first. He passed the rope under his right thigh and over his left shoulder so it could be payed out smoothly and gradually. He stepped onto the slope and began to descend. The rope held firm. He went down two-thirds of the way, about fifty feet. Then he pulled himself back up.

"Your turn," he said. "Go all the way. I'll follow you."

She took the rope from him. "Here's what you need—" he

began. She stopped him with a raised hand. "Daddy, I know how to do this." He started arranging the rope. She pulled away. "Daddy, you're wasting my time."

Giving up, he stepped aside. She passed the rope under her thigh and over her shoulder, just as he had. She stepped over the rim. "See you at the bottom, Daddy."

He watched her descend, then took the rope and followed her down. At the bottom, they looked around. Where they stood appeared less like a clearing now than a field of dense head-high underbrush. Bard grabbed a fallen branch and began to slash a trail. Advancing, they scraped their faces against sharp bramble and tripped over hidden ruts.

"There," Molly whispered. She had a hand on his elbow. "There, through that willow thicket."

The low wood-frame cabin, aged but well kept, ten feet by fifteen feet at most, stood in a small clearing, surrounded and almost obscured by a ring of sycamores. A pair of rusted troughs lined the cabin's east side, still partly filled with feed for Ollie's pet sheep. A water tank rose some twenty feet behind the cabin, crowned by a small satellite dish. Hard by the west side was a piece of machinery Bard did not at first recognize. Then he did: an old Ingersoll-Rand generator, wired through an Army-surplus charger to a pair of six-volt forklift batteries.

"We might even have power for the computers, Molly."

He pushed open the front door, which had no lock. They stepped inside. They looked around, blinking in the dusty gloom. "This is cool," Molly said. "Like a tree house."

All four corners were furnished with big stuffed multi-colored pillows. Braided throw rugs covered the floor. Thick cylindrical candles filled the windowsills. Shelves and drawers lined two of the walls. Framed topographical maps covered a third, each a quadrant of Chumash County. Against the fourth there rested a battered upright piano. In the center of the room stood a long table.

A long, empty table.

"Damn," Bard said. "Where are the computers?"

Molly walked over to the piano, sat down, and began to play. Bard recognized "Twist and Shout."

"Ollie taught you that also?"

"Yes."

She started to sing. When she finished, Bard said, "He must have been pretty cool."

She looked at him. "So are you, Daddy."

He began a dance step, improvising, trying to mimic the moves she made at home while listening to her headset. Molly rolled her eyes. "Daddy . . ."

"What's wrong?"

"You've got to move to the music."

"So show me how."

Molly tried to look put out, but rose and came to him. "Here, this way." Her left hand went on her hip, her right hand into the air. She twirled and swayed.

He tried it but got his limbs tangled.

Molly cracked up. "You forgot to put your hand on your hip. You also forgot to twirl."

In slow motion now, she showed him. He tried to copy her.

"No, no," she said. "Move in a *circle*."

He tried again.

"Okay, I think I got it."

Together they danced. Bard counted to four, stepped, turned. Again. Four, step, turn. Twirl, sway, step. Molly was grinning. "You're the bomb, Daddy." Four count, step—

Losing his concentration, Bard tripped on his own feet. He lurched forward and banged against the piano, which began to slide. He looked up and saw that the wall behind the piano, now exposed, was covered with three oak panels.

Bard regained his balance. He walked over, ran his hand along the panels, and tapped gently. He punched the edge of one. As he expected, it popped open. He peered inside of what now revealed itself to be a built-in cabinet.

"Here we go," he said.

There was just one, but that was enough. On a deep shelf sat a Dell Optiplex 6XM 5133 with a nineteen-inch monitor. Behind it Bard could see a welter of cables and power cords, which fed into a Newpoint twelve-outlet surge suppressor. He pulled on the shelf. It slid out, forming a desk.

"Hey, Molly," he said. "Looks like this baby is hooked up and ready to go."

Ollie's batteries still had juice. At the press of a button, his computer started to whir and boot. Then it stopped. A box appeared on the screen. The computer was demanding a password.

"Any ideas, Molly?"

She sat beside him, tapping her forehead with her fingers. "He had an old ragged pet sheep named Walter."

Bard typed in WALTER, then Walter, then walter. Nothing.

Molly tapped harder on her forehead. "He loved Mozart."

Bard typed MOZART, Mozart, mozart. Nothing.

Molly stared at the screen. "His favorite writer . . . Try Chekhov."

Bard typed CHEKHOV, Chekhov, chekhov. Nothing.

"Ooooh." Molly jumped up, arms clawing the air. "I can't stand this."

"We just have to be patient and keep at it."

"For how long? This could go on for days."

That was true, Bard had to admit. He'd been relying on Molly's intuition, he realized now. Her intuition, and even more, her connection to Merta.

He stood up. "Tell you what. I'm going to leave you alone. You stay here by yourself, thinking about Ollie, trying to imagine him, how he thought, what he felt. I'm going to sit outside, right near the door."

Molly took his seat at the computer. "Good idea. You do that, Daddy."

Stepping outside, he found that the fog had lifted. Dappled woodland sunlight filtered through the sycamores. Broad swathes of purple lupine abounded. Birds called, gulls and coots and sandpipers. What a sanctuary Merta had here. Yet he'd let the world in. Computers, a satellite dish. Why?

Bard circled the cabin over and over, widening his arc with each round but staying close to Molly. For all the danger, he was glad to have her with him. She wasn't any safer sitting at home with Sasha. If he managed to gain entry to Merta's computer, what would he find about his ex-wife? A sordid account of her ruthless ascent? The prices paid, the bargains struck? For a passing moment, Bard wasn't sure he wanted to crack the computer's code.

His thoughts turned to the maps on Ollie's walls. They intrigued him. He liked maps, too; he studied charts of his favorite places when he felt the need to be transported. Was that Ollie's habit? Or did his maps carry some other import? It was tough to question a man in his grave. Bard had always thought himself fairly adept at interrogation. Merta presented an uncommon challenge.

What Ollie cared most about, what he loved—that would be the key to his password. Not his favorite pet or composer or author. Something that mattered more to him. Most to him.

Bard thought of what the school guidance counselor told him. *Loved to be with the kids. He tried to act reluctant, but oh was he pleased when we asked him to teach them music.*

Bard turned back to the cabin. He pushed open the front door. Molly, hunched over the keyboard, was rocking with impatience. "Nothing works," she groaned.

"What did Ollie love most of all, Molly?"

She frowned. "I dunno."

"Children."

"I guess."

"Try it."

She typed in CHILDREN, Children, children. Nothing. CHILD. Nothing. KIDS. Nothing.

She rolled off the chair, ending up flat on her back on the floor. "I'm useless. You might as well shoot me."

Bard knelt at her side. "Molly, stay with me now. And let it all out. You were one of his favorites, weren't you?"

"Yes . . . I think."

"Did he have a special nickname for you?"

"No."

Molly sat up. "But he did have a nickname he used for all

of us. Something he called just about every kid. It was like he couldn't remember every kid's name, so he stuck to one."

"What, Molly?"

"He called us all Mushka."

"Mushka?"

"Yeah, I don't know, it was just his word."

"With two *o*s, or a *u*?"

"I think *u*."

Bard wheeled to the keyboard. He typed in MUSHKA. The computer beeped merrily; the screen winked and filled with icons. My Computer; My Briefcase; Recycle Bin; Internet Explorer; Acrobat Reader; Real Player; Microsoft Word. Bard knew computers from the sheriff's department, but not enough for this. He moved aside. "You're on, Molly."

Molly sat down and stared at the screen. She clicked Start, then Programs, then Windows Explorer, which gave her Merta's directory. She found two word processors, Word 97 in Windows, Xywrite III+ in DOS. She opened both and scrolled down endless lists of files and folders that gave no hint of what they contained.

Gago.clp; 3LQ.prn; 90999.kr; ashlyn.nts; corny.ltr; dlite.txt; hayes.seg.

She opened "Corny.ltr." It was a note to a teacher at the school, thanking her for help she'd given at a piano lesson.

She opened "Gago.clp" It was a scanned-in magazine article about bad puns.

"This also could take days," she said. "Even months."

"Any way to search for specific references?"

Molly nodded as she punched keys, returning to the main desktop. She clicked Start, then Find, then Files or Folders. A box opened up, asking for a name. Molly looked over at her father.

"Try RC Cummings."

She typed it in. Nothing.

"Try Lillo."

Nothing.

"Try Albert Donner."

Nothing.

Bard thought of a grinning face in a newspaper photo. On a whim, he said, "Try Bruce Hightower."

Nothing.

Bard kicked at the wall. "It's got to be there."

Molly stared at the screen. "I think it's hidden."

"What do you mean?"

"Certain security programs will hide stuff for you. Files or whole folders. You can't see them in the directories."

"How can you get to them?"

"Through the security program."

"Where's that?"

Molly was tapping on the table as she peered at the screen. "Somewhere here in the computer, right before us. It can't be hidden. You have to be able to go through it to get to the hidden stuff."

"But it can be disguised?"

"Bingo. Way to think, Daddy."

Molly began scrolling through the folders in the My Documents directory. She opened one randomly, and saw nothing but ordinary data files, all tagged with the Microsoft Word icon. She opened another, and saw more data files written with Word. She opened a third, a fourth, a fifth. All the same.

In the sixth folder, she stopped. A file's name caught her attention. *Conrad.* "Besides Chekhov," she said, "Ollie always talked about Joseph Conrad."

Bard recalled Conrad from his limited time at Chumash State. He toyed with a notion. "Conrad wrote *The Secret Sharer*. Not a bad title for a security program that hides stuff."

Molly stared at the file's adjacent icon. It wasn't a Word document. It wasn't any kind of data file. The icon indicated it was a program file, an application. "Ollie could have changed the icon," she said. "Maybe he forgot. Or maybe he wanted to leave a sign."

Molly double-clicked on the file. In an instant, a program launched. A box appeared, asking again for a password. Molly tried MUSHKA. No. She tried Mushka, then mushka.

Nothing. Molly closed her eyes. Bard put a hand on her shoulder. "Go ahead," he said. "Try your name."

She glanced up at him as if to explain. He pointed to the keyboard. She sat for a moment, then typed MOLLY. The computer whirred and the box disappeared, replaced by a full screen. At the top were the words "Secret Sharer." Under those words was a directory of Merta's hard drive, not unlike the one called up by Windows Explorer. Except this one, Bard and Molly quickly saw, included several folders not visible before.

They scanned down the list. There it was, one labeled RC Cummings. It had a graphic attached that resembled a belt. Molly double-clicked but it wouldn't open. She looked up at the top of the screen and saw an Unhide button. She highlighted the Royce folder and clicked the button. The belt disappeared. Again she double-clicked on the folder. This time it opened a list of files on the right side of the screen.

Royce1, Royce2, Royce3, Lillo1, Lillo2 . . . Each had numbers to the right indicating the date it was last modified. The most recent, Bard saw, had been worked on the day Merta died.

"Open that one," he said, pointing.

Molly double-clicked once more. Microsoft Word launched, then the file opened. There it was: *SASHMEMO*.

Bard didn't want his daughter to see this, whatever it contained. "Okay Molly, I'll take over now."

"Good luck." Molly sat where she was. "I want to see."

"No."

She argued with him only when she thought she might prevail. Now she saw there was no point. Rising, she pointed to a spot on the screen. "Click there," she instructed.

He sat down and reached for the computer mouse. Once more he whispered his prayer. *Talk to us from the grave, Ollie.*

NINETEEN

The memo took the form of a letter to Sasha.

My dear Sasha:
 *I am so sorry. What has befallen you is all my fault.
There are reasons, though, for what I have done. These
you must understand. Tomorrow I will explain face to
face, but I want also to put this in writing.*

Bard turned from the computer. Molly was sitting cross-
legged on one of the cabin's corner pillows, absorbed in the
Game Boy she'd carried in her back pocket. Bard turned back
to the computer.

 *This all began when I noticed those strange com-
modities trades that RC Cummings had instructed Lillo
to execute. Then came the request to backdate certain
transactions on Lillo's letterhead.*
 *My dear Sasha, although you professed not to under-
stand the reason, it was clear they wished to obscure the
true buyer of certain big land parcels in the county. You
will recall how we analyzed this over one long weekend.
It gave me such pleasure when you finally decided to
deny RC Cummings's request. But they came at you
again, stepping up the pressure. You will recall how riled
I grew when you told me of these repeated requests.*
 *What you don't know is what I did later that evening. I
came back to your office for a file I'd left there. I let myself in with the key you so kindly gave me. In the few min-*

utes I was there, the phone rang. I recognized Albert Donner's voice, leaving a message on the answering machine. He was being none too subtle. I'm sorry to report what I did next, Sasha. I'm not proud of this, but it is a fact that I can be a cantankerous old cuss at times. I don't like bullies on the schoolyard, and I don't like bullies in the business world. So I picked up the phone. I didn't identify myself, didn't say who I was. I just demanded that he stop pressing you to do shady deals. I went further. I threatened to report RC Cummings to state regulatory authorities. I told Donner to back off or else.

That shut him up, my dear Sasha. I'm afraid so. It was then that RC Cummings fell silent. It was then that Lillo's business dried up. Oh my God, dear Sasha, I felt so responsible. As I watched you being pushed nearly to bankruptcy over the following months, I felt compelled to do something to make amends. There was no way to reconcile with RC Cummings. My only option was to find out what they were up to. That would give you leverage, I imagined. With leverage, I believed you could regain all the business that Lillo had lost.

What did I do, dear Sasha? I began to look at the land parcels for which RC Cummings wanted fake documents. Some things you can find simply by poring through public records available in courthouses. Some things you find on the Internet. Such a marvelous invention, the Internet.

Here is what I found, dear Sasha: Our very own county commissioner, Bruce Hightower, owns all those land parcels. Bruce Hightower is not just the local politician who welcomes venture capital into Chumash County. Bruce Hightower is the source himself of that capital. He is the investor. He is principal owner of RC Cummings, which is not a venture capital firm at all. It's a front for Bruce Hightower.

My first insight came when I took a look at that bluff above Pirate's Beach. A Nevada corporation called Xenon owns that land. It was transferred to Xenon from another Nevada corporation, Nirvana, which in turn received the land from a third corporation, Astoria. Who is the president of Astoria? None other than Bruce Hightower. He is listed merely as an employee of Astoria, but if so, he is a highly regarded one, for he is also its vice president, secretary, treasurer, and sole director.

My dear Sasha, I eventually found Hightower's footprints all over Chumash County. Shell companies controlled by him have funded much of our recent development. The monies were funneled through RC Cummings, and on through Lillo. Such layers were needed to obscure the fact that our friend was conveying laundered millions from all over—Panama, the Turks and Caicos Islands, Switzerland, the Netherlands, Antilles, the Cayman Islands. How do I know? Well, for one thing, our friend is playful about naming his shell companies. Too playful, perhaps. One of Hightower's shell companies is named, of all things, MotherShip.

When I came across that name, I understood everything. You see, dear Sasha, although my own job with the U.S. Customs Service mainly involved sitting on the British Columbia border, I had colleagues who worked much more exciting beats. Operation Cash Extraction, for one, which aimed at getting back money from retired drug runners who have laundered ill-gotten funds into the legitimate economy.

I made a few phone calls. It wasn't hard to unwind the tale. In the 1970s, Hightower was one of the biggest and most innovative marijuana smugglers of his time. He helped pioneer the "mothership" smuggling technique. Imagine, Sasha—a big freighter full of dope would unload on the high seas to a handful of medium-sized boats, which then relayed the product to smaller craft that blended in with recreational boaters. My dear Sasha, the motherships made Hightower a smuggling star. They also made him a very rich man.

Then his luck changed. He got caught in a sting operation. To escape a lengthy prison term, he turned informant for the DEA. Part of the deal was, he had to hand over all his ill-gotten gains. What did he produce? The grand sum of $420,000. That's right, dear Sasha. He insisted that was all he'd made.

There were many in Customs who scoffed, of course. But the prosecutors agreed to believe Hightower because they wanted an informer. He served just twenty months before being released with a new identity. He obviously arrived in Chumash County with his entrepreneurial instincts quite intact. It seems clear that he had a mind to go straight—and to launder his drug stash through legitimate businesses.

My dear Sasha, no doubt you're wondering right now what I did with my newly acquired insights. Here's where the story gets fun. In my Customs job, I will confess to you that I longed at times to do something more exciting than uncover a family's hidden bag of forbidden apples. I longed at times to join my more adventurous colleagues as they pursued their drug smugglers and money launderers.

They had such techniques, Sasha! There was one fellow in particular. He would slip alone into an elevator with his target and whisper the name of an obscure shell company known only to the smuggler. What an effect! Often the smuggler would crumple at the sound of that one word. Some would vomit, right there in the elevator.

I couldn't help it, Sasha. I wanted to do that just once. I wanted to create that moment. So I planted myself in La Graciosa's central plaza at midday, when I knew Bruce Hightower would be heading to lunch. I rose as he passed by my bench, accidentally bumping into him. In his ear I whispered, "Mothership."

Oh, Sasha, I wish I could tell you that Hightower crumpled or heaved. Alas, he showed not the slightest response. He apologized for bumping into me, and walked on.

That happened a little past noon on this very day,

Sasha. Now, near dusk, I sit at my computer writing you this memo. Although Hightower didn't react to me, I'm sure he is agitated. I'm inclined to take precautions. I'll explain more tomorrow—I must stop now, for I have Molly's friend, that lovely young Marilee Cooper, coming for a piano lesson. For reasons of security, I don't want to e-mail or fax you this note. I want to put it in your hands. So I will call you. We'll meet tomorrow morning.

I've reported all that I've learned, Sasha. It's my fondest hope that much good for you comes from what I've done. Here is your leverage, Sasha dear. Here is your way back.

Bard turned from the computer to find he was alone in Merta's cabin. Molly had slipped outside without him noticing. He had no idea how long she'd been gone. He jumped up, pushed through the front door. The fogbank had returned on the late-afternoon breeze. It hugged the ground now, obscuring even the ring of sycamores at the edge of the clearing. He burned his lungs shouting for Molly. Listening for a response, he heard too many to sort out—creaking branches, rustling leaves, the crunch of twigs.

Bard tried to imagine Molly's mind. Where would she go, what would draw her?

The rope, of course. She'd go play there if she were bored. She'd turn the rope into a swing.

Bard plunged through the haze toward the slope where they'd rappeled. "Molly . . . Molly . . ." Why wouldn't she answer? Why wouldn't—

Emerging from a willow thicket, he found himself within feet of the rope. It dangled from the tree above, untouched. Bard looked around, peering into the mist. He froze. A gray lump lay curled against the base of a nearby sycamore. A gray lump with long dark blonde hair. He fell to his knees before Molly. She was breathing. He could see no sign of injury. He rolled her over. Her eyes opened. She yawned.

"Sorry, Daddy. I got tired. I guess I fell asleep."

Bard collapsed next to her, using the tree as a backrest.

Molly sat up and rubbed her eyes. "Did you find what you were after in Ollie's computer?"

Bard wondered how to answer that.

That Sasha indeed had resisted RC Cummings left him washed with relief. He felt fairly certain now that she was harboring no secrets. She hadn't seen Merta's memo; she didn't know about Hightower. She must be so perplexed, so isolated. Bard regretted his manner with her in recent weeks. What moved him most was Ollie's obvious appreciation for Sasha.

If only Merta's other revelation were as helpful—or welcome.

Not many in Chumash County would want it disclosed that illicit drug money was financing their great boom. Both the power brokers and rank-and-file citizens had compelling reasons to keep Bruce Hightower's past hidden. New construction gave work to contractors, architects, electricians, plumbers, carpenters, masons. New stores drew shoppers, hired clerks, enriched merchants. Mounting tax coffers funded schools, repaired roads, built libraries. Everywhere property values rose as prosperity fed on itself.

No, the citizens would not want it known what was fueling Chumash's fine renaissance. So they wouldn't want it known that Bruce Hightower killed Ollie and Marilee. More precisely, they wouldn't want it to be true. They wouldn't let it be true. Jed Jeremiah had to be guilty.

One question remained: How wide was the conspiracy? How many in Chumash County knew about Bruce Hightower?

Bard thought of all the county big shots who assembled on the podium with Hightower at Pirate's Beach, then again at Jimmy's office, issuing warnings. He thought also of Howie Dixon, always carrying water for his keepers. Then there was Angela Stark. You'd have to assume she knew about Hightower, but men with pasts have fooled plenty of women. Bard couldn't say where Stark stood, couldn't imagine.

Nor could he fix on his next move. It would be neither wise nor useful to bring Ollie's memo to Angela, or to anyone else in power. He'd be showing his hand to folks who shouldn't know what cards he held. Rather than thank him for the news, they'd likely come after the messengers. Bard could think of no more effective way to put Sasha and Molly in peril.

Taking the memo public, handing it to Jimmy, would be just as foolish. The memo didn't prove anything about the murders, after all; it only besmirched a county hero with uncorroborated accusations. Besides, even if true, Hightower had paid his dues. The drug smuggling happened so many years ago. It was only grass, not hard stuff. Hightower turned, Hightower informed, Hightower helped the DEA. What's so wrong? people would say. What's the big deal?

The roasted bodies, of course. They were the big deal. The roasted bodies, and Jed Jeremiah just steps from Death Row.

Bard stood and helped his daughter to her feet. "Come on, Molly girl. Ready to rappel?"

TWENTY

Cassie Teal stared at the intercom sitting on her desk. "Could you repeat that, please?"

Again the receptionist said: "Douglas Bard is out here. He wants to see you."

Cassie tried to fathom what she'd just heard. She and Doug had kept their meetings a secret since the trial started. That is, until his ex-wife moved in and they stopped meeting altogether. Whatever Bard wanted now, it was too late. There was no point.

"Tell him I'm not available," Cassie said. "Tell him to leave."

A moment later, the door to her office burst open. Doug Bard stomped in, followed by a worried receptionist.

"It's okay, Delia," Cassie said.

The receptionist retreated. The door banged shut behind her.

"She's probably on her way to Angela's office," Cassie said.

"Angela can go to hell."

"Easy for you to say."

"I haven't talked to you since that night you left my house."

"There have not been any opportunities since."

"Let's make one."

"Shall we retreat to your cabin? Would Sasha mind?"

"Come on, Cassie."

They stood looking at each other. They could hear footsteps in the hallway. Somewhere, a phone was ringing. Cassie reached for her sweater.

*   *   *

Near dusk they sat on the side of the ancient volcano called King's Peak. The hikers were all down now, and the turkey vultures had ceased their endless gyrations. Far below, La Graciosa's lights were blinking on as children turned up driveways and front doors closed on the fading light. Across the ravine a bellicose cow mooed while its sisters stood still, listening.

Cabrillo came by here in 1542. He saw seven pcaks, all in a row, with broad valleys on either side. The early explorers called them the "Seven Sisters." Ever since, geologists and students have stared at them, walked across them, chipped away at them. The surrounding mountains were mere youngsters, sedimentary ranges no more than one million years old. By contrast, the Seven Sisters—remnants of volcanic plugs formed deep in the earth, then thrust up and exposed by erosion—were at least twenty-three million years old. They'd resisted the ravages of time and wind and rain, for they were made of granite, fine grained and hard.

To get here, Bard and Cassie had driven to the end of a dusty fire road, then ducked under barbed wire and walked up a grassy slope covered by wood chips. Beyond a grove of oaks, the trail became less obvious, the slope steeper. Footing had been tricky on granite boulders made slippery by a dusting of soil. Coming down would be trickier yet. Yet the view was worth it. King's Peak towered above the others. Turning their heads, Bard and Cassie took in the crashing surf, the splintered piers of Pirate's Beach, the vast white Chumash Dunes, the oak-thick inland hills, the twinkling streets of La Graciosa. Behind them, far to the north, the sky and coast disappeared into the mist.

"What a place," Cassie said.

"Best I could think of."

She was rocking slowly. "Sorry to be bitchy before. But I can't help wondering about your life with the family."

"Their lives are in danger, Cassie."

"Sasha still means so much to you."

Bard looked away. "Why do you say that?"

"It shows. You're not such a mystery to me."

"Only to myself, then."

"Doug—"

"It's like this. Sasha is Molly's mother. And Molly is the air in my lungs."

Cassie stopped rocking. "Who would guess that Douglas Bard is a poet."

Bard said, "Sasha was long ago."

"Your cabin is still kind of crowded, Doug."

"Yes." Silence. Then, "Cassie, I found Ollie Merta's memo."

She absorbed that, fixing on the view as if unwilling to abandon the dunes and the mist. "And did it unlock all your mysteries, Doug?"

"It told me who killed Ollie and Marilee. It also told me why everyone needs Jed Jeremiah to be the killer."

She pulled her legs up and wrapped her arms around her knees. "I guess you have a story to tell."

"Yes."

He gave her everything. Merta's challenge to RC Cummings, his research into the land parcels, Bruce Hightower's background, the whispered encounter on the plaza. The piano lesson with Marilee. The promise to deliver a memo. He watched her as he spoke, vainly looking for a sign that he was affecting her. His voice rose, grew impatient. "Merta signed his own death warrant, don't you see, Cassie? Hightower knew he'd been uncovered. He couldn't have that. God knows how many millions he's laundering. Merta had to be silenced. The stakes were too high. And not just for Hightower. Also for all those who run this county. They couldn't let this get out. A county built on drug money! Imagine, Cassie! There goes our oasis. There goes our boom. There goes everything."

Cassie's eyes stayed with the view. "It would be way more than an embarrassment. They'd all have to hand everything they owned over to the feds. Forfeiture is one of the drug laws' most powerful features. Whatever you buy with drug money, you lose. Autos, boats, shopping centers, cattle ranches. It's written right into the statutes."

"Will you help me now, Cassie?"

She didn't appear to hear him. "Of course, money laundering isn't easy to prove. Showing the transfer of money is usually a snap. The problem is proving that the money came from a particularized criminal source. You have to prove that the source of the money was ill-gotten gains from specific criminal activities."

"Merta said U.S. Customs had Hightower on their radar," Bard pointed out. "There must be a solid paper trail."

"Not necessarily. There usually isn't one. If you're smart enough to make a few hundred million, you're smart enough to obscure how you did it."

Cassie turned to him. "You know, Doug, up until now, I've always thought Angela Stark was simply a smart relentless prosecutor, playing hardball but abiding by Chumash County's particular rules."

"If so, the rules have evolved."

"Yes. Angela runs Dixon. But who would have guessed that she had a keeper?"

"You assume she knows all about Hightower? That she's protecting a killer by prosecuting an innocent man?"

A glow showed in Cassie's eyes. "The most dangerous emotion is love."

"Even for Angela Stark?"

"Yes. Even. A person consumed by passion can do just about anything. Particularly someone who's deeply frustrated."

"You sound as if you're familiar with the type."

"Come on, Doug. Everyone has keepers of some sort. Even if they're buried deep inside."

Bard drew closer to her. "Cassie, I'm not sure who all in our county is part of this, but there still are some folks we can safely turn to."

"Do tell."

"The jurors."

In silence, Cassie resumed her rocking, arms around her knees. "It's too late, Doug."

"How can you say that?"

"Jed Jeremiah finally blew. In the courtroom today, he jumped up. He announced he wanted to plead guilty."

Bard found it hard to breathe. "Jesus Christ. Right in front of the judge? Right in front of the jury?"

"Yes."

"What did Brody do?"

Cassie's mouth curved into a faint smile. "Louis Brody's job is to be his client's advocate. So Louis Brody has decided to support his client's wishes."

Late at night, Angela Stark reached for the remote control. Why not play it once more?

On her television screen, Louis Brody and Jed Jeremiah sat facing each other across a narrow table in a jailhouse conference room. Something like a smile played across Jed's face.

"How many more times do I need to say it?" he asked. "I don't want to fight. I want you to stop defending me. I want you to give up."

"I can't just give up, Jed. That's now how it works. We have to fight."

"But I killed them, Brody. I want to confess."

"We've gone over this, Jed. Why would you want—"

"I am the sum of my sins, Brody. I cause death. I'm dangerous. You ought to know that by now."

"Tell me again just what you did."

"I've told you often enough. I've told myself, too."

"You strangled Merta and the girl? Then you burned down Ollie's house?"

"It was his own fault. He wouldn't stop poaching and trespassing. He wouldn't leave me be."

"The little girl wouldn't, either?"

"She saw me. She was screaming. I put my hand on her mouth to shut her up. When I stopped, she was dead, too. I killed them both."

Brody studied his client. "As you know, Jed, the state won't plea-bargain."

"So plead me into first-degree murder. That's what I want."

"Jed—"

"What does it matter, Brody? They got me. The daydream, the footprints, the witnesses. What a great show. I just don't want to watch it anymore. Like I told you, I want to control my own destiny."

"We still have a chance."

"For chrissake, don't you see?" Jeremiah's eyes blazed. "You're defending a guilty man."

"So what?" Brody looked unwell. "It wouldn't be the first time."

"But you can't abide that anymore, can you, Brody?"

A tremor played across Louis's face. "I'm your lawyer. My job is to represent your interests."

"Exactly, Brody. I couldn't have put it better. So here's my interest—to be in control. Plead me guilty or just plain quit lawyering. That's what I want. Goddamn it, Brody, be my advocate."

Louis's head tilted back. Minutes passed. He appeared to be examining the ceiling. Or was he praying? Angela Stark leaned forward to see better. She almost felt sorry for the man. What a dilemma. Which to serve, his client's desires or the state's demand that he be a zealous adversary?

On the screen, suffering contorted Brody's features. "How can I do this, Jed?"

Jeremiah didn't answer.

"Is it that you just want to accept responsibility, Jed?"

"Yes . . . responsibility, sure, that's it."

"It's not so much a death wish, is it, Jed? It sounds to me more like an inclination to accept what's coming."

"Don't worry, Louis. My life isn't that valuable to me. My life is only an existence. No, it's not even an existence."

Brody spoke as if to himself. "It's sort of like if I were a doctor. It's sort of like having a terminal patient in the hospital say he no longer wants life support."

"Exactly. I have that right."

"Still . . . It would feel like I'm abandoning you, Jed. If I don't fight for you, I'm abandoning you."

"No." Jeremiah leaned toward him. "Just the opposite, Brody. You'll abandon me if you ignore my wishes."

"Just the opposite?" Brody peered into Jeremiah's eyes as if on a search mission. Angela had watched this scene twice before, but still she held her breath. "I hadn't thought of that. I suppose you could put it that way."

Jeremiah reached for his lawyer's hand. "Don't abandon me, Brody. Everyone else has. Not you."

Louis examined their entwined fingers, Jed's gnarled and bent, his a smooth pink. "Abandon you . . . ?"

"Don't. Not you."

Still Jed clutched his hand. The union appeared to hypnotize Brody. Minutes passed. Finally he spoke, so softly that the hidden microphone almost couldn't pick up his voice. "Okay, Jed. I won't abandon you. I'm not going to ignore your wishes. I can't do that. My job is to represent your interests."

Angela watched Jeremiah ease back in his chair. Just as Brody said, it was like granting a terminal patient his wish to exit. That's what Jeremiah resembled now—a patient who is told the pain will soon end.

Angela hit the pause button. She sat still, studying Jed Jeremiah's face.

From a corner of the district attorney's office, Cassie Teal watched thin bands of early-morning sunlight poke through her window blinds. The light crept across one wall. The days were growing shorter now, summer was turning to fall. Soon they'd be finished with all this; soon they'd be off to new cases, different thoughts. The notion comforted Cassie.

She looked across the room at Angela Stark and Howie Dixon, sitting at the conference table. Angela was reviewing a file. Howie was doodling.

"What a sweet spot we're in," Stark said. "Brody will be here in a few minutes. He'll try to get a deal. But the poor man has no leverage."

Cassie said, "I wonder what finally pushed Jed to blow."

"Had to have been the daydream," Angela proposed. "That nailed the case shut."

"It did," Cassie said. "Didn't it."

Dixon stopped doodling. "Also didn't hurt that the judge gagged Bard."

"That, too," Cassie agreed.

A knock at the door interrupted them. Louis Brody stepped into the room. He glanced at Cassie first, then the others. "Your whole team's here."

"It seemed appropriate," Angela said.

Brody approached them slowly. He chose the chair next to Cassie. "Well, I guess it's no secret why I'm here."

"Tell us anyway," Angela suggested.

Brody looked around the room. "My client wants to plead. We'd like to stop the trial and cut a deal."

The DA offered a sympathetic smile. "But in fact you've already stopped the trial, Louis. And your client has already pled."

"He said he wanted to, was going to, but it's not been formally entered or accepted yet."

"It will be tomorrow."

"Yes, well, I—"

"It's no use," Angela continued. "You're trying valiantly, Louis, but there's nothing you can do now. I'm sure you see that. You will just have to plead into first-degree murder."

Brody paled, hearing it put so baldly. "Pleading into first degree without a deal is the definition of incompetence."

Without thinking, Cassie put a hand on his arm. "No one can blame you, Louis. Everyone saw what happened in the courtroom. Your client blew up on you."

Brody stared at her hand. "Can't we do something here? Can't we negotiate?"

"Not possible," Angela said.

With distaste, Brody caught the gleam in Stark's eye. He shook his arm free from Cassie. "What a game we all play. All our roles stink. I wonder how any of us sleep at night. Whatever we pursue, it sure as hell isn't justice."

"I sleep just fine," Angela said. "You know what the definition of justice is on the street? 'You get what you deserve.'"

"Yes," said Brody dryly. "I suppose that's right."

Dixon said, "Louis, if it's any comfort, in these last days Jeremiah has been regularly confessing to everyone in the jailhouse."

No, it wasn't any comfort. Brody's voice rose. "I've spent

hours with Jed. Hours. You know what I've learned above all else? That Jed looks to his past and his future with equal torment."

Cassie wanted to respond, but could think of nothing to say.

Brody hesitated, as if waiting for something unforeseen to develop, then rose. At the door he stopped and looked back at all of them. "I want you to know that I'm not abandoning Jed. I'm standing by him. I'm representing his interests."

The others sat in silence after he left. Dixon, his hand on his stomach, spoke first. "Jesus . . . When this is all over, I'm going fishing up at Shasta."

Cassie closed and locked the door when she got back to her office. She sat down at her desk. From a drawer, she extracted a file, and placed it before her. She stared at its cover. *Spiky Samuels, Docket 80224.* There was no need to open it. She knew what it held.

No longer could she ignore the matter. No longer could she ignore that she'd perjured herself before Judge Hedgespeth. *I told Mr. Samuels there could be no deal. I told him that we couldn't promise him any special treatment.*

With reluctance, Cassie opened Spiky's file. There it was, right on top. A confidential presentencing report. Near the bottom of the page, one sentence: "DA Angela Stark and Sheriff Howie Dixon have requested that the sentence on Spiky Samuels be postponed until the Merta-Cooper murder case is completed."

Poor Louis. He'd tried his best with Spiky.

You pled guilty to a motel robbery nine months ago, but haven't been sentenced. Do you have any knowledge of why you haven't been sentenced?

No, I haven't.

Has the state made any promises or agreements with you? Have you been given immunity in this crime?

No, I have not, not as I know of.

You are absolutely certain that you haven't been given any immunity, is that correct?

I'm certain.

So you just decided to cleanse your soul?

Yes.

What a hoot. Angela had even been planning to run with this in her closing argument. She'd shared a draft with Cassie. That would have been something, watching Stark march before the jurors. *There was an attempt made by defense counsel to impeach Spiky Samuels. You all heard that. Impeach means to reduce his credibility somehow by showing that for some reason or another he isn't telling the truth. And I submit that there have been no promises made to Spiky Samuels for his testifying in this case. He had absolutely nothing to gain by testifying against Jed Jeremiah.*

At least they'd be spared that particular courtroom show.

Cassie picked up Spiky's file. She held it in her hand for a moment, then turned and slipped it into her briefcase.

She felt isolated. Wasn't anyone else bothered? What about Howie? He must be feeling it. Sure. He can't wait to escape. Can't wait to go fishing up at Shasta.

Cassie froze. *Fishing up at Shasta.* Something tugged at her. *Fishing. Shasta.* She reached for her scheduling book and began flipping through the pages. Hadn't Dixon been fishing up at Shasta once before? Wasn't that the weekend she'd tried so desperately to track him down? And wasn't that also the weekend—

Cassie stopped flipping. There it was. She stared at her penciled entries, a snapshot of the not-so-distant past. She picked up the phone and punched in a number. "Douglas," she said. "We have to meet."

She handed him the Spiky Samuels file first. Bard rifled through it impatiently. She leaned over, pointing at the last line in the presentencing report. "That's proof we cut a deal with Spiky. Both Angela and I denied it in open court when the judge asked. So did Spiky, up on the witness stand."

Bard studied the documents again. He slapped the papers against his hand. "Am I missing something? I don't get it. This is naughty, but it'll hardly get a mistrial. Who cares about Spiky? He's not what the case rests on, especially now that Jed is pleading. We need so much more than this."

They were sitting at the kitchen table in Cassie's house. Bard had walked over from the plaza, hoping to go unnoticed.

"Well, I guess I care," Cassie said. "Since I'm one of the naughty ones."

"So go confess on Sunday."

"I'm not Catholic. In fact, I don't go to church."

"Well, then," Bard eased up, "we might be compatible after all."

Cassie took back her file. "Since you're such an expert about the law now, what would you say the case rests on? That is, if Jed hadn't blown up?"

"The bootprint and Eddie Hines's testimony hurt, but Brody at least managed to counter them. He had more trouble with the daydream. That was devastating."

"Yes. Angela and Brody agree."

"Well then, there you have it."

Cassie's eyes stayed on him. "It's no good on either side, Doug. You can't have clean hands in this business."

He waited for her to continue. When she didn't, he asked, "What's up, Cassie?"

"What's up is, I'm a mole now, too. Out in the cold, just like you."

"Are you going to explain?"

"Yes, goddamn it. Of course. That's why I called you."

"Okay, then."

She began drawing an imaginary line on her table. "Something Dixon said this morning triggered my memory, sent me back to my scheduling book. There was a weekend months ago when I needed to reach Howie. I had a trial starting on Monday, and only Howie could fill in some holes. I absolutely had to talk to him. But I couldn't. He wasn't in town, and he wasn't reachable. He was upstate on a three-day fishing trip at some godforsaken lake high in the Shasta National Forest. No phones at the campsites, cells don't work up there, nothing. Best I could do is leave a message at a small grocery store way the hell down the mountain. He never got it, never went down the goddamn mountain."

"I'm sure there's a point here," Bard interrupted, "but again I'm missing it."

"Yes, there is a point here. You know when that weekend was, Doug? It was the weekend that Jed supposedly told Baynes and Akers about his horrible nightmare."

"Yes . . . So?"

"Don't you see, Doug? Baynes says they called Howie and told him all about it, right away, that very day. But Baynes could not possibly have talked to Howie. It didn't happen. Which means the daydream business didn't happen."

"Dixon testified that he got a call?"

"Yep."

"Jesus. I know Howie rolls with the current. But I didn't think he'd get in this deep."

"Howie helped frame an innocent man."

"You think so? Why's Jed confessing then?"

"We've all driven him off the cliff, that's why."

Bard thought of Jed aching over his wife's death. "The cleansing power of confession helps, too."

"Yes," Cassie said. "I've heard more than a few false confessions. People thinking that punishment, rather than penance, is their path to absolution."

"What can we do?"

"As a prosecutor, I'm obliged to hand over exculpatory evidence to Louis. Then the ball is in his court."

Bard worked that over in his mind. "Obliged, my ass. Prosecutors overlook that duty all the time. I'm sure Angela expects you to do lots of overlooking. You'd end up out in the cold, just like me."

"So be it."

"No. You want to be a prosecutor. You want to put the bad guys away. You don't want to defend killers."

"That's true. But I have no choice here, Doug."

Again he thought things through. He rose. "Yes, you do, Cassie."

*　　*　　*

Louis Brody acted as if he weren't there. Bard didn't care. He kept talking. "If everyone is not in agreement on how the game is played, you can't be doing this, Louis. Pleading into a capital charge when you know they're coming at you with a syringe is lunacy. You're not going to be an adversary, but the problem is, they are."

Brody still wasn't swayed. He said, "My client's interests come first. I'm obliged to represent Jed, what he wants. I can't abandon him. I won't abandon him."

Bard thought of Cassie, protecting Hernandez's interests as the county searched for a girl's body. How tangled things could get, being someone else's advocate. "Look at it this way, Brody. If you don't fight for the defense, the whole system breaks down. If you stop playing your role, the game just doesn't work. You have to fight, goddamn it. Even if you don't want to."

Brody found that amusing. "What you're saying is, the state's interest in a just society takes precedence over a defendant's autonomy. Since when have you become so concerned about the state's interest?"

"It's not the state I care about. It's the defendant."

"Is that so?" Brody's amusement grew. "When Cassie fought for Hernandez's life, you denounced her all over the county."

Bard tapped a foot against his chair. "We're getting off track here. I didn't come to argue theory."

"Why did you come?"

Bard reached into the satchel at his side. He tossed the Spiky Samuels file onto Brody's desk.

"Exculpatory evidence for you."

Brody opened the file. As he read, Bard talked. "There's proof there that Angela Stark cut a deal with Spiky, which means she lied in court to the judge."

Brody had his finger on the relevant sentence. "It also means Cassie lied."

"Yes."

Brody closed the file. "Too little, too late, Doug."

"There's more."

"Oh?"

"The whole daydream business is a lie."

"I've always assumed so. But the judge, in his great wisdom, allowed it in."

"I have evidence that will convince him otherwise. At the least, he'll reverse his ruling. He might even throw the whole case out."

"But Jed has confessed, Jed is pleading."

"Jed hasn't formally pled yet. He just said he wanted to."

"And he's going to. There's no point. You're wasting our time."

"The daydream business is what pushed him over the edge."

"That's one possibility. I can think of others."

"We have a chance here, Louis. A chance to pull Jed back."

Brody hesitated. That prospect stirred something in him. "You really think Hedgespeth might toss this out based on what you have?"

"It's possible."

Brody ran his fingers along the edge of his desk. "This is a hard one."

"No argument about that."

"I've made a commitment to Jed."

"Give me a few minutes here to explain what I have."

"What's the point, Doug?"

"A few minutes."

Brody threw up his hands, surrendering more than agreeing. "A few minutes."

TWENTY-ONE

Would there ever be a morning bathed in stark bright morning light? Not in La Graciosa, it seemed, at least not this season. Doug Bard stepped slowly through the thick gray mist, sensing where the park benches were, the bear statue, the winding creek. He didn't mind. He wanted to take his time as he approached the *asistencia*.

They'd let him in the courtroom today. He'd already testified, so no longer was a pending witness. Bard had no idea what to expect. All he knew was, Louis Brody had his hands full with Jed Jeremiah. Client and defense attorney had been holed up most of the weekend. Once, Bard passed Brody on the plaza. Louis just shook his head and rushed by.

Bard was halfway across the plaza now, the *asistencia* a dim outline before him. He heard muffled voices. A face loomed, coming from his right, then two more. Bard's path so closely intersected the trio's, they nearly collided.

Sheriff Howie Dixon. Dixon, walking with Marilee's parents, Harvey and Cynthia Cooper.

All of them stopped, frozen by confusion and the damp gloom. Bard nodded his greetings. He wanted to tell the Coopers about their daughter's friendship with Molly. He wanted also to warn Dixon about what was coming. *Fix what you've done, Howie. It's not too late. Save yourself. Save who you are.* The words wouldn't come, though. Bard couldn't bring himself to speak.

"Well now, Doug, looks like it's just about over," Dixon was saying.

The sheriff turned to the parents for affirmation. Their arms were wrapped around each other. Shawls circled their necks, protecting against the morning chill and whatever else might assail them. They were staring at Bard.

"If it's almost over," Harvey Cooper said, "it's no thanks to this detective here."

"I'm not a detective anymore, Mr. Cooper."

"Good thing."

"Mr. Cooper—" Bard stopped, then decided to keep on going. "You must know that my daughter Molly was a close friend of Marilee's. She and I have mourned together over Marilee. We've also worked together to learn what really happened."

"What really happened?" Cynthia Cooper looked as if she might slap him. Her shawl slipped to her shoulders. Strands of hair, graying now, fell across her face. "In court this morning, a man is going to stand up and plead guilty. Isn't it clear what happened?"

Bard glanced at Dixon. The mist had burned off a bit, enough for them to see each other clearly. "What do you think, Howie?"

Dixon hitched his belt up. "Come on," he told Marilee's parents. "It's time for us to get inside the courtroom."

The jury box was empty. After Jeremiah's outburst, the judge had sent the jurors home and scheduled a bench hearing. Hedgespeth alone would decide whether to accept Jeremiah's plea. Jed's competency would be one issue. Whether he'd been fully advised of all his rights would be another.

Hedgespeth, gazing out at a packed courtroom, did not appear to relish the task thrust upon him. He would much rather moderate an exchange between two adversaries, then let twelve citizens of Chumash County decide about truth and justice. He had no choice, though. Whether to accept Jeremiah's plea was not something he could leave to jurors.

"Everybody ready?" Hedgespeth inquired.

On the state's side of the lawyers' table, Angela Stark rose. "Yes, Your Honor."

Louis Brody was already on his feet. "The defense is ready."

Doug Bard sat in the last row, Jimmy O'Brien by his side. He still hadn't told the editor that he'd found Merta's memo. Bard couldn't trust what Jimmy might do, what anyone might do. Jimmy would be furious when he found out, but it couldn't be helped.

"Word is," Jimmy whispered, "Jed wouldn't talk to the shrinks they lined up to judge his competency. I don't see how Brody is going to play this."

Bard nodded but said nothing. He studied the back of Brody's head. Louis had listened and absorbed, but hadn't committed to anything.

Bard looked around the courtroom. The spectators were a fair cross section of Chumash County—ranchers, fishermen, merchants, housewives. Most, agitated by the latest turn of events, were frowning or whispering, clutching each other's hands. In the second row sat the Coopers. Farther back, a contingent from Marilee's school stared intently at the judge. And in a far corner, Bard now saw, Bruce Hightower leaned against a wall.

"What I think we need to do," Hedgespeth began, "is have Mr. Jeremiah rise and repeat more formally now his desire to plead guilty. Then I will ask a few questions to make sure he understands what he's doing, and is acting on his own volition, with the benefit of counsel. If we can satisfy those issues, we'll move on to the medical experts. What I'd like—"

"Your Honor." Brody was approaching the bench. "With your permission, Your Honor, I'd like to ask for a continuance of this hearing."

A low murmur coursed through the courtroom. Angela Stark leaned forward. Hedgespeth lowered his glasses. "Mr. Brody," the judge asked, "what is this about?"

"A new matter has come to my attention in the past two

days, Your Honor. I need more time to explore information
I've just received."

"So your client does not intend to plead guilty?"

"Your Honor, I'm not saying that. I'm only speaking for
today, for this moment. Right now, I'd like a continuance.
Give us a couple days, give—"

"No!" Jed Jeremiah had jumped to his feet, although he
was handcuffed and shackled at the ankles. Two bailiffs took
a couple steps toward him. Jeremiah raised a hand.

"I want to get on with it right now," he demanded. "I want
to be done with it."

Brody, trying to pull Jed down to his chair, appeared more
resigned than surprised. "I say again, Your Honor, I ask for a
continuance."

Jeremiah shook him off and looked toward the jail guards.
"Let's get out of here," he commanded. He began marching
in shackles toward the courtroom doors.

"Mr. Jeremiah!" Judge Hedgespeth called out. "Hold on
now there. Hold on or I'll have to chain you to your chair."

Jeremiah stopped midway toward the door. He stood in a
sort of no-man's-land, away from the lawyers' table, away from
the spectators, away from everyone. He glared at Hedgespeth.
"What my attorney is doing here today is not according to my
wishes or interests. My desire is to just go ahead and get it
over with. Two days or two months isn't going to make any
difference, so let them do what they have to do."

Hedgespeth couldn't hide his dismay. "Mr. Brody, what
have you to say? How shall we proceed? Do you and your
client wish a recess to discuss?"

All eyes fixed on the defense attorney. *A nebulous legal
wilderness*—that's how he'd described his situation to Bard.
This morning, he'd hoped only to delay a reckoning, but Jed
was proving too impatient. Brody clutched the edge of the
lawyers' table.

"Your Honor," he said. "I'm facing a quandary. I'm pulled
between what Jed Jeremiah is telling me, and what my instincts as a lawyer tell me. I don't want Mr. Jeremiah to think
that I'm abandoning him. All I'm saying is that I believe we

should have a brief continuance. I certainly hope that Mr.
Jeremiah realizes I'm still working for him. I—"

"No!" Jed shouted. "I don't realize that. I want to plead!"

Hedgespeth slammed down his gavel. "That's enough out-
bursts in this courtroom. Mr. Jeremiah, Mr. Brody, there will
be no more warnings. I will have the defendant chained and
gagged if I must."

Brody managed to pull Jeremiah into his chair. He
clenched Jed's shoulder. "Your Honor, can we at least have a
recess for a few minutes?"

"No, sir!" Jeremiah yelled. "No, sir, I want to plead right
now."

"Bailiffs," Hedgespeth called. "Bind and gag the defendant."

The guards approached the lawyers' table. Brody stepped
between them and his client. "No," he said. "You can't do
this. You just can't."

Hedgespeth showed no expression. "It's your choice, Mr.
Brody. This is your call."

For a moment, they all stood frozen, the defense attorney
facing the guards, the judge watching from on high, the defendant seated behind his lawyer. Then Brody turned and
looked at Jeremiah.

"Okay," he said. "Enough. I cannot countenance this treatment of my client. I cannot countenance his being bound and
gagged. I came here this morning determined to honor his
wishes. I wanted only a brief delay. But Mr. Jeremiah insists
that he be heard immediately. He and I have talked for hours
these past two days. I have advised him of all the consequences, and still he desires to go ahead. Based upon that, I
will honor Mr. Jeremiah's wishes."

Brody gazed up at the judge with tortured eyes.

Now it was Hedgespeth's turn to hesitate. Brody's choice
didn't appear to be what the judge had anticipated. He peered
at the defense attorney. "Are you sure now, Mr. Brody? Have
you considered your proper role in these proceedings?"

"My proper role?" Louis took a step toward the bench.
"What would that be, Your Honor?"

Hedgespeth fumbled with papers before him. "Well, now—"

Brody interrupted. "Am I merely a puppet in the state court system, Your Honor? An actor reading a script? Can the system always require me to push back when the defendant doesn't want to push back?"

"Mr. Brody—" Hedgespeth began again.

"Just how many motions do you file? How many objections do you raise?"

"You have a job—"

"It just seems to me that defense attorneys sometimes let their egos and ambitions get the best of them. It seems to me that defense attorneys sometimes ignore ethical boundaries in their drive to win at all costs."

"Well now," Hedgespeth observed, "you could say that about both sides, couldn't you? All the more reason to keep pushing from your end."

Brody shook his head. "It's no use, Your Honor. My client insists upon pleading guilty. I will support him. I will not abandon him."

Hedgespeth looked at Angela Stark. "Does the state have any position?"

The DA rose. "We came to court today to hear a plea entered, Your Honor. We are prepared to go forward."

Still the judge didn't act. He shifted in his seat, wincing. Jimmy whispered to Doug, "Hedge's gout is acting up again."

Bard could barely breathe. He leaned toward Jimmy. "Someone has to do something if Brody won't. Someone has to stop Jed from pleading."

On the bench, Hedgespeth was gathering himself. He tapped his gavel to quiet the murmuring. "Okay, this is unusual, but we will proceed with this hearing. What I'd like—"

"Your Honor, if I may, excuse me."

The judge lifted his eyes toward the voice that had interrupted him. So did Bard, peering over a dozen rows of spectators. Everyone in the courtroom now was staring at the state's side of the attorneys' table.

"Your Honor," Cassie Teal said again, "may I approach?"

"What now, Ms. Teal?" Hedgespeth asked.

At Cassie's side, Angela Stark was reaching out for her deputy. Cassie ignored her. She took three steps toward the bench. "Your Honor, forgive me, but I feel obliged at this point to speak out, as an officer of the court."

Hedgespeth peered over his glasses. "Speak out on what matter, Ms. Teal?"

For a moment, Cassie's head turned slightly toward the spectators. Bard wondered if she was looking for him. "Your Honor," she began. "I am not expert enough to say whether Jed Jeremiah is competent to enter a plea, but I do feel that the state's case has pushed him toward taking that action. Most particularly, the evidence put on by the state about the defendant's so-called daydream. What I—"

"I object. Just what's going on here?" Angela Stark was on her feet, calling out to the judge.

Hedgespeth held up a hand. "You'll have to wait a minute, Ms. Stark. A representative from your office already has the floor. You can't object to what your own office is saying."

"But I—"

"Ms. Stark, sit down."

Angela, eyes fixed on her deputy, slowly sank into her chair. Cassie continued. "What I am obliged to report is that new evidence has come to light about that daydream. New evidence that contradicts what Sheriff Dixon and his two deputies testified to about that dream. I believe this new evidence demonstrates that the daydream never happened, could not have happened."

Cassie looked over at Louis Brody and Jed Jeremiah. "I'm obliged by the rules of law to hand this evidence over to the defense. I'm sure this is something both the defense and the court will want to examine."

From behind Cassie, Angela whispered words only her deputy could hear. Hedgespeth silenced her with a wave. "Ms. Teal, what exactly are you doing? Taking over the defense attorney's role?"

"Not at all," Cassie replied. "I'm playing the prosecutor's role to the hilt. Pursuing truth and justice. Isn't that my job?"

"We're after a conviction," Stark said out loud. "The jury decides what's true."

Cassie turned to her. "My convictions are more important than a conviction."

Hedgespeth was gulping from a glass of water. "That's enough, that's enough. This isn't a law school debating society. As far as I can tell, this is still a court of law."

Everyone fell silent, waiting for him. Hedgespeth sat hunched over his notes. "Okay, Ms. Teal. This is a bit unusual. I need some help sorting things. Why don't you just tell me a little about this new evidence."

Cassie reached for her briefcase. From it she pulled a file. She opened it and leafed through the pages. "Your Honor, you may recall deputies Victor Baynes and Andy Akers testifying that they called Sheriff Dixon right after hearing about the daydream. You may also recall that Sheriff Dixon corroborated, testifying he took their call. I have reason to believe that this couldn't have happened. I have reason to believe that Sheriff Dixon was not reachable by phone or any means of communication the weekend Jed supposedly talked about a daydream."

Murmurs again coursed through the courtroom. Angela was scribbling on a legal pad. Brody and Jeremiah were staring at Cassie. Hedgespeth was tapping his gavel. "How do you have reason to so believe, Ms. Teal?"

"That weekend, Your Honor, I desperately needed to reach Sheriff Dixon on another matter. I could not. He wasn't in the county. He was fishing high up in the Shasta National Park. There were no telephones, no way to reach him. I know because I tried all weekend long. I tried—"

"Your Honor!" Angela was again on her feet. "I object. Cassie is testifying now. She absolutely can't do that. She—"

"I'm going to permit this," Hedgespeth interrupted. "Ms. Teal is making representations as an officer of the court. The jury is not present, she's just talking to the court. She can do that without taking the stand. Ms. Teal, continue."

"That's just about it, Your Honor. I have my calendar

and scheduling book right here. That's how I realized what weekend we were talking about. I can produce those if you wish."

Hedgespeth made a note. "That would be fine later, if it gets to that. Right now, what I very much want is to hear from Sheriff Dixon. Is Howie available? Is he around here somewhere?"

"Your Honor," Cassie said. "I believe he's down the hall in his office."

Hedgespeth turned to his bailiff. "Please go get the sheriff. Tell him I want him in the courtroom. And absolutely do not tell him what this is about."

Doug Bard vainly tried to catch the sheriff's eye as he walked into the courtroom. Stepping slowly toward the bench, Howie Dixon stared straight ahead.

"Sheriff," the judge said, "I need you to take an oath and get up here on the witness stand for a moment."

Dixon glanced at Angela and Cassie. The DA held up her hands. Cassie looked away. Howie grimaced as he took the stand.

"Sheriff," Hedgespeth began, "would you kindly raise your right hand? . . . Do you swear to tell the truth, the whole truth, and nothing but the truth, so help you God?"

Dixon's voice was low and hoarse. "Yes, I do."

"Okay then," Hedgespeth said. "The lawyers here, for certain reasons, aren't in a position to do the questioning. So I will just ask you a few questions myself, if that's okay."

"I guess so."

"You guess so." Hedgespeth nodded. "What I need to ask about is the phone call you received from sheriff's deputies Baynes and Akers concerning the defendant's so-called daydream."

Dixon reached for the glass of water at his side. The judge continued.

"Do you recall where you were exactly when you received that phone call?"

"Let's see, it was the weekend . . . I guess I was in my den. Maybe watching a game on TV."

"Do you recall what game?"

Dixon began scanning the courtroom. Again Bard tried to catch his eye. *Don't make it worse, Howie. Fix it while you can, Howie.*

"Oh no, I couldn't—"

"Well, was it football or hockey or baseball?"

"I guess it was football, that time of year."

No, Howie, Bard thought. *Stop, Howie.*

"Was it morning or afternoon?"

"Let's see now. I'd say afternoon."

Save yourself, Howie. Save who you are.

"And then the phone rang?"

"Yes, it was Victor—"

"Your Honor." Cassie Teal was on her feet and approaching. "I've got to object."

Hedgespeth gaped at her. "You've got to what?"

Cassie said, "May we have a sidebar?"

Hedgespeth lifted his eyes to the ceiling, then waved Brody forward. The defense attorney joined Cassie and Angela at the end of the bench farthest from the witness stand.

"This simply isn't proper," Cassie began in a low voice, screening her mouth so Dixon couldn't hear. "The sheriff needs to be advised of his rights."

Hedgespeth said, "You or Ms. Stark can do that as soon as I've finished with my questions."

"That would be too late," Cassie argued. "Sheriff Dixon has a right to counsel at this point. He needs to be advised of the possibility of his jeopardy and his self-incrimination by further testimony."

"You're too much," Hedgespeth said. "He's up here because of you. And now—"

"All the same," Cassie interrupted. "Rather than commit perjury, he has the right to invoke his Fifth Amendment rights."

The judge's expression mixed irritation with grudging admiration. "My, my, Ms. Teal. I'll be damned. You are something. I don't need but one lawyer in this courtroom. You can play all the roles."

Cassie pulled a strand of hair out of her eyes. "If need be, I guess I can, Your Honor."

Hedgespeth worked things through in his mind. "Okay then. You're right, Ms. Teal. Yes, the sheriff needs to get himself a lawyer. We'll have to stop. Let's go back to open court now."

The lawyers retreated to their chairs.

"We're going to suspend matters," Hedgespeth announced. "What I've heard very much concerns me, but I'm unable to make a ruling. I don't want to continue the trial or accept the plea right now. And I can't keep on with the current line of questioning. I want the defense to look into the matters raised by Ms. Teal and I want Sheriff Dixon to get a lawyer. Until then, proceedings are suspended. A continuance is granted."

Bard glanced at Jeremiah. Jed was pouring words into Brody's ear.

Cassie rose again. "Your Honor."

"Something else, Ms. Teal?"

"There's the issue of the mental health reports, Your Honor."

Hedgespeth reached for a file. "Oh, yes. Mr. Brody, I see in here that the defendant has refused to talk to any psychologist or psychiatrist. I ask that you try mighty hard to get that issue resolved."

Brody, pulling away from Jed, said, "I've already tried, Your Honor. My client refuses. What I can say is—"

"You can't say anything!" Jeremiah rattled his shackles. The sound of metal against metal clanged across the courtroom. "I'm the only person that knows what happened, so how can you say anything? I'm as competent as anybody in this room. That's not my problem. There isn't nothing shaky about my mind. I just want to get it over and done with."

Hedgespeth slapped his gavel. "You may soon get your

wish, Mr. Jeremiah, but not today. Continuance granted. Proceedings suspended."

Jeremiah sat still now, watching as Hedgespeth rose to leave the bench. "Oh, I'll get my wish," he called out. "If need be, I'll get this over and done with all by myself."

TWENTY-TWO

Everything Doug Bard could think to do he'd already done.

There was no prudent way to ask anything more of Jimmy. Nor was there a point in turning to Cassie. She'd coolly accepted his praise for rising in court with new evidence—and just as coolly deflected talk of what she'd done for Howie Dixon.

Bard had tried to visit the sheriff. But Howie had a lawyer now, paid for by the county, hired up in San Luis. No one talked to Dixon anymore.

Bard didn't even try to see Jed Jeremiah. Jed was way out of bounds. Jed, in fact, was on suicide watch. He'd tried once already, just as he'd promised Judge Hedgespeth. A weak attempt, using a broken piece of plastic on thick weathered wrists, but afterward, Jeremiah had promised: I'll get better at this.

So might Bruce Hightower, for that matter. Hightower, or whoever the commissioner might next send after Sasha and Molly.

No matter how things broke, there were perils. Time was of the essence. Bard couldn't count on the courtroom any longer. He had only one course left.

The steering wheel spun in his hands. He'd been driving aimlessly through Chumash County, trying to still his mind. Now he turned toward Apple Canyon. A full moon guided him to his cabin in the woods. Sasha stood at the door, waiting.

She and Molly were packing up, getting ready to return to their home in the highlands. "Parting again," Sasha said.

"What nostalgia. My knight in shining armor, that's how I thought of you that first summer."

"Sorry I let you down."

Sasha's eyes filled. Her hand went to his shoulder. He wasn't sure whether she was offering or seeking succor. On her wrist was a silver bracelet he'd given her in another world. "Come in," she said, stepping aside.

It felt like entering a sanctuary. Something had changed with them after he read Merta's memo. They weren't at war, they weren't on guard. They saw each other more clearly, and knew now that the danger lay elsewhere. They had closed ranks. For the time being, they were again a family.

Sasha and Doug sat before the fireplace. "What's going to happen?" she asked.

He had only the seed of a notion. "Who knows? Jeremiah will likely kill himself or a jailer before the court hearings are over. He'll have plenty of time. Now that Dixon has a lawyer, this could stretch out for quite a while."

"But Jeremiah didn't kill Ollie and Marilee. We know that now." She paused. "I know that now."

"It wouldn't be the first time an innocent man gets sent to Death Row."

"Jesus, Doug."

Molly wandered out of the bedroom, on the way to the kitchen. She gave her father a quick hug. "Can't talk, Dad, my buddies are all live on AOL. Love you."

He tried to grab hold of her. "What can I use as bait? How can I lure you from that computer?"

She laughed and tugged free. "Daddy, you're cute." In an instant she was gone.

"Doug," Sasha asked. "What can we do?"

"What can we do," he repeated. His eyes were on Molly's bedroom door. Such a preteen she was. *What can I use as bait? How can I lure you?*

That was it. Yes. Bard jumped to his feet. "It's not smart or safe for us to expose Hightower, so we have to get him to expose himself. We've got to lure Hightower from behind his cover."

"How, Doug?"

"Bait. We've got to bait the trap."

"With what?"

"That's obvious. Ollie Merta's memo."

Sasha's eyes widened. "You've always said it would be dangerous to reveal we have it."

"There's no safe ground anymore, Sasha."

She didn't flinch. "No, of course not."

They silently shared the room, each exploring possibilities. After a moment, Sasha said, "I'll be part of the bait. I've got to make it known to Hightower that I have Ollie's memo."

Bard looked at her. Another surprise. Those closest to you sometimes were the hardest to figure.

"No way," he said.

"Come on, Doug."

"You're not going to be part of the bait."

"I want to do something."

"No."

"Okay, what then?"

It was obvious now. Bard rose. "I'm going to sell jail."

He looked so comfortable, standing alone on his terrace, surveying the black sea. Head back, chin forward, hands in the pockets of his khakis, a forelock of hair hanging in his eyes. Not cocky but confident. Optimistic, to be more precise. Even now, in this situation, Hightower appeared at ease with himself and the world.

Bard thought, you need such an approach to be a successful entrepreneur. Whether it's smuggling marijuana or reimagining the Central Coast or killing an adversary, you need a certain assured vision, a certain expectation about the future. Hightower's was the American way, foot on the accelerator, unhampered by doubts or qualms.

He'd showed nothing when Bard revealed that they had Ollie Merta's memo. He'd reacted much as he did when Ollie murmured *mothership* in his ear.

"Can I get you something to drink?" was Hightower's first

response. His next was, "It's so nice outside, let's go sit on the terrace."

Hightower's home surprised Bard. He hadn't expected something so distinctive. Even more than the architecture and the furnishings, he liked its isolation. They had that in common. From the terrace, Bard took in the stunning view of surf and sky and winding coastline.

"How'd you buy this place?" he asked.

A faint smile, amused, not the least rattled. "Do you mean did I acquire it with laundered, ill-gotten drug money?"

"Something like that."

"Well, Bard, I suppose the answer is yes."

"I see."

"Are you horrified, Bard? Are you repelled?"

"Not much can horrify me anymore. You get accustomed to things in my business."

"So sanctimonious. You didn't strike me as the type."

"You misread me. I'm not troubled in the least by all the grass you moved. That's not why you need to confess."

"Confess to what?"

"You tell me. Time to talk."

Another faint smile. "Is it, now? Next you'll tell me it's all for the best. That I need to get the load off my mind."

"Do you have a load?"

"Don't we all?"

"So walk me backward into the past."

"Ah, the past." The thought of it plainly tantalized Hightower. He turned from the sea looking lit from within. "Sure. Why not revisit the past?"

He talked on and on, unable to hide his longing and sheer exuberance for a time in his youth when there were no rules, only possibilities. Imagine what it was to be a college kid in the sixties, he urged. He'd been twenty in 1970. That's when it started. No, not then, before. But that's when things turned. He got caught that year at the Mexican border trying to sneak forty pounds of pot into the United States. For that he served eight months in jail. Once released, he wandered up to Canada, then to the South Pacific. He taught sixth grade; he worked as a recreation director.

"Yes, Bard, it's true, believe it or not, that was my intended career path. Volleyball nets, basketball courts, baseball diamonds. A delight. Might have stuck with it. If only I hadn't had such a bright idea."

"Mothership?"

Hightower appeared pleased that Bard knew. He was off again, full of explanation about how it worked. Merta had described it fairly well, but Hightower provided the detail and color. The pitching and heaving, the fog, the nerve-jangling adrenaline-fueled paranoia as big freighters unloaded on the high seas. Then the medium-sized boats, surfing up and down ten-foot seas. The smaller craft, weaving among the recreational boaters, creeping toward shore. Making land. Delivering the goods.

Recalling it all, Hightower celebrated his lost world.

"The motherships changed everything, Bard. Suddenly all sorts of brilliant characters were smuggling tons of marijuana. You had real-estate developers, you had police officers, you had fishing guides, you had yacht salesmen. Even the blue-collar workers finally got their trickle-down economy. Burly men who tossed one-hundred pound bales of 'square grouper' from freighters. Fake scamboat crews that sailed the product to canal-front homes. That's not to say the white-collar professionals didn't cash in, too. Realtors sold and resold waterfront homes to mask what was going on. Lawyers set up trusts to hide domestic ownership. Bankers moved illicit wealth to secret offshore corporations. Everyone prospered, Bard, everyone. Oh what a time. You didn't just prosper back then. You also got high."

"And you, for one, got rich."

"Yes, Bard, very rich. What can I say. I had eighteen-wheelers full of grass rolling all across the country."

"Then your luck changed."

"Yes." Hightower began to lose his enthusiasm for the story. "You seem to know it all. No need to revisit, then."

"How did you happen to land in Chumash County?"

"Look around you, Bard. Come here." Hightower pulled him over to the edge of the terrace. Doug, eyeing the crashing surf a hundred feet below, feeling this man's hand hard on his back, leaned away. Hightower didn't seem to notice. "There's a time warp here on the Central Coast," he was saying. "The worst of modern popular culture has passed us by. Look at this! Everything is so natural. Everything is to proper scale, everything is in proper relation to the surroundings. A throwback, Bard. That's what we have. That's why I came here."

"To build all over the county? To develop stores and condos and housing tracts?"

"You can't stop time, Bard. I've said it over and over. What you can do is decide how the changes come. Look at what I've done here. Be honest. This isn't stucco cookie-cutter trash. The condos at Pirate's Beach look as if they've grown out of the hillside. So will the homes on the bluff out there, if they ever get built. That's the way to go. If not my way, there would have been some other fellow's way, some much more awful way. I've protected Chumash County, Bard. I've protected and preserved."

Hightower stood on his terrace, feet planted, head back, enthralled with his vision of the Central Coast.

"Why develop at all?" Bard asked. "Why launder through real estate? Why not go with the high-tech venture capitalists?"

"Hah! Not a chance, Bard. That's all ephemeral, that will all evaporate. What I build here will last and last. What I build here will forge a community. A real community, not something fake that exists only on a computer screen. You can walk along the streets of Chumash County. You can talk to the people face to face. You can attend their planning meetings. You can see their schools, their shops, their lives. People here are prospering once again. People are happy. Is that so bad, Bard? Tell me now, is that so bad?"

"It's all built with illegal drug money."

"There you go again, Bard. Sanctimony doesn't fit you."

"As I said, you misread me."

"Maybe so, but I'm not interested in seeing if we can stir up great gobs of guilt. The fact is, what I did shouldn't have been illegal. We're not talking crack here. My brand of grass just got people high."

"All the same, it must have been unnerving when Ollie Merta bumped into you on the plaza. What did you think when he whispered 'mothership' in your ear?"

That stopped Hightower, for the first time since Bard had arrived. He sat down. "What did I think?"

"From the way Ollie describes that moment in his memo, it must have been something."

Hightower reflected. "Yes, it was something, Bard."

"Your cover was blown."

"Yes."

"What happened?"

"Sorry, Bard, I don't feel overwhelmingly compelled to tell you."

"You're going to have to talk sometime soon. This is coming out."

"Actually, it already has."

"Only to me and Sasha so far. It's got to go much further."

"No, no, you don't get it; Bard. When I say this already has come out, I mean I've already unloaded. I've told my story."

Bard waited, uncertain what he meant.

Hightower continued. "You've got no hammer over me, Bard. There's nothing to reveal. I've already gone to the DEA and U.S. Customs myself. They and my lawyers are in the midst of negotiations even now. I've acknowledged that I still possess many millions of those ill-gotten gains that so offend you. We've given the authorities an accounting."

Bard labored to get his bearings. Nothing made sense anymore. If Hightower had nothing to keep secret, then why would he care about Merta's memo?

"Here's the deal, Bard. I'm going to hand over a mighty bundle in exchange for freedom from all further legal action. Close to thirty-five million, believe it or not, thanks to a few wise investments over the years. They get all I've got, and I get to walk."

Bard tried to cling to his thread. "Why not cut this deal

long ago? Why kill Ollie Merta then? Why kill Marilee Cooper? Why let Jeremiah go down?"

Hightower was plainly stunned. "You're kidding. You think I killed those two?"

"Merta was killed just hours after he bumped you on the plaza. It's obvious what happened. You had to shut him up. Most likely you didn't plan to kill him. Most likely things escalated once you got there."

Hightower was still trying to adjust. "You think me capable of murder, Bard?"

"Killing Merta wasn't enough. You had to destroy his records, his computers, his proof. That's why you burned down the house. It wasn't just to cover up the murders. You had no idea what he had, where he had it. So everything in the house had to be destroyed."

"Even a little girl?"

"Yes, even a little girl. A little girl who witnessed what happened."

Hightower appeared fascinated now. "Bard, you're so far off. I ran some righteous grass twenty-five years ago, that's all. I'm not a killer."

"I think you are."

Hightower had recovered his insouciance. He leaned back in his chair. "You're missing the point, Bard. Or rather, ignoring the point. I've gone to the feds. I have nothing to hide. So I had no reason to quiet Mr. Merta."

"You went to the feds after Merta died?"

"Well, yes."

"Remorse. Covering your tracks. Something like that."

"Remorse?" Hightower looked as if he'd never heard of the word. "Come on, Bard. I didn't cut the deal before Merta showed up because I wasn't overly eager to hand over thirty-five million dollars. Especially to folks who will probably burn through it in a day on some damn fool jet bomber cost overrun. Surely you can understand."

"Why go to the feds at all?"

"Finally, a good question." Hightower gazed out to sea. "The answer is not so hard to understand, really. I had this quite uncomfortable monkey on my back for years. Then Merta comes along, whispers in my ear. It was something I'd always expected. Now here it was. I didn't understand how Merta knew about me, but he did. I went home that night figuring this fellow was about to blow a whistle, or maybe try blackmail. So I decided right then, that night, to open my own purse before he did. In a way it was a great relief. To get it off my back. To get it over with finally."

"But then Merta dies in a house fire. You're off the hook. There's no reason to go to the feds."

"Yes, that's what I figured when I heard the news. An incredible coincidence. An incredible stroke of luck, if you want to be so heartless as to call it that. So for a while, I held back, did nothing. Tried to pretend everything was back to normal. But it wasn't, Bard. Couldn't be. I'd already made my decision. I'd already felt what it was like not to carry around so much weight. That was too good a feeling to let go of."

"Better than thirty-five million dollars?"

"As hard as that is to believe, yes. Especially after Merta. He made real what I'd always feared. In the weeks after I bumped into him, I lived in an inferno, always waiting for another guy to whisper in my ear. That's not a way to live. Don't you see, Bard?"

The thing was, he did see. He sensed Hightower was telling the truth. It was all such a jumble, though.

"So you finally decided to go to the feds."

"Yes. With my lawyers as a shield, of course. I didn't throw myself at their mercy, exactly. We proposed a deal."

"Then it turns out Merta didn't die in a house fire. It turns out he was murdered."

"Yes. Which I confess did make it weird, Bard. Angela has just been consumed by that case. I sometimes think Merta's ghost hovers above my bed."

Bard thought of the visit he and Molly made to Merta's hidden cabin. Ollie's ghost lingered there, too, speaking to them from the grave. If only they could hear, and understand. Bard felt as if he were again wandering about lost in Merta's dense mountain forest. A cold hand seemed to be gripping his heart.

"So who killed Ollie Merta?" he asked.

Hightower was at the edge of his chair now. "Why doubt it was Jed Jeremiah? As I understand, he's burning to plead. And Angela's so certain. She's absolutely driven about this."

Angela's so certain.

The cold hand gripped him tighter. A notion began to tug at Bard. He couldn't shake it off. He'd almost forgotten. Besides the bootprint on Ollie's door, there'd been those two other prints, in the dirt below a window. Prints the DA had suppressed. Prints made by a woman's shoe, size eight.

"Bruce, did you tell Angela about meeting Merta on the plaza?"

"Yes, of course, right away. That night. I was all shook up. Mighty agitated, I have to admit. Saying foolish stuff. Embarrassing to think of now. I just lost it for a while."

"Before then, had Angela known about your past?"

Hightower frowned, finally sensing Bard's direction. "Up until that evening, she didn't know a thing. I told her everything that night. I had to, couldn't help it. She saw me so upset. I had to explain what Merta meant, how he could affect my life."

"You told her it was Ollie Merta on the plaza?"

"She told me, actually. I sort of recognized him, but didn't know his name. She did, soon as I described him."

"How did Angela respond to all you said?"

"She was wonderful, actually, once she understood. She listened. She tried to calm me. She told me everything would be okay."

"And then?"

"Then?" Hightower searched his memory. "I think we had a party to attend that night. Yes. Up at the country club, a charity ball of some sort. I dreaded going, but felt obliged. Angela drove separately so she could leave early. Had to work late at the office, she said."

Bard thought of Angela at Merta's burning house, wearing not business clothes but three-inch heels and a black-matte jersey dress. The dress clinging to her body, the neckline scooped. "So you parted ways at the party? Didn't see her again that night?"

Hightower had heard enough. "Now look, Bard, what are you driving at?"

He wasn't driving at anything anymore. He'd arrived. Just one more turn. "Does Angela know you've gone to the feds? Does she know you're negotiating a deal?"

Hightower was on his feet. "No, she doesn't, as a matter of fact. To be honest, I don't share everything with her anymore. We've sort of cooled things. Taken a few steps back."

"So she still thinks you have something major to hide?"

"I guess . . . I assume so."

Bard rose also. "Where's Angela right now? I'd like to talk to her."

Hightower paled at the question. "I assumed you knew, Bard. I assumed your visit was connected. Sasha called Angela earlier this evening. Told her there was something critical she'd learned about the Jeremiah case, something she had to share with her."

Bard gripped the back of his chair. Sasha, Sasha, Sasha. Determined to make her own amends, to avenge Ollie's death, to prove something to an ex-husband. Insisting, as always, on her own way.

"Where are they meeting?" Bard asked.

"Angela just said she was going to see Sasha."

"Where? Where?"

"I don't know."

"Think, Hightower. Goddamn it, think."

"Apple Canyon. She was going to Apple Canyon."

Bard turned for the door. "My house."

All was dark now. The midnight fog had rolled in, obscuring the bright evening sky. The road down the coast twisted in and out of wooded hollows. Bard had to break and slow or risk fishtailing into the sea. He glanced at his watch. Angela had left Hightower's more than two hours ago. How long had she been with Sasha and Molly? He'd called the house, but no one answered, not even the machine. Maybe Angela had cut the phone lines. Maybe Angela had yanked a cord.

Bard tried to imagine the scene. Sasha, describing Ollie's memo, saying this was something Angela had to know. Stark no doubt choosing to act surprised, then coolly asking to see the actual document. She'd want to put her hands on it, hold it, feel it. After that? There was no way to figure, at least not by applying reason. Would Angela try once again to cover everything up, to protect Hightower, to save their lives together? The stakes would certainly seem high enough to her.

The most dangerous emotion is love . . . A person consumed by passion can do just about anything. That's what Cassie had said. Bard agreed. Who wasn't obsessed? Who wouldn't kill, given the right cause? It was such a thin line dividing those who contained themselves and those who did not.

He was threading through Apple Canyon now, trying to recall the shape of Angela's hands. They would have fit easily around Marilee's neck. But what of Merta's? There must have been a struggle first. A glancing blow, something to leave him dizzy and weakened. Or had he been asleep? No. Angela would have talked to him first, tried to glean what he knew, what he meant to reveal.

As she no doubt has been doing tonight with Sasha. Sasha and Molly. This time he didn't hesitate; Bard punched the knob on his glove compartment and reached for his Glock. At the same time, he lifted his foot off the accelerator and let himself roll into the final bend of the road. Before he got there, he came to a full stop. He'd walk in tonight. No point announcing himself.

As he stepped out of the car, the forest closed around him. He fought to keep his bearings in the gloom. Thick branches scraped his face. He'd lost the road somehow. For guidance, he had only the faint yellow glow of the house, showing through the dense foliage. He lunged toward it, using his arm to cut a path. He tripped over a tree trunk, twisting as he landed face forward in a bed of moldy leaves. He rose, ignoring the pain already clenching his ankle. Another ten steps and he broke through into the clearing at the edge of his driveway. He was halfway to the house when he thought to pat the pocket where he'd stuffed the Glock. It wasn't there. He turned back to the forest. It must have slipped out when he fell. No time to go back, and no use anyway in the dark. What the hell, Bard thought.

At the front door, he stopped to listen. He could hear the low murmur of voices. He looked through the window. Sasha and Molly were both on the couch. Angela was sitting between them. Bard reached for the doorknob. It twisted in his hand. He stepped inside.

"What a surprise," he called out. "A visitor."

All three turned at once to look at him. No one moved. "Oh, it's you," Sasha said.

He slowly approached them, limping. The ankle was throbbing now. "Hey, Molly," he said.

Molly smiled back but looked wan. "Hey, Daddy."

He sat down in one of the corduroy chairs and spun it to face the couch. He fought to keep the pain from showing in his face. "So, what's up?"

Angela cast glances about the room. She'd come in jeans and hiking boots, uncommon for her. Around her shoulders hung a brown cape. Finally she fixed on him. "Forgive the intrusion, Doug. But Sasha invited me here."

"It's no intrusion," Bard said. "Have you found the trip out worthwhile?"

"I should say so."

"I tried to call. No one answered, not even the machine."

Sasha looked at Angela before responding. "We were outside for a while. And the machine seems to be broken."

Bard decided to let someone else bring up Merta's memo. To Angela he said, "I've brought you a message from Bruce Hightower."

Her voice was steady. "You've been to see Bruce?"

"Yes."

"Pray tell, what's the message?"

"He wants you to know there's nothing to hide anymore. He's gone to the feds. They're cutting a deal."

Angela showed nothing. "I don't know what you're talking about."

"I think you do."

She was studying him now, trying to measure his words. Bard looked down at her hands. They were on her lap, folded inside a blue kerchief, as if she were holding something, hiding something. The small bulge, he estimated, was just about the size of a supercompact handgun. Was that why Sasha and Molly sat so mildly by her side?

"You are mistaken," Angela said, looking away.

She offered that with such unforced certainty, he wondered for an instant if he'd once again miscalculated. Then her hands moved, slightly, and beside her, Sasha flinched.

"There's no mistake," he said. "Hightower told me everything."

Her eyes gave her away. " 'Told me everything,' " she said. "What do you mean by that?"

"I mean he told me how Ollie Merta whispered to him on the plaza. How he came to you that night so upset. How he told you about his past. How you promised him everything would be okay. How you two went off to a charity ball. How you left early, on your own."

She digested all that, then shook her head. "Why would he tell you such things?"

Bard wanted Angela to blow up. He wanted her to lift her hands out of that kerchief. "Because I let him know we found Merta's memo. Because I accused him of killing Ollie and Marilee. Because he needed to set the record straight."

"Nonsense!" Angela's hands jerked. "I don't believe you even spoke with him."

Sasha and Molly hadn't moved. They sat listening, watching. Bard found he couldn't keep his eyes off Angela's brown cape.

"You killed Ollie and Marilee," he said. "You killed them to protect Hightower. You killed them to save your life together."

"That's outlandish."

"Not at all. Hightower means everything to you. It's you two against the world, isn't it, Angela?"

"You're nuts." Angela's hands moved toward her waist. "You come at me with such wild accusations. 'I know' you say. 'I know.' You don't know anything. Nothing at all."

Her cape started to slip off one shoulder. She reached for it with one hand.

Bard watched. Of course. Her brown cape.

"It's over, Angela. Remember the witness at Ollie Merta's house? Sally Dyle, the school counselor? She saw someone who moved like a dancer, someone wearing brown. We assumed it was a deer. But what if we put you in Ollie's forest wrapped in this brown cape? Bingo, Sally will say. That's what I saw."

Angela shook her head. "It wouldn't hold up. Wouldn't even be admitted."

"Then there's what Hightower would say in a courtroom. How Bruce would testify to protect himself."

She froze, saying nothing. He'd found the opening.

"He's pulled away, hasn't he, Angela? You killed for him, you're prosecuting an innocent man for him, and yet he isn't there anymore. He told me he was finished with you. He told me, Angela."

"You fool." Her eyes were hot coals. "What do you know?"

Bard watched Angela's lap. His ankle felt on fire. The pain radiated now into his calf and shin. He wasn't sure he could stand or walk.

"Here's what I know," he said. "I know you killed Ollie and Marilee." He decided to gamble. "Also Benjamin Mire."

She flared, all reflex. "No, not Mire. He knew nothing. That was a real accident. His furnace blew up."

They looked at each other. "Okay, then," Bard said slowly. "Ollie and Marilee."

She was trembling. "You make it sound so sordid."

"I'm sure it didn't start that way. I'm sure it wasn't meant to be that way."

Her fists stayed clenched in her lap, but she looked tired now. When she next spoke, her voice sounded faraway. "I could have wallowed, I could have taken weeping to my bed. Instead, just like Bruce, I chose to act, to shape our fate. I was on a mission of mercy. Bruce was in such pain. I wanted only to save him. And yes, to save us. I meant only to stop that man from ruining our life together."

Bard shifted his weight in the chair, trying to test his ankle. "How did you intend to do that?"

"I thought I could reason with him. Either that or scare him. Mostly, I needed to find out what he knew."

"Ollie resisted?"

Her lip curled at the memory. "He was such an ornery old cuss. He teed off on me. 'There's right, there's wrong, there's corruption, there's integrity.' That's what he shouted. So horribly self-righteous, so mean-spirited. And so excited about bringing Bruce down. He talked as if Bruce were a mass murderer. Think about it, will you, Doug? Merta wanted to ruin our lives so he could play the big shot for once. He said he was going to report all of us the very next morning. Bruce, me, RC Cummings. 'I have the goods,' he cried out. 'I know everything.' "

Angela looked at Sasha. "He also told me, 'I work with Sasha Bard. Sasha knows everything.' "

Bard said, "You must have wanted badly to see what he had."

"Yes, I did. He mentioned a memo he'd written. A memo for Sasha. I started searching for it, all through his drawers and papers. He came at me, swinging a broomstick. I grabbed at the broom, rammed it back at him. He fell to the ground."

"He was stunned then. You could do what you had to."

"What I had to. Exactly. Well put, Doug."

"Which eventually included prosecuting Jed Jeremiah for the murders."

A flicker of a smile. "Your fault, Doug. I wanted to call it an accident. You made it a murder."

"Yes, that's true . . . And now here we are."

"Not for long," Angela said. "I'm leaving."

"You plan to just walk out of here?"

"No." Angela nodded at Molly. "I'll have to take someone

with me. To guarantee safe passage out of Chumash County. I'll be okay once I get to a big city. I can lose myself in a big city. I've always been able to lose myself in big cities."

"That's foolish. You won't get far."

"Better to try than surrender."

Angela reached for Molly's arm. Bard lunged, but his leg gave way. He pitched forward, landing on his belly. When he looked up, Angela had the gun out of the kerchief, aimed at Molly. Just as he suspected, a Colt Agent .38 spec. Small ebony grips, silver meds, super compact. Perfect for a lady's purse.

"A second little girl," he said. "You don't want that, Angela."

She didn't, he could see that. A single tear ran down her face. "I didn't even know Marilee was there. Then she came out afterward, screaming. I was just trying to quiet her down."

"Molly's not screaming," Bard said. "Look at her."

He knew he could count on his daughter to maintain. Her cool blue-green eyes gazed at them all, as if there were no gun in her ribs, no wild woman at her side.

"If only Marilee hadn't screamed," Angela whispered.

At that instant, Molly's forearm slashed through the air. The edge of her hand cracked into Angela's wrist. The gun clattered to the floor. Molly picked it up. She handed it to her father. She said, "Thank God I took karate lessons."

TWENTY-THREE

It being a Friday night, the bar was full at JB's Red Rooster Tavern, so Bard and Cassie and Jimmy settled at their favorite table next to the potbellied stove. As Jimmy signaled for a waitress, Bard turned to watch Dave Murphy bang out his tunes.

"Give us three brews," Jimmy called.

Cassie shook her head. "Make mine a martini."

Bard said, "Make mine a Black Bush."

Jimmy looked horrified. "Jesus, I'm with a bunch of lushes."

Cassie whacked him on the back. "Come on, we're celebrating. We have reason."

"Yes," Jimmy agreed. "We do."

His journalism had much to do with that. When finally handed Ollie Merta's memo, he'd first bellowed at Doug for holding it back, then gone to work. The state attorney general's office had stepped in hours after the *News-Times* spread the memo—and Bard's account of Angela Stark's confession—across its front page. Within days, all charges were dropped against Jed Jeremiah. Two weeks later came Angela's indictment for the murders of Ollie Merta and Marilee Cooper. By then, Bruce Hightower had finalized his deal with U.S. Customs. It was hard to say what stunned Chumash County more, the revelations about their DA or their county commissioner.

At least the feds weren't going to make the county forfeit everything Hightower built. In fact, Hightower's deal came with a pleasant bonus: U.S. Customs announced it was giving half the seized $35 million to the Chumash County Sheriff's Department, since by law local government entities are entitled to get money proportional to the work they did in money-laundering cases. That Doug Bard's labors had mostly come after he quit the force was a fact he and county officials together chose to obscure. The version offered the feds was that Bard had continued serving the department as an independent consultant.

They were all independents now. Jimmy, summoned by the *News-Times*'s owners, quit halfway through a division publisher's denunciation of his "irresponsible, uncorroborated reporting." Cassie Teal, offered the interim DA's job until the next election, decided she'd rather go back to defending accused killers.

"Who's paying for these drinks?" Jimmy asked. "We need someone at the table who has a job."

Bard sipped his beer, saying nothing. His mind was on Howie Dixon. Unlike them, Howie didn't have the luxury of choosing his own fate. He resigned quietly, hoping to avoid perjury and obstruction charges, but the AG's office filed against him anyway. No longer provided a lawyer by the county, Dixon had been forced to sell his treasured seaside property up the coast to pay for a defense attorney. Bard knew he shouldn't care, but it weighed on him. If only he'd said something to Howie on the plaza that last day.

"Who's going to defend Angela?" Cassie asked.

The others looked at her, appraising. When she realized what they were thinking, she held up a hand. "No way, guys. I'm not detached enough. Nor experienced enough."

Jimmy slapped the table. "I have it then. There's only one lawyer for Stark. Greg Monarch. I'm going to haul him out of retirement. I'm going to—"

Bard stopped listening. The sight of a tall, muscular man entering JB's Tavern had caught his eye. He wore a cowboy hat, which obscured his wild tangle of hair but not his thick beard. Jed Jeremiah marched to the bar, elbowing aside those in his way. "Whiskey," he called out, in a voice loud enough for Bard to hear.

Glass in hand, Jeremiah turned and scanned the room. His eyes fixed on a pair of women at the jukebox, then moved slowly along the tables. Jed spotted Bard just as he brought the glass to his lips. He looked away, and swallowed the whiskey in one gulp.

The music had stopped. Dave was taking a break. The piano sat unattended. As Bard watched, Jed rose from his stool and stepped toward the Fischer upright. Not until he was by its side did anyone else notice. Jed was clutching a stuffed duffel bag in one hand. He wore a shabby red windbreaker and looked as if he'd been living outdoors. He eyed the unattended piano for a minute before sitting down.

Bard recalled the stories, how he'd learned to pound pianos in all the honky-tonks he'd visited.

Jed started playing. It took several minutes before the drinkers began putting down their glasses. At first, it sounded as if he were improvising. Only gradually did those listening realize what he was doing. He was, in late summer, playing "God Rest Ye Merry Gentlemen." But he was inflating and transforming it with a harnessed anger quite unlike the Christmas spirit. Jed rode an inner wave, looking at no one. He did not smile or turn his head. There was only the piano and himself.

By now everyone in the tavern had stopped talking. A few glanced around to see who else was noticing. The moment continued and extended until Bard thought something had to peak. Instead, Jed cut loose and took it higher, working the old upright for everything it had, for more than it had.

Then it was over. Jed stopped. From around the tavern came a smattering of applause. He ignored it, or didn't hear. He jumped up, grabbed his duffel bag, and walked back to the bar.

Bard rose and approached. Jeremiah didn't move. Bard took the stool next to him. He said, "Good to see you out and about, Jed. Nice work on the piano."

Jeremiah didn't appear interested in responding. He signaled for another whiskey. When it came, he tapped the glass with his knuckle. "You started this," he said finally. "And I guess you ended it, too. Put me in jail, got me out."

"Something like that."

"Don't know whether to shoot you or thank you."

Bard eyed the bulge in Jeremiah's windbreaker. "Come on, Jed. If you pull out that piece, you're going to end up in jail again. You don't want that, I don't want that."

"That's true."

They each worked on their drinks for a while. Bard said, "You sure made it hard on those of us trying to get you out. Pleading guilty and all. Tantrums in the courtroom. Why'd the hell you do that?"

"I'd had enough. Just wasn't going to sit in that cell forever. Or that courtroom. Got so wrathy, I flat out didn't care. Thought I'd have some fun, jack the system around a little before it got to jacking me."

" 'When you kill me, I still won't have done it.' That's what you told me up on the mountain. I kept thinking about that. Couldn't let it go."

"Funny thing is, after a while, I got to thinking I truly was guilty."

"How come, Jed?"

Jeremiah drained his glass. "Hard to say. Guess I've always felt that way."

The two men eyed each other. Jed said, "Know something, Bard? I was trying to jack you most of all. Make you crazy like me. Make you see what you did."

"If that was your goal, you got there."

"Well then, maybe I can crawl back up my mountain and live in peace."

"You do that, Jed." Bard climbed off the stool and turned to leave. The thought of Jeremiah alone in his cabin stopped him. He turned back to the bar. "Keep this in mind, Jed. You're not guilty."

For once there was no fog in La Graciosa. Late-night stars lit the creek-side path where Bard and Cassie strolled. Let me walk you home, he'd said. Now, words escaped both of them.

They smelled the jacaranda and the kelp, and glanced about. Bard recalled another night, long ago.

"You've still got the heebie-jeebies?" he asked.

She recalled also. "From time to time. Not always. Getting better."

"What about your patience level?"

Now she was lost. "For what?"

"Foolish men."

"Ah yes." A sideways look. "Getting better at that also."

They walked on. "Any regrets?" he asked.

"About standing up in the courtroom?"

"Yes."

"None."

"I couldn't believe it when you insisted Howie get an attorney."

"You think that was wrong, Doug?"

"Actually, no. Don't tell anyone, but I was relieved."

She took his hand. "We are a pair, I think."

"An unemployed pair."

"Ah well. We can fish in the creek for dinner."

"You could have stayed on, Cassie. You joined the DA's office because you wanted to be on the right side."

"Come on, Doug. There's no place on Earth that guarantees you're standing on the right side."

"You think of Angela much?"

Cassie stopped. They were in front of her cottage. "More than I should."

They stood where they were, each waiting for the other. Finally she asked, "Want to come in?"

Yes, he did. Not now, though. Not yet. "Could you leave the door unlocked? I'll be back."

Past the heart of town, he drove into the eastern foothills, climbing through the chaparral grasslands, threading among the dense stands of Spanish oak. Sasha and Molly had moved back to their house. Their family once again was apart.

Sasha opened the door at his knock. Molly came, too, standing by her mom. He studied them. Molly was almost as tall as Sasha now. She looked like her, too. They could pass as sisters.

"Thought I'd come say good night," he said.

Sasha arched an eyebrow. "No need for protection here. No threatening messages this evening."

"Maybe I'll phone one in. If that's what it takes."

Sasha smiled at that, and waved him through the door. The three of them sat in the living room on the blue silk sofa. Sasha was prospering, better than ever. She'd remodel again soon, Bard imagined. Or maybe trade up to a fancier house.

"You both did so well with someone holding a gun on you," he said. "I'm mighty proud of you."

"Hello?" Molly said, making a face. "Did we have a choice?"

Bard leaned over, ran a hand along her cheek. "Guess not."

Sasha asked, "What are you going to do now, Doug?"

"I'm not sure. The sheriff's department is pretty grateful for the windfall I got them. They might take me back."

"You want to go back?" Molly asked.

How far back, Bard wanted to ask. Ten years? Fifteen?

"I'm not sure," he said.

Molly had hold of his hands now. She was sliding onto his lap. Her arms went around his neck. "You going away again, Daddy?"

He held her, not breathing, not moving. Sasha watched. He wanted time to stop, time to vanish.

"Oh, Molly girl," he said. "I'm going to miss you when I go."

ACTUAL INNOCENCE

Greg Monarch has no choice but to take the case of the fiery, impetuous Sarah Trant, an ex-lover he hasn't seen in two decades. Five years ago, Sarah was found guilty of slashing an old man's throat in central California's sheltered El Nido Valley. Now, six months from execution, she turns to the one man she hopes can save her. Greg failed once before trying to rescue Sarah from her private demons. This time, however, the demons may not be just in her head.

**Chosen by the *Los Angeles Times*
as One of the Best Books of the Year!**

"A winning story packed with bizarre plot twists, high-octane action, bizarre characters, and a slam-bang finish.
A thumbs-up choice for mystery fans."
—*Booklist*

Published by Ballantine Books.
Available wherever books are sold.